Acclaim for Nick Tosches's

IN THE HAND OF DANTE

"An incendiary novel.... The most audacious thing about *In the Hand of Dante* is the author's furious delivery of rare aesthetic bliss."
— Troy Patterson, *Entertainment Weekly*

"A masterful, unique novel.... Tosches has written a riveting read, a surreal, complicated work altogether equal to the controversy it will generate." — Dylan Foley, *Philadelphia Inquirer*

"If you are weak of heart, put this down. Of course, if you want an absorbing book written by a masterful writer, by all means, pick it up.... Tosches pulls it together in wicked, outrageous style."
— William McKeen, *Orlando Sentinel*

"Nick Tosches dumps the sacred and profane inside a cocktail mixer and shakes 'em up, hard."
— Steve Murray, *Atlanta Journal-Constitution*

"Like reading *Naked Lunch* spliced with pieces of *The Confessions of Saint Augustine*. It's jarring at first, but it grows on you, as the book's design begins to make more and more sense.... *In the Hand of Dante* jogs the mind, and in the end it earns a distinction that can be claimed by few recent novels: This is a book that deserves a second read.... Tosches seems the perfect writer to tackle the subject of Dante's emotions." — Jenny Shank, *Rocky Mountain News*

"Astounding.... A staggering work of genius.... Tosches is a gifted showman.... You'll likely find yourself compulsively reading."
— Chauncey Mabe, *South Florida Sun-Sentinel*

"Tosches writes with the flourish of Faulkner and the grittiness of the toughest pulp fiction." — Curtis Ross, *Tampa Tribune*

"Tosches is as elegant and substantive a writer as is working today. . . . A singular American writer unafraid to wrestle with monstrous themes and to examine his own deep fearsome wounds — and break your heart with the beauty of language at the same time. You'll love it, you'll hate it, you won't be able to put it down."

— Dennis Love, *Book Street USA*

"Everything about Tosches's work is outsize. . . . He writes to the stars and gutter at the same time." — Steve Erickson, *Bookforum*

"A grand, expansive treatment of themes Tosches has chased throughout his career: the act of creation, God and faith, love and death. . . . *In the Hand of Dante* breathes vivid life into Dante Alighieri. . . . Tosches limns an empathetic portrait of Dante's love and faith and doubt and foibles as he strives obsessively to hew from his soul *The Divine Comedy,* an epic that ascends from fundament to firmament, using the vernacular (caged in troublesome terza rima) to touch the face of God."

— Mike Miliard, *Boston Phoenix*

"A fascinating performance. . . . The contemporary narrative is a thrill-a-minute crime story."

— Fred Chappell, *Raleigh News and Observer*

"Tosches positively struts as he parades his impressive research into the personalities, manners, politics, artifacts, and language of the period, creating a whirligig that sweeps readers through the history of, among other things, rhetoric, classics translations, anti-Semitism, printing, papal stratagems, and Florentine politics. . . . It's a dazzling performance." — Bill Bell, *New York Daily News*

"Tosches is a great writer. . . . The novel includes many poetic interludes and much meditation on the nature of art, commerce, and beauty. But — always true to his roots — Tosches also deals up plenty of punchy New York encounters in barrooms and streets. The corruption and sin that lie at the heart of Dante's masterwork and most of Tosches's writing is never far away."

— Jeff Hinkle, *Tucson Weekly*

"Not for nothing has a cult of devotees gathered around Nick Tosches. . . . He combines the starkness of Jim Thompson and the grittiness of Charles Bukowski with a highly literate sensibility."

— Elizabeth Bukowski, *Wall Street Journal*

"A thrilling novel." — Elissa Schappell, *Vanity Fair*

"It's *The Name of the Rose* meets *The Sopranos,* scripted by Kathy Acker and starring Dennis Hopper, reprising his role as *Blue Velvet* psychopath Frank." — Joy Press, *Village Voice*

"A well-rigged, neo-gangster thriller with a dash of historical novel thrown in. . . . It is appropriate that Tosches, a great psalmodist of the American vulgar, should gravitate to Dante, the political fighter and preeminent poetic advocate for the vulgar tongue. . . . What bullfighting was for Hemingway, Dante will be for Tosches."

— Maureen McLane, *Chicago Tribune*

"This novel's true wisdom lies in its poetry, the same 'fatuous writerly nonsense' the author denounces even while indulging (beautifully) in it. . . . *In the Hand of Dante* becomes an inspiration: To write more like the author. To watch *The Godfather* trilogy again. To read Dante, most of all."

— Tiffany Lee-Youngren, *San Diego Union-Tribune*

ALSO BY NICK TOSCHES

Hellfire

Power on Earth

Cut Numbers

Dino

Trinities

The Devil and Sonny Liston

The Nick Tosches Reader

Where Dead Voices Gather

The Last Opium Den

In the Hand of Dante

Nick Tosches

BACK BAY BOOKS
LITTLE, BROWN AND COMPANY
Boston New York London

To Russ Galen

Originally published in hardcover by Little, Brown and Company, September 2002
First Back Bay paperback edition, September 2003

Library of Congress Cataloging-in-Publication Data
Tosches, Nick.
In the hand of Dante / Nick Tosches — 1st ed.
p. cm.
ISBN 0-316-89524-5 (hc) / 0-316-73564-7 (pb)
1. Dante Alighieri, 1265–1321 — Manuscripts — Fiction. 2. Manuscripts — Collectors and collecting — Fiction. 3. New York (N.Y.) — Fiction. 4. Sicily (Italy) — Fiction. 5. Criminals — Fiction. 6. Authors — Fiction. 7. Theft — Fiction. I. Title.
PS3570.O74 I5 2002
813'.54 — dc21 2002020712

10 9 8 7 6 5 4 3 2 1

Q-MART

Book design by Cassandra J. Pappas

Printed in the United States of America

In the Hand of Dante

LOUIE PULLED OFF HIS BRA AND THREW IT down upon the casket.

There was residue on his hand. He hated that. He held forth his hand to the one bitch who was still on her knees. She closed her eyes and licked the scum from his hand. As he stood over her, he could smell her hair, which had the same dirty cloying stench of that coconut-oil shit those fucking Haile Selassie cabbies used inside their taxis. And he could feel the sticky grease of whatever cheap shit she wore on her lips. He withdrew his hand from her.

Downstairs, on West Twenty-sixth Street, he stood awhile in the night. It was the dead of August, that time in New York when the daylight sky was an oppressive low-lying glare of white, and the dark of night was a haze of starless ashen pallor. Louie felt at one with it. He lighted a cigarette and drew smoke. It was late. But not for him.

Humidity and his own sweat began to gather on his skin. He looked at the moist glistening amid the hair of his bare forearm. He looked longer at the hand that held the cigarette. He didn't know which was worse, the traces of his own detested bodily fluid or the slime of that bitch's tongue. This would clean him, he told himself, feeling the gathering of humidity and sweat increase. All he needed now was a good breeze from the river. That would be nice. He began to walk. He had not tucked his shirt into his trousers, and he had not buttoned his shirt, and he did not do these things now. He carried his jacket of fine, fine cotton and fine, fine silk, the one that he had paid two grand for in Milano. It had been made for him, by whatever the fuck his name was. It was the color of the deep blue-green sea, and was almost weightless; but as he carried it, he could feel the sag of weight in one pocket.

It was his favorite jacket. It was like wearing nothing, and you could wear it with anything, and only a guy with class would see it for what it was. And it was the color of his eyes. Broads loved his eyes. Even now, even now that he was an old fuck, the broads still loved his eyes. Some were scared of them, but some loved them.

Louie paused a moment when he reached the corner of Sixth Avenue. He lighted another cigarette. He turned downtown. He kept on walking.

Yeah, sixty-three fucking years old last May. And here he was, walking down the avenue like a kid. He liked to walk, at night, alone, even in this heat. It was nice. These nigger punks passing him by in the street: they got nothing on me, he told himself. It was true. It really was. It was like the man said. You're only as old as you feel.

He thought of that broad in St. Louis: that broad with no arms. He thought of that job in St. Louis: that son of a bitch would not go down.

May. April. March. February. January. December. November. October. September. August. Well, ain't that a fucking pisser. He was conceived in this fucking weather. Who the fuck would fuck in this weather? Without even no fucking air-conditioning? Jesus Christ.

But what the fuck was he talking about? He used to fuck in this fucking weather. Without no fucking air-conditioning. Yeah. He remembered those smacking sounds, that puddle of sweat in what's-her-name's belly, him coming down on her hard and fast, endless fucking hours, his own sweat-drenched gut coming up from that pool in her belly with a loud fucking smack, again and again, faster and faster, harder and harder, louder and louder, like the suction blast of a goddamn force-cup plunger unclogging a fucking toilet bowl.

Yeah, maybe he was getting old, after all. Conceived in August. Maybe that's why he didn't mind this heat, this stillness of dead, heavy air that others could not take. Yeah. Conceived in August. Sixty-three years ago. No. Sixty-four years ago.

What the fuck had he ever conceived? It had all ended up on his right hand or in some cunt's yap. Dead-baby juice. And now it was too late. Born alone, die alone. He was better off that way. Shit, knowing him, he'd pay some broad to hold his hand when he died. Money bought anything.

He made it to Fourteenth Street before he knew it. More niggers, more spics. Shit, in the old days you wouldn't see a nigger below Fourteenth Street. Then the basketball courts, the Jew cunts who go for the dark meat; next thing you know, it ain't a fucking neighborhood, it's a fucking nigger dumping ground. But he didn't blame the fucking niggers. Who wouldn't rather fuck some kike bitch, no matter how fucking ugly she was, than a goddamn nigger broad? Who wouldn't rather be here than there? The trouble was, these days, here was there. But, no, he didn't blame the niggers. He blamed these white motherfuckers who had come in from the sticks with their nigger-loving ways. They deserved what they got. And he blamed it on the cops. He remembered when the neighborhood kids had taken pipe-cutters to those basketball poles. He remembered when the neighborhood kids had taken baseball bats to those nigger skulls. In the old days, the cops would have covered for them. But these cops now, they were different. They weren't from here. They were from those fucking cop suburbs, and they didn't know shit about nothing. They didn't even know where the fuck they were. They were worse than the niggers.

Fuck them. Now that there were no more neighborhoods, no more neighborhood ways, no more neighborhood people, fuck these white assholes. He was with the niggers. He was. Every time they killed a cop, he felt good.

No. Fuck them all. He wasn't with nobody. He kept walking. There was a pang of pain in the groin muscle that he had pulled more than a year ago. It was like it had never really healed right. It hit him every once in a while, like a knife, on the inside of his right thigh, just below his crotch. You get older, things don't heal fast.

He crossed Bleecker Street to Carmine Street. The humidity and his sweat were heavy on him now. He made the sign of the cross on his forehead with his thumb as he passed Our Lady of Pompeii, and the humidity and sweat on his forehead felt like holy water to his thumb. He ambled to the other side of the street, to a shit restaurant with an ugly paint job. It was closed, and the kid was inside by himself, sitting at a table with some paperwork and a drink. Louie rapped on the door. The kid saw who it was, and he stood and came fast to unlock the door.

"Makin' the rounds, my friend?" the kid said. His voice and manner lay between deference and fake casual cheer. He was about thirty-five, with beady eyes and a moustache.

"Don't call me that."

At these words, the fake casual cheer faltered for a moment, and Louie let it falter in silence. He turned away from the kid and strode to the table where the kid had been sitting. He draped his fine, fine jacket over a chair, then he sat, pushed aside some of the paperwork, and lighted a cigarette.

"Give me a drink and an ashtray."

The kid went behind the bar. The fake casual cheer had returned to his manner, but it was more subdued.

"We got this new grappa. It's great."

He raised some stupid-looking fancy-ass tall tapered bottle for Louie to see.

"Fuck you. Save that shit for the suckers. Just give me a Dewar's and water on the rocks. And fuck the ashtray. I'll use the floor."

The kid came to him with the drink and an ashtray. He set them before Louie, and he sat with him.

"How's life?" the kid said.

Louie stared at the kid's moustache. The kid must have grown it in the year or so since he had seen him last.

"Back in the old days, when I was a kid, the old-timers used to say the bigger the moustache, the bigger the man."

The fake casual cheer again grew unsettled.

"Now, these days, I see a guy with a moustache, I figure he's either a cop or a faggot. Or both."

"I guess I better shave it off then, huh, Lou?" he said with what remained of his unsettled fake casual cheer.

"Nah." Louie waved his hand and shrugged with a grimace. "Leave it. Your father's a cop, right? Maybe you got that half-a-fag cop streak in you. It suits you. The moustache."

The kid said nothing, for there was nothing that he could say. Being Louie had its privileges, and Louie indulged them often.

He crushed out his cigarette, drank, and spoke again.

"You know, your uncle's a real fuck-up. I mean, don't get me wrong. You're a fuck-up too. But you're small change. Your uncle, he's a real fuck-up. He had this joint, did good for a while, pissed everything away gamblin'. He comes cryin' to my friends. They help him out. He keeps fuckin' up. He's runnin' cryin' to the bank over here to cover his checks to Con Ed every third time he gets a shut-off notice. My friends don't like that. Your uncle is one sick stupid fuck. And that is all that he is." Louie looked at the kid's paperwork, which was mostly racing charts and scribblings. "You know the story."

Louie drank, lighted another cigarette, smiled faintly. "Now that I think of it, he's got a moustache too. Maybe God didn't give him that walk of his for nothin'." He drank. "Anyway."

He pulled the weight from his pocket and laid it on the table: a Walther PPK nine-millimeter semi-automatic pistol in a sealed plastic sandwich bag.

The kid saw a black gun about six inches long in what appeared to be a crumpled evidence bag.

"Don't you think you ought to put that away?" he said. "What if some cop walks by and looks in?"

Louie sneered. "When's the last time you seen a cop walk? They don't walk no more. They go to the gym like the rest of these fruits, but they don't walk. Shit, the last cop I seen walkin' a beat, it was a broad. About five foot two, this butch haircut that came up to my belly-button; looked like one of them ugly little Halloween gourds with all the little bumps on her face and everything. New York's finest. Like your old man: a worthless ugly little cunt."

The kid no longer looked Louie in the eyes. No one knew Louie, not really, except maybe Louie and except maybe his boss, but everyone knew not to fuck with Louie; and everyone, except maybe Louie and except maybe his boss, feared him without really knowing why.

"Anyway. My friends, they figure that if I throw a scare into this piece-of-shit uncle of yours, maybe he'll get the message."

The kid nodded uneasily, and he offered to get Louie another drink.

"Take it easy," Louie told him. "It's like the great Buddha said: Moderation in all things. The Eightfold Path." He sneered at the kid's moustache. "You ever take it up the ass? You ought to try it sometime. Might make a man out of you." He looked at the kid's averted eyes. He liked seeing things in people's eyes that had never been there before. But he was getting tired, and enough was enough. He looked at the cigarette he was smoking. There were a few drags left, and he took them. He ground out the cigarette. "So," he said. It was more like a heavy, weary sigh than a sound of any meaning.

"Like I say, you and your uncle, you're two of a kind. Two little lyin' degenerate cocksuckers. And I know you been robbin' him, sellin' the stock to other joints, a few bottles here, a few bottles there. Chickenshit stuff. Nickels and dimes. But, then again, you're a chickenshit little cocksucker. You rob just like your father, who's another chickenshit little cocksucker." He paused, drank the last of his drink. The melting ice felt good on his lips. "Your mother, God rest her soul" — he wiped at his lips with the back of his hand — "she was just a cocksucker. And not a very good one at that."

He looked for anger in those beady eyes, but that anger was occluded by fear. Louie tilted his head slightly, studying the rest of the kid's face.

"You're funny-lookin', you know that? How'd you get a broad to marry you? She must be a worse fuckin' loser than you. I never seen her. Your kids neither. I never seen them. You got a picture?"

The kid withdrew his wallet. Louie snatched it from his hand. He removed the money that it held — it was not much — and he stuck it in his own pocket.

"Is this her?"

The kid nodded. "We love each other," he said, as if he meant it. Scared people say the stupidest shit.

Louie glanced at the picture. "Yeah. She's funny-lookin' too. Yeah. You look like one of them, what do you call them, one of them things that catch the rats, yeah, what do you call them, yeah, one of them ferrets. And she looks like a pig. Can she suck cock at least? I mean, any better than your mother could?" He looked at another picture, a picture of a young boy and a younger girl. He seemed to ponder it. "You cross a donkey and a horse, you get a mule. I guess this is what you get when you cross a ferret and a pig. How old's the little girl?"

"She'll be ten next month."

"Like I said, I never met them, your wife, your kids. Maybe I should take a ride out to Jersey one of these days and pay my respects. I could find out if your wife sucks cock any better than your mother. And what did you say, the girl was ten? You know, it's funny, the older you get, the younger you like your meat."

He drew phlegm from his lungs into his mouth, and he spat on the picture. Then he drew more phlegm from his lungs, and he spat into the face of the kid.

The kid began to cry as he wiped the phlegm from his face with a table napkin.

"What is it you want me to do?" he said.

"Two things. First — and like the arresting officer says: think about this before you answer, because it may be the most important answer you ever give in your life — how much money is in this shit-hole right now?"

"Just the take from tonight. About twelve hundred."

"That's pathetic."

"It's all credit cards these days."

"How much of this twelve hundred did you already dip into?"

"You took it."

"Empty your other pockets too."

The kid put about a hundred and eighty dollars and some coins on the table. Louie took it and put it in his pocket.

"Now, where's that twelve hundred?"

"In the kitchen."

"Let's go."

Louie rose. The kid rose. The kid began walking, to the left of the bar, to the narrow passage that led to the kitchen. He could feel Louie close behind him: very close behind him.

On the kitchen wall, there was a cheap ugly picture in a cheap ugly frame: one of those Virgin Mary things that these kitchen spics went for.

"How come they call all these shit joints Italian restaurants?" Louie snorted. "I mean, you can't find a wop in any one of these fuckin' kitchens. They're all fuckin' Dominicans, Ecuadorians, this, that, the other fuckin' thing. These ain't fuckin' Italian restaurants, none of them. They're fuckin' spic joints. Who eats this shit, anyway? Jews?"

The kid raised his arm and reached behind the picture and removed an envelope and turned to give it to Louie, who held in his right hand the gun in its plastic bag, and who with his left hand took the envelope and shoved it in his back pocket. The kid did not ask about the second of the two things that Louie wanted him to do.

"Now, remember what we were talkin' about — about makin' a man out of you? Get on your fuckin' knees."

"Lou, please, I'll do anything you want me to do, but —"

"Then just fuckin' do it."

The kid knelt slowly on shaking legs. This was not real, and yet it was. He felt the hard floor beneath him, the hard wall behind him. They were real. His eyes were closed, his head was somewhat bowed.

Through the crotch of his trousers, Louie grabbed and loosened his balls, the cramped sagging folds of which were stuck together and stuck to the cramped folds of his underwear, until they were free from the paste of the gathered humidity and sweat;

and with his forefinger he raised aside his shrunken cock, and it was as if once again this dank, bunched trinity of cock and balls could breathe and feel the good, drying air. It felt nice.

"Now hold your ankles nice and tight like a good little girl. That's a good girl."

Louie pulled the trigger through the plastic bag, and that was that. He stepped back. Perfect. It was funny: if somebody was kneeling and you did him close and straight through the head, really close and really straight, just so, with no second shot to jack him, he would stay kneeling. But if you tried to set up some collapsed fucking discombobulated fucking stiff to make him look like he was on his knees when he went, it was a real fucking pain in the ass. And it never looked right. Never.

This looked nice. Louie noticed that the little cocksucker was kneeling with a hole in his head directly under that stupid spic *porcu Madonna*. Forget about fucking nice. This was fucking art.

C*'èrano nove cieli: non sfere celesti, ma cieli della terra, cieli di nube e di soffio d'aria.*

There were nine skies: not heavens, but skies. All of what truth he knew had begun with the revelation of this ennead.

With eyes drawn to them, he had come well to know them through his years beneath them. The first of the skies that he had come to know had through those years become to him the rarest of all. This was the great sky of illimitableness. As every of the skies had four aspects — its coming, its being, its passing, and its night — so this sky of illimitableness came from darkness with most dulcet light, in which one discerned the hue of pale rose, as one could discern the blue of the sky itself, the blue of all skies, the blue of the nine skies within the veins beneath the skin of those among us who were of angelic color.

There had been such a vein of blue where the soft aureate curling wisps remained ever free at the left of her forehead: tameless, unclenched, and uncommandable, while all else of her tresses had been dressed taut and twined. He once had seen a droplet as of dew — an infinitesimal liquescent pearl of the aqua rosmarina with which her hair was combed: to him it was the very dew of the morning of illimitableness itself — a droplet whose rainbow had entered his eye and there since dwelt, impressed upon and immanent in his vision, as an *ad gloriam* of her.

Her. She whose movements and the movements of the skies had since become one.

The sky of illimitableness had been revealed to him before she had been revealed to him. In the meadow, with his young, supple spine to the pulse of the earth, having seen it so many times, he had at last perceived it, opening to him as the nebulous abundant white infinity-blossoms of great clouds parted, opening to him the blue that was the blue of the All. He had felt then the pulse of that earth as if he had none of his own, and it was as if the breath of him were taken from him by what had opened to him; and as yet another billowing Eucharist of white, more radiant than the others, but unseen by him, rolled away, and, lost in wonder that had made of him wonder itself, without pulse of self and without breath of self, but containing all breath and all pulse, he was blinded by the golden planchet aflame of the sun, and was then without all sense that birth had given him, and he had felt what lay beyond that to which we are born.

Then this miracle had passed, and young Dante Alighieri again had been simply a child with supple sapling spine to the earth. But the child had lain all the day and into the night, waiting for the return of what did not return, and seeing the aspects of the sky subtly change, as if its vastness were of soul and sigh.

The stars then had beckoned him to read their myriad secrets, and were without moon.

I SPEAK TO YOU AS AN AOL TIME WARNER product.

I never envisioned that I would live to say these words, which both repulse and strangely amuse me. Then again, I never imagined that I would live this long, period. But imagining ends, and fortune bears two faces, neither of which is unveiled until the end. I now feel nothing of repulsion or of strange amusement. I feel only the fatal awaitance of that final unveiling. For I now know that, one way or another, I will not be here to utter these words again in the span of near seasons. For I now know that, one way or another, I, Nick Tosches, will not be here, period.

I can speak no more of this to you now, because there is nothing more that I know of it. The veil has not yet been raised. But I can, and I will, tell you what brought me here.

I draw deep breath and exhale and disperse the dark of my past into the dark of the here and now, and I breathe forth only the dark of this tale. For as much as no one has ever broken and entered into that dark church within me, and as much as I have always craved the presence there of the soul of another, this dark church has nothing to do with the tale I must here tell, except in that it has to do with me.

Dark: a word so old and weary with use that it has all but lost its meaning. And yet, again and again, I here find myself drawn to it. My life on this earth has not been without its light, its happiness, its love, and its joy. But these too are words so old and weary with use that they have all but lost their meaning. I have at last grown comfortable with such words, as I myself have grown so old and weary with use as to have all but lost meaning. So I will speak to you in such words, from this old and worn darkness that now overglooms old and worn light, old and worn happiness, old and worn love, old and worn joy.

As there is nothing left to lose, I here turn the key and throw open the doors of this church, hiding nothing, and with no truth to fear. I will not labor over words. Such labor, like the sweet afternoon with which I begin my tale, is now behind me.

And, God, it was a sweet afternoon. Every afternoon was sweet. It was summer. I had left New York behind me more than a month ago. First Yucatán, then from Cancún to Cuba.

Late at night, the sway and rhythms of *son* and *danzon*, *rumba* and *mambo*, the striking of claves and beating of drums, would enter me through the shutters of my room at the Hotel Santa Isabel in La Habana Vieja, and I would descend to the Plaza de Armas, to merge with what had entered me. I would wander to where the sway and rhythms faded, to where danger seemed to loom silently in the hot night air: to the deserted black decay of the Castillo de la Fuerza, the squalor of the waterfront. I felt an odd calm, as if lingering to meet an evil that had crept away at my coming. Then I would return to the sway and rhythms, until they too, disbanding, fell away to silence; and I would ascend to my bed.

In the sweltering glare of day, I would retreat to take a shave at the barber on Calle Obispo, an establishment that dated to the age of the conquistadors; and I would roam amid the vendors who crowded the shaded arcade of the plaza. I sought among them for remnants of the Havana that died with the end of the Batista regime. I sought especially for *fichas casino*, antique chips from the old casinos. But my mention of such things unsettled the vendors, for these things were the artifacts of a forbidden history. Eventually, however, one of them placed a call for me, and then, for a price, he gave me the name and address of a man whom he described as an outlaw historian and collector.

I visited with this man, Lázaro, for hours into the night. As I was an *americano*, and as I dared to make my way to his apartment near a bad corner of Calle Compostella, he felt that I presented a rare opportunity to speak freely and without risk. I was interested only in buying pieces of his collection; but listening to him, even as he knew that I understood not much of what he said, was a part of the price. He was unwilling to part with many of the pieces that I coveted most, but in the end I managed to bargain successfully for a black-and-white photograph of a naked woman ribboned with the title MISS MODELO 1957, held aloft, one hand on each of her comely thighs, by a beaming Presidente Batista. This was nothing, however, to the casino chips: the Havana Riviera, the Habana Hilton, the Casino de Capri, the Casino de Sevilla, the Tropicana, Wilbur Clark's Casino. The most astounding chip of all bore no name: encircled with a border of deep crimson and set, also in deep crimson, in a round of white, its bold symbol said more than words. The symbol was the *Hakenkreuz*, the Nazi swastika. It was, Lázaro told me, from the long-forgotten Casino Aleman, which had stood since its founding in 1862 at the intersection of Prado Promenade and Neptune Street.

From Havana, I went south, from the Cuban mainland to Cayo Largo. At one end of this island lies the most beautiful and pristine stretch of beach in all the Caribbean. Near the other end, where the road ends and wilderness begins, scattered above the shore, are a group of ramshackle cabins which collectively bear the name of the Isla del Sur Resort. I shared my cabin with innumerable lizards. Outside, there were large iguanas, which moved about quietly, and large land crabs, which scratched and clawed and crunched their way quite noisily along the stony paths. Slung between two porch-posts was a woven hammock, which I also shared with innumerable lizards. I rented a motorcycle from the island's only gas station. I left the motorcycle near the road, as it could not handle the terrain that led from the road to the cabin.

One morning, I set out to go deep-sea snorkeling from an old shrimp-boat at the other end of the island. I got on my motorcycle and swerved out onto the road, but I swerved too fast and I swerved too wide and I swerved too low, and I spun out and was thrown into a patch of gravel and burs on the other side of the road. I looked up, and I saw the motorcycle coming down fast upon me.

Every straining movement to escape drove the gravel and thorny burs more deeply into my flesh, and shifted upon me the crushing weight of rusted metal, rattling engine, and spinning tires. Then I was out from under, and slowly, shaken and shaking, I rose. I began to pluck the burs from me. It was then that I saw that my left knee was torn open. The gash was deep, but it did not hurt and there was not much blood. I knew that this was not good.

I long ago had been stabbed to the bone in the metacarpal thenar of my left hand, and it had not hurt and there had not been much blood; and then the hand had gone cold, swollen, and turned gray. In the emergency room, the doctor — some guy dressed in white, anyway — had told me that this was called venous clotting, and that you could die from it. He had told me to bring the tips of the thumb and the forefinger of my grotesquely swollen hand as close together as I could.

I had forced them to within two inches of each other, and he had grasped my hand in both of his hands and then squeezed. The blood that then had shot from me had hit the ceiling. Then he had sewed me.

So I knew what to do. I braced myself with my right hand on the upturned handlebar of the motorcycle, and I bent my left leg a bit, grabbed it at the ankle with my left hand, and swiftly jerked it until my heel hit my ass. Blood squirted and began to flow. There was no sewing that I could do, so I wrapped my T-shirt around the knee, righted the motorcycle, and rode off down the road.

Aboard the boat, I unwrapped my knee. It did not feel too bad, and it did not look too bad. The boat dropped anchor and a couple of old guys smoking cigars lowered the stern-board. I gestured to my knee and in a pidgin Spanish I asked *el capitán* if it was all right to swim with this open wound.

"*El mar cura todo,*" he said. His grin was wonderful to behold: teeth of deepest antique tawny, adorned here and there with softly gleaming gold, set in a face as tough and brown and veined and wrinkled as maduro tobacco hung to dry.

The fish were beautiful. I luxuriated in moving slowly among them. Then, in the silent clarity beneath the surface of the sea, there appeared some fish that were drab and common-looking. There issued a plume of blood from my knee, and I realized that these drab and common-looking fish were gathering some yards away, where the plume of blood dispersed and evanesced. I realized simultaneously that these drab and common-looking fish were barracudas. My gentle, roaming breast-stroke ceased. I spun and churned.

Butterfly-stroke, crawl-stroke, death-stroke. I was without breath as I clambered aboard.

"*Tiburón?*" inquired *el capitán.*

"No," I told him. "Barracuda."

His grin was wonderful to behold.

I sat and had a smoke. My knee now looked bad. My knee now felt bad.

The only medical facility on the island was a dispensary out at the airstrip. A nurse swabbed my knee with a white substance that soon hardened like plaster. By the time I reached my cabin, all I could do was hobble as far as the hammock and heave myself into it.

The humble soul who was the attendant of this place had observed my unsteady wincing gait, my plastered knee, and my collapse into the hammock. Lying there with my leg outstretched, feeling my knee throb with pain, I now observed him. In the distance, he was making his way up a tall palm, climbing-loop in his hands and machete in his belt. After a while, the fronds obscured him. Two coconuts fell to the grassy sand.

He smiled as he approached me. He sat at the edge of the porch, and he laid the coconuts on the ground before him. With strong, deft strokes of the machete, he pared the top of one big green coconut, then the other. He laid them on their sides and, with one powerful blow of the machete to each pared top, he opened them. He stood and drank from one of them, and he placed it in my hands. The kindness of this young stranger, and the quenching warm water of the fresh-cut coconut, were gifts from the gods. The young man placed the other coconut on the wood slats of the porch, against the post of the hammock.

He smiled again and was gone. That evening, and in the days and evenings to come, he brought me food as well, from the large cabin that was the cooking-house and eating-house.

I lay there for days, with nothing but the sound of the waves and the comforting visits of the young stranger who smiled; and I smoked and I suffered and I slept. Never was pain so lovely.

The nurse from the dispensary came to see me. My knee had swollen so badly that the swelling had fractured and cracked open the plaster. She seemed uneasy at what she saw. She felt my forehead, she listened to my heart, and she sniffed at the openings in the plaster on my knee. She spoke to me, and I understood little of what she said, but I did understand the word *gangrena*.

Cayo Largo was a narrow island. Its northern shore, barely more than a mile from where I reclined, was mostly mangrove and swamp where only mosquitoes and their diseases thrived. This hot and humid island with its malarious and miasmal atmosphere just a southerly wind away was no place to risk infection of any kind. The nurse had hoped that the weekly medical-supply transport plane would bring more medicine, perhaps even *antibióticos*; but it had brought nothing that could help me.

Medicine and groceries: it was hard to get these things in Cuba. Paper was hard to come by, too. The nurse carried little ruler-torn slips of cheap scratch-pad paper, each slip stamped in faint purple ink with the words SERVICIOS MEDICOS. On one of these slips she wrote the name of the medicine that I must obtain: *Sulfadiazina de plata*. Her handwritten capital *S* was very delicate and very pretty. She said that I must return to Havana to get this medicine at once.

One of Compañia Cubana de Aviación's sporadic flights between Cayo Largo and Havana would be leaving tomorrow morning. Most of Cubana's fleet of twenty-six were Russian-surplus death crates, such as the two-propeller Antonov-24, one of which had recently gone down near Santiago, killing all forty-four persons aboard. Cubana was now really on a roll. After the AN-24 crash, two more of the airline's Russian-surplus planes had crashed in a single week, killing forty-seven.

I had been lying here for three days. I wanted to keep lying here. *Gangrena.* Compañia Cubana de Aviación de la Muerte. The miasma of death little more than a mile to the north, awaiting the right sultry breeze. I did not care. I wanted only to lie here.

On those occasions when I made my way to the latrine, or into the cabin for any reason, I placed all pressure on my good leg, and in my left hand I grasped the walking-stick that the good stranger had carved for me from the hard branch of a hard tree at the edge of the wilderness. Now I left the hammock and did not take the walking-stick in hand. For a while I merely stood, letting the pressure grow equal on both legs. Then I raised my good leg. Then I walked. The shore was deserted for as far as I could see. I lurched and staggered and strode and stumbled to the sea. The breaking waves hurled me down. I sat there, legs out, head back, bracing myself with straightened arms upon the firm wet sand, feeling my legs sway as the sea, again and again, rose upon me and washed over me. My knee burned as if it were aflame in the sea, as the wild gritty froth tore and scraped and laved the last of the plaster from it, and then, again and again, macerated and flushed the bare livid wound with the salt of that wild froth. I raised my head and looked into the sun, which in its slow descent was turning the sea to furious gold.

"*El mar cura todo,*" I proclaimed. But these words, like my great laughter that followed them from a place within me unknown to me, could not be heard amid the fury of that golden sea.

AFTER A FEW DAYS' MEDICAL ATTENTION and shuffling amid the horrid heat and filth and poverty of Havana, the sway and rhythms of the night no longer entered me, for I heard them as they were: a disingenuous imitation by rote, *para los turistas*, of a joy long dead; an annoyance, a noise that merely kept me from sleep.

I was still unaware that this is what really had been entering me all the while: death.

This dead music that only weeks before had drawn me forth into the dead of night, and to those places where death seemed to lurk: it was now as nothing. All of it — that which had drawn me, and that to which I had been drawn — nothing. Yes, faint wisps of death had entered the veins of my being, but those veins now thirsted for the true sway and rhythms, the true night and the true hidden shadows of the true thing itself, rather than the mere lifelessness and the torpor of indifference toward danger that had been the faint wisps of weeks ago.

It was in the music of the sea to the south, in the almighty roar of creation and destruction, the endless vagitus, lullaby, and threnody of the waves, whose tides bore away every dying soul, that I had found the true sway and rhythms of the true thing. Lying there alone in that hammock in the black of night, it was to me as if the stars, like glintings of infinity, and the clouds, like gatherings of shades, drifted and wove to the music of that roar, that vagitus, that lullaby, that threnody of those soul-delivering and soul-taking waves of that vast and deadly and godly song that was without beginning and that was without end. Lying there alone in that hammock in the black of night, the strange thirst in my veins had been quenched, as the thirst of my ailing had earlier, in the light of day, been quenched by the warm water of the fresh-cut coconut that had been brought to me by the kind young stranger. Lying there alone in the black of night, I felt the sea to be the great old stranger: the great old stranger that was beyond any epithets of kindness or of evil, just as its entrance into me was beyond both my will and my understanding.

"Listen," I whispered one night — to myself, or to company unseen and unknown, or to the thirsting mysteries in my veins, or to the congregation of ghosts of that church within me — "they're playing our song."

But how long had death been in my veins? Had I entered this life in an amniotic shroud? Had my own vagitus been threnody as well? A memory has been long with me, perhaps longer than any other, and it may tell of something.

I was six years old when I first took the life of another.

Did I really just write those words?

Jesus, how they reek of the cheap rhetoric of cheap solemnity.

This writing racket makes a hard habit to kick. It will ride you to the throe of the end. Look at Henry James as death approached: articulating through the slobber of a stroke, drivel and dribble as one, unstanchable: "So here it is at last, the distinguished thing."

It was Flaubert who said it best, giving us the perfect diagnosis of the writer's disease in words that have been engraved in me since I came to perceive that most writing, foremost among it the greater part of the most revered of it, is but little more than artful whoredom:

"Turns of speech," said he, "conceal mediocre affections: as if the fullness of the soul might not sometimes overflow in the emptiest of metaphors, since no one, ever, can give the exact measurements of his needs, nor of his conceptions, nor of his sufferings, and the human word is like an outworn, battered timbal upon which we beat out melodies fit for making bears dance when we are trying to move the stars to pity."

He agonized endlessly, Flaubert, to conjure *le mot juste*, the perfect word to express what he sought to say. It was twenty years after he wrote the above that he finally found, as evinced by his last finished fiction, that the perfect words were the simplest words, those words so old and weary with use as to have all but lost their meaning. Ezra Pound took up the call of *le mot juste*, only to look back upon the great work of his long life as failure. "I have tried to write Paradise," he said at the end of the poem that he had begun fifty-seven years before. But to write Paradise lay beyond the greatest powers of the greatest poets, for, as Pound in the wisdom of his years finally saw, Paradise lay beyond words. Thus what had begun those many years before with an Homeric surge, "keel to breakers," into the sea, was to end:

Let the Gods forgive what I
have made
Let those I love try to forgive
what I have made.

No, there could be no Paradise for words, not for one who had glimpsed Paradise:

Do not move
Let the wind speak
that is paradise.

At times the sound of this wisdom seems to me to be even more beautiful in the Italian translation of Pound's daughter, Mary de Rachewiltz:

Non ti muovere,
Lascia parlare il vento
Così è Paradiso

Le mot juste is silence. If I can not now go forth into the silence of this wisdom — as I very soon shall go forth — I must here and now cease to be a writer in the wretched sense of that profession. I must here and now leave all of artful whoredom behind me. I must proceed with simplicity. And there is no time to grant grace to that simplicity, as there remains time neither to gaze back upon what I have written nor to pause nor to ponder. I can not regard as a book these words that issue from me, but must regard them as testament or testimony, lest care hinder them from carrying this tale to its end. And as I do not know how much time is left to me, so much more recklessly must I move forward. My own end must not come before I bring these words and this tale to their end; for they are not only a part of my own ending, not only testament or testimony, but also a letter-bomb that must be delivered, a letter-bomb that will blow away the face and hands of what we call culture and what we call history. There is a good chance that even if I bring these words and this tale to their end, they will be suppressed or outright destroyed, especially as I shall not be here to contend with. But I must not dwell on this; and, besides, these words will be entrusted to one whom I trust above all others, and to whom a letter-bomb of truth might be considered a form of literature that transcends. So, I must move forward, leaving grace and literary concerns behind me, riding hard on the mare of honesty alone, which overwhelms those lesser things. No, this is not a book and it does not represent me as a writer. And why should that even matter? Most of those who read me can not tell the good work from the bad. Soon I shall be gone, and then soon I shall be forgotten. Perhaps two or three books out of a dozen or so, maybe a scattering of poems: let these represent me. Then again, as I say, why should it even matter? Hemingway said it well: "Posterity can take care of herself or fuck herself." It's probably the best line the fat faggot ever wrote. So, then, this vestigial treacle from my days of whoredom — these locutions about taking the life of another, and all such trifles — must here be abandoned. I disgust myself with such fatuous writerly nonsense. I'm going to have a smoke, make some coffee, take a shave. Dawn has come. It's Sunday morning. The Lord's day.

All right.

I was six years old the first time I killed somebody. He was maybe two years older than I. It was an overcast and rainy afternoon. It was on a deserted street near the glass factory, which was more like a glass dump: high rusted corrugated tin fences swelling and sagging from the big heaps of shattered glass that long ago had burst and overflowed from them. No one ever seemed to work there, and there were no signs of industry, but they still called it "the glass factory." These were the good old days: when you could look to farthest downtown and see nothing but open sky and the grand old buildings of another age; when urban blight — the abandoned or bustling warehouses and factories, the vacant lots, the decaying piers, the alleys, the child's endless treasure-trove of it all — was as romantic and magical as any enchanted woods in a picture-book. Now, the downtown vista has been destroyed and dominated by the immense twin towers of absolute ugliness and blandness and mediocrity, lesser structures of ugliness and blandness and mediocrity rise upon landfills, the abandoned or bustling warehouses and factories have become luxury properties filled with "*living-spaces*," the vacant lots have been filled with more of the same, the alleys have been occluded, the foreboding decaying piers have vanished and been replaced by "*friendly recreational spaces*" and dismal "*esplanades*," and even the children are no longer children, but blobs of *New York Times* "Living"-section papier-mâché mush, products of "*parenting*" in these "*living-spaces*," leashed and tethered for "*structured activities*" or "*quality time*" in the "*friendly recreational spaces*," malnourished by the pabulum of "*political correctness*," computers, television, and a "*balanced diet*" with occasional "*treats*" and "*munchies*," with nowhere to prowl, no imagination, and no freedom, having emerged from an aerobically fit and ultrasonically scanned womb, bearing a modish name, and doomed to the common fate of lifeless sterility in a sterile and lifeless place.

But again I wander, and I must not. Besides, who cares about such things? There was a time when I myself cared about this world and this race; but that time is behind me.

So, anyway, this kid was pulling one of those little red metal wagons, which was old and beat-up and filled with stacks of old and sodden newspapers. I don't remember if he was holding it openly or if he drew it from the wagon when I came upon him, or he upon me; but I remember him holding the butcher's knife toward me, and I remember what he said.

"Hey, kid, wanna die?"

I was scared. But, as I realized later, it was not the big knife that scared me, and it was not the boy that scared me. It was the question that scared me. It was the eerie sense of indecision, or, more, the vague, unsettling awareness of that eerie indecision, that scared me. I was a child, and I could not then articulate this, or comprehend it, but I felt it, and it scared me.

My grandfather's brother, who was in the rackets and was a mystery religion unto himself, had recently advised me that whenever I was alone and saw a stranger approaching, the first thing I should do was to look about me in the gutter for a discarded beer bottle or soda bottle, the base of which I should then break off against the curb, thus leaving in my hand a fine and jagged weapon. Now here I was. I had not even seen this stranger approach, and I was standing in a rubble of jagged glass with nothing in my little hands. So I kicked the boy in the shin as hard as I could. He dropped the butcher's knife. I picked it up. I stabbed at him. He fell backward over the pull-bar of his little red wagon and landed face-up on the pavement. I jumped on him, straddling his scrawny belly, and I opened his scrawny throat with the blade of the butcher's knife, which took from him his voice, and then his life. I had not killed him, but only his question. He went with it.

Even as I did this — slit his throat rather than pierce his heart, as a child might be expected to do, construing the heart as the most vital organ and the best place to fatally strike, even if he had but a child's notion of where it was — I felt that I was influenced by a gesture that was common to my grandfather's brother, and his brothers, and others of my family: the crescenting of thumbnail or outstretched forefinger across the throat. It was most often a gesture of opprobrium or threat or deadly intent toward another — "*ti scanno*" — but my grandmother, who was from Abruzzo, and who had married into this strangeness of brothers from Puglia, used this gesture to express her sense of being fed-up to the point of suicide, or omnicide. Only now, lying in a sweat in Cuba, wondering how long death had been in my veins, did I begin to feel that, while this familial gesture very well may have influenced the manner of this childhood deed, there may have been a more instinctive and immediate influence: a reflex. The boy's question had come from his throat.

I walked some distance before I saw that the bloody knife was still in my hand. I would have loved to have kept it, but I knew to get rid of it. I dropped it through a street-corner sewer-grating. The blood on my right hand was already sticky and turning brown. I figured it best not to wipe it off on my shirt or pants. I was unsettled, shaking, but I felt no guilt or shame for what I had done; and in all the years that since have passed, amid all the guilt and senseless shame that have haunted me, I never once felt guilt or shame about that overcast childhood day. And while my dreams have always been unpleasant and peopled largely by the dead, he has never been among them.

What troubled me deeply was that in the coming year, I was to receive my First Holy Communion. Preparatory to this, we lowly public-school kids were forced to attend Sunday-school, purportedly to get a minimum effective dose of the religion that the parochial-school kids got daily. Not only that: they actually forced us to attend Mass as well, every week before Sunday-school, and the nuns would actually go to the church to see that you were there, and if you were not, they would not allow you to come to the Sunday-school class down the block at the parochial school, and if you got barred from Sunday-school, you would be barred as well from receiving your First Holy Communion. So this whole routine of God and sacrament and sermons and nuns was getting to me, and what was getting to me more, increasingly so, was what it was all inevitably leading up to: First Confession, without which there was no First Communion. What was a seven-year-old kid supposed to confess? "Bless me, Father, for I have sinned." But then what? The good nuns coached us with stock sins: "I stole"; "I was disrespectful of my mother and my father"; "I disobeyed my mother and my father"; "I" — *what? Quick, give me another.* I mean, when you got right down to it, how much did a seven-year-old child have to work with? I mean, even the ever popular "I committed self-abuse" was not yet in the repertoire. It would be another five years until I started jerking off, smoking, drinking, and robbing in earnest; and by then, believe me, I wasn't doing any confessing to anybody. But at six, this whole sin and sacrament and confession thing really had me going. These nuns were *bad.* If you failed to confess a sin, God might strike your mother dead. A boy once kicked his dog and did not do penance for it, and he was stricken lame. A boy once chose to go to the movies instead of to confession and then, walking back from the movies, he was run over by a truck and, dying thus in a state of sin, went directly to Hell. A boy did this, a boy did that. A boy, a boy, a boy. It was always a boy. If you listened to these nuns, who at night were probably lapping one another's cunts and dipping into the poor-box, girls were without sin. It was as if Eve was away doing charity work when Adam ate that apple. Even later, when puberty reared its head, the "self-abuse" bit was never insinuated among the budding target sex, several pubescent members of whom were doing their best to lessen our own load in the self-abuse arena. I mean, like, after all, it was *her* hand. But by then you knew the ropes: you knew which priests to stay away from — "How often?" "What *kind* of impure thoughts?"

But, as I say, at six the idea of getting into that box with one of these guys was really giving me the willies, and the nuns had done a good job. Every sin was another wound to the crucified Christ. I did not believe any of this, but, still, it gave me the willies.

And now here I was. I knew murder was one of the big ones. Top Ten. I mean, as far as commandments go, it wasn't really *up* there — it was down under "Honor Thy Father and Thy Mother" — but it was there, all right: "Thou Shalt Not Kill." I remember, a few years later, I actually looked at the Bible. We had been made to memorize the Ten Commandments in Sunday-school, and now here I was reading them in the Bible. It sounded familiar at first: "Thou shalt have no other gods before me." But then it went on: "for I the Lord thy God am a jealous God." Why didn't they make us memorize that part? Or at least reveal it to us. I mean, "for I the Lord thy God am a jealous God"? What was this? The Mosaic version of "You Cheated" by the Shields? "Runaround Sue" by Dion and the Belmonts? "The Ten Commandments of Love" by Harvey and the Moonglows? I mean, this God in this Bible seemed so obsessed with making sure that the collective chosen piece of ass of His chosen race didn't glance sideways at another god that He would never notice a murder here or there. I mean, this "Thou Shalt Have No Other Gods Before Me" went on and on, a hundred words and more, and, bang, bang, bang, as if He were just trying to fill out the tablet: "Thou shalt not kill. Thou shalt not commit adultery. Thou shalt not steal."

But, at six, the very notion of merely going into that box and opening my mouth gave me the willies. The notion of going in there and saying that I had killed somebody turned my mind white with fear. Even if He, the Lord my God Himself, placed murder beneath working on Sunday or dishonoring thy father and thy mother, this notion turned my mind white with fear.

I went looking for my grandfather's brother. He wasn't at the club, but he was at the garage. There was never a car in this garage:

only him, even though this was not even his garage. He was sitting there on a lawn chair, wearing Bermuda shorts, old crocodile shoes without laces, no socks, an old white-on-white dress shirt with French cuffs, unbuttoned, unlinked, and untucked. He was wearing a cocked fedora — cocked not to the side, but to the back — and he was smoking a guinea rope. He looked as he often looked.

"Hey, old-timer," he said.

"Hey, Unc," I said.

"You look like you seen a ghost," he said. "What happened?"

He looked at the dried, dark brown blood on my hand, but he didn't say anything.

"I killed some kid," I said.

"When?"

"Just now."

"Where?"

"Down by the glass factory."

"How?"

"I cut his throat."

"Was he from the neighborhood?"

"I never seen him before."

"Where's the shiv?" He saw that I didn't understand him. "The knife," he said. "Where's the knife?"

"I threw it down the sewer."

"Go wash yourself." He gestured to a work area near the wall behind him. He sometimes received visitors at the garage. At times he sat with them in the open at the entrance to the garage, and at times he led them to the privacy "in back," as he said. There was a sink there. As I washed, I felt better already. He was my real priest, and he had not raised his voice or damned me.

"Why'd you do it?"

"He had this big knife and he asked me if I wanted to die."

"So you didn't start nothing. He did."

"Yeah."

"How do you feel?"

"O.K. Now. I feel O.K. now."

"You gonna make a career of this now, or what? You feel like a little tough guy now?"

"No."

"Good. 'Cause you ain't. Remember what I always told you. The golden rule. Love thy neighbor."

"Right."

"And you don't be like this kid you ran into. You don't give no malarkey to nobody."

"Right."

"Right. You don't give no malarkey to nobody? And what's the rest of that, like I told you?"

"Don't give no malarkey to nobody and don't take no malarkey from nobody."

"So, you didn't take no malarkey."

"Right."

"And you're sure he ain't from the neighborhood."

"I never seen him around here before."

"C'mere."

I moved closer to him and he tousled my hair.

"Unc?"

"What?"

"Do I have to tell what I told you when I make my confession?"

"What're you talkin' about, 'confession'?"

"For my First Holy Communion."

"Oh. That. God's everywhere, right?"

"Right."

"And He hears everything, right?

"Right. He sees everything, He hears everything."

"So who's more important, God or the priest?"

"God."

"So God just heard your confession. You said it out loud. I heard it, God heard it."

"Is that the way you do it?"

"That's the way I do it."

"So that's it? My sin is gone?"

"You didn't sin. The little *citrull'* who pulled the knife on you for no reason: he's the one who sinned. God punished him through you."

"Thanks."

"We're buddies, right?"

"Yeah. Buddies." I was smiling now, and there was a smile in his eyes too.

"Just remember," he said. "What goes on between us and God, things like this, they're special. You can't tell nobody about these things. That's a sin. A bad one."

I understood. And, above all, I was absolved.

I never did tell anyone, and it was another thirteen years before I killed anybody else.

But that doesn't have anything to do with anything.

"Hey, kid, wanna die?"

And so it was that this memory and this question returned to me in Cuba, in my hammock feeling death and the sound of the sea enter me. *Gangrena.* In the middle of the night, after I heard that word, I found myself whispering it, rolling and trilling the *r* absurdly in an exaggerated and comical Spanish accent, to the swollen knee of my raised and outstretched leg: *gangrrrena.*

Gangrene. Amputation. An unpleasant malady. An unpleasant treatment. At this point in my life, however, I lived every day with the threat of amputation. Diabetes. It doesn't get much play among the AIDS-and-breast-cancer crowd, but it kills more people each year than both of those other things combined. AIDS afflicts about three quarters of a million persons in the United States, and breast cancer about two and a half million: a total of fewer than three and a half million. Diabetes afflicts sixteen million people in the United States. AIDS kills about thirty-odd thousand Americans each year, and breast cancer about forty-odd thousand: a total of about seventy-five thousand. Diabetes kills about a hundred and eighty thousand Americans each year. The annual government research budgets for AIDS and breast cancer total more than two billion dollars. The annual government research budget for diabetes is less than three hundred and fifty grand. You look at the figures and you tell me that disease is not a fucking fashion industry.

So, what happens to diabetics? Let's say, to put it mildly, they tend to die young. Most of these deaths are caused by complications of the disease: a nasty array that ranges from blindness and diabetic coma to hyperglycemic stroke and kidney failure. It is the almost inevitable condition of diabetic neuropathy that leads to amputation, or, more commonly, amputations, plural, as the spread of the neuropathy, from the extremities through the limbs, is sought to be contained or controlled by amputation after amputation, from toe to foot to knee to hip, and then perhaps again, chopping in increments or severing whole another limb, and so on.

My diabetes was diagnosed at a late stage, a few years ago, after I dropped fifty pounds in three months and figured I was croaking. I was told that if I maintained perfect control of my glucose levels, I had a fifty-percent chance of making out all right. Controlling one's glucose level is not merely a matter of careful medication but also of rigid dietary strictures. It is not just a matter of laying off sweets and pasta and bread and booze and fruit juices and such, for, as everything that one ingests, except water, turns to sugar in the body, it is difficult to control one's glucose level and still eat a decent meal. I loved to eat, but I went with it for a while. Then I saw that no matter how much I lived in deprivation, my numbers, as they say — my glucose-level readings — were not much improved. Metabolism varies from one person to the next, and the exact nature of diabetes is multifarious and mysterious. It is not just a matter of the body's inability to produce insulin. Sometimes, as in my case, cells do not absorb or process the sugar in the blood, and this greatly compounds the difficulty of dealing with the disease.

Then my dick blew out: something to do with blood vessels, part of that old black magic called neuropathy. Fortunately this aspect of neuropathy did not involve the amputation of the offending appendage. I am not sure if penile blow-out is the proper medical term, but it is both one of the primary symptoms and one of the most common complications of diabetes in men. But so many men, who do not drop fifty pounds in three months, and who are unaware of blow-out as an indicator of diabetes, are prevented by shame from going to the doctor, and thus, undiagnosed and unknowing, they may literally die of shame. Fuck them.

For me, as I say, the blow-out came later. It was very upsetting. It was not that I was much interested anymore in fucking — I had seen the light and was by this time a blow-job man through and through; a true connoisseur of blow jobs — it was that, even while I didn't want to fuck, I wanted to be able to fuck. Of course, being unable to fuck, I immediately wanted to fuck again. First I tried shooting myself up, in the dick, with this stuff that my urologist gave me. Then I tried these pills. Then I figured: fuck all this shit. I was glad that I had fucked three different broads every day for years in the toilet of the same gin-mill. I was glad that I had fucked the wife, girlfriend, mistress, mother, and daughter of every guy I knew. If it was over, so be it. I recalled something that Frank Costello was supposed to have said; something about there being only so many bullets in the gun. *Solo pisciare*, as the guys from the other side used to say, *solo pisciare*. I walked about singing that old Mississippi Sheiks song, "Pencil Won't Write No More," the verses of it that I could remember.

> I just worry and I wonder,
> baby, everywhere I go;
> just thinkin' about my old pencil:
> it won't write no more.
>
> Everybody's a-thinkin':
> what a time you once had;
> it can't be no more
> because the lead is gone dead.
>
> I used to write with my pencil,
> I would always leave my sign;
> now the lead has gone dead,
> I can't even draw no line.
>
> Oh, I really believe
> this is goin' to take my life;
> can't find the lead in my pencil
> even with my Rawl pocket knife.

The other side of this record was "I Am the Devil," which seemed to complement it well.

> Yes, I'm the Devil,
> oh, and I don't care none.

Fuck me and fuck my dick. But I was pissed off at the disease that had retired it. I refused to allow it to take away the pleasure that I derived from eating. To take away a well-used dick from a degenerate was one thing, but to take away pasta from a wop was another thing by far. And for what? A fifty-percent chance to prolong my life? That was a toss of the coin. Where was the savvy in that chump's bet? And to prolong what kind of life?

"I can't believe this," said the lovely young lady that was mine at the time.

We were at a good Italian restaurant, and I had just finished off a meal fit for the Devil — yes, I walked about singing both sides of that old record — and now the owner had brought me exactly what I craved for dessert.

"I just can't believe this," said the lovely young lady that was mine at the time. "You'd rather have that hot-fudge sundae than me."

Had this comment been made to me several years before, I would have told its maker to shut the fuck up and leave me the fuck alone. But I was now a sober and gentler soul, and I considered her words and her feelings, and I responded soberly and gently and honestly.

"Well, if you put it that way, I have to admit: yeah."

"What are you going to do if you end up commuting to dialysis in a wheelchair?"

"Then I'll find out if you *really* love me. Now, please, let me enjoy this in peace."

And so. *Gangrena*? Fuck it. I'll eat it for breakfast. I'll pour the discharge over vanilla ice cream and make a hot-gangrene sundae.

But there was more going on inside me. In that hammock, in the middle of that night, after I heard that word, *gangrena*, after I found myself whispering it comically toward the swollen knee of my raised and outstretched leg, I found myself whispering to that same knee:

"Hey, kid, wanna die?"

Yes, something was going on inside me. I was not five years

old. I was fifty. But regardless of whatever wisdom age had brought me, I might as well have been five, for, though I could feel this thing within me and without me, and I could hear it in the sea, and I could see it in the stars, I could not understand it.

"Hey, kid, wanna die?"

Some of the forbidden casino chips that I got in Havana were from the time of that fatal question, and they may have been moved across the felt of a blackjack table on that very day, at that very moment, held and passed by unknown distant hands as the blood dried on my own: other times, other souls, other demons within them. I had those forbidden chips in a small pouch. It was time to play.

LOUIE WAS NOT IN THE FUCKING MOOD for this fucking shit tonight. He had just ordered a fucking pizza and was settling in to watch the fucking ball game, and now this. He simply was not in the fucking mood for this shit tonight. He had been in a good mood. He was looking forward to this fucking pizza. Half plain, half onion and garlic. He had already turned on the oven, so he could lay the pizza box on the stove right away and keep it nice and warm and crisp while he finished it off nice and slow and easy, watching the game. Then the telephone had rung. That cheap ugly plastic piece of shit. And there was only one fucking person in this whole goddamn fucking world who had his number.

"I just ordered a pizza," he told him.

"You just ordered a pizza."

"Yeah. I just ordered a pizza."

Then there were no more words: just a harsh and impatient sigh in Louie's ear.

Louie hung up the telephone, and he sighed his own sigh, which was also harsh, but disgusted and resigned rather than impatient. He was sick of this shit. This is what happens: a guy gets too much power, too much time on his hands, and this is what happens. Forty years ago, this guy was borrowing twenties off him; now every little bug up his ass, you got to drop everything and come fucking running like a nigger slave. His Royal Majesty requests.

So here he now sat, as summoned.

"It's good to see you, Lou."

The son of a bitch sounded like it was a pleasant fucking friendly surprise visit; like it was, oh, fuck the pizza, fuck the ball game, fuck the nice quiet night at home, let me mosey over and drop in on this fucking *braciol'*-buster and see how he's doing.

"Is that real?"

The last time Louie was up here, there was an Our Lady of Pompeii Church calendar that advertised Perazzo's funeral parlor on the bottom of every month hanging on the wall behind his desk. Now there, Christ, some kind of fucking —

"Rembrandt. Self-portrait."

Louie looked at it pensively. "You know," he said, studying it, "if I had a snout like that and I was doing a self-portrait, I think I woulda done a little cosmetic surgery with the paint there." He turned his eyes from it. "What's somethin' like that worth?"

As Louie turned his eyes from it, Joe Black turned toward it, in a different way than he used to turn to look at the calendar to see what day it was.

"How do you put a price on beauty, Lou?" Joe Black turned toward him with a smirk.

Louie was going to say something, but he didn't.

"Did you hear about Aldo Chink?" said Joe Black. "They found him dead up on a Hundred-fifteent' Street. In church. Heart attack. Kneelin' there prayin' and —" Joe Black snapped his fingers.

What the fuck was this? It was like: fuck you, fuck your pizza, fuck the ball game; here's my Rembrandt, Aldo Chink croaked in church.

"Fuck Aldo Chink."

"Ah, come on, Lou, he was all right."

"Fuck him. I mean, these people kill me. This son of a bitch dirty rat cocksucker collapses in some fuckin' pew, and it's like, oh, poor guy, he croaked while he was kneelin' there prayin'. He prob'ly ducked in the fuckin' joint 'cause he saw a fuckin' shylock comin'." Louie lighted a cigarette, shook his head in mild disgust. "Fuck Aldo Chink."

"Yeah, I thought I should have the Kleenex ready."

"What do you want me to say? He was a cocksucker when he was alive. Now he's a dead cocksucker. The son of a bitch owed me three grand."

A few breaths passed in silence.

"You seem down, Lou."

A few more breaths passed in silence. Louie sighed, without emotion, a drained sort of sigh.

"Nah, I don't know. I'm tired, that's all, Joe. I'm tired." His words were subdued. They came forth honestly and tiredly, like a part of that drained sort of sigh, from that tiredness of which he spoke, that place inside him, of tiredness and worse, from which he had earlier this night hoped to escape. "I mean, it seems like yesterday, Joe, you and me, we were kids. We were out there shinin' shoes for those old-timers there outside the Full Mooners Club. Now we're the old-timers. And you're sittin' there under

Jimmy Durante's grandfather, this Rembrandt there, whatever the fuck it is, and I got a cold pizza waitin' for me back at my place. I mean, don't read me wrong. I feel good that you're sittin' there. I got no complaints, really. Except maybe that quick draw on the Ameche that you're developin' there." The words ended: "I'm just tired, Joe. That's all. I'm just tired."

Then there were more breaths of more silence. Louie was about to ask why Joe had called him to come here tonight, but Joe spoke first.

"If you're tired, Lou, you should take a rest."

"It ain't that kind of tired, Joe. It's like: *tired*."

"Do you like that painting, Lou?" Joe Black cocked his head toward it without looking at it.

"To be perfectly honest, no. I think it's an ugly piece of shit. And I know you do too. Otherwise, you'd have it on another wall, where you could see it, rather than hangin' it behind you where you don't have to look at it; hangin' it over your head like a crown for other people to see."

"Yeah," Joe Black said. "Ten million bucks' worth of ugly. Can you believe that shit? Strange fuckin' world, hey, Lou? Strange fuckin' world."

"Well, at least I know you didn't pay no ten million bucks for it. For that kind of money, you could get somethin' good."

"No, no, you're right. But what I'm sayin' is, it's strange what people will pay for. It's strange what people will pay a lot for. When I say a lot, I mean a lot.

"That's why I fucked up your pizza tonight, Lou. I fucked up your pizza to tell you that you're going to be a very wealthy man. This may be the hardest work you've ever done, but when it's done, if we bring this one home, you'll never have to pull a trigger again in your life except to go out in a tweed jacket to clip a pheasant. This is big, Lou."

"How big?"

"Bigger than anybody ever dreamt anything could be."

"What is it?"

"Something nobody ever dreamt of."

"What kind of money we talkin' about?"

"Your end?"

"My end."

"Between one and two million. Maybe more. Cash. Tax-free. Nice, clean bills."

"Christ, what do I have to do, kill a fucking army?"

"We're going to have to hush a few mouths. Just a few lullabies along the way."

"When's payday?"

"A few months after we start."

"And when do we start?"

"Soon. I just got the word I was waiting for before I called you. Lefty's looking for this guy he knows: some writer, a friend of his, half legit, the key guy we need to move this along. Like I say, soon."

"A friend of his? What, we got friends now? Who is this guy?"

"I don't know," Joe said dismissively, wincing as if there were a burning of slight, familiar aggravation in his chest or his gut. "Some guy named Nick."

"Nick? This is a world of fucking Nicks."

"What is this? What the fuck do you care what his name is?"

"It ain't got nothin' to do with nobody's name. It's that word *friend*."

From a drawer of his desk, Joe removed an envelope and passed it to Louie.

"For now, like I said, take it easy awhile. There's ten grand there. Think of it as the three grand Aldo Chink owed you, plus seven for luck. Think of it as a *friend*. Better yet, just think of it as money."

Louie slipped the envelope into the inside breast pocket of his fine, fine jacket of fine, fine cotton and fine, fine silk. He stood and patted the breast of his fine, fine jacket.

"Joe, my friend, I await your call."

He made it home by the top of the seventh inning. The score was tied. The pizza was good.

THE FULL MOON RED IN RISING TURNED silver and white within an hour's span.

THE PRIEST WAS IN HIS SEVENTIETH YEAR. For most of his life, he had wanted only to serve God.

For as long as he could remember, he had not felt himself to be a part of this world. He had seen very little of this world. Alcamo. Palermo. Rome. He had not travelled much beyond the provinces of these places.

Long ago, in the spring and summer when childhood left him, he had lain high upon a hilltop. Below him, the old vines and the new vines and their sweet-ripening grapes lay glorying in the sun. To the north lay the Golfo di Castellammare and the Tyrrhenian Sea. To the northeast, about fifty kilometers away, along the sea-coast, lay Palermo. To the southeast, about the same distance away, inland, lay Corleone. To the east, between those two places, lay Piana degli Albanesi.

This hilltop place, where pale wild roses still grew, was said to be where Ciullo d'Alcamo, the divine Cielo, had encountered the muse that inspired him to write what was among the earliest and most beautiful verse to be inflected in the Sicilian language. In that spring and summer when childhood left him, the boy who lay there wondered if the pale wild roses were much different at all from the roses that Cielo had looked upon perhaps seven hundred years before.

White butterflies fluttered and lingered amid the flowering stalks of lavender, as aeroplanes flew low overhead, shrilling down their bombs of destruction. In the heat of summer, not long before the invasion of Palermo, the aeroplanes bombed the railroad facilities of Alcamo. He could see and hear and feel the deafening explosions that shook the very hill on which he lay. Yet he felt neither fear nor concern. It meant nothing to him.

"*Rosa fresca aulentissima . . .*"

He whispered these words endlessly: the first words of the only poem by Cielo to have survived. Over the course of those warm and sunny days, he brought the poem to memory: a hundred and thirty upon thirty lines, whose closing words — *chissa cosa n'è data in ventura*: this thing that is not given in fortune — were like the surrender of the petals of that *rosa fresca* to the winds.

His whispering was in a meter that the poem seemed to summon naturally from him. He knew nothing then of the language of scansion and metrics. Only later would he learn that his whispering had been of *strofe pentastiche*, composed of three *alessandrini monorimi* followed by a *distico* of *endecasillabi a rima baciata* diverse from the rhyme of the preceding three lines. And when he learned this, he learned too that his whispering had been in perfect accord with the form and rhythm of the poem. He was not so proud as to feel that this proved any preternatural instinct for poetry on his part. He felt only that it proved the greatness of the poet, whose spirit was so sublime as to reach through the centuries to reclaim his voice from the mouth of a boy, and whose prosody was so brilliant that his poem could be neither wrongly perceived nor wrongly uttered. One needed to know nothing of the Alexandrine monorhymes of Old French *laisses*, or of eleven-syllable lines called hendecasyllabics, or even of the *rima baciata* — the "kissed rhyme" — of rhyming couplets. No, one needed to know nothing but the power of the rose and the power of the wind that is fortune. These powers were of God, and though his poem was one that spoke through the romantic motifs of his time, it was closer to these powers, and to God, that Cielo brought us with his words.

These words, and the fresh-burst rose most fragrant and the winds of fortune they evoked, possessed a greater force than that which rattled in destruction through the skies. This great and beautiful island had been beset and invaded without end, since the dawn of history, by the passing powers of the ages. This is what had made the soul of this great and beautiful island so strong and so indomitable. The metal locusts could take his life, as they took the lives of so many around him; but they could take no souls, and they could make the soul of this place only more strong and more indomitable. For him, that spring and that summer, there was no war. There were not even the seven centuries that had passed since the rose that now enraptured him had first enraptured Cielo. For that rose was the rose that lay beyond this world.

He had left the countryside and the little town of Alcamo. There had been the seminary in Palermo, then the cassock. There had been the parish duties and the studies and the teachings at the Università. It was through his years of work at the university, amid the thousands of old and rare volumes of the recently bequeathed Castegna collection, that he had been brought to Rome, as a subaltern in the Archivio Segreto of the Biblioteca

Apostolica Vaticana. This work held little appeal for him, as the Archivio Segreto was a place of documents and of very little poetry. But he did his work well, and his increasing consultancy to librarians of various collections of the Library brought him after some years to the attention of the prefect, who was a medievalist and who looked with a smile upon the priest from Alcamo.

"*Rosa fresca aulentissima*," spoke the prefect slowly and pleasantly, then was silent in the luxuriance of what he had spoken.

His guest luxuriated in silence as well, then finished the line — "*ch'apari inver' la state*" — and then the two men went on together until they both felt bound by what fortune had and had not given them. For while they were both but priests undestined to become prelates, they both also had been blessed to sense the rose and the wind.

No, it would not be theirs to wear the Gammarelli-tailored crimson robes and the scarlet biretta. And they knew that many of those who did wear this finery looked down upon them and did not look toward them as brothers.

The younger priest, who now was well past his fiftieth year, told of the hilltop near Alcamo: the hilltop of the pale wild roses and the legend of Cielo's muse.

"It is a place where no one can look down on you but God," he said.

For the first time, his eyes wandered from the eyes of the prefect. Then he spoke again:

"In a way, I feel as if I have never left there. That hilltop. I feel as if I am still there."

"Do you return to Alcamo often?"

"In the summer, when the Library is closed. Or to christen this niece's son or that nephew's daughter. Or to bury this brother-in-law or that uncle. I have so many brothers, so many sisters, so many cousins. I have lost track of their ever increasing progeny."

"They must be very proud of you."

"To tell you the truth, I often feel that they look upon me strangely. Not down upon me, but strangely. I feel that my chosen path in life seems strange to them. I am good for christening the little ones, for marrying the bigger ones, for burying the dead ones. But I am of no use when it comes to placing money in their hands. And when I am with them, I am the only one who shows little concern to argue about which dead aunt made the best bread, or which dead neighbor made the best wine."

He smiled, and the gentle laughter that played within him could be seen in the movement of his belly.

"I'm sure that if I did appear one day with a red sash round my cassock, I should stand much better for it in their eyes."

"My association with the Vatican is all that redeems me in the eyes of my own family. They often seem incapable of introducing me to anyone without mentioning the Vatican in the same breath."

"I get a bit of that too."

"That's what that day in November is all about: that day when the Most Holy Father sits there in the Sala delle Udienze Paolo Sei with another seat next to him, and we can all stand in line to have our photograph made with him. He tilts his head toward you as if awaiting or listening to your counsel very intently, and before you can so much as address him, that's it — click — the photographer has snapped the picture, and you're ushered out while the next sitter is ushered in. A week later, you can purchase all the prints you wish, matt or glossy, priced according to size, and get them out in ample time for Christmas."

"And tell me, have you done this?"

"I confess. Yes. And it brought my sister great satisfaction and much prestige among her neighbors."

The other laughed warmly.

"Lest you judge me too harshly, I tell you that I have known at least two prelates that have put such photographs in gilt rococo frames and hung them on the walls of their own chambers. One of these men had framed photographs from two different sittings, and they were mounted to flank the lower part of the grandiose crucifix that was the centerpiece of his living-room."

"I would have more respect for a Borgia catamite."

"Well, I believe that, where you would have respect, the particular Most Reverend Eminence of whom I speak would feel envy instead."

The priest smiled as the prefect spoke. Then he did not smile.

"The Borgias," said the priest. "They have served well as the sable-collared scapegoats of our collective sins. The Church seems to have embraced and perpetuated their infamy as if to say: here is the dark stain on the purity of our soul. All opprobrium is directed to them, and the innumerable other dark stains of two thousand years are hidden behind the lurid tapestry of that opprobrium. Even the history of this Library, as set forth by the Vatican and accepted and endlessly repeated by popular historians, hides its true origin. We are told that the Library was founded in 1475 by Sixtus IV, who in fact merely established the three original rooms of the old Library on the ground floor of the pontifical palace. This allows the Vatican to bring no light to bear on Boniface VIII. For, while it was Boniface who was the true founder of the Library, in 1295, the first year of his pontificate, almost two centuries before Sixtus IV, it was also Boniface, the war-lover, who openly ridiculed all belief in life after death, and who dismissed his sexual congress with young women and boys as no more a sin of the flesh than the brushing together of two hands. This is why Boniface is not acknowledged as the true founder of the Library: for to acknowledge him as such would be to acknowledge Boniface himself, rather than to hide him beneath the tapestry of the Borgias, whose poison rings and evil intrigues and incests and murders serve to divert the eyes of history from Boniface and the rest.

"Yes, the Borgias have served their Church well, for they are the cherished scapegoats that have been used to embody and obscure the sins of every dark pontificate before them and after them."

"And, of course," said the prefect, "they were Spaniards. Outsiders. This has made it all the more fitting, all the more convenient."

"I must confess that there are times when I feel that the most horrible of the Borgias' sins was the pillaging of the Library, the stripping of gold, silver, and jewels from the bindings of unique and beautiful books, to fund the war-chest of worldly power. True, the Library lost more when Gregory XII sold rare manuscripts to enrich the papal treasury by five hundred florins in 1407; but desecration is far more sordid than sale."

"None the less, though the gold and jewels of their own worldly grandeur have been taken from them, most of those pillaged books themselves remain.

"I wonder what it says of us, to treasure and adore bindings more than what they bind."

The prefect's gaze wandered to the grand windows that overlooked the courtyard trees.

"But that is what the Vatican is," he said. "The throne and crown, gilt and jewelled beyond the wealth of the ages, of a glory whose true throne and crown are spirit and soul alone. The papacy for nearly two thousand years has done to the glory of God what for a passing moment the Borgias did to our books, the one by encrusting the spirituality of the Church with precious stones, the other by prying out precious stones that encrusted the sacredness of the spirit of words, which, like the sacredness of the spirit of God, has little material value in the marketplace.

"But if we ponder it in a certain way, the Borgias, in spite of themselves, perhaps may be regarded as more holy than most, for, rather than defiling with gold and jewels, they tore away the gold and jewels that defiled. Are not the words of your Cielo all the more beautiful, all the more pure without gold and jewels? When you tell of that hilltop of the pale wild roses and Cielo's muse, there is no hint in your memory of precious stones or veins of golden ore in the humble rock of that place. So it was with this Church, which was to have been built, as ordained by Christ, on the humble rock of Saint Peter. Too often do we behold with greater awe the sculpted rock of Michelangelo and Bernini than we do that humble rock of the spirit that brought them to be. Too often do we behold with greater awe the beauty or the rarity of a book's form than what lies within."

Form and essence. Flesh and soul. The priest of Alcamo had dwelt often on these distinctions. To embrace essence and soul was to live in the light of the spirit. To embrace or even to crave form and flesh was to live in lust. The Borgias had desecrated books. The all-encompassing lust of Boniface — for empire and every worldly indulgence — included a passion for books. For the priest of Alcamo, who had remained celibate all his life, books had become the form and the flesh to which he had succumbed in craving and embrace. He caressed the skin of illuminated parchment as other men caressed the skin of painted women. The scent of old leather bindings was as intoxicating and as seductive to him as any perfume. To remove Petrarch's notebook from the Library vaults and lay his hand where the poet had rested his own living hand in writing was an ecstasy more of carnal sensuality than of the soul. Such was his lust, such was his sin. But unlike Boniface he did not dismiss it as nothing more than the brushing together of two hands. Almost daily had he confessed this lust to God, and almost daily had he repented it; as all the while he had increasingly indulged and surrendered to it. What he held in silence from the prefect was this and more: that the wrought gold and jewels of the binder's most luxurious art were to him as captivating and beyond all thought of despoiling as were to the looting Borgias themselves the gold and jewels that adorned their dear and diabolical Lucrezia.

And, above all, he held in silence the sin of his theft. It was his greatest sin, and yet for it he felt no shame.

He was a child of that magical hilltop. But he was a child of other hilltops as well.

It was Don Giovanni Lecco of Piana degli Albanesi who had spoken into the ears of those who served him in Palermo that the boy of Alcamo was destined for the gown of the scholar and the gown of the priest. Don Lecco then was young and robust, and he spoke more with rifle and silence than with words. All knew the tale of how, under his own family roof, he had killed his own father, who had crossed him, then had dragged the body out so that it lay in the street close to the threshold of the open door; and then for days had killed without pause all who came, from nearby and as far as Palermo, to claim it for respectful burial as it lay bloated and rotting, until the street was filled with the stench and litter of many bodies that lay bloated and rotting, until at last from Palermo there came three men dressed not in mourning black but in suits of white linen, and these men did not remove their hats in respect as they stood at a distance from the grotesque body of the man they had served, and one, who was their leader, raised an open hand to the figure of the armed son in the doorway while his companions aimed handguns to the street and fired each into the corpse of the father, facing then the son and removing then their hats in respect, then slowly approaching and entering through the door, which then closed for the first time in days. Only then did the town's two police officers enter the street, and, with them, the carriage to carry off the bodies. As the mother told it, the whole mess had happened because the son had discovered that his father had been unfaithful to her.

That was long, long ago. Few could recall the bloodshed. Many could recall the kindness. Don Lecco was a good man.

Piana degli Albanesi was a place where the Canon of Lek still held sway. The legendary Lek had brought the tablets of the law to old Albania. This law was the law of the blood feud. According to the Canon of Lek, a man under the roof of his own home could kill anyone under that roof. As descendants of Albanians who had settled in these parts centuries ago, the people of Piana degli Albanesi believed above all in two things: the Church and the Canon of Lek. They who knew of such things knew that whatever honor the so-called honored society of Sicily possessed came from the code of the blood feud of their ancestral land. Like those of his shared ancient blood who revered him, Don Lecco was fiercely proud of that ancient blood. It was with great satisfaction that he allowed others to infer from the Italianate echo of his name that he was a descendent of the great Lek himself.

At eighty-nine, Don Lecco strode strong and silent with a cane. He lived alone in a house of thousand-year-old stone with an aged maid and an aged cook and an aged guard with an aged wolf gun. The thousand-year-old stone lay covered in ivy, and it looked upon a garden that lay in the shade of thousand-year-old trees. There was a fountain said to be from the days of ancient Roman empire: once a spouting dolphin, but now worn away to a moss-covered shapelessness that gently trickled on the lily-pads beneath it. The old walled garden led to a narrow gated passage that led to the street.

Whenever the priest from Alcamo returned to Sicily, he visited Don Lecco and celebrated Mass for him. Don Lecco was different from the rest. He always seemed proud of him and of his calling.

As the time neared for the celebration of Don Lecco's ninetieth year, the priest located within the vaults of the Greci collection the bound sixteenth-century manuscript known as the Buzuku Book of the Mass: the oldest document written in the Albanian language, which from distant antiquity until then had remained purely verbal, recorded only by the wind and the unwritten code that bound a man's word by oath alone.

And he stole it.

And old Don Lecco, who could read not a word of it, held it to his breast and drew the priest closer that he might kiss him.

He had returned to Rome feeling that he would never see old Don Lecco again except to bury him. He saw himself burying the book with him, placing it under the little blue pillow on which his lifeless head rested. He saw himself saying Mass over him in the august and simple perfection of the old Latin liturgy, as both he and old Don Lecco liked it. He saw himself speaking with no prepared eulogy, but from his heart. He heard himself saying, "Don Lecco was a man of God."

This had been only a few weeks ago. For an instant, it had passed his mind to tell the prefect of the stolen book. The manuscript was unique, yes. But there existed three photocopies of it in the archives of the Albanian National Library; the Vatican had published a facsimile edition of it; and yet another edition had been published in Tirana.

If the prefect believed that we too often beheld with greater awe the beauty or the rarity of a book's form than what lies within, then, by his very belief, the priest had stolen nothing.

It was he himself who had been robbed. He had robbed himself through his own innocence and estrangement from this world. A boy on a hilltop who lived in a poem and sought to serve God. An old man discarded among books with a vague sense of sin in a place where God's name was everywhere and yet one had to gasp for even a trace of His presence. Seventy years. Where had they gone?

He was sick of this place. He wanted to return to Sicily. He wanted to return to life, and he wanted to leave life as he had entered it: lost in a poem. Somewhere. A small church in the hills of his homeland, where the breath of God was deep, where an old priest could celebrate his Mass in Latin at every dawn and spend his days in prayerful peace in the balm of that breath. He would miss only the scent and touch of the wealth of books. But this might be a blessing, a final purification. And the poem of his youth, Cielo's flowing words, still lay in the sanctum of memory.

The prefect appointed him senior curator of the Library. There were many large old brass keys strung on an old brass keyring that was large enough for the priest to put his fist through.

The holdings of the Library occupied seven levels. The lowest level had been a stable until 1928, when Pius XI sold the horses and replaced them with automobiles as the means of Vatican transport. But hundreds of years before it was a stable, it was a gallery for the promenades of Julius II, and as such was built with various niches to display a number of classical Greek and Roman statues. When work was undertaken to convert this structure to accommodate part of the Library's ever growing and now overwhelming holdings, most of these niches, as well as the building's entries of open arched travertine, were wholly or in part bricked-up and buttressed for reinforcement so a large central supporting column could be erected.

After some days of wandering and luxuriating among the labyrinthine stacks and vaults of the upper levels, discovering which key unlocked which door, he made his way down to the lowest level. There was a door before him, which he unlocked. He switched on the overhead lights, and he could see the big pillar and the many aisles and stacks of steel shelving, now laden with books and archival boxes, that had marked the beginning of the Library's belated entrance into the twentieth century. All seemed to have fallen to neglect, and to have become a repository of neglect: soiled derelict volume upon soiled derelict volume, unmarked and sagging soiled box upon unmarked and sagging soiled box. It was little wonder, he reflected, that no full and comprehensive catalogue of the Library's holdings had been accomplished.

Far to his left, in the dimness, near the shadow of a niche that was partly bricked-over and partly filled with cobweb, he discerned another door. It was of crude upright planks nailed across by three crude vertical planks. To this door there was no lock, there was no key. There was no handle with which to pull.

He pushed upon it, but it was stuck shut, or somehow sealed. He searched about for something: he knew not what.

He returned to the door with an old wooden library ladder that he found lying at the base of a collapsed shelving unit. Heaving forward several times against the door with the ladder as a battering ram, with as much force as his age afforded him, he managed not to burst open the door, but did break away one of the rotten upright planks.

Reaching and probing through the breach, he discovered that the door was mysteriously held locked by another plank set as a crossbar against the other side of the door. With some effort, he managed to raise this inner crossbar from its braces with his forearm. He heard it fall loudly and tumble resoundingly downward upon what sounded to be steps of the same heavy but rotten wood. He then pushed the door open, and what little light fell behind him in this cranny of the vast hall allowed him to see the first of these plank steps, which led to utter darkness. He felt about for a light switch, but there was none.

The priest stood awhile, and he stared and he wondered: a subterranean vault without light, sealed impossibly from within.

Early the next morning, he returned with a strong battery-powered lamp inside his black leather briefcase.

He made his way with care down the decayed plank stairs, the lamp in one hand to light his way, the other hand against the wall of stone to steady him, testing each step with one foot before lowering the other, peering keenly through his bifocals as he moved. His last step took him to a floor of natural bedrock and a low-ceilinged narrow passage that led to a vaulted chamber.

It was here that he saw the true base of the column that seemed to have been raised on the floor above, but which, as he now saw, had actually been set securely and unseen on this bedrock below. Yet this vaulted chamber was doubtless much older than the column; and if the workmen in the course of their labor had come and gone through the door above — which, as well as the stairs, they likely had built in makeshift fashion to accommodate their labor below — they also likely had come and gone through another passage of their own device, for judging by a bricked-up door-frame of wood to the east of the pillar, they also must have dug a passage from the open courtyard ground, which now revealed no evidence of any such entry.

It had to have been by means of this latter passage, bricking it up and filling in the earth behind them, that, after the column had been set and the floor above had been buttressed from beneath at the corners of this subterranean chamber, they had left for the last time, evidently having been instructed by Pius XI to bar the other door from within — as if so that only a ghost might open it — before they rose from the earth through the other passage, which then was to be concealed.

This was all the more curious, as there seemed to be nothing here but litter left behind by the workmen: many crumbling cast-away newspapers from the summer of 1928, wine bottles and beer bottles and soda bottles, cigar butts and crumpled cigarette packs, food wrappings, broken tools, bent rusted nails, and shims and scraps and shavings of wood — all of it blanketed with the dust of a tomb.

In fact, the priest reflected, this forsaken and forgotten underground chamber indeed may have been designed as a tomb, for built into the recess of one wall was a rectangular stone basin, very much like a Gothic sarcophagus to which no chiselling or slab of effigy had been laid. This basin of stone seemed to have served the workmen as their first trash receptacle, as it was piled full with a heap of their detritus. It seemed that after this sarcophagal midden heap had overflown onto the ground, the workers had taken to tossing the trash about haphazardly.

With a piece of dirty stick, the priest poked and stirred through the heap of trash: maybe there might be among it some plans, notes, or construction documents that might shed light on the history of this underground chamber.

The priest felt the stick hit something of heavier substance. He churned and swept aside the trash. Several grime-covered parcels lay stacked in the corner of the big stone box. Each of them was wrapped in age-blackened heavy cloth and bound by age-blackened rope. The parcel that lay topmost had apparently been opened by the workmen, for it was carelessly and loosely rebound. The priest opened it and found within it a collection of the death-bed confessions of various popes from the eighth to the twelfth centuries. Having opened this parcel and found nothing but old and drab-looking documents that they could not read, the workers presumably had cursorily closed the parcel and tossed it back to its place with the same disregard and disinterest with which they had tossed their successive daily newspapers upon it.

These documents, no matter how truthful they were — in fact, one of them purported to be the final confession of the last of the Sicilian popes, Stephen IV, as transcribed from the account of his chamberlain, who, as it later became known, had tortured the dying pope most gruesomely — were of very great historical value.

As he opened the parcels and saw that their contents bore several notations, seals, and marks dating to the third decade of the trecento, he assumed that these documents were perhaps part of the lost Library of the Avignon papacy of John XXII. As he was now in his seventieth year, this struck him as a serendipity, for John XXII had been crowned at the age of seventy, in 1316, and lived to hold the papal chair for eighteen years, until death came to him, in 1334. The priest wished only that God should bless him with fortune: not to possess the crowned power of a John XXII, or the uncrowned power of a Don Lecco, but only to be granted the years that they had been granted.

Pope John XXII was a free-thinking man. Petrarch described his papal court at Avignon as a thriving center of scholarship and literary life. Under his pontificate the Library grew extensively, and in 1327 a complete inventory of it was made. The disappearance of this inventory meant that there could be no definite identification of these, or any other, manuscripts with the Library of John XXII. Furthermore, nothing from the Avignon papacy was believed to have been reclaimed by Rome until the fifteenth century. The catalogue of the Library that was then compiled, under the direction of Nicholas V, was also lost to history.

The parcels were indeed curious: one contained accounts of intercourse with the Devil; another, accounts of intercourse with Jesus, collected from nunneries in Lombardia; another, an early codex of the most obscene verse of Catullus. And, tucked beneath the rope knot of each of them, and lying near to the one that had been opened, there was a paper card of heavy stock, now softened and darkened and pallid where it had lain beneath the rope, bearing the same words in the same flourishing olden hand: DAMNATUM EST — NON LEGITUR.

These manuscripts and the mysteries they summoned were overwhelming. Who had damned these things not to be read, and when and why had they been thus damned? After all, since the Renaissance, far more damnable and blasphemous documents had lain unhidden in the Library. How many parcels such as these still lay secreted and unknown in the undelved winding innards of this place?

The parcel on the bottom was the largest and heaviest, and as he lifted it, the priest could feel that it held a box of some kind.

Then the beauty of the box lay before him, and he raised its lid. A white butterfly settled for a moment near his thumb at the edge of the open casket. So absorbed was the priest that the manifestation of a butterfly within this tomb-like chamber gave him not the slightest pause. Then the butterfly was gone.

The priest saw a parchment sheet scrawled with lines of measured words, wild with strokes of angry deletion, dense with strokes, calm or triumphant, of words overwritten on words. He riffled through the cask. There were hundreds of pages, most of parchment, a few of paper, all apparently scrawled by the same hand with the tempest and serenity of creation.

Through his bifocals, with lamp held close, he brought the scrawl of the first line into clarity. The penultimate word of this first line had been scratched out and altered several times; but he knew the word that he would find penned above those scratchings as soon as his lips moved in whispering the beginning of that line.

Nel mezzo del cammin di nostra vita

His breath rushed from him, and he feared that his heart might stop; for never before had he experienced a miracle.

ON THAT NIGHT WHEN THE STARS HAD beckoned him to read their myriad secrets and were without moon, the hunger in the pouch of his boy-belly was slight, sated so were blood and being by the thrillsome richness of what had taken him, entered him, timeless hours ago.

Besides, he had a goodly-rent piece of *pane sciocco* and a goodly-rent piece of *pecorino*, stolen from stalls near the old eastern wall. He would never forget the taste of that day's bread, which was strong with the fresh-milled grain of that early summer's harvest and the taste of that morning's stone oven, or of the cheese, rich with the ewes' milk of verdant spring. He remembered them ever after, and it was as if they were verily in his mouth when he remembered them. But that thing that had taken and entered him, it eluded his memory in fine. Was it manhood that had taken and entered him? Soul-hood perhaps? Only years later, after other such days, would he know them as what they were: the holiest of days, the rarest of days, the days of illimitableness.

It was in accord with this system of the astronomy of the soul, this system of the nine skies, that he had arranged and measured the words of his first, little book, which had come to be known — wrongly and falsely, but better thus than not known at all — as the libretto of *La Vita Nuova*, after a phrase he had used in the rubric of its first page. *Incipit vita nova*, he had written, in Latin, amid the *lingua volgare* of his opening words: *Here begins new life*.

But how truly Pliny had warned of *fors varia*, the manifold hazard of copyists!

In the transforming of the words *vita nova* into the *lingua volgare* and the imposing of them upon his work as a title, these words had become *La Vita Nuova*. If he had wanted to evoke a new life that was more clearly defined — *a* new life, *the* new life — he would have rendered the words in the *lingua volgare* rather than in Latin, whose ambiguities, as here its fecund forgoing of articles, like small shades of mystery set within the majesty of the lucid precision of that language, are let to drift, enhancing that majesty, through the prism of subtle possibilities. Nor had he claimed this new life for himself. It was not *mea vita nova*, but simply, and enormously, *vita nova*. They knew nothing, those who obtruded their fool words and meanings on what was already writ.

In truth, the phrase had wended to him from the Latin of his olden Bible. Therein did the Apostle Paul exhort the Romans: "*nos in novitate vita ambulemus*." These words struck him, in Latin and — *noi dobbiamo camminare in novità di vita* — in his own tongue as well. Yes, he felt, as if a secret truth in these words whispered through him: we must walk in newness of life.

At the heart of his little book lay a long *canzone*, flanked by four brief sonnets afore and again by four brief works after. Nine skies. A heart of nine. In the long *canzone*, he rhymed a dream of a tremulous earth, a dimming sun, a star's appearance — *apparir la stella* — and birds in flight falling dead from the sky. As the years passed, he came to feel that it was not a good *canzone*. As the years passed, he came to feel that it was like much else that he had wrought, and like unto his very life as well: longer than it was good.

In those days when the work of the little book was being drafted, he cherished his friendship with Guido Cavalcanti. "*Mio primo amico*," he called him in that little book. Never, however, did he declare the elder maker, as he knew him to be, *il miglior fabbro*, the better maker. It was through the benison of Cavalcanti's acceptance and support of him that the young maker had gained his earliest recognition and respect. Then, when Cavalcanti saw that his protégé could stand aright of his own, and when his protégé became a posed and disingenuous purveyor of confections and revealed himself to be no *primo amico* but to himself, Cavalcanti saw him indeed. What was it that Guido had said of him, through that beautiful, violent mare of his verse? "*Dante, un sospiro messagger del core.*" Dante, a sighing messenger of the heart. Yes, and more. Oh, God, if only to steal and ride that mare, whose thews and soul were one. If only to steal, or to kill it.

THE REMOTE SEA AND HAMMOCK OF CAYO Largo had raised an indwelling to the very base of my throat. Fuck dead New York and all the world — the true gangrene — that I had left behind. I needed a farther sea, a farther hammock. I, like you, am a fucking god; and each of us, as such, must find the one true healer, Paean, physician to the gods. I had found him, in the sweet afternoons of those many sweet afternoons, in the sweet nights of those many sweet nights, lying as the magic of the sea and the wisps of death and the breezes through the palms were one. What I now felt in the depth of my throat, that indwelling that I felt rising to whence words come: it was Paean working his cure within me. It was he, and no nurse speaking of *gangrena*, who impelled me to that farther sea.

In the end, I found it: south of the equator, near the Tropic of Capricorn, in the distant Pacific, in the Leeward Islands of the Tuamotu Archipelago of French Polynesia.

Bora Bora. It had been merely a name to me, and little more than a year ago I could not have told you where on earth it was, other than that it was some faraway place. But to lay eyes on it as one neared it by sea was to lay eyes on something that claimed both soul and senses, for what one saw, set against the pale and the deep shades of every celestial and oceanic blue, were lush verdant cliffs and peaks of forested plains like altars to which no man has ever ascended — and the color of it all is unique and so unlike any other that the name of this color, *poe rava*, the miracling of darkest green and blackness, is found only here, and is used to describe the rarest and now all but vanished of the natural black pearls whose giant mothering shells once populated the coral massifs of this place. And both of and towering above this miracling of color, reaching into the clouds, there lies Mount Otemanu, the Mountain of the Bird.

The great volcano that was the great mother of this place thundered for more than four million years before sinking to form Bora Bora. It is a thundering that echoes in the crashing of the sea on the surrounding coral reef. There is only one passage through the thunderous reef into the serene and blue lagoon, the sea of Bora Bora, which is said to be the most beautiful lagoon in the world. As the thundering waves upon the reef seem to echo the volcano that mothered this place, so the serenity of the lagoon within the reef seems to echo the myth of this place, whose name, Pora Pora in the Maohi language, describes it as the first blessed child of peace to be drawn forth from the ocean after the creation of the isle of Raiatea.

As one enters into the lagoon, the thunder fades to lovely silence, and, if the warm breeze is right, as it was for me, there drifts in it, from the growing magic of the color so rare that its name resides only here, the ambrosia scent of jasmine and gardenia that is the scent of this place.

On the island itself, the creamy white gardenia blossoms and the violet blossoms and the red blossoms and the pink blossoms and the yellow blossoms of countless other flowers, countless other scents, came forth in sun and shadow from the lush deep green. Tall palms bent toward the sea where the lush deep green gave way to soft white sand in stretches of beach and hidden coves. There stood the open monuments to a darker magic of the sun: the faded petroglyphs, the raised and smoothed and worn coral altars, the *marae* of human sacrifice practiced late into the nineteenth century, when the scent of blood-offering and cannibalism mingled with the scents of the white blossoms and the violet blossoms and the red blossoms and the pink blossoms and the yellow blossoms.

I took a luxurious faré of Tasmanian oak and cedar, rattan and bamboo, a pandanus-thatch roof lashed to big fir beams. The thing was built on stilts a good way out over the pristine lagoon, with a narrow plank walkway bridge connecting it to the shore. There was a fine big four-poster bed, an overhead fan, a big cast-iron tub, a teak sundeck from which I could dive into the clear blue water, not far from a pristine reef, or on which I could sit and gaze at the setting sun and the luxuriant constellations. Early every morning, a young native girl brought me arrangements of enticing fruits of exotic flavor and flowers of subtle perfume, and wooden bowls of fresh *monoi* — a lotion of fragrant white gardenia petals macerated in purified coconut oil — with which to nourish and soothe my skin. And, more than once, she visited me at night, bringing only a single piece of fruit, or a single flower, and herself.

Shit, there I go again: *writing*. Fucking *writing*. Even I got fucking sucked into that one: *bringing only a single piece of fruit, or a single flower, and herself.*

Fuck that shit. The bitch gave decent head, and that's that.

On some days, I would motorbike along the sole road that circled the island, and I would go to a café of a few small tables set out in the open shade and sun near the little village of Vaitape. I would sit there and drink good coffee and smoke and look up at Mount Otemanu; and I would feel it all: the power of the mountain and the beauty of the sky and the delicate fragrant breeze and the umbrage of the big blade raised above the throbbing chest. I felt like Gauguin, a hundred years after him, amid the same phanopoeia of breeze and of colors whose names were immanent. He, too, had been dying and loving it.

The quiet of this place, the beautiful quiet of it all — it was as rich, almost, as the colors. *Quietus*: discharge from life; death, or that which brings on death. There was no word in French, no word in English that quite cast this nuance of subtle release upon that often dreaded thing.

And, yes, the hammock. Every morning, I would saunter along the path that wound among red ginger and the Bougainvillea of pink and of orange, the red Coeur de Marie and the white hibiscus, piny iron-trees and rosewood, and the soft growth all around of nature's fair purflings whose names I'll never know. It was this little path, wondrous and so overgrown with charm, that led from the bridge of the faré to the secluded beach where a sole hammock hung from two towering tamanu trees. This was the hammock of the sweet afternoon with which, I said, many useless words ago, my tale begins.

The suff of the lagoon was an endless liquescent sigh, beneath the blue and golden light of endless sky. The clouds were the creamy white gardenia blossoms of that boundless lush blue. The sigh of the gentle lagoon, the sigh of the moving clouds, the sigh that swayed the palms were as one and all-embracing.

In the morning I lay with my feet to the south, and in the late afternoon, as the sun in its arc transmuted shade and light, I lay with my feet to the north.

At midday, when the blazing sun turned platinum-white, I went into the lagoon. Where the brilliant lapping water rose only to my thighs, I was surrounded by all the teeming swirling colors of a god gone mad with the prowess of creation: fish of every dazzling iridescence of the spectrum, every dazzling form and size.

My knee was now healed, and where the lagoon deepened, I swam rather than stepped; for with each deepening the dangers amid the beauty grew: the spiny, poisonous starfish known as the crown of thorns; the benign-looking venom-fanged cone shell; the long, sinuous, sucking sea-leech with its slimy skin of toxic mucus; the stinging anemones in all their dahlia-like loveliness; the bottom-lying stonefish with its dorsal fin of thirteen poisonous spines that bring instant and crippling agony; the long-needled diadem urchins.

I did not tarry much along the shallow reef, for it is in the shallows that the giant moray makes its home. It is a ghastly sight to see it emerge from its coral cavern: sometimes ten feet in length, as big around as a cow, with powerful jaws and a cavernous mouth of razor-sharp teeth.

And I did not swim to the deepest reaches, to the big reef where the great waves broke, for the one passage through the thunderous reef into the serene and blue lagoon is the one passage for shark and man alike. No one knows exactly how many species of shark populate these islands. There were times, in the brilliant lapping water that rose only to my thighs, that the teeming swirling colors of the fish that surrounded me would suddenly disperse and vanish, and one or more gray sharks could be seen prowling, their fins gliding gently through the translucent surface of the water, their bellies within inches of the soft lagoon bottom.

But most of the time, as I softly swam, there would be only the myriad teeming swirling colors of creation swimming around me; and, as I lingered amid the lapping near the shore, I would feel the ticklings of their myriad tiny kisses.

Then, always, I would return to the hammock. My heart beating well and good as I left the lagoon and the sunlight, and laid me down in the shade. I would have a smoke and look at the endless blue sky and the lagoon, feeling all of life that was in the lagoon, all of wonder that was in the sky. On the horizon, beyond where the crystal lagoon deepened to richest blue, billowing waves broke high and mighty on the reef of Motu Toopua.

The black bark of the tamanu, with their moss of deepest green, was the color of this paradise, the color of the towering Mountain of the Bird, the color of the rare and true black pearl of nature's making. Mingling with that moss of deepest green was other moss, which was the color of palest moonlight, of faint lime and fainter silver hue. Amid the all-embracing sigh, that bark was an enchantment unto itself, and I became lost in it. How old were these trees? No one knew. They seemed as timeless as the power of the mountain and the beauty of the sky and the delicate fragrant breeze. They were here when the coral massifs were rich with black pearl. They were here when the big blade was raised above the throbbing chest.

White terns and dusky petrels flew in silent song. In the black boughs and dense sheltering leaves above me, other fair small birds ascended and descended, appeared and disappeared, bough to bough, through breaches of pure blue. It was in the pleasant light of the late afternoon that, through those breaches of pure blue, the indwelling that had been raised to the base of my throat was drawn forth from me.

My heart skipped a beat. I shall never know if this sudden stillness of the heart, this taking of my breath, was caused by what was drawn forth from me, or if it was caused by the sudden flight from the trees of the fair small birds, which seemed to flee at the very moment of that exorcism, that epiphany, that drawing forth.

Fifty years ago, when there were many here yet alive who remembered, and perhaps longed for, the umbrage of the big blade raised above the throbbing chest, a little boy far-away had been asked a question that had shaken him and haunted him: "Hey, kid, wanna die?" Now, these fifty years later, in the all-embracing sigh of this sweet afternoon, a grown man answered clearly:

I did not care. I truly did not care.

I looked up through the breaches of blue where the birds had flown and sung. Yes. I was dying, and I did not care. I was not dying in the sense that we all are dying, the sense that our brief journey from the womb brings us daily closer only to the common end. I was dying in the sense that the timetable of my particular journey lay before my eyes, with the approximate date of arrival indelibly stamped; dying in the sense that I had been sentenced to death by a disease whose prognosis grew steadily worse. This did not distinguish me from a great many others, who shared a similar fate, or whose fate was worse.

But I did not care. And in not caring, I was free.

I looked slowly at the paradise that surrounded me, and I felt deeply the paradise within me. "Death row," I whispered. "I'll take it." I laughed quietly a good long while.

I had made peace with my daughter a long time ago. I was nineteen when she was conceived. Her mother, who was twenty and who was beautiful and who wanted marriage and a child, used to clutch my buttocks and hold me to her as hard as she could when I was upon her and about to ejaculate, so that I might forsake control and not withdraw from her. She usually was not successful, but once in a while she was. And thus my daughter had come to be.

I'm pretty sure that I know when it happened. It was the day that those guys landed on the moon, and it must have been on a weekend, because her mother was not working that day. Me, I never worked. I was a thief and a drug-dealer. I couldn't care less about this moon thing, but to everybody else, including her, it seemed to be some kind of big deal. So I figured that I would make it a big deal too. I would make sure that I was getting my cock sucked at the moment that this moon thing happened. I indulged her by situating myself so that she could watch the moon thing while she went down on me. The direction of her attention did not much matter: she was a wonderful girl and a great fuck, but she wasn't much in the blow job department. But I sat there with my can of beer and my reefer and I pulled it off with perfect timing. "*One small step for man, one giant leap for mankind.*" There. Ah. Oh. Yeah. Take that. It wasn't so much her mouth into which I released myself at that moment. It was the mouth of all mankind. God only knows how many times we ended up fucking that day and into that night. All I know is that after more than five or six long and strenuous fucks, I would usually find a small drop of blood mingled with the watery drizzle of the last of my semen, and this was one of those times when I saw blood. And, with all the beer and reefer, her clutch was successful every time. So I'm pretty sure, considering when my daughter was born, that it was that hot summer day, when man and mankind first defiled the moon, that she was conceived. A few weeks later, when the hoped-for emotional response on my part was not forthcoming — it was more like, "Hey, baby, whatever comes out of you is yours" — her mother wasted no time in finding a sucker who within another few weeks was conned into believing that it was the seed of his love that pullulated inside her. Anyway, about fifteen years after my daughter was born, my old love and I crossed paths. She was still beautiful, and she was without bitterness, although she did seem hurt that, only a few years after we had parted, I had married someone else. This marriage had been one of the least significant and least memorable affairs of my life. (I call it an affair because, even at my most writerly, I have never lapsed so low as to use the word *relationship*, which to me is now a part of that vapid and sterile Lifestyle Glossary of mankind's giant leap toward mediocrity.) It was, this short-lived marriage, nothing more than a symptom of the ever worsening alcoholism that clutched me deeper and held me harder and more closely than any human hands. I did not have to elucidate this to my old love any further, as she herself could see what a wretched drunk I had become. We spent a few days and nights together over the course of a few months, and she saw for herself: a few pills and a few beers early in the morning to calm the shaking and banish the threat of seizure, then out to the gin-mill for all of the day and all of the night, then to the after-hours joint, then either home to sweat and to stir or directly back to the gin-mill if it was after eight o'clock, when the after-hours joint closed and the legal gin-mill opened. Besides the beer and pills, I was good for maybe two bottles of Scotch and a few bags of dope along the way. I usually took no meals, using scraps of food as I used cocaine: only to enable me to stay awake to drink more; but as I was with her, I took her to dinner, and this meant a bottle of wine or two and a few brandies as well; and what food I ate and kept down only increased my ability to take in more booze throughout the night and day to follow. All the while, she just sat with me, drinking Evian or some wop equivalent. Of course, I wasn't really with her. A drunk is never really with anybody or anything except the booze. But her presence and her voice were comforting. She said that what really scared her about me was that I never seemed to be fucked up, only distant, as if the booze and the heroin had become a sustenance without which I might die, while at the same time no one could do what I was doing and continue to live. I told her I was all right, that I was only drifting awhile. After those few days and nights together, she told me that she couldn't bear to see me anymore; she couldn't bear to see what I was doing to myself anymore. She had given me two small photographs, one of her and our daughter, and one of our daughter alone. I looked at them every once in a while. Then I looked only at the picture of the girl alone. She was the prettiest thing I'd ever seen and not wanted to fuck. I mean that. Her eyes and her smile had an innocence and strength that were as beguiling as they were pure, and in their happiness there seemed to lie the secret of a melancholy that only she and I could feel and share. It brought me almost to tears, and it brought me most surely to love. Some sixteen years ago, I had abandoned her before she drew breath; abandoned her in a way that was as heartless as infanticide. Was my soul any different from the souls of those old pagans who laid their unwanted newborns, so tender and so tiny, upon the open rocks, then turned away and left them exposed to the elements, that the gods might bear the onus of their fate? Yes, I had abandoned myself as well, to the rocks of my own demons. But it was I who had laid me down; I myself who, of my own strength and will, had strode to those rocks. As I looked at the image of this little angel who had survived to smile after I had left her and turned away never to look back, I felt a sense of sin, and of loss. There was no penance to wash away this sin, no way to reclaim what I had lost. How could she ever even feel herself to be my daughter? She was the daughter of God's kindness and her mother's goodness. I was just a vague melancholy within her, the unknown ghost of a long-ago summer's day, a ghost of something that had been without kindness and had been without goodness. And yet, even in the sadness of my sense of sin and my sense of loss, I felt that my abandonment of her had been a blessing for us both, for if indeed I had been her father in presence, that smile never would have blossomed; and in my self-centered irresponsibility, I had escaped, or at least forged a key that allowed me to come and go as I more or less pleased, from the bleak damnation of what had seemed to be my own predestined fate. Though never quite having raised myself wholly from the gutter in the years since I had left her in the womb, I had written three books. Yes, I may have been drunk most of the time, but I never drank when I wrote. Never. One of these books, *Hellfire*, had gotten a lot of praise. I was redeemed. Fuck you: I wasn't a drunk, I wasn't no goddamn dope-addict; I was a literary fucking genius. And, as it happened, it was not long after first laying eyes on the image of that little angel that I received my first respectable advance, for a book called *Power on Earth*. The little angel's mother had told me that the kid wanted to be an archaeologist or a doctor or a librarian. So, I called up the kid's mother and I told her that, whatever it turned out to be, archaeologist or doctor or librarian or none of the above, I wanted to pick up the tab. I would only blow it anyway, I told her, and she would never have to tell the kid where it came from. In the end, God only knows what she told the kid; but about a year later, that little angel, somewhat bigger and more beautiful, was standing in my arms laughing and crying and shaking her head all at once. At first she called me Nick, and then she called me Daddy; and she asked me if it was all right to call me that; and I told her it was the best thing that I had ever heard. The stretches of work got longer, the benders became less frequent; and she and I came to know and love each other. It was a gift, and with it came a new awareness of the magnitude and multitude of gifts that life can offer if only we forsake our ideas of life and open our hearts just enough to let in the breeze of the holy mystery that life truly is. Then the breeze became a chill. It was summer's end, and she had just entered Princeton, even though she still didn't know what she wanted to be. When I kissed her good-bye, I realized that her smile no longer had that secret melancholy that I had sensed when I first saw her image, and I wondered how long it had been gone, and how I could not have noticed this before.

This was the smile of beatitude, and I felt blessed that a part of me was of her, and that, through her, this part of me would flourish as something better than I would ever be, and that, through her, it would savor a purity of breath that I would never know, and that, through her, I would live long after I had ceased to be. I don't know what my own smile looked like, but it felt good.

Then it was over. She was gone. And they never caught the motherfucker who did it. Three days before they found her, in the scrub off the Garden State Parkway. I had them close the casket after I kissed her.

Time passed, and my feelings drifted to feelings past. I remembered feeling like one of those who laid their unwanted newborns, so tender and so tiny, upon the open rocks, then turned away and left them. I remembered feeling that my daughter — our daughter — was the daughter of God's kindness. Then remembrance left me, but feeling did not. I stood before the centuries-old crucifix on my wall, the one that my grandmother had brought over from the other side. I stood there and I looked at it, and I felt nothing of those open rocks or of God's kindness; but I did recall a verse from the Book of Psalms: "*Happy shall he be that taketh and dasheth thy little ones against the stones*." And I kept looking at that thing on the wall, and I said, very slowly and with no anger at all, "Fuck you, God. Fuck you." At the time, there was a brand of heroin that came in dime bags stamped in red with the letters D.O.A. A few days later, I daubed one of those little glassine packets with some rubber cement and stuck it to the carved loincloth that hid the high holy privies of the kike on that cross.

So, as I said, I had made peace with my daughter. I had no other ties of blooded love on the face of this earth.

My mother was gone, my father was gone. All the old ones from the other side were gone. Those whom I loved, I loved. Those who loved me, loved me.

But fuck them. Fuck you. Fuck me. Fuck that kike in a diaper nailed to that cross.

Even in paradise, these words came easy. Especially in paradise; for they too, these words, were part of the all-embracing sigh. I blew a kiss to the breeze, to the endless blue sky, to my daughter.

The title of an old gospel song was never far from my feelings: "This World Is Not My Home." Not the meaning of the song, just the title. My home was not up yonder, hereafter, through heaven's open door. It just was not here.

I was sick of looking into vacant eyes, sick of hearing vacant words from vacant people.

So, yes, somewhere, early on, I became a writer. It seemed an unlikely thing. In my neighborhood, books were not read. There were few books, many bookies. My father discouraged me from reading, on the grounds that it would "put ideas in your head." There was, of course, a certain wisdom in this. Ideas and thought are wretched folly from which few escape. But, then again, one can only go beyond them by going through them. They are the passage that separates the wise guys from the men of wisdom. Sometimes they seemed so close, the wise guys and the men of wisdom. "I don't do thoughts," said Eddie D. from the projects. "The Great Tao," said Ch'an Buddhist Master Niu-t'ou Fa-Yung thirteen centuries earlier, "is free from thought." So close and yet so far.

I wrote terrible things. One of my first pinches as a teenager was for stealing books. The sonnets of Shakespeare were in that batch, and it was to be a long time until I finally got to read them; and longer still until I came to perceive at their heart the one line that said it all: "O learn to read what silent love hath writ."

The greatest poetry is wordless. The greatest poets are those blest and humbled by this truth.

Again: "I have tried to write Paradise" — I can not forsake these most theophanous of Ezra Pound's words; I shall bear them to my end — "Let the wind speak / that is paradise." To learn to read what silent love hath writ, to bow to the power of the breezes. To embrace these things is to live, and to know that what one can write is as nothing before that silence and that power is to begin to write. Fa-Yung again: "How can we obtain truth through words?"

These were things I came to understand only after the long night yielded to light.

But, anyway, there I was boosting books. I couldn't tell the bad from the good. I kept trying to read and to like *Moby Dick*, but I never succeeded and felt that it was my failing. How could I become a writer if I didn't "appreciate" the great American novel? So I pretended that I had read and liked it, and, over the years, I actually may have conned myself into believing it. Ultimately, I simply embraced the sad truth that it simply was not much of a book at all. In 1829, aboard the whaling ship *Susan*, Frederick Myrick of Nantucket, the first scrimshander to sign and date his work, had etched into the tooth of a sperm whale all to which Melville had so beautifully aspired: "Death to the living," reads the scrimshaw, "long life to the killers." And that is that. Melville never escaped from the passway of thoughts and ideas; Myrick may never have entered it. As much as I admire Melville and his vision and what he wanted and tried to do, it is Myrick's scrimshaw that speaks to the ages. And whence did Myrick steal those words? The true originators are lost to us. How many centuries or millennia before Homer or Sappho did someone behold the dawn or the moon and see it to be "rosy-fingered"? As Ecclesiastes had it: "The thing that hath been, it is that which shall be; and that which is done is that which shall be done: and there is no new thing under the sun." And whence did the Preacher steal that wisdom, and whence who before him? "Originality is but high-born stealth." These may be the only words written by Edward Dahlberg that are worth remembering; and, again, who knows where he got them.

Immature writers plagiarize; mature writers steal. But while I was the former, I did the latter. Above all, I stole from myself. Words and phrases that enamored me, whether I had come upon them or they had come to me from within, were endlessly repeated, recycled, ridden like horses until they were dead. As I had been a thief in boyhood, I became, while learning to write, a fool of a thief who stole from himself. I wrote five books on a stolen typewriter.

Why did I want to become a writer? It was only many years later that the true answer, or what I believe to be the true answer, came to me. I thought of myself as a tough guy. Writing, in this regard, seemed a respectable racket. Hemingway and others like him had rendered it so: a manly art — whatever the fuck that was. I mean, shit, none other than W. H. Auden had noted, in the late forties, that America possessed "a culture with dominant homosexual traits."

Manly art. Only after I became a writer did I come to see this lie for what it was.

I came to writing through cowardice and fear. Deep inside me, I needed to communicate my feelings, and there was no one to whom I could. In the old neighborhood, honest expression was a sure means to ostracism. Besides, it wasn't in me. To look someone in the eyes and talk from the heart was beyond me. Writing was thus a way of communicating without looking anyone in the eyes. It was far from a manly art. It was a cowardly art. Then again, maybe the two are the same.

But Hemingway, for all his ridiculous fraud, made money: a lot of it. He followed *The Old Man and the Sea* with a series of similarly written advertisements for Ballantine ale ("I would rather have a bottle of Ballantine Ale than any other drink after fighting a really big fish"). And that was something that I surely wanted to do. I'm not talking about writing beer advertisements or fighting really big fish; I'm talking about making money. I wanted to make money. It was something I needed to do.

That's what it was: cowardice, theft, hard times. A true love for the sounds and colors of words, the rhythms and meters of lines, the evocation through them of the ultimately inexpressible, came later. With it came the true love and awareness of that silence and that wind and the gods and demons they enlaced.

I was nineteen years old, not long before my daughter was born, when I was first paid for writing. Before that, my friend Phil Verso was the only one with whom I shared all of what I wrote. We had known each other since the eighth grade, before the publication of the book that would deliver to me what *Moby Dick* had failed to do, the book that woke me and freed me and inspired me: *Last Exit to Brooklyn*, by Hubert Selby, Jr. I was fifteen then; and Selby, who became a dear friend, continued many years later to wake me and free me and inspire me in ways that had little or nothing to do with writing. Of the three living writers whom I consider to be great — Peter Matthiessen and Philip Roth are the others — it is Selby whose art and whose soul reach the highest, and it is he whom I most respect, as a writer and as a man.

But before there was Selby, there was Verso. Phil and I ran together, robbed together, got shot at together, drank and took dope together, laughed together. The laughter is what I remember and miss, for everything else seemed for us in those days and nights to end in laughter. All of what I wrote in those days is long vanished except as tantalizing shards of half-buried memory; but the laughter of those wicked days still echoes clearly, and, though the echo is forlorn, it is more tantalizing than the shards.

The heart and holy place of our world was Hubert's Museum on West Forty-second Street. At street level, Hubert's was a faded pinball arcade and shooting gallery; downstairs there was a freak show. Outside, in front of the joint, a man, or a boy, could connect with anything. Many of the twisted and surreal little things I wrote were inspired by the twisted and surreal spirit of that place. Phil loved them. I can still see his face, hear his open evil laughter as he read them. He was my conspirator and my first, and therefore most important, supporter. He remained so through the years. Even prison could not kill his laughter, and in later years the words and tales I stole from him were many. When he read my first novel, he recognized himself and exulted that he had "made it as a character in Nick's book." His kid brother told me this at Phil's funeral, a month before what would have been Phil's fortieth birthday, a few days after Phil went down in "one of those things," as he used to say, on a hot summer night in Coney Island.

By then, unlike poor Phil, unlike my poor daughter, I had prevailed. I was more fortunate than most as far as this racket, and life itself, were concerned. But I was coming to see the wisdom of what I had mistaken as the folly of my father's mean-eyed old-world backward ways. I should stay away from books — "that shit," he called them — for they would "put ideas in your head."

And he was right. He truly was. They had put into my stupid fucking head the stupid fucking idea that literature was still a thing of noble fucking value. Through those books — through that shit — I had entered a different world, a sort of parallel neighborhood, in which Homer and Dante and Samuel Beckett were as big a deal as my grandfather's brother, and bigger still: as big as those old-timers at the club whom my grandfather's brother rose to embrace. But this was not true. And the grand irony, as I now, much later, had discovered, was that it was less true in the world of publishing than it was in the old neighborhood.

Now there was nothing. Yes, I had escaped, or at least forged that key that allowed me to come and go as I more or less pleased, from the bleak damnation of what had seemed to be my own predestined fate. But now I could no longer remand myself, or return for solace and comfort, to the old neighborhood places and ways. For there now was no neighborhood. There was "*quality of life*," which meant no quality of life: no life, period; no nothing. And there was no world where Homer moved or was revered by the masses. There was Oprah's Book Club.

In thirty years, I had seen the publishing racket reduced to a drab, unimaginative, and unsuccessful form of corporate salesmanship that grew every day more devastating in its mediocrity. Where once there had been rare sparks of life, signs of intelligence, and at least a lingering respect, if not a concern, for the powers of what T. S. Eliot called "the sacred wood" of poetry, you would today be hard-pressed to find a senior editor in New York who had heard of Eliot's *The Sacred Wood*, let alone read it, let alone followed the stream of this darkening grove, back past Böcklin's haunted painting of that name, past Orsini's *bosco sacro*, past the *silva sacra* of pagan Rome, to peer into the unknown sylvan source, and to find along the way that the word *silva* in Latin had a more obscure, and in this context more magical, meaning as well. To Quintilian, *silva* denoted the raw materials for writing, among which we surely might see the powers of the sacred wood as foremost. I dare say not one such editor might be found. And, yet — without the volumes of the *Institutio Oratoria* of Quintilian, without the literary essays of Eliot, without a true, second edition of Fowler, without a Liddell & Scott, an *Oxford Latin Dictionary*, or even an *Oxford English Dictionary*, without a guide to scansion and meter, or likely even a guide to the fucking subway — they go forth. With little else than the latest edition of *The Chicago Manual of Style* (replete with "recent changes in style, usage, and in computer technology," and sporting a fine typographical error to prove this new commitment to bow before the cheap, plastic *silva* of the new WordPerfect postliteracy), a cheap suit, a satchel to attest to their industry, and maybe something like, oh, I don't know, *The Art of Editing* or *Creative Editing* — because, see, this is where the *art*, the *really* creative part comes in — and, of course, a copy of our newspaper of record: respectable, informative, reliable, astute, and perhaps the only shit-house rag on earth that would be stupid enough to print an image of Saint Andrew being crucified, identifying the image as that of "Two Jews with peaked Jews' caps tying Christ to the cross." (Yeah, I know, these late-breaking stories, sometimes you can slip up a little on the details. Besides, you know, all these fucking Christians look alike. Sure, it's got his name, S. Andreas, right there on the goddamn cross, but, still, you know, these things slip by.) Yes, the world's dignified gray rag of record truly sets and reflects the editorial standards of our day. Jews' caps.

This, essentially, is to what it all had come down. After takeovers, buy outs, and mergers, there remained only half a dozen or so editors of any importance. This was because Random House, Knopf, Pantheon, Crown, Vintage, Bantam, Doubleday, Dell, and others were now all owned by Bertelsmann of Germany. Viking, Penguin, Putnam, and others were now owned by Pearson of Britain. Simon & Schuster, Scribner, Pocket Books, and Atheneum were all owned by Viacom; Warner Books and Little, Brown were now owned by AOL. St. Martin's, Henry Holt & Co., and Farrar, Straus & Giroux were owned by another kraut conglomerate, Verlagsgruppe Georg von Holtzbrinck; Rupert Murdoch's News Corporation owned HarperCollins, Lippincott, Morrow, Avon, and others. These six corporate entities now controlled about seventy-five percent of the adult book market; and four of these six controlled about two thirds of the market by themselves.

Only two of these six corporations, AOL and Viacom, were American, and both of these were based predominantly in media other than traditional publishing, which was to them but an insignificant and vestigial appendage.

Thus, as publishing was the primary business neither of Viacom nor of AOL, it could now be said that there were in effect no major American publishers left in America.

I had been a shylock; I had been a bookie: I knew my way with figures, without calculator or scrap of paper and nub of pencil. The arithmetic here was quite simple. AOL Time Warner was valued at more than two hundred billion dollars. AOL had revenues of about five billion dollars a year, and spent about a billion dollars a year on advertising and direct marketing.

Time Warner Trade Publishing, which comprised Warner Books and Little, Brown, had revenues of about three hundred million dollars a year.

These book-publishing revenues equalled little more than one tenth of one percent of the value of AOL Time Warner.

Warner Books had begun, some forty years before, as a publisher of pulp paperbacks. But the house that had begun, in 1837, as Little and Brown of Boston had been, once upon a time, independent and venerable: a hundred percent of itself unto itself. Now its revenues were less than one tenth of one percent — a mote in the eye, a minuscule morsel between the teeth — of the Moloch of mediocrity that was the world's largest entertainment and media conglomerate; and the revenues in full of Time Warner Trade Publishing were less than a third of what AOL alone spent on promotion.

In the old days, when corporate profits fell, the cutting knife would be turned first to advertising. Now things were different: the mote could be flicked from the eye, the vaguely irritating morsel picked from between the teeth and spat aside, with the greatest of ease.

Synergy. That was the word they liked. Synergy. It was all a matter of synergy.

Twenty-five years ago, more than fifty publishing houses held among them the same market share that now was controlled by six global companies. In those days, when there were autonomous publishing houses whose true business was publishing, editors possessed autonomy in turn. Their bosses, the publishers who ran the houses, were figures of flesh and blood, rather than unseen bureaucracies. The term "publisher" now was just another job title, and there was no "publisher" who had the power to act independently. The power had shifted to the business departments, whose ineffective calculations of demographics, marketing potentiality, and projected profits decided the fate of books. The racket no longer had much to do with writing. Books were products, and those products that were judged, more often wrongly than not, to represent the lowest common denominator of the taste of the populace were deemed to be of the most value. What the Nobel-laureate physicist Lev Landau said of cosmologists, that they are "often in error but never in doubt," could far more than justly be applied to these new business-school arbiters of publishing, these subliterate Uriah Heeps in their blue-chalk-stripe shirts with white cuffs and white Eton collars, these golem whose tastelessness in dress perfectly reflected their tastelessness in books.

As my late friend Sal Scarpata, who did not live to see forty, once said, "Remember all those creepy-looking assholes that couldn't get the girls when we were kids? Well, now they're out to get even with us."

Yet — often in error, never in doubt — the golem never forsook the arrogant delusion that they could predict and manipulate the consumption of the masses; and, no matter how wrong their own balance sheets proved them to be, the unseen bureaucracy seemed not to question this delusion.

Those who bore the title of publisher or editor or both, who once had stood above the golem, were now pressed to serve them. Every book that they wanted to acquire and publish now had to be slutted to fit the paradigm of the golem's delusion. It had to be presented as a product whose nature was of a tried and true formula of current marketability. It might be labelled "daring," in the manner that detergents and oral-hygiene products may be labelled "new and improved" or even "revolutionary," but, like those detergents and oral-hygiene products, regardless of label, it must be consumer-safe, with tested and approved artificial fragrances and colors. It may be "shocking," "brutally honest," "outrageous," "wild," or "nightmarish," as these have become the acceptable flavors of mediocrity; but, while being "shocking," "brutally honest," "outrageous," "wild," or "nightmarish," it must never be offensive or aberrant, nor must it venture in any way beyond the pale of the petting zoo of the accepted. Above all, it must possess the promise of meeting those loftiest and most discerning ideals of mediocrity that might win it the imprimatur of our newspaper of record, which, though it may crucify the wrong Jew every once in a while, knows well enough to dismiss Philip Roth as distasteful while receiving goyim such as John Grisham and Stephen King as real writers.

To survive, editors had no choice but to serve the golem. Even if they had entered the business with literary souls, even if they still paid lip-service to literature, the truth was that the only way now for them to rise was to serve the golem. Spirit, imagination, courage, individuality, profligacy: no more. A love for the classics might be professed, but the truth was that no editor could or would publish these books today. The truth was that these classics were still in print and still sold, if often not read, only because they were on the required-reading list and therefore on the compulsory-purchase list of almost every victim of the diploma-mill racket. They were not Oprah material, these books, not the stuff to which this other racket, publishing, had by now devolved to the point of no return.

Book sales, and reading, were decreasing. About half of all sales were now controlled by four major chains of stores. It was a joke. No publishers. No stores. No nothing.

My friend Bobby Tedesco used to say, "There are only two kinds of people in this world: the Italians and those who wish they were."

It now seemed that it could be similarly said that there were only two kinds of books in this world: Oprah books and those that wished they were.

I had just published a new book. To me, it was not much of a book. I had not intended it to be. I had wanted to pick up a few hundred grand, and that was all. But to say that it was, to me, not much of a book is not to say that it was not a great book compared to what else was being published. The critics, as usual, were very kind to me, and the book got an award, and even hit a few bestseller lists, which no book of mine ever had done.

The week that my book appeared on the bestseller list of the *Los Angeles Times Book Review*, my friend Jerry sent me a copy of that list. My book was near the bottom of the list, but it was there. My publisher had only one other book on the list, at the top of the list, a confection of recipes and decorating tips. Sure, my book could not compete with this sort of book, which was a "*good*" book. My book was an attempt to redeem the soul of a man — big, bad, black Sonny Liston — whom history had damned to Hell. I called the book *Night Train*, which was the title of Sonny's favorite song, and which I long had felt to be the perfect metaphor for the doomed brief journey to the end of the night that was Sonny's life. My publisher, however, felt that, even though I had conceived this as my title some years ago, it might cause the book to be overshadowed by another, recent book, by

Martin Amis, that bore the same title. I had reluctantly accommodated the publisher with a different title, *The Devil and Sonny Liston*, under which it now appeared. (Ironically, though Martin Amis is British, my publisher in Britain felt no such qualms. When my book was released there bearing the title *Night Train*, it surpassed Amis's book as the book with which the title was more popularly associated, and since then the two books have coexisted in Britain without problem or confusion.)

But this was not about my perhaps not-so-good book — that is to say great book — and Amis's perhaps better book. It was about my book and the book of recipes and decorating tips. I believed that as my book — which, yes, I admit, lacked in decorating tips — was a serious attempt to redeem the soul of a man in the eyes of a world that, for all its hypocritical political correctness, still unadmittedly but deeply fears and despises what is big and bad and black, and that as it was at least a real book — if perhaps written from the not-so-sacred whorehouse on the outskirts, rather than the purest heart, of the sacred wood — my publisher should have been somewhat pleased that I had lent a touch of dignity to their representation on this bestseller list.

But this was not the case; and it was then that I discovered that, except as a public sham, publishers now no longer seemed to care about even the wisp of respectability, even if it garnered a wisp of commercial success amid a meadow of praise.

According to my publisher — speaking not to me but to my agent — the book had not been well-received. Furthermore, it had not met "sales expectations." All things considered, it had been for the golem a rather disappointing venture.

So there I had it: my first bestseller was as nothing to those recipes and decorating tips.

This was the season when I knew that, for me, this racket was over. For thirty years, I had fought, and I had prevailed. But as I had prevailed, so the enemy had gotten bigger and more monolithic. Now one either knelt before it bearing the frosted cake of surrender and oblation, or one perished.

I had known my editor for seventeen years, since the days when he had worked in the fine old offices, rich with fine old wood, of the fine old house of Scribner's, when there was still an old man Scribner walking the fine old creaking floorboards. True publishing still lingered, and these fine old offices of wood overlooking Fifth Avenue were a mellow place where my editor and I could feel and relish the air of that place of the soul and the ages, that other place, that place of aspiration, that other wood that was sacred and unhewn.

Now I had breathed the air deeply and fully of that sacred wood, and I wanted no other air within me.

He was the best possible editor, in that he only very rarely attempted to edit me. As no writer can write until it is understood in all humility that the wordless breeze of which Pound spoke possesses powers of poetry that no writing or writer can ever attain, so editors must come to similar understanding. The greatest editors do not edit. They find good writers and they conspire with them to bring them freedom and gain. Maxwell Perkins, who worked at Scribner's with Hemingway, F. Scott Fitzgerald, Thomas Wolfe, and others, today bears the title of "editor of genius." If Perkins ever came into contact with genius, his end of it lay in allowing those writers who could construct their own sentences to go unhindered in doing so. How could Saxe Commins, the senior editor of Random House under Bennett Cerf, have imposed himself on William Faulkner or W. H. Auden or William Carlos Williams? How could Barney Rosset have tampered with William S. Burroughs or Hubert Selby, Jr.? How could James Laughlin have siphnianized Ezra Pound or Paul Bowles? They could not have because they would not have. Therein lies true editing.

But the golem who had usurped the editors' power had made all but impossible this sort of conspiracy between writers and editors. In the old days of publishing, as in the old neighborhood days, there had been values, and a sense of standing together against what threatened those values. There had been a sense of kindredness, a sense of devotion, a sense of breathing together. The Latin prefix *con-*, expressing joint action, connection, partnership; the Latin infinitive *spire*, "to breathe": *conspire*, "to breathe together." Then came the rise of the golem, who knew nothing of values, be they the values of bygone publishing or of bygone neighborhood ways: the golem, who breathed with no one.

So, I was disheartened to hear that the words of the golem had come forth from the mouth of my old friend and editor. Long ago, we had aspired together and conspired together. About two years after we had met, when Scribner's had been acquired by Macmillan, and old man Scribner no longer walked the fine old creaking floorboards, my friend and editor had accepted a new position at another house only on the condition that his prospective employer agree to publish my first novel. That was the beginning of new life for both of us.

Now, fifteen years later, what was I hearing? I was hearing words that seemed to say, "Fuck this 'literate, poetic' bullshit. Fuck you and your 'rare humanity' and your 'great' books. Frosted cakes and wardrobe tips: that's the *real* sacred wood. Go bake us a cake, and then maybe you'll be worth something to us."

As it happened, the next volume by me that he was to publish — twenty-five years' of arcane notes, investigations, and musings reworked into a book about the poetic impulse from pre-Homeric times to the present day — seemed to me so utterly bereft of commercial potential that, stating this outright, I wondered in the very pages of the book how I could "hope to con the most benighted and gullible of publishers into paying a decent dollar for it."

But prior to publication, during the early production stages of the book, the golem had doubts of their own — doubts far more bizarre than mine. It was feared that the title that I had given the book — *Where Dead Voices Gather* — was such as to cause confusion, whereby the book might be mistaken for a novel rather than a work of nonfiction. Surely, it was assumed, now that this matter had been brought to my attention, I would share this most understandable concern and consider the addition of a suitably deadening subtitle, by which my book might be rendered distinguishable from fiction.

In my years, I felt that I had either exhibited or witnessed every stupidity within the repertoire of the higher vertebrates. But this was a new one. I began to compose a letter of response, and I found that with every word and punctuation mark, my anger grew:

> I got to pondering the matter of your request for a subtitle. This led to more pondering, until I saw and felt the light, and that most holy and terrible of all things came forth from it: honesty.
>
> Regarding your expressed reasoning for a subtitle, i.e., that the title as it is might "confuse" potential buyers, who might be led to believe that it is a novel:
>
> 1. I should like to know of a single bookstore that does not clearly segregate nonfiction from fiction.
>
> 2. Any title that draws a potential buyer to a book, whether through "confusion" or not, is a good thing. What is the brilliant marketing idea at work here? That we should not want to bring a potential buyer who is interested only in fiction, or only in nonfiction, close to the book through "confusion"?
>
> 3. One would already have to be very close to the book to even read the subtitle, which surely would be smaller, subtler, and less overwhelmingly blatant than the sign NONFICTION, under which, or near which, the book would be encountered.

4. Could anyone so stupid and benighted as to suffer the "confusion" of which we speak ever even be considered a potential buyer of this book?

5. I am aware of the wellspring of humanity that is the ichor of the sages of marketing, but I have never encountered such tender care and concern over the possibility of inconveniencing one who might "mistakenly" approach, or, God forbid, browse a book, and then turn away from it, or buy it as the case may be. Is the risk that such a "mistaken" soul might actually buy the book to be avoided?

6. The idea of confusion here is wrong, untenable, and idiotic. The title does not present confusion. Rather, it presents mystery, which attracts us all, even those too dumb to notice the big signs NEW NONFICTION and NEW FICTION that sadly demarcate every major bookstore in this sadly demarcated age.

7. Who gives a fuck what they think it is? It is a fucking book.

I just can't buy or fall for this nonsense, which I find to be ridiculous, disturbing, and abjectly moronic.

Simply put, there will be no subtitle. But fuck that.

Assuming that you will immediately set about preparing the book for publication exactly as it is in its final version, I will recommend to you a good and literate typesetter, who will be able to render any classical elements in an expert and efficient manner.

Otherwise, fuck that too, and on to the main event.

We both know that this book is certainly more important to me than it is to those who reign, and I must protect it, and I impose this duty neither on you nor on anyone else, but only on myself, which is where sole responsibility lies. For this book represents me, as will the forthcoming novel represent me; and nobody is going to fuck with me, cut me up, drag me down, or ruin me — nobody except me. I will and shall either stand or fall, flourish or perish, but it will be as me.

What is beyond my control, the damage or destruction that can be fated me by the ever more oppressive forces of the post-literate industry of mediocrity, of which publishing has become but a vestigial appendage — so be it; but what is within my control — my inner fate — so be it, too. I should like to convey to the confusion-prone my apologies, pride, and gratitude for not having authored that collection of recipes that bested me on the Nonfiction (clearly labelled to prevent confusion) bestseller charts of the hick L.A. *Times*.

That which I have been writing from my heart, and that which I will continue to write from my heart, can not and must not be tailored even a stitch to reflect either the heart of another or the false plastic heart of this marketplace that once was a world. These books of mine can be edited no more than a leopard in the wild can be manicured.

You have spoken of your late-kindled love for Homer, a love which I share. Note that in the *Iliad* he evokes only the aid of the goddess in writing, and in the *Odyssey*, only the aid of the Muse. They are one, and they are the only one, and they are immanent: the possibility of invoking or suffering another's influence is unthinkable. Of course, large parts of the *Odyssey* are poorly wrought, and larger parts of the *Iliad* are all but unreadable. There is no editor who would not have razored the Catalogue of Ships wholesale or in part from Book II of the *Iliad*, any more than any editor would have let stand the First Book of Chronicles in the Bible itself. These are facts obscured by the reverence that we embrace without pause for these books. It is true that these works all might have been so much the better for editing; but they were and are leopards, which we choose to call books, but which will continue to inspire and move and awe long after the toxic perfumed waste of louche novels and confections, which some of us also choose to call books, have done their damage and are forgotten.

(By the way, how is the *Iliad* to be reckoned, as fiction or as nonfiction? As Schliemann and others to this very day have shown, there has been great confusion on this matter. Surely a subtitle would have helped the book along a bit in the course of the last eighteen hundred or so years.)

I think of the joy and inspiration and deep effulgences I have had from reading William Faulkner, who, with all his flaws and outright alcoholic sloppiness and mistakes, simply refused to be edited once he had learned how to write (after his first two, unbearable novels), and how fortunate he was to have editors, first Harrison Smith and then Bennett Cerf, who had the courage and wisdom *not* to edit him. ("You're the only damn fool in New York who would publish it," said Alfred Harcourt to Smith about *The Sound and the Fury*. And, of course, no major house would publish it today.) As Faulkner said, "I get drunk, I get mad, I get thrown from horses, I get all sorts of things. But I don't get edited. I'd rather see my wife get fucked by the stableboy." Without that credo, and without the bravery and blind faith of Zen-brilliant no-edit editors such as Smith and Cerf, Faulkner would have been transformed into just another forgotten mediocrity, and we would have been deprived of a greatness fine as breath. There would, really, have been no Faulkner. Yes, he was different. Yes, he was commercially unviable. Until he won the Nobel Prize, his books got worse reviews and turned less a profit than mine. (Which likely means nothing other than that he was a better writer than I am, and his books were better than mine. As I've said, I need to write a bad book to get the money that I need to return to writing good ones.) But he was, to use a word he loved, unvanquished.

Of course, those were different times, when publishing companies had real, individual bosses, and when those bosses were human beings who had balls and loved books and knew when not to fuck with what they loved, no matter how strange or singular or unwholly understood the object of that love. Now there is no individuality and no bravery, and the Bob Cratchits of yesterday are the tyrants of today, suffering all from the arrogant delusion that they know how to make money while in reality they are going down the drain, staring at the momentary bottom line while Harry Potter and the next Faulkner alike pass by them unnoticed. Those who cower beneath these financial and cultural bankrupters dwell always in danger of losing their jobs; and that is a sad and a bad thing.

(As one who is strongly opposed to censorship, I am repelled by the idea that I may end up being forced to be published under the aegis of America Online, which, as you may or may not know, is the most vehement supporter and enforcer of censorship on the Internet. I don't know if you feel any moral disgrace or self-loathing in finding yourself aligned with an active enemy and suppressor of free speech, but I surely do. The only ray of hope I see is that AOL, being so mismanaged, and with its stock value having fallen by almost fifty percent within the last year, may, in its need to raise cash, sell us off to a less disgraceful massa. I mean, I signed a contract to write a book, not to betray my fucking principles. Homer would puke on us; Faulkner would piss on us. If we had a conscience, we'd do it for them.)

But there are still leopards, and they still have their claws. They also dwell always and increasingly in danger of losing their jobs; but in their case, their jobs are them. And, to a leopard, one's soul is a sacrosanct and invaluable thing, and it will kill or be killed to hold and protect and honor that thing.

In other words, while I hope always to have in my life those very few editors whom I have come to respect and to whom I have come to feel closeness and friendship, there will in my life, when it comes to my books, be no more editing.

The dice that bear the numbers of my life are in my hand, and they are mine to roll. I really do not give a fuck anymore. And thus I win.

This is simple English, simple honesty, simple truth. And, lest anyone be confused by lack of subtitle, it is nonfiction most pure.

Please feel no need to reply in words to any of this, for no such reply is desired and no further words pertaining to any of this will be forthcoming from me.

Sincerely,

NICK

Jesus. Yeah. Faulkner. His story said it all. For every writer, every publisher, every editor, every reader: his story said it all.

"I have written THE book, of which those other things were but foals," he had told Boni & Liveright, the publisher of his first two, God-awful novels, after finishing the manuscript of *Flags in the Dust*, in the fall of 1927. He was right. And the book was published in due time, in the summer of 1973, eleven years after he was dead.

The house of Jonathan Cape and Harrison Smith did, however, publish another of his great books, *The Sound and the Fury*, in the fall of 1929. Depression or no depression, bestsellers then, as now, could and did sell in the millions. *All Quiet on the Western Front*, also published in 1929, would sell more than three and a half million copies throughout the world in the span of eighteen months. *The Sound and the Fury* sold one thousand seven hundred and eighty-nine copies.

When Harrison Smith saw Faulkner's next book, *Sanctuary*, he responded aghast: "Good God, I can't publish this. We'd both be in jail." Smith eventually summoned his courage, and when *Sanctuary* was published, in early 1931, it sold more than six thousand copies — a degree of commercial success that Faulkner would not see again for another eight years.

Random House acquired these books when it acquired Smith's company and became Faulkner's publisher in 1936. As Smith had shown bravery, conviction, and devotion, so did Random House. Though it took almost thirteen years, from 1931 to 1943, for *The Sound and the Fury* to sell another thousand copies, bravery, conviction, and devotion paid off. For Random House, *The Sound and the Fury*, and the rest of Faulkner's novels, became in years to come one of the most profitable and prestigious treasure-troves that any publisher could dream ever to possess.

The catch, of course, is that, while Random House has justly prospered from its bravery, conviction, and devotion, the sweat and suffering of Faulkner's own brilliance and bravery have, as they say, earned out only after he has taken his place beneath the dirt.

I'm sick of these sons of bitches who moan and groan about how they work so hard for their fucking families. They're full of shit, every fucking one of them. Only the artist works truly for his loved ones and descendents alone. And that is because they are the only ones who get to see the fucking paycheck. Artists are not paid hourly. They are not paid weekly. They are not paid monthly. They are not paid annually. They are paid posthumously. In life, there is nothing: not even decent down-payment, not even the token gesture of a ten-percent lagniappe.

So next time you're going to show me a picture of your ugly fucking wife, whom I probably fucked and forgot twenty years ago, and your kids, who, yes, have the misfortune of looking just like you, and you're about to tell me how hard you work for them, just do me a favor: stick it up your fucking ass. The same goes for that old bag cocksucker mother you talk about taking care of. Shit, when she croaks, there'll probably even be a payday in *that* for you. Fuck you people with your paid vacations and your pensions and your rich mommies and daddies and your bullshit about how hard you work and how much you sacrifice. The only worthy sacrifice you can make is to kill yourself. I hate every one of you motherfuckers who ever inherited a dime, or who stands to inherit a dime. You're the scum of the earth, because you can't make your own way on it. Even if you pretend to make your own way, you've got that net under you. You're dilettantes of real life.

It feels good to say these things.

Free. As only one on death row can be.

Anyway, go fuck yourselves. I'm talking Corncob Willie here.

Yes, his story says it all. For every writer, every publisher, every editor, every reader: his story says it all. Yes, for every reader too.

"Now, Mr. Faulkner," she said, "what were you thinking of when you wrote that?"

"Money," he replied.

Or how about this one, regarding a particularly convoluted passage in one of his works:

"What does that mean, Mr. Faulkner?" he asked.

"Damned if I know," Faulkner replied after a moment. "I was readin' that the other day and wonderin'. I remember I was pretty corned-up when I wrote that part."

Or just read *The Wild Palms*, in which that wind, the wind of Pound's final wisdom, is the great fatal force. You would need to read no other novel after it. I myself robbed the final page of the manuscript of this novel from its vault in the Manuscripts Division of the Alderman Library of the University of Virginia, in Charlottesville. It is among my holy things, and I shall hate to leave it behind.

I have them gathered about me now, my holy things, as I write this. I feel no need to tell of them.

But, God, to have had or to have known an editor or a publisher who had upon his wall those words:

Good God, I can't publish this. We'd both be in jail.

And there, atop a bookcase beneath it, a copy of the latest printing of the latest, handsome Vintage edition of *Sanctuary*, the ever profitable, required-reading "literary classic" that once was unthinkable and that once took thirteen years to sell what it now sells in a week.

Yes. And nearby it, on another wall, the fine, fierce words of Revelation:

I know thy works, that thou art neither cold nor hot: I would thou wert cold or hot. So then because thou art lukewarm, and neither cold nor hot, I will spue thee out of my mouth.

But it could not be. This fucking horse was dead.

Not long after reading the riot act to my publisher, I came even to feel betrayed by my agent, who had been my conspirator, ally, and cohort of almost twenty-five years. First there was the matter of some big-deal fat-ass bitch agent who was working with us on our moving-picture deals. I had caught her in a lie. And, as if the malignance known as Hollywood were itself not but one great lie, this had angered me, and I would have nothing more to do with her. My agent, however, did not sever his own ties with her, on the grounds that she had done well by us and was of use in his dealings on behalf of his other clients. This rankled me. Other clients?

Yeah. Another fat-ass bitch, that movie agent. Oprah. That editor: he had a fat ass too. Even my agent was getting sort of wide in the bottom. Do you have a fat ass too? What is it with you people and your fat fucking asses? All you pear-shaped fucks. I should have toted a fucking theodolite from the get-go, to measure all these distended fucking buttocks and calculate trouble before it came.

Fuck him. Fuck her. Fuck the other guy. Fuck you, whoever you are. Fuck you all.

Perhaps I should have greater sensitivity to the feelings of others. Perhaps I here have been hurtful to many. But I will not go silent to my fate.

So, yes, fuck you all. May you all rot in Hell. And I above all, for I was the worst and greatest fool among you.

I was getting old. Diabetes had killed my dick and was killing me slowly throughout. I was prohibited for popular consumption.

But I still had my sense of humor, and I still had my love for the breath of this world.

I felt that God had kept me alive for something. Thirty years seemed to have vanished from me like the glimpse from the corner of my eye of something lovely and wild. When I laid my head to the pillow at night, I was visited more and more frequently by the image of myself as a youth seeing a breach of light in darkness, and sensing in that breach the thrilling promise of all things possible and limitless. These visitations of the night were fleeting but brought with them an ever greater and more whelming sense of sadness and of loss. The thrilling promise of all things possible and limitless was gone. I was old now, and I was lonely. But at the same time, I recalled the many times, after youth had passed and the dream of writing became the truth of writing, that I had come to wretched and nightmarish consciousness lying immobile on floorboards in pools of coagulated blood, often not knowing if the blood was mine or another's, or that I had come to a more sedated consciousness, in intensive-care units, my wrists bound to bed rails and pierced with the taped-over needles of intravenous tubes; the times that I had lain in coma for days, as callers were advised that I likely would not make it through the night; the times that I was told by doctors in hospitals that I would be writing my own death certificate if I returned to my ways, and that the next time I was wheeled in on a stretcher, the sheet would be covering my face; the times that I was told in rehabilitation clinics that I didn't have another detox in me; the time in one lock-up joint when, in a compulsory group-therapy exercise, we all had to compile our own substance-abuse histories and then write them on a blackboard, and when the day came that I wrote mine, this black guy whom everybody feared — this guy had done so much crack that his kidneys had exploded and he was now on dialysis; and, while almost everybody in this joint was black, this guy, even on dialysis, had the brothers as scared of him as he had us few pale-ass motherfuckers scared of him (it was not only, among the brothers, a matter of who was going to marcel his hair or light his cigarettes or launder and press his britches: it was a matter of who was so fortunate as to be chosen to do so) — he broke out in tears and, as if from a pew in a country Baptist church in Alabama, where he was born, he cried as if he were a wholly different man suddenly prostrate before the ways of the Lord: "Nick, oh, my God, Nick, thank God you're still alive!"

Maybe he was crying for himself. Maybe he was in all true and welling compassion crying for one whose every organ should have exploded but who was spared by the same grace of God that had at least saved his own life.

We became good friends. Then, on the outside, we lost track of each other. But he's never left my heart, and I can see his face now as I write this. I hope he got his transplant, and I hope he is alive. There are some who I want to believe will breathe well and strong and long after I myself soon cease to do so; and he is one of them, and like the others, he is in my prayers of gratitude.

Don't get the wrong idea. As I say: there are some. Most of you I would rather send or see sent in my place.

And, yes, I came to believe, ever more deeply, and with ever greater thanks, that God had spared me — for something. I came to believe that God had kept me alive to deliver forth all that I could; that He had kept me alive to surrender myself as a vessel, that I might let flow to others, through my writing, the gift that I had received: the gift of the awareness of the immense blessing of the every moment and the every breath that we are given; the gift of the awareness that we are the destroyers of our own lives, the breakers of our own hearts; that freedom lies only in the absolute honesty that fear strangulates within us; that all the pretty pills and all the fraud and whoredom of psychotherapy and mass-market spirituality in this world are as nothing compared to the ancient words of the Gospel of Thomas — "*If you bring forth what is within you, what you bring forth will save you. If you do not bring forth what is within you, what you do not bring forth will destroy you*" — and that these words are all of truth and wisdom that need be known.

I swore that I would never write another false or worthless word, and that I would write only to my fullest powers and toward purest end; and that what I wrote would be neither tempered nor censored nor contrived: not by me, not by anyone, not by anything. Even if it might touch upon and draw the light from only one soul beyond mine, then lie lost two thousand years in the desert waste, this was how it must be. I had been kept alive for this: to make what I could, and thus be free, in fidelity and in gratitude and in dignity.

And that is when it ended. That is when I felt the garrotting of God's mitten strings around my neck. I had strayed too far from the prim garden of propriety where those yapping poodles called writers are confined. There were all sorts of poodles: the so-called serious, literary poodles; the so-called challenging poodles, whose own repressions and self-absorbed posturings saw to it that their little dances at the edge of a very blunt razor remained well tethered and resulted in no bloodshed; the so-called probing poodles; the so-called whimsical poodles; the so-called outrageous poodles. Yes, all sorts of poodles. And, confined for so long to this garden, most of them had inbred, so that what little distinction among them had once existed had now all but vanished. They all knew to change the pitch of their yapping and to shed a tear whenever a Kennedy hearse passed by.

For honesty is the anathema of our age; and to express what bears not the imprimatur of the overseers of the stuffing of that à la mode gray paper-pulp mulch that fills the holes where hearts and minds once were is regarded not as virtue but as sin. The fig leaf of shame that covers the loins is as nothing to the masquerade by which we cover in shame all that is real within us.

The truth shall set you free, as one Jew once told the other Jews who had gathered to him. And, yes — what eternal beauty, what eternal wisdom lie within those words. The truth shall set you free. But it can land your ass in jail, take the bread from your table, and place the bell of the leper round your neck as well.

A buddy of mine, a gentleman young in age but of the old school, works on the block where the last Kennedy death-circus occurred: where those lonely sick souls gathered to stand staring at a nondescript building, its front littered with a heap of cheap flowers, in the hope of being validated by the passing notice of one of the encampment of television news-vans. He told me of running into another friend of the old school late one night while the circus slept. "What's up?" my buddy asked him. "Nothing," his friend said. "I'm going down to that Kennedy thing." My buddy was taken aback. "What the fuck are you going to do down there?" he asked. "Pick up some flowers for the old lady."

When I heard that little story, I realized how much of myself I had lost. It had never even occurred to me to get flowers, to cut out the middleman, the Korean deli-owner around the corner, who was raking it in selling those cheap bouquets to those oh-so-sensitive souls who normally would walk over a corpse if it was black and shabby, or if they didn't recognize its face from the cover of *People* magazine. In that little story, in that theft of flowers, that raising of them from meaningless tourist trash to gifts for the living, there was more of honesty, humanity, and purity than in all the ghoulish mawkishness — I use the word with its true root in mind: *mawk*, Middle English for *maggot* — surrounding the lurid sideshow midden of idolatry.

If we are willing to laugh and be entertained by corporate-devised moving-picture confections of murder and drug-addiction, why does that same corporate factory deny us the opportunity to read a book by a true-voiced killer who exults in murder, or a book by a drug-addict who offers us, say, *The Addict's Way: Reflections for Junkies in a Hurry*? How can we delight without guilt in a false image of evil while denying delight in its reality? Are we that steadfastly false, that deluded in the conviction of our own lack of evil? Yes, surely, different packaging for different lies. But a culture governed by fear, servility, and deference is doomed, as is any writing, or any life, governed by those same forces. Hypocrisy is not the problem. Hypocrisy is merely the veneer of the problem. The problem is stupidity.

Anyway, so be it. Fuck this one-horse universe of the Demiurge, this world of lies that have become the marrow of the walking dead that once was a humanity that dared to speak its name. Fuck this mediocrity-worshipping world where a third-rate blowjob from Westchester is adored beyond Isis, Aphrodite, Sappho, the Virgin Mary, and my Aunt Gertie combined.

The publishing industry, which was supposed to be the means that brought me and readers together, had become the wall of dead culture that kept us apart, the living from the living. Fuck the Berlin Wall and fuck Pink fucking Floyd. It was the wall of mediocrity that needed to be brought down.

Yes, there were all sorts of poodles. But none of them were threatening.

Anyway, as I say, that is when it ended. I could no longer even hear the poodles yapping in the distance. There was nothing now but silence. A strange sort of silence. The sort of silence that has a name only in that arcane and old language of the Mafia, the language known, when it is known at all, as Baccagghiu. The word is *stagghiacubbu*, and is defined in Italian as *silenzio profondo*.

In this profound silence, I knew that if I could not make what I could, and thus be free, in fidelity and in gratitude and in dignity, I could at least be free, in fidelity and in gratitude and in dignity. I myself could be banished, but my dignity could be banished only by me.

Lest these words sound saintly, in the same breath that they came to me when that silence descended, there came also the knowledge that, for me, dignity was not enough, for I was one greedy, money-hungry motherfucker. My first steady gainful employment, at the age of fourteen, was as a barroom porter, mopping up and picking cigarette butts out of urinals, for twenty dollars a week. Many years later, I had gone on to make and to blow millions. Sure, I could still make my poetry, and I could still go free with it into the night, where spirits opened; but there was not much money in that. If I was going to pass what dwindling time there remained to me in the *stagghiacubbu* of that wisdom of the wind of paradise, I was going to pass it in a freedom not only of the soul, but in the freedom that only money can buy.

My agent and I knew that I could cash in for a good few million if I were willing to commit myself to one great cold, calculated whoredom. That is, if I were to relinquish all morality and all pride and all that I held holy, and dedicate myself to manufacturing a pure-bullshit bestseller.

It was odd; as a younger man, I never had a compunction about actually, literally robbing people. And even as my agent and I spoke, though I did not ever want to spend another night in jail, I might easily have agreed, if the right people were involved, to actually, literally rob one of the publishing conglomerates. Or, fuck that — the golem kept no cash on hand, anyway — just blow up the fucking building. But I had great trepidations about using writing as a means of robbery if it involved the debasing of writing and my own self-humiliation.

"You're always saying you don't give a damn about posterity," my agent said.

"Yeah, I know. But between now and posterity, I . . ." I what? "Remember, a long time ago, Christ, it seems like ages ago, I had written about a hundred pages of my first good book, and you were trying to sell it, and I would've taken ten grand, five grand, anything, and everybody was turning it down, and we were sitting in some Chinese joint uptown, and you asked me, 'If I can't sell this, will you finish writing it anyway?' and I paused awhile and I thought about it and I said, 'Yeah. But then I won't sell it for less than a hundred grand,' and you looked at me awhile and you looked sort of puzzled and you said, 'Why?' and I said, 'Because I'm a prick' — do you remember that?"

"I remember that."

Then I didn't say anything. I knew he was right.

"Look," I said, "I know I've been fortunate. I'm probably doing better than eighty percent of the writers out there."

"It's more like ninety-nine percent."

Jesus, this racket was more pathetic than I thought. If only I hadn't blown all that money. If only I had held on to it. But what the hell else was it for, if not to blow? I was on my way out, and I tell you one thing: I never saw a Brink's truck following a hearse.

Like all notions that were born of the love of money, it was tempting. Maybe I could do it my way.

Looking back on it all as I lay in that hammock, amid the unique lush rare deep color whose lush rare name applied to it alone, in the deep powerful silence whose deep powerful name applied to it alone, laughter rose from me to singing birds above. But looking ahead, looking to the remaining lot of my life that awaited me in New York, no laughter rose from me.

I had spent many years in thrall to the fear of death. But now, strangely, the prospect of an early death did not disturb me. The death of my daughter had inured me to the coming of my own death. It was as if in taking her from this world, death had bitten from me the fear of it, leaving only a loathing and an enmity in its place.

And I had come to feel, too, that to live in fear of death was to experience death with every pang or twinge of fear rather than just the once, and that all fear of death was but the fear of life: that when the fear of danger holds us from doing, we do not live. It is not what we do in life that kills us. It is what we do not do that kills us.

Besides, I had been written off for dead so many times that, to believe my doomsayers, I was running on swag breath, anyway.

So, as the doctor said, a few years.

Maybe I was right in believing that God had kept me alive for a reason. But maybe I was wrong about the reason.

For, yes, I had fought, and I had prevailed; and, yes, as I had prevailed, the enemy had gotten bigger and more monolithic. I could not be vanquished. I would not be vanquished. But neither could I vanquish that which no longer contained blood to shed.

I felt as if I had failed. There was not a human soul left on the battle-field to conquer or to convert. I had not disembowelled the dead horse of this culture.

Then again, if Ezra Pound couldn't do it with those three lines of his, in those days when there was still blood to be shed, no one could.

As the Fool in Yeats's *On Baile's Strand* proclaimed of mad Cuchulainn, so the fool that was I whispered of myself:

> "He has killed kings and giants, but the waves have mastered him, the waves have mastered him!"

But as I lay in my hammock whispering in gentle meter, I knew that, unlike mad Cuchulainn, I had not rushed in my madness to war against the waves of the sea.

The sea was my savior.

A few years. I should maybe merely count my blessings. All great blessings came unseen. Maybe what had been raised from me had opened me to a greater blessing.

Shit, who was I kidding? I was not going to go down singing my own fucking threnody with a string of fucking daisies around my neck. Fuck Yeats.

> To be, or not to be: that is the question:
> Whether 'tis nobler in the mind to suffer
> The slings and arrows of outrageous fortune,
> Or to take arms against a sea —

The sea, the sea, the sea. Always, always, always the sea. Fuck Shakespeare too. He was as nothing to the promise of that greater man born but ten weeks before him and felled at the age of twenty-nine, before ever a *Hamlet* there was.

Shall I die, and this unconquered?

That was the fucking spirit.

Come, let us march against the powers of heaven,
And set black streamers in the firmament,
To signify the slaughter of the gods.

God, yes, that was the fucking spirit.

Come, let us charge our spears, and pierce his breast
Whose shoulders bear the axis of the world,
That if I perish, heaven and earth may fade.

Man, I did not recall the lines that followed, and I still do not. But what more could be said than this? Fuck God and fuck His world. If I am to go down, then may this whole shit-house of a universe and the motherfucker of a God who made it be brought down with me.

Fuck Shakespeare and that faggot, pondering, penny-a-word bullshit. And may God and the Devil both kneel with open mouths before great Marlowe's young balls.

What form did this death assume, that of which Marlowe had his damned and damning Tamburlaine pass from this world in wrath? All that is said of this are words of the physician who addresses him:

I view'd your urine, and the hypostasis,
Thick and obscure, doth make the danger great.

Diabetes is a disease characterized by urine that is thick and sedimentary with glucose.

To die with all of this unconquered.

Like the melancholy of dimming light through old stained glass, what was to me sadder than slow-nearing death itself was to know that my daughter, who had gone before me, would not be there to warm my hand in hers at the hour of my death. There were many who loved me, but blood alone was blood.

No, the sea was not my enemy. The sea was my solace, even though it contained all the sadness that ever was. As I lay in my hammock on that sweet afternoon, while death knit silently in the shade not far from me, I saw a small bird standing at the water's edge. I watched this little bird for a long while, mesmerized by its few slight steps in the soft white sand and the long stillnesses of its own mesmerized stance as it gazed out across the sea. Then I saw it suddenly take flight, higher and farther, out over the ocean, diminishing slowly in the vast blue sky, until it vanished.

As I watched, I knew what I would do.

I had written two novels about the vanishing neighborhood and that underworld of it, which I knew. Although I had denied it, both of these novels were very autobiographical. Though the second of them was far more popular than the first, I always liked the first one more. Maybe this is because the second one was written during a long descent into the black of a night from which I almost did not emerge. The few times that I have looked at it — mostly to answer translators' questions — the coldness of that black night returned to my veins in a very unpleasant way. But that book ended right: without hope. The first one, *Cut Numbers*, the one that I held more dear, was more intimately autobiographical, but I had laid to it an ending that was sanguine. I know now that I did this because I wanted to believe that my own future might be so. It was as if I felt that, through a sort of word-magic, if I wrote my future, it might come to pass. As I see it now, the book ends, in a way, with my own unconscious prayer.

The book received a good deal of acclaim (even though nobody bought the fucking thing), but the greatest praise, to me, was that it was the only book that had ever been read by Vinnie Moustache, who held down the corner of Downing and Bedford and was one of the very last of the true old-timers. I remember his ongoing critiques as we stood together on that corner, outside Dodge's joint, on those mornings after those nights when he had read in my book.

"I hated to see Joe Brusher die," he had said to me one morning, about one of the characters in the book.

"Jesus, Vinnie," I said. He knew the real character on whom the character in the book was based. *Nobody* was sorry to see this guy die.

"No, no," he had said, "don't get me wrong. It's just that he was so real, and now I know he ain't gonna be there to read about in the book no more."

That was the best review I ever got, right there on the corner of Downing and Bedford.

A few years before, I was still having to tend bar to make a living, even after two books.

"Don't worry," Vinnie would say, "if this book-writin' shit don't work out, *quann' u ventu v'ène*, we'll put a fuckin' coat on ya."

Quann' u ventu v'ène. That meant *quando il vento viène* — when the wind hits. As for the coat, Vinnie sported a wide-collar camel-hair wraparound, which had been custom-made for him in 1940. As he told it:

"Yeah, these two little fuckin' kikes from up the garment district, they owed me money. But they were stand-up kikes. They couldn't cough up the scratch, but they didn't hide. They came right up to me in the joint one morning, unrolled this big piece of brown paper on the pool table, told me to lay down on it. So, I'm layin' there like Christ on the fuckin' cross, and they're goin' round me with these fucking big black crayons and shit. They shuffle out, come back a few days later, they got this fuckin' coat. 'Here, just like we made for George Raft. Black lining for him, gold for you. So whadaya want, the coat or the money?' I took the fuckin' coat. Then whadaya think this one little kike says to me on the way out? 'We can do it in vicuna too, but we only owe ya a hundred bucks.'"

Forty-odd years later, the coat was still looking sharp. And I tell you, I had to have the lining replaced, but, now sixty-odd years later, that coat still looks sharp, and I've never seen another one like it.

Anyway, these guys were always on my side. There were a lot of good times. I remember the first time there was a big picture of me in one of the New York papers. I was walking down the street that day, but it was the opposite side of the street from the club.

"Hey, ya famous fuck!" one of them yelled out from the doorway of the club, loud enough to bring old ladies to their windows three floors up and half a block away. "Get the fuck over here where ya belong and get fuckin' incriminated!"

Though I know that very few of these guys actually read them, free signed copies of my books were much in demand among them. It got to be a comedy. Most of them always needed a second one a week or so after they got the first one, and it was always the same thing: "Aldo Chink took mine and never gave it back"; "I lent it to Sammy the Rat and he left it in the fuckin' gin-mill"; and, perhaps my favorite, "Right after you give it to me, I hadda go out, see Angelo; turn my back on it for ten fuckin' minutes, the fuckin' rats eat halfway through the fuckin' thing."

Good times, bad times. Just a few summers ago, when Vincent Gigante was on trial and *Time* magazine wanted to know what I thought of him, I told the truth: "I'd rather have him as a neighbor than any cop in the Sixth Precinct."

I told the guy from *Time* magazine that Vincent Gigante's conviction would be a death knell for the neighborhood.

And I was right.

I also knew that some men can exist in a changed and hostile environment without being seen, just as stone faces sculpted high above the streets on the window-arch keystones of old tenement buildings are rarely noticed by those who pass day after day beneath them. I knew several such men. I knew one of them very well. We had been close since we were kids. And now he, like one of those unseen stone faces survived from another time, was pretty high up there himself.

I envisioned him beckoning me to him. I recalled the old days, the old ways.

It was not even a decision.

There was not the merest change of pulse, the merest stirring of the soul.

There was only the knowledge that one life had ended and a new life had begun.

In my heart, I was home.

I had been sober for years. I had been there, clear and present, in the every moment of my downfall.

No: that is wrong. For I was still unfallen.

I had been there, clear and present, I should say, in the every moment of the downfall of the racket into which I had so foolishly and so long ago strayed.

I had embraced serenity and honesty as my terrible swift sword. But where serenity and honesty do not exist, they are without meaning or power except to oneself; and where every soul is false, such a sword is but a vapour.

Still, I had the gift of this breath, the gift of this moment. I had it all.

Maybe in tasting both of spiritual and material wealth I had tasted of that forbidden tree of knowledge. My spirit may have led me to the beauty of this journey that had freed me, that had laid me down in this hammock of serenity and enlightenment in paradise. Yes, it was my spirit, my soul, that had led me here. But it was money that had bought the ticket and was covering the thirty-grand tab.

When I lay in my hammock in the late afternoon, with my feet to the north, I could see the dwindling light in its descent draw forth softly the endless black-pearl nuances of the distant looming peak of Mount Otemanu. Earlier in the afternoon, when I lay in the shade, with my feet to the south, I could see, if I let my gaze stray to follow the curve of the beach, an open-air thatched hut. This curve of beach had a name: Pofai. And this thatched open-air hut had a name as well: Pofai Bar.

This spirituality shit had gone far enough.

The wisdom to know the difference.

Goddamn fucking right.

I eased down from the hammock, strolled down to the little thatched hut by the sea.

"Dewar's on the rocks."

The Polynesian bartender seemed to speak French but little English. There was nobody else there but a couple of honeymooners who were drinking bona fide tropical drinks through straws. They, too, spoke French. The broad had nice tits.

"That sugar will kill you," I told them.

They looked to me and chirped: uncomely sounds for human beings.

I drank down the Dewar's, pushed forward the glass, threw the Polynesian bartender a smile.

"Half measures avail us nothing," I said.

He brought me another. I raised it to the sea and to the sky and to him.

"To my thick and obscure urine," I declared.

He grinned a grin of enthusiastic agreement: good to see white foreign fool have good time; put *beaucoup de francs Pacifiques* in *pareu.*

I wondered where that little bird was, out over that big blue sea.

I again pushed forward the glass, again threw a smile. I could begin to feel it now: the slow sweet tongue licking the slow sweet burning beneath my skin. I imagined the little bird awaiting me on my window-sill back in New York. Again I raised my glass.

"To the slaughter of the gods."

FOR THIS, SHE HAD DIED. FOR THIS, IN the bloom of her purity and goodness, she had been sacrificed, as if by the same *mano destra* that now held the pen. For this, she had been taken: not for the divine poetry of the stars without moon, but for the dismal, doomed scribblings of a fool upon the scraped skins of beasts and tallowed latrine rags. Beholding his right hand, he saw it was the killer's hand that held the pen. Beholding his right hand, he saw it was the coward's hand that held the pen. Yes, as the oldest of the *trobar-clus* of the oldest *trovatori* had laced it in melody most fair: the brave man does it with a sword, the coward with a word of love. For this she had died, and with her that part of him that might have lived to make, in flesh and blood and breath and grace, the only work, the one true and greatest work, that God had given man to write.

LOUIE STOOD LEANING WITH THE BASE OF his spine to the porcelain edge of the kitchen sink. The fat-lady panties he wore were black and sheer and ill-fitting. He was otherwise naked. He tried to adjust the gusset of the panties to cover his cock and balls. As he looked down to do this, he saw that his toenails needed to be clipped.

"Now, here's what you do," he said. "You sit there, right where you are, and you tell me what a pretty pussy I got. You tell me I got the prettiest pussy you ever seen. You keep tellin' me that. You smoke your cigarette and you drink your drink, and you keep tellin' me that, and you lick your lips and you tell me you wanna eat my pussy."

Louie drew the cigarette from his mouth and flicked ashes behind him into the sink.

"How old are you?" he said.

"Nineteen," she said.

"You think this is, like, *strange* or somethin'?"

She shrugged hesitantly. "I seen stranger," she said.

"Like what?" he said.

She shrugged hesitantly. "Guy wanted me to play dead."

"Play dead? *Play* dead? What the fuck's that all about? You want a dead broad, you just kill the bitch. That way, you don't gotta pay her, either."

His words brought an unpleasant chill to the young lady who sat nearby, and she inhaled haltingly.

"Not that I give a fuck about what you think is strange," Louie said. "I'm just curious, that's all. About what people think's strange and ain't strange. I'm curious."

"Curiosity killed the cat," was all the girl could think to say.

Louie flicked more ashes behind him.

"Maybe that's why you don't see no cats around here."

He watched her look nervously about, as if she were noting the absence of cats. Louie knew that she wasn't looking for anything: she was just nervous, that's all. He had her now the way he liked them: a little scared. His eyes narrowed; he tossed the cigarette butt behind him, into the sink.

"Now tell me 'bout my pretty pussy," he said.

HE KNEW PROFOUNDLY THE POWERS OF the threes. As from the minstrels of Languedoc he had been led into the field of sweet beauty of the Provençal troubadours, so from the banished Jews of that region he had been led into a field of stranger beauty, forbidden and hermetic, that lay beyond. For the land of the language of Occitan was more than the wombing-place of the troubadours' lovely new song, still wet with the dew of first morning on the parting petals of the rose of its heart; it was, too, the *primum scriptorium secretum* of that most aged wisdom of that the Hebrews called by name cabbalah. It was the holy man Isadore the Jew of Languedoc who first set down in the ancient characters of his kind these secret teachings that until then had been passed down through the ages by hushed tone alone. In these teachings, he believed, one might breach the innermost veils of Scripture, to which Augustine had alluded.

If it had been their misfortune to have been purged from the songful tales of Languedoc, so it had been his fortune, else he never should have met and come to know, in Venezia, as one exile only could know another, he who went by, though it was not his, the name of Isaiah.

Of the *mysteria* into which Isaiah led him, that which mesmerized him most was the *mysterium* of the gematria, that domain of the cabbalah which treated of the hidden numberial measures and powers of words.

Like unto the echo of the name itself, Isaiah seemed himself to be a figure of Testament. His long wisping beard had passed the years of whiteness and entered those years in which further age yellows the whiteness of hair as it does that of ivory or of bone. He wore always the Jew's cap and cloak of black, in heat as in chill, and these too seemed to have passed from one antiquity to another, till their shabbiness had taken on the dignity of reliquary cloth. He lived meagerly, drawing what little few coins he did from a small group of students and reverents. He lamented softly and without bitterness that there were so few students.

"Sofia is their true mother, yet they turn from her, never to know her," he said of the children of his kind. "Pharaoh, as the book of Exodus tells us, killed every first-born among the Jews; but the false god of this new world, which is gross commerce, shall claim them all, every-born, and no Moses set adrift in swaddling amid the bulrushes shall escape and rise to lead and rejoin them to God."

He spoke in a strange chymistrie of tongues: part Latin, part Franco-Latin, part *vernacolo*, uttering amid the all a word once and again of Greek or of Hebrew or of Arabic, causing his auditor to draw unsteady inference or to seek explication in asking. At times the old man stared into the large stone of dark ruby set in its band of gold on the third finger of his left hand, as if lost in contemplation of what lay in its shifting hues. The stone seemed not so much to absorb or reflect dark and light, as to contain and diffuse the hues thereof unto and from itself. Indeed, in the glow of the sun, the stone did often grow dark, and in nightfall or guttering candlelight, the stone was often luminous to behold. It was while he was staring one dusk into this stone that his auditor, after long silence, asked him why he concealed his true name.

"So that no man might know it," he said, and said no more.

If he lived meagerly in one sense — a close *cassetta* above a leather-tooler's shop in a vicolo behind a synagogue, to which he seemed to keep his back ever turned — he lived most richly in the sense of the codices that claimed more of what little space there was than did the *paletta* on which he slept.

Though most of these books were in Latin, and many of these familiar to his visitor in title if not in text, there were books most ponderous of ancient Greek, and of course of Hebrew, and most beautiful and alluring to behold of all, works of the most exquisite Arab calligraphy on the finest uterine vellum.

"*L'arabo é l'ebreo nuovo*," the old man said enigmatically: the Arab is the new Jew.

Many of the texts were not finely made. Some were crudely rendered by hands that were not those of scribes, and just as crudely bound. But these, he said, were most precious of all, for they held learning and wisdom of which few were aware. One of them he claimed to be the work of Isadore himself and known only to its successive owners, of which he was but the fifth since Isadore. No owner, including himself, had ever copied or allowed it to be copied, for this was forbidden in direst terms at the head of its incipit, and so this text remained unique. There were also scrolls of Hebrew, and a great, well-scriven illuminated Bible in the languages in which it was written. This Bible was more than the Old Word of the Jews; it contained as well the New Word of the Christians, as was easily discerned even by one who had no Greek.

The silent curiosity of the old man's companion must have been manifest in countenance, for the old man uttered without the asking that the figure of Jesus intrigued him. In saying the name, he said it as the Lord himself would have given it: *Yeshua.*

The one who called himself Isaiah would gaze at times upon his books as great and comforting treasure, troved to provide and care for him, as wife, from infirmity to grave. At other times he would raise a guarded forefinger to his temple or bring the same to his chest, and with a wan smile would say that the true vast and grand library, with chambers beyond number, was within the palaces of memory or heart.

As if impelled by occult communion, the old man's visitor brought his hand gently to pages and codices and scrolls he could not read. The old man showed no disapproval; and yet his visitor sensed the old man himself must never be touched, in embrace neither of gratitude nor of friendship nor of respect. Amid that bank of books that claimed the better part of the old Jew's cell, one was fastened by lock and clasp. When he moved his fingers over the time-worn brass of that lock and clasp and the hard thick leather it secured, his host said simply and with no tone of import, but beyond enigma, in three words and as many tongues, "*Caveat u sirocco.*"

More and more the poet sought emmisarial duties in Venezia from his lords. More and more he sought opportunity to tarry there beyond the duration of his missions.

It was after some visits, during which little was revealed of the secret teachings, that the old man commanded him to swear on oath that he reveal neither what might be revealed nor the revelator himself. This oath was to be sworn under penalty of death, and was sealed by laying lips on the Bible which held the books of both men's faiths. The poet knew that such an oath was implicit and self-contained in their intercourse. For a Christian to be found in communion with a Jew for the seeking of what the Church of State would doubtless see as the *ars hermetica* of a *magica* most heretical, unholy, and black, could mean anathema and death by neck undone, or worse, by fiery spit, no matter how wholly he believed his seeking to be pure and in love of wisdom, no matter how wholly he knew his heart and soul and life to be of God and Christ. The Jew would be the first to meet his end, then the Christian.

"But by this oath," as the old man said, "we both might be saved from death; so we might then live to die."

During his previous visits, the poet had brought with him leaves of his verse, believing at first that the old man might demand to see such testament to the caliber of his soul's work, then later bearing them in the increasing hope that he would, if not demand to see them, then at least express an interest to see them. On this day of the oath of death, he unstrapped his folio and passed the leaves of words to the old man of his own will and desire. The old man read the first of these leaves with soft but sonorous voice, in perfect meter and felicity of rhyme. He read then the next, again with soft but sonorous voice, in perfect meter and felicity of rhyme. He then but glanced at the third, then passed them gently whence they had come, saying nothing either in voice or in countenance.

No word or gesture had ever stricken the poet so deeply, or so unnerved him, as this want thereof. Only later did he perceive that in suffering this seeming dismissal had he felt more shame than anger or indignance, and thus had been brought low, to humilitas, as no deed or word ever could so have brought him. The old man had expressed nothing: neither that the first leaves did not inspire him to read the third, nor that the voiced leaves were good or bad or worse or shone with brilliance. But while the old man had expressed nothing, his own soul had roiled with fear and unsureness and damnations of himself. This had been the first lesson taken under oath: the power of nothing. It was but the introit, in the form of a silent blow of nothingness, to a long and learned discourse on the revelation of the *cifra*, and on the unspoken nature of the Logos.

When he parted that morning from the old man's cell, he paused to behold he who held open the heavy-timbered door. Age had not much bent him, and the men's eyes met easily. He asked the old man why he was doing this.

The old man gently closed the door and returned to his bench, which was of the same heavy timber. Time had not much bent him, but it had wearied him. He sat slowly, as if careful of his bones, and he beckoned the other to join him.

He spoke in a Venetian dialect so faithful in its Latinity that one would have been pressed to comprehend him without a knowledge of the pagan-most mother tongue.

"As has been scriptured, the Jew is the chosen of God. But we are obligated to look more closely.

"Chosen as and for what? To be punished? To suffer in bondage? For, as it has also been scriptured, the first of the race of man and the first of the race of women, known by name as Adamo and Heva, were of the chosen, and were the first to transgress against Him. Perhaps the tribe of Israel of their descended generations was chosen both to suffer and to teach: to suffer for the sin of the father more so than others in His universal damnation, and to teach the knowledge that had been tasted, and that had been passed down from fallen father to fallen son through the death after death after death after death of their damnation's decree. If this be true, that he was chosen to teach, it then follows that there came a time, the time of the revelation of His choosing, when the fateful taste of knowledge was judged by Him to be dispersed among all of those in thirst of this knowing among all the variegated tribes of man, including those that had been blown away like seed from the tree of generations of knowing. Why this might have been — that the knowledge whose forbidden knowing had brought man to damnation was now deemed to be known to man by He who had damned him — is not of that knowledge. This is why I search the words of all beliefs and all wisdom, the least of which is to be found in the books which your Church has decided to embrace in the gross and ungodly self-interest of the furtherance of its own earthly hierarchy and rule.

"Other than that, it is a mystery or a lie. I know myself no more than you about this matter of the chosen. Thus, in fine, as to whether it pertains to your question of why I do this, I know myself no more than you."

With the palms of his hand, the old man rubbed his knees through the cloth of his robe, and looked downward as he spoke again.

"When you ask why I do this, you speak as one to whom your Church's virtue of charity remains unknown. It is as if you have been never before either the benefactor or the recipient of kindness. It is as —"

The poet made as if to voice words of clarifying exceptance, but, at the utterance of the first vowel of the first-person singular, he was told to be still, in a most abrupt and unkindly way.

"It is as if," resumed the Jew, "you question the very air as to why it gives you breath."

The old man's hands ceased to move upon his knees, and he made straight his neck, and he himself was still; and it was then that the poet spoke, tentatively at first, then freely.

"I meant no lack of gratitude by my question. Believe me: my gratitude is great. It is only that I have never known one of my kind to be welcomed into the realm of your wisdom."

"Perhaps they are of great number, those of your kind who have been welcomed into the realm of wisdom. Perhaps they are of great number, but, like yourself, have been sworn to secrecy under penance of death. Or perhaps *you* are the chosen. Perhaps it is yours," he said slowly, "to suffer and to serve."

After a small silence the old man spoke again.

"Besides," he said, "little of what has been spoken here thus far has not been rendered into the language of your Church."

"I have no Aristotle," he said, by way both of confession and comment, "but only so far as his words have been repeated and elucidated by Tommaso d'Aquino."

The old man shrugged at the mention of Aristotle. "As for your countryman Tommaso d'Aquino, whom I knew in Paris, he was a well-meaning man and of great learning, but I found more of wisdom in the humble, ill-writ little book of your Gregorio of old than in the whole of Tommaso's *Summa*."

The elder breathed, the elder spoke.

"You have got your Ptolemy, no doubt, by way of many Latin treatises. You have got your Pythagoras by way of the Arabs and Alan of Lille. You have got your Plotinus by way of Eusebius."

"But I have no Plotinus."

The old man stood, as wearily as he had sat, his eyes upon three great volumes that lay beneath many others. Each in turn, he began to remove the volumes that lay atop them. The poet stood and helped him in his labor. At last, the first of the three great volumes confronted them. The old man gestured to it more with beard than with hand.

"Do not return here until you have studied it well."

The poet hove the ponderous book to the bench, and the two men sat with the book between them.

"You are very good of heart to entrust me with this treasure."

The old man gently stroked his beard with the knuckle and nail of his left thumb.

"No," he said. "These books all bear curses of a sort, and evil will befall he who steals them or causes or allows them to fall to harm."

The poet said nothing. He stood again, gathering his folio and the great book, as if to leave.

"How shall I ever pay you?" he asked. "As you know, I am a man of meager means."

It was then, as he seemed to subtly nod in understanding, that the old man seemed as well to smile, which the poet, having never witnessed him to do so, felt might be merely the play of advancing light upon his face.

"When it comes to paying, we all become men of meager means."

He seemed more burdened than pleased with the matter of payment that had been broached. Then the two stood, with neither smile nor play of light, lingering.

"The true price, the price of truth, will in course be reckoned and revealed; and it will not be drawn to my account."

The old man's hands were again upon the heavy-timbered door.

"As for me, I will take what gold, but nothing of silver, as you have to give, or can however get."

Having taken a mortal oath, and bearing a book that bore a curse, he stepped from the dim light of the *vicolo* into the open piazzetta, where the sky, as he knew before seeing it, was one of calling.

Never had he known such a one for death and mortal curses such as he in black with his back to the six-pointed star: the star made of two trinities; the two-trinitied star.

My bender did not last long. To make one's way to America from Bora Bora one first had to make one's way to the big airport in Tahiti. I staggered around Tahiti for a few days, drinking and gambling. Whatever the fuck the name of the main city there is, that's where I was. Beautiful Tahiti. What a fucking tourist-trap dump. "I don't speak no English, mahn, only French and Tahitian," one of these beautiful Tahitian people told me: a big, haughty, nasty, jive-ass door-monkey at the neon entrance to some ragged carpet-joint whom I had asked if the joint had blackjack tables. "Fuck you," I told him. He became highly perturbed and drew a big switchblade and snapped it open. "I thought you don't speak no English, mahn," I said, spitting back at him his own nasty-ass pronunciation. I snorted an arch laugh at his knife, which I knew he had drawn in stage-threat intended as much to impress his small coterie of fellow haughty, nasty, jive-ass Tahitians as to scare me. He didn't like that, either. So much for beautiful fucking Tahiti.

I couldn't drink on the long flight home, because I couldn't smoke on the long flight home, and I can't drink without smoking. I was so loaded, I thought of chartering a private jet, but the price was almost a hundred and fifty grand, and I knew, even in my stupor, that I didn't have that kind of scratch to blow. So I drew back the big reclining sleeper-seat into full-bed position, doped myself to unconsciousness with Dalmane, MS Contin, and Valium, let the nice Air France lady place a nice big soft pillow under my head and spread a blanket and a comforter over me, and I sank into the abyss of oblivion.

At home I escaped the road to the hospital by commencing immediately to taper off with my customary regimen of white wine and heroin, decreasing the dosage of heroin daily, from a bundle to a dime to nothing, and, after a few days, also daily decreasing the white wine, from two bottles to two glasses to nothing.

I had been away for a long time. My assistant, Michelle, had kept everything in order during my absence. We had a rule of dealing with all correspondents. Unless they came to us with a pure and loving heart or with money, we ignored them. This made life, and business, much, much simpler.

She saw that I was sickly, but she didn't say anything, because she also knew that I was in recovery. She said only that I was very tan, and she asked me where I'd been. "A lot of beaches," I said, "a lot of hammocks, a lot of lizards." I asked her if any money had come in. She gave me an accounting of a few small checks. She said that Russ, my agent, and Danny, my foreign-rights agent, had an offer from Germany for three hundred thousand marks for something or other. She had long ago learned that these were the kind of deals that meant little, as I would not soon, maybe for years, see any of the money from them: a percentage went to my agent, and the rest went to my American publisher, toward paying back my advance.

"And you missed a couple of deadlines," she said.

Deadlines. Dead-lines. Dead lines.

"No." I sort of laughed. "No. Not really."

THIS WAS WHAT HAD BROUGHT HIM TO Sicilia: to know — the desire for which the Gnostics had been damned.

The fire-light of the tower of the port of Trapani vanished behind him in the dead of night; and, as the ship rounded towards the ancient island that still bore the old Arab name of Gazirat Malitimah, he felt and was robed as one who was damned, and the appearance of the isle in the light of the crescent moon was that of an isle of the damned, or of the dead, or worse.

BACK IN NEW YORK, AS FORTUNE, OR FATE, had it, I did not have to seek out my old friend Lefty, because he was already looking for me.

Lefty knew well of my obsession with Dante. Back when we were drunkards together, he had sat silently nodding, feigning interest, as I at times maundered endlessly about what I then held to be the most beatific emanation of the human soul. No drunk ever truly listens to anybody: it is all between him and the drink; the rest is just part of the meaningless world beyond that all-consuming drink. Still, he remembered those Dante jags.

He asked me if I was in the mood to get rich.

"Oh, I guess I could get in the mood," I said.

He told me to get half a dozen passport photos and meet him at the club next Tuesday.

In the old days, I would have asked him which club. There were two on Sullivan Street, two on Thompson, two on MacDougal, one on Bedford, another on Downing. Now there was only one.

Tuesday came. I gave him the pictures. He told me to meet him the next Tuesday.

And so it was that we now sat together in Joe Black's place with this guy called Louie.

I had seen this Louie character around now and then through the years. He was one of those guys who, just by looking at him, you knew never to ask: what's his story? And thus you pretty much knew his story.

"Is that real?" I said, gesturing to the painting on the wall above where Joe Black sat.

"Rembrandt. Self-portrait."

"Do you like that painting, Nick?" Joe Black cocked his head toward it without looking at it.

"I got to tell you," I said. "To me, it's a piece of shit. I mean, don't get me wrong. I'd love to own it. Just long enough to sell it. But, no, to be perfectly honest, I don't like it."

"I think we're gonna get along," Louie snorted.

"How about *The Divine Comedy*? You like that, Nick?"

I had been working on my own translation of the *Commedia* for more than a dozen years. In the course of those years, I had come to perceive something of Dante the man — not the unquestioned, infallible god that centuries of reverent scholarship had made of him, but the man whom his contemporaries had remembered in none too glowing a light — and, more so, to perceive the *Commedia*'s great flaw. It was a flaw of form. Dante had chosen a cage of rhyme and meter so confining that no majestic creation could survive within it, so often did it necessitate unnatural affectation to accommodate structure, so often were soul and beauty and power sacrificed to sustain the structure of the work, as might be done by one so cold as to value artfulness above art. As no beautiful wild bird born to soar free could survive in a cage, so it was with the beautiful wild bird of his poem.

And the whole Beatrice routine grew rather tiresome, trite, and ridiculous as it went on and on. Botticelli seemed to share this view: in his sketches for the *Paradiso*, the figure of Beatrice becomes ever more monstrously larger, dwarfing the figure of Dante himself.

On one hand, I agreed with George Steiner, who held the *Commedia* to be the supreme work of its millennium. On the other hand, I sometimes found myself agreeing with Goethe, who railed against it as a stultifying, miscast mess. (These were words that, in any case, I always felt more fitting to describe the second part of Goethe's own *Faust* than any other work.) But as the *Commedia* became to me less glorious a poem, it became to me all the more glorious a monument to the impossibility and futility of man's most noble creative aspirations.

"Yeah," I said. "I used to love it. Now I like it."

"What changed?"

"You look at anything long enough, you see what's wrong with it. A broad, a poem, your life. You look at anything long enough, no matter how beautiful it is, and you see what's wrong with it."

"How would you like to look at the real thing?"

"What do you mean: 'the real thing'?"

"The real thing. The original manuscript."

"Yeah, I sure would like to see that. But it doesn't exist. It probably got thrown into a fireplace to keep somebody warm about six hundred and twenty years ago. There ain't even a single scratch that exists of anything that Dante ever wrote in his own hand. Nothing."

"If it did exist, what do you think it would be worth?"

"It would be priceless. A thousand of those fucking things maybe." I gestured to the Rembrandt. "I mean, it would be the greatest literary treasure of all time. It would be like the Vatican trying to put a price on Michelangelo's *Pietà.* It's impossible, unthinkable. Nobody could ever afford it."

"We'll make it affordable."

Thus spake Joe Black.

The upstairs Magnifica Class section on the flight to Rome was less than a third full. The first thing that Louie did was move away from me to a different seat.

We are all born alone, and we all die alone; but Louie seemed to like everything in between the same way as well.

With the tickets, Joe Black had given me and Louie two fake passports each. The passports had different fake names, one to be used on our way over, one to be used on our way back. Each of the passports was partly filled with various stamps of entry and exit, and the fake names on them matched the fake names on the tickets, which had been issued as individual one-way tickets, coming and going. All we had to do was keep the right ticket with the right passport and remember our fake names. All other identification and credit cards had been left behind. Each of us had been given about ten grand in lire, and we were to pay for everything in cash.

"You ever take that flyin' sardine can to Palermo?" Louie asked me when we arrived in Rome.

"Yeah," I said. I hated that flight.

"I can't handle it. I got us a Gulfstream," Louie said.

The first thing he did when we sat down on the couch seats of the Gulfstream was to light a cigarette.

The pilot asked him to please wait until we were off the ground.

"Shut up and keep your eyes on the road," Louie told him.

I lighted a cigarette then too, and Louie nodded with vague approval.

The traffic in Palermo was bad. Some sort of religious shit.

Church after church marching statues out into and through the streets, followed by processions of mournful-sounding bands — horns and drums and cymbals — and mournful-looking parishioners, most of them women.

"They're worse than Jews, these fuckin' *sicilian*'s, with all these high fuckin' holy days."

Stained glass and bleached blondes.

We lay by the pool of the Villa Igea, surrounded by gardens and trees, overlooking the harbor. The sun was strong, the sky was blue, a few soft white clouds drifted by.

"We're livin', kid," Louie said.

Some guy came by. His shadow fell over me. He dropped a carpenter's canvas satchel to the ground near Louie.

"The driver will be outside the gate tomorrow morning at eight," he said. He handed Louie a folded wad of five-hundred-thousand-lire notes, bound by a rubber band. "Here's for taking care of the driver."

The next morning, we checked out at eight. Each of us had only an overnight bag, and Louie was now carrying the carpenter's satchel as well. We walked through the open gates of the walls of the hotel grounds. The driver opened the back door, and Louie and I eased into the car.

As we ascended into the hills, the winding road narrowed. We entered the very small town of Piana degli Albanesi. I had been here before. This was one of those places — like Castelvecchio di Puglia, where my grandfather and his brothers came from — where the wops had names like mine.

The car pulled up to a narrow gated passway between two buildings of decaying stone.

The gate was open. Louie entered and I followed him. The passway opened to a big walled garden that seemed so old, overgrown, and untended that it had begun to claim the big old house, whose facade was covered with the dense leaves of climbing vines. Near the staircase of the house, an old man slept in a wooden chair with his mouth open and his hands resting on a wolf gun in his lap. Beside him slept a dog that was his counterpart in age, and which was barely able to open one eye as we passed.

The door was open, the screen door beyond it was shut. Louie stood aside. I knocked gently. An old priest shuffled forth to greet us. He was very happy to see us. Louie and I shook hands with him. He led us to the parlor, where, in an easy chair, a very old man slept. Faint sounds came from another room. Slow, aimless kitchen sounds.

The old priest brought us to where the very old man sat sleeping. He cleared his throat. The very old man continued to sleep. He spoke the words "Don Lecco" in a low voice. The very old man continued to sleep. He spoke the words "Don Lecco" in a louder voice. The very old man stirred. He adjusted himself somewhat in the easy chair. I extended my hand to him, but his own hand merely made a lackadaisical gesture for us to be seated on the nearby couch. He then held his forehead for a while, and then, with some exertion and the aid of the old priest, he rose to his feet. He stood still for a moment, and he breathed deeply, with a seeming sense of great self-satisfaction, as if the act of standing had restored him to the stature of a god.

He moved very slowly to the big old Conforti safe that stood against the wall to his left. The safe was dark brown, but large areas of the paint long ago had flaked away to reveal the darkened steel beneath. He laid his hand to the combination lock and gave it several very slow turns, then he put the force of both hands to the latch and moved it downward. The ponderous steel door made a deep clicking sound, then creaked open.

The very old man returned very slowly to his easy chair and made another lackadaisical gesture toward the safe.

The priest opened the safe wider and took out a fine-carved

antique casket and laid it on the coffee table before me and Louie. Next to the box, he placed two letters, one in Italian, the other in English, from the Biblioteca di Palermo, entrusting the accompanying manuscript to the bearer of these letters and authorizing the loan of the manuscript for study abroad by "our American colleagues" for a period not to exceed six months.

I put on my reading glasses and removed the lid from the box.

Could this be real? I stared at the first sheet of parchment, then carefully shuffled through it, pausing here and there. Crossed out on page after page were the words that had spewed forth ignivomously from the poet, then been reworked, lessened, trifled to accommodate the form of meter and rhyme. Years ago, in my translation of the poem, I had come to the conclusion that the *terza rima* form must be abandoned. Yes, because it was impossible to English the Italian words into such a rhyme scheme without forcing even greater decorative affectations than this chosen form had demanded in the original; but also because I had come to see that the form was wrong, period. Now, here before me, obscured by scratchings and scrawlings, lay evidence of what might have been an uncaged *Commedia*, the wild bird of it soaring free in rushes of *vers libre* that might have cast to Hell the formal breastplate of poetry itself.

How could these pages not be real? And yet if they were, it was a miracle.

Louie asked if he might have a cup of tea.

The priest assented happily and went off to the kitchen. He returned and said the tea would be brought in a moment.

Louie turned to me.

"Do you feel that all is right?" he said.

"I feel that all is right," I said.

Louie smiled to the priest. I put the lid back on the box. Slow footsteps could be heard, and an old woman appeared with a silver tray, a small silver teapot, two delicate-looking teacups and saucers, two small silver spoons, and a diminutive silver bowl of sugar from which protruded a diminutive silver spoon. As I moved aside the box to make room for her to place the tray on the table, Louie slowly opened the canvas carpenter's bag, as the old priest eagerly watched him. There was no greed in the old priest's look of eagerness: just a kindly and humble yearning for a kindly and humble sunset to his life.

The old woman laid the tray on the table and smiled, as if it were nice to have a guest once again. At the same time, Louie reached into the bag, raised a black gun with a black silencer affixed to it, and shot the old lady in the gut.

He then shot the priest, who stood more in sadness than in horror.

Then with the slightest turn of his wrist he shot old Don Lecco where he sat.

It all seemed to happen in less than two seconds.

Louie removed a second gun from the bag and stood.

"Put that box in the bag and clear out the safe," he said.

As I emptied the safe of its few contents, I could hear Louie put a second crackling whooshing shot into everybody. He peered through the window. The old man was still in his chair, the old dog by his side.

"Let's go."

With one silenced gun in each hand, he shot the old man and the dog in their heads simultaneously from behind.

We moved quickly through the garden, quickly through the passway, and into the waiting car.

I went through the other stuff that I had taken from the safe. There was a codex of Catullus, a small parcel of documents that seemed to be the confessions of early popes. There was a bundle of about twenty million lire. There was a golden diamond ring. There were envelopes of personal papers. Louie slipped the ring on his finger. We split the money.

On the outskirts of Monreale, we pulled into a dilapidated auto-repair garage with a lone gas pump outside. There was a fat man in a rocking chair, in the shade of the garage eave of rusted corrugated tin. We got out of the car. Louie nodded to the fat man, and the fat man nodded to Louie. There was a big rusted metal drum rotted through with holes of corrosion and about half full with garbage and ashes. Louie gathered up some dirty newspaper pages, wadded the paper into the drum, doused it with gasoline, tossed in our first set of passports, then tossed in a lighted match, and we stood there and watched the passports curl and burn away to nothing. I threw in the envelopes of personal papers from the safe.

Louie looked about him and gestured to the fat man with a slight shrug and upward palm. The fat man gestured to a large greasy tarpaulin that lay within the entrance to the garage. Louie summoned the driver from the car. They entered the garage together, and as the driver stepped onto the tarpaulin, Louie shot him dead.

He wiped the guns with motor oil and a rag, then left them wrapped in the rag on a workbench. The fat man was now standing in the garage entrance, and a taxi had pulled up next to the sedan.

The dishevelled taxi driver nodded to the fat man, and the fat man nodded to him. The driver removed our three small bags to the trunk of the taxi.

Aboard the Gulfstream, Louie took a deep drag and let the smoke come forth from him slowly. He looked about the cabin, at the nice plush carpeting and the little end tables with their vases of pretty flowers, the fancy little curtains on the windows, and the legs of the sole attendant, who brought us our ashtrays.

"We're livin', kid," he said.

THREE YEARS HE HAD LABORED, AFTER THE vision of the three beasts, to write — to draw from the stars — perfect words of perfect souls and perfect meter and perfect rhyme.

Three years of labor until he had them: betraying no labor, flowing and natural as a soft rain that spoke, each *prismina* of each droplet whispering rainbows of meaning beneath a sky turning dark without the reader seeing it, feeling it, until the final sigh of the last word evanesced from calm to foreboding silence:

Nel mezzo del cammin di vita nostra

The dark woods — the *selva oscura* — had been real. He had revisited them not long ago in a vain attempt to recapture the spirit that now seemed to have been drained from him. They were to the west of the old road from Firenze to Pisa. Yes, as it only now occurred to him: to the West, the land of the dead.

In youth, he had told of encountering three beasts in these woods. Sometimes he even told of slaughtering one of them with blade and force, his murderous growl so fearsome that the others fled through the piney scrub and thicket. It was a lie: fear would have overcome him. But from this lie had come the three beasts of his poem.

It had taken him some months alone to arrive at *vita nostra* from *vita questa* and, originally, *vita mia*, which bore the same measure of sound and of meter. That arrival of *vita nostra* had brought about, or had been brought about by, a sky of intensest summoning. He was borne and strengthened for days by it. The idea of the One: from *my* life to *this* life to *our* life.

The soul, the beasts. He had never forgotten what he had read in the olden translation by Chalcidius of Plato's *Timaeus*, wherein Plato explains that man has two souls: an immortal one, resident in the head, and a mortal one, "subject to terrible and irresistible affections," that was "tethered like a beast untamed in the belly." How wondrous a phrase: "a beast untamed in the belly." And all our souls, mortal and immortal, were but rays of the one great soul of the universe. The life of the soul of one was the life of the soul of all: *nostra vita.*

But this arrival was as nothing to the coming to him of the third beast, born of vision and not of design: the third beast, completing the triad, the trinity, the *sacerdotum mysterium* of the three.

A beast untamed in the belly: *'l veltro*. It was a word that some old men had used to describe a wolfen creature; but to him its sound evoked all the feral willfulness and all the craven hunger for freedom and seeking of that beast of the soul in the belly: *vengo, voglio*, *volo*, *trovo*, and many such verbs were summoned by it, along with the power of the wind, *il vento.*

And, in the grand scheme of his work, to end each of the trinitied tercets of its triptych, he would turn to the stars, *le stelle*, delivering the reader to where the *mysterium tremendum*, the expressing of the inexpressible, lay in wonderment.

It was only years later, working through the last of the poem's three cantiche, the *Paradiso*, seeing the sky of night, which had been the sky of works and days, turn morbidly to the sky of gloom, that the stars themselves finally revealed to him in their silence but one of their myriad secrets. It was the only one that he, in his vanity, and arrogant false-godliness, needed to know:

Non muovere — do not move. The felling secret passed through him smoothly, chillingly, fatally as a sword — *you can not write Paradise. It is here, in the stars, already writ, and you may read of it, but you can never express it or author it except through the genuflection of your silence.*

We were over the Atlantic, almost home, before I asked him.

"Why'd you kill the dog?"

He looked at me.

"Why'd I kill the dog?" he said.

"Yeah. Why'd you kill the dog?"

He looked at me.

"Because dogs bark," he said.

A few minutes passed, and Louie spoke again.

"Fuckin' priest takes it in the heart. Nice old bag who brings us tea. Old-timer out there takin' a fuckin' nap with the fuckin' mutt. This fuckin' Don Lecco thing, that'll probably start a fuckin' war in Palermo. And you ask me about the fuckin' mutt. We don't need some mutt barkin' at us while we're sneakin' our way out of a massacre. Simple as that."

A few minutes passed, and he spoke again.

"You like dogs?" he said.

"Yeah," I said.

"Me too," he said. "I mean, real dogs, like that one we shot. I don't like those little fuckin' mutant things you see in New York. But I don't think real dogs wanna be cooped up in apartments. It ain't natural. Those dogs wanna run free. I think people that keep big dogs in the city are stupid creeps. They're killin' their own fuckin' dogs, but they're doin' it slow and mean. If I lived in the country, I'd have a dog. A real dog."

"What do you mean: 'that one we shot'?" I said. "I didn't shoot that dog, you did."

"You were an accessory. You're an accessory to murder in the first degree."

A few more minutes passed in silence.

"You know what's disgusting, though," he said. "Those broads in the street, in New York, who hold newspapers under their dogs' asses while the dog shits. That makes me wanna puke. Or you'll see some really good-lookin' piece of head walkin' by with a mutt on a leash, and you see that she's got a little plastic bag of dogshit in her hand. Man, it's disgusting."

His face contorted with revulsion. This was the first true emotion I had witnessed in him. And it was an emotion that I shared.

"Yeah," I said. "Dogshit broads."

"And the thing is, you don't always know. A broad might be a dogshit cunt, but you don't know unless you actually see her in the street with that bag of shit in her hand. Like maybe that good-lookin' bitch, that stewardess, on that Gulfstream. She could be strokin' your cock, and you wouldn't even know: it could be her dogshit hand."

"I just wanted to fuck her legs," I said. "That would've kept her hands out of the picture."

"You wanted to fuck her legs?"

"Yeah. I like fuckin' broads' legs. I mean, don't get me wrong, they got to be great legs. That broad, she had great legs."

"You're a sick fuck. But I'm sicker."

"What would you have done with her?"

"I was thinkin' about tyin' her up and pissin' on her. But that was probably only because I had to take a leak. Because after I took my leak, I wasn't thinkin' that no more. I was thinkin' about tyin' her up and holdin' a gun to her head and makin' her beg to suck my cock."

"Do you do that a lot?"

Louie raised his hand slightly and turned it waveringly a few times.

"This leg thing," he said. "Is the hosiery on or off?"

"Oh, on. Definitely on."

"I can see that," he said.

"You still think it's strange?"

"Ah, this is a strange fuckin' world. But I'll tell you one thing. Anybody who knowingly has any kinda physical contact with a dogshit broad is definitely fuckin' sick. A guy that fucks a stiff, he ain't nothin' compared to a guy that holds hands with a dogshit broad."

"You ever do that, fuck a stiff?"

"I thought about it. We're talkin' broad stiffs here — I don't go that other route. Anyway, yeah, I thought about it. I mean, I look at it this way: they're quiet. No bullshit, no nothin'. I jerked off one time on a broad stiff. God, she was pretty. Like a fuckin' angel, except for the hole I put through the side of her head. And a few times I took their underwear."

"What'd you do with it?"

"What would you do with it? I used it to jerk off. I ain't gonna wear no dead broad's underwear, I can tell you that much. Besides,

I only take their underwear once in a blue moon, when they're real dolls; and a good-lookin' broad, her underwear would never fit me. And there ain't many good-lookin' broads I get sent out to do, anyway."

He looked away wistfully, through the little window, into the clouds.

IT HAD TROUBLED HIM GREATLY THAT HE was unlearned in the languages of Scripture and of the great writers of ancient Hellas. The books of Augustine were revered by him, but it was the literature of the pagan Greeks that had so enamored and entranced Augustine, and this literature remained beyond him. He could not so much as give halting voice to the pronunciation of the sounds of the Greek alphabet, save for those few words that had been Latinized in the Bible of Jerome.

And as Jerome himself had plainly and clearly said: "Holy Scripture is like a beautiful body concealed by a dirty gown. The Psalms are as well-sounding as the songs of Pindar and Horace. The writings of Solomon have *gravitas*, the book of Job is perfect. All these books are composed in hexameters and pentameters in the Hebrew original. But we read them in prose! Consider how much Homer would lose in prose!" These words from the learned heart of Jerome still haunted him. He knew the first and greatest of epic poems only through the crude rendering known as the *Ilias Latina*, which had been dismissed and denounced to him as a misbegotten and egregious regurgitation of the true and original.

Of those languages in which ancient wisdom and the most provocative of modern learning were enclosed, and through which they were revealed — Hebrew and Arabic — he also knew nothing. What he gleaned of it from the sages and scholars who were conversant in these tongues had perforce to be communicated to him by them in a *sbagliazio* of Latin and the *lingua volgare*, neither of which possessed the exactitude of vocabulary particular to this wisdom and learning. As certain terms and phrases central to this wisdom and learning had no Latin or vernacular equivalent, the sages and scholars to which he turned were behoven in their generosity to coin such equivalents, or often, when this was not possible — as when the hidden numinous power and meaning of a Hebrew character or phrase lay self-enclosed and expressible in and through that character or phrase alone — to strive for even the vaguest approximations of equivalents.

How could one as bereft of erudition as he, a beggar at the gate of Logos, the Word in its every sense, ever be a maker in the revered and classical sense, let alone one who aspired to the grandeur that he set out to attain?

He had no choice. He must write in the language that his own soul spoke. He lent to this the cloak of justice in his composition *De Vulgari Eloquentia*.

If he was without the Greek of Homer and Testament, pagan and early Christian, he was certainly not without the Latin, pagan and Christian, of Cicero, Ovid, Virgil, Augustine, and other masters. From Cicero he had learned the laws of rhetoric, which Quintilian had amplified and to which Augustine had hewed in Christian light.

Man's eloquence, said Tullius, should reflect the timbre of the nature of the matter he addressed. In recounting everyday affairs or in giving narrative to a homely tale or fable, a simplicity of plain but well-wrought words was befitting. In delivering forth praise or guilt, warning or dissuasion, rhetorical figures, such as antithetical isocola, anaphoras, and other subtle ornata, were to be interwoven with the simplicity of the straightforward. For arousing the passions of men and evoking the eternal forces, words and style of the greatest dignity and power must be deployed.

While Augustine rejected Tullius's classification and differentiation of subject matters — to a Christian, said he, every mode and every aspect of life was holy and inseparable from the almighty matter of eternal salvation — he embraced Tullius's laws of style, joining them to corresponding Christian purpose: the simplest, to teach; the intermediate, to praise or to vituper; the loftiest, to persuade or to save souls.

Yet, in affirming Tullius's division of styles — the low, the intermediate, and the sublime — why had Augustine failed to remark upon this division as forming that most sacred of adumbrations, the triad, which foretold and mirrored the Trinity itself in pagan prescience, as Virgil had foreseen the coming of Christ in his *Eclogues*?

Just as the Incarnation brought together man and God, the low and the sublime, so he had sworn beneath a sky of illimitableness that he would make a *poetria* as great as any that had ever been, likewise bringing together the low and the sublime, *humilis et sublimis*, working with the spectrum of the trinity of styles, to set before man and God what was at once of the loftiest heights and the lowest depths — *peraltissima humilitas* — and the sum of the skies, timbrous with such subtlety that the three laws of rhetoric would therein be thriced, and indeed all would be as thriced upon thriced, summoning the perfection of creation in every way — *Dominus, Filius, Spiritus Sanctus* — down to the very sacring-bells of the trinitied rhyme of its *terza rima.*

It would possess what could only be called, in a trinity of words with the sound of a prayer, *divinae mentis aura*, the breath of divine mind. It would be, as Augustine had said of the Holy Scriptures, *res incesso humilis, successu excelsa et velata mysteriis*: a lowly thing at first, but then sublime and veiled in mysteries.

As the sky of illimitableness could not be summoned by will, so true enlightenment could not come elsewise but through the fleeting, fluttering, momentary contact — *ictu* — an illumination of but a breath, after which one must return to the *humilitas* of life, ultimately to the *humus*, the dirt, that is the common source and end of *humanitas*. It was through the trinities upon trinities of his invocation of the *divinae mentis aura* that he prayed to bring forth *ictu* from ictus.

He knew, under certain skies, that God breathed into him. He knew, under certain skies, that God breathed within and breathed forth from him. That breath, he swore and prayed, must and should not be wasted.

So he had prayed for strength and for power, and for the breath of God to flow forth from him. On his knees on hard stone in the great church in Mediolanum, where Ambrosio had baptized Augustine; on his knees on hard stone in the Templum Vaticanum in Roma and the church of San Marco in Venezia; on his knees on the floors of many churches; on his knees in the dirt and rock of many open or tree-sheltered places; on his knees in the copse of the *selvaggio* of the vision of the three beasts; so he had prayed. *Dammi la forza, dammi il potere, dammi la Sua spira, faremi un vaso della Sua volontà.*

Those were glorious years, of prayer and of power and of *poetry*. A sea was within him, and the wind that brought it rage or calm was that divine breath, and the fierce waves and gentle seductive purling stillness of the words and meter of that rage and that calm came not by design of the laws of rhetoric but in preternatural concord with them. Even in his struggling, when no words or even the colors thereof came, strength was with him.

Then, slowly, he came apart.

With the deepening of his Christianity had come a deepening of his understanding of prayer. It was, he felt, the mystical marriage of *humilis et sublimis*, in its purest and most intense and miraculous emanation, in which man spoke directly to God. As the pagan rhetoricians often deemed it vile to treat of lowly matters in a style sublime, or of sublime matters in lowly style, so these sensibilities were as nothing to the damnable sacrilege of speaking in words of ornata to the Lord. One must pray most plainly, simply, and directly from the soul, disallowing all rhetorical contrivance. And even in so doing, if a man's soul in this manner should petition the Lord for his own welfare, gain, or worldly furtherance, insofar as these things might be sought as ends unto themselves rather than as means to serve God and fellow man, then he who thus prayed did so commit the greater sacrilege and was all the more damned. For the only prayer was the prayer to serve the will of God and the powers of righteousness, and to seek for oneself only as regards that serving, and to give thanks for the blessing of that holy servitude. Many believed that it was meet and good to pray for the welfare of others. While he saw no wrong in this, he saw much folly, as he never knew of a man to be saved from death, loss of eternal soul, or the gallows through prayer on or in his behalf. That the most innocent child should be stilled and taken to grave seemed to him empirical proving enough that the unheeding and inviolate will of God, which we should pray only to serve, could not be bent by even the purest, guileless, sincerest, and *humilisimus* of askance for the good either of a single unborn soul or of all mankind. Prayer, he believed, was autochthonic, self-fulfilling. It was the habitual, heartfelt prayer for the strength to serve that in itself reinforced and replenished that strength. It was the habitual, heartfelt prayer to serve as a vessel for God's will and breath that sculpted us as such on a well-turned potter's wheel.

Thus he had long believed, and thus he had likewise been aware that such belief brought him close to the gaze that the Church reserved for those looked upon or hunted as heretics. Within himself, however, he felt neither guilt nor shame nor the taint of heresy. Sooth be said, he found more heresy in the gross and common conception — common, it seemed even unto the Church of Rome itself — that prayer was a sort of cheap metal currency through which the favor of God might be bought or curried.

And it was during prayer, as the prodigious reverberation of this belief overtook him, that he came apart. His heart stopped for a breath, and there was a sudden cataclysmic emptiness in the stead of that beating and that breath, and he trembled.

He had been praying to himself: praying not to the God that dwelt without, praying not to the God that dwelt within him, but praying to the God that was him, he was sundered by the terrible truth, descended of a sudden, that it had always been thus.

It was beneath the mosaic of God the Pantocrator. The sky of his madness came upon him then for the first time; and it was the beginning of the end.

JOE BLACK SEEMED TAKEN ABACK.

"*Authentication*? What do you mean: 'authentication'? It looks old to me."

I could picture hauling this thing around with a sole piece of documentation: "It looks old to me," bearing the signature, name, and title of "Joe Black, *Pezzo Grosso*."

"It looks old to me too," I said. "It looks *real* to me. But that ain't enough. We need paperwork. High-class paperwork. As much as we can get."

"Oh, shit," Louie moaned. "Here I am, committin' nine kinds of mortal fuckin' sins and takin' all sorts of fuckin' no-smokin' plane rides, and this thing might not even be *real*? I gotta tell ya, I am getting truly fuckin' sick of this no-smokin' shit."

"Don't worry, Louie, I can take care of this part myself," I said.

Joe Black looked to Lefty.

"If we're gonna do this, we gotta do it right. Nicky knows how to do it right. That's why he's here."

"See," I said, "we at least have to prove that this thing is from the time that Dante wrote it."

"And how do we do that?" Joe Black said.

"We take it to the University of Arizona for carbon fourteen dating, and then we take it to a place in Illinois that's the most respected technical-analysis joint in the world. But first I have to go back to Italy. I need dated documents written when and where Dante would have written this, so that the parchment and ink can be compared. I need to have the watermarks on the paper dated. See, we have no handwriting to which to compare this handwriting, so we need as much circumstantial evidence — as much authentication — as possible."

"How you gonna get those dated documents?" Joe Black said.

"Steal them," I said.

THE SUDDEN HORRIBLE THOUGHT THAT SHE she had died for this. Or worse: that God, responding to the Luciferian vanity of his willfulness to write paradise, had answered him with the inspiration he craved by delivering her to death, through him, for him, upon his soul — the cruel proving to him that there was no inspiration for one who sought to make or to illuminate what He alone could and had made, and unto itself illumined. As he had witnessed, felt, been borne, on that long-ago day unto night of illimitableness — blessing rare and enough for any man's life — he had wanted not only to read the stars of that night, but to write them.

Her death had brought him nothing but his own miserable aching death in life itself.

IT WAS BELIEVED TO BE IN VERONA, UNDER the aegis of his patron Cangrande della Scala, that Dante completed the first two cantiche of his poem, the *Inferno* and the *Purgatorio*: the first perhaps in late 1313 or, more likely, in 1314; the second, by the end of 1315.

Dante later spent the remainder of his life in Ravenna, beginning in 1318, under the patronage of Guido Novello da Polenta. It was believed to be in Ravenna that Dante completed the *Paradiso*.

I travelled under my own name. I brought with me, secreted beneath the bottom panel of my cheap green vinyl travelling bag, the few pages of the manuscript that were drafted on paper, and, in my wallet, the identification cards that I had been granted by the Vatican Library during my research there a few years before. These cards of authorized access to both the Archivio Segreto and the Biblioteca Apostolica Vaticana bore the seal of the Vatican and attested to the honorary doctorate that the Vatican had bestowed on me. They served as impressive credentials, especially to the directors of libraries, and most especially to the directors of Italian libraries.

I went first to the Archivio di Stato di Verona.

I dressed well and wore a dark blue shirt. I said that I was seeking details of certain early trecento political affairs, and that I thus desired to examine official documents from the court of Cangrande della Scala.

The director himself was also well-dressed. I liked that. Archivists and librarians were the keepers of what remained of culture. They were men and women deserving of dignity but rarely receiving it. It was good to see one who seemed fully aware of the dignity he was due, and who received it, if only from himself.

Three folders were brought to me. Nothing was bound: I did not need the single-edged razor that was in my pocket. I searched only for documents that were sealed and dated. I chose one from 1313, one from 1314, one from 1315. When no one was looking, I slowly unbuttoned my dark blue shirt, and I slipped them in.

I strolled out into the sweet sunlight of Via Franceschine, and that was that.

I then went to the Archivio di Stato di Ravenna.

Same dark blue shirt; same story, except that I now desired to examine documents executed by Guido Novello da Polenta.

Again I did not need the razor in my pocket. Again I chose three sealed and dated documents from those that were brought to me by the director's assistant: one from 1316, one from 1318, one from 1321. As I located and selected the last of these, I noticed a letter that was dated somewhat later in 1321 but which was on paper rather than on parchment. I took this too.

I strolled out into the sweet sunlight of Via Guaccimanni, and that was that.

I then travelled south, through the high green hills, to the small town of Fabriano, on the river Giano, where Italy's finest paper had been produced since the late thirteenth century.

In studying the manuscript, I had discerned that the writing on the few pages of paper — they were all near the end of the *Paradiso* — appeared, but for a few scratched-out lines, to be in a distinctly different hand than that of the parchment pages of the manuscript.

This was a great mystery. It also potentially posed a great problem. On the one hand, no forger would ever do such a thing. On the other hand, it begged an explanation. I detected the same similar, vague watermark on these paper pages; and now I thought I detected this same, vague watermark on the paper document I had lifted in Ravenna.

At the Museo della Carta, I met with the man who was the heir and successor to the vast and arcane knowledge and singular research of the scholar Zonghi, whose lifetime of work on the history of paper and paper-making in Italy had yet to be surpassed.

"The precise origin of watermarks," he told me, "will never be known to us. It seems that certain individual craftsmen in the employ of the paper-makers began at some early time to use their own individual drying-screens; and, either by design or accident, the wire mesh of one such screen came to leave an identifying mark on a particular craftsman's paper. This craftsman's paper must have been of especially excellent quality, leading paper sellers to place orders specifying paper bearing that particular mark. Soon all craftsmen of pride began to work distinguishing symbols into their screens.

"The turning-point in paper-making came when linen replaced wool as the fabric of which undergarments were made. As the most commonly discarded of cloth goods, old undergarments were, with animal parts and hemp, one of the primary ingredients that went into the paper-maker's cauldron. Linen made an incomparably superior paper, and the aristocracy began employing it instead of parchment in the course of their everyday affairs. It was then that many courts and noble families began to order fine paper bearing elements of their own crests or seals as watermarks, and this distinguished their paper from all others. By this time, paper-makers had come to employ women — *filigamiste* — whose job it was to fabricate watermarks."

I passed him the few paper pages of the manuscript. He placed the first sheet on a light box and studied it through a loupe. He did the same with each page in turn. He nodded, then took down a thick book from his shelves, opened it, and found what he was looking for.

"These sheets are part of a small order that was placed only once. He then read from the book:

"*Una risma, tipo di miglioramento, ai 34 bolognini.*"

He shut the book.

"This *filigramatica* represents the eagle that Guido Novello da Polenta bore for his coat of arms. The order was received at Fabriano on the first day of May 1321, and it was delivered to Ravenna on the third day of the following month."

I passed him the paper document from the Archivio di Stato di Ravenna.

"From the same order," he said.

AS STONES THAT GLEAM IN THE SEA LIKE precious marvels, when garnered and laid to dry, turned to drab and unmemorable objects to be left behind or cast back into the sea, so were the words of this thing, written and so perceived in the tide of night and beheld anew, as nothing, in the morning light, when the ink of them was dry. So it was on most mornings, to be sure: those mornings that were not of the ever more rare days, the days of the sky of illimitableness, or the days of the sky of signs, or of the days of the sky of vows, or of the days of the sky of the dead's unrest, beneath the ground and in the wind, or of the days of the sky of summoning. The days of signs stirred him, invigorated him, be they of the signs of the comings and goings of seasons, or of those more arcane signs of which the ancients knew much that since had been lost. Yes, he loved these days. Even as he hated the season whose coming the signs might signal — the wretched malarial summer or the harsh chilling rain of this region to which his fate had brought him — he loved the signs themselves: the wildflower bloom and breezy blushing skies of spring's final strophe, the smoky wood scents and rustling sweet winds through grape-ripe dry leaves of autumn. Of those other, arcane signs — the hues of the moon, the flight of certain birds, transformations and prodigies of clouds and beasts — he felt at times that his understanding so little of them served only to increase all the more the awe and mystery they held for him. Jews and Saracens had taught him much of what had been lost, recovered by them, and held close by them; but they themselves had uncovered and knew but little.

The days of the sky of vows were the days of willfulness. On these days, he took pen in hand, as a sore-shouldered and world-weary field-man might take scythe in hand, going forth with naught but the doomful vow of what must be done.

The days when the spirits of the dead were not at rest stirred him like the days of the signs, for within him were the dead of his own life and the deathward parts of him, and these, amid the unquiet dead whose *movimenti* he sensed in earth as well as tenebrum of sky, drew him into a darkness that bore and drew from him strange *sentori*, words, and sentences, dark but lovely or most terrifying.

When he woke to the sky of summoning, it was as if to the call of a cock at dawn that crowed for him, a call that confirmed his own true calling. It was then that he lifted the pen not as a sore-shouldered and world-weary field-man his scythe, but as a reaper of marvels, rising to behold before him as far as could be seen flowering grain unlike any that had ever been brought to harvest, a harvest that was his and his alone, as the ordained vessel of the power and glory of its making.

Of the other four skies — the sky of works and days, the sky of sin, the sky of gloom, and the sky that a man saw last and only once — the first was that which imbued by far the vaster parts of the lives of all who lived: sky upon sky of soullessness, passing and forgotten as one breath follows another, neither with awareness nor with gratitude, but simply with being and with doing, like and as a grub, divorced from the great gift and miracle of the every breath of the every moment of the every day of the every season of the every year of this, one's only life, the sum of which existed in the present breath alone, and the length of which, likewise, could be measured by the present breath alone, and the value and worthiness of which lay alone in the sense of sacrament, and the depth thereof, with which the present breath was drawn. For this breath was the only gift, the only life we had, and there was not promise of the next — life is but a breath, Job tells us; and, as the Psalm says, we all stand as a mere breath — and thus a man who by the passing of the waxing and waning of the moons and the seasons may be said to have spanned an hundred years, he may indeed never truly have drawn his first breath of life, and a child brought to the grave after but few summers may, having drawn but a single breath under the sky of illimitableness, be said to have lived longer and fuller than he who is reckoned to have an hundred years; longer and fuller than he who, even if he be a king, is as seed spent on the ground and washed away by rain. For there was no time. *Tempus fugit*, it was said, but it was breath that was the wingèd thing: it was breath that fled. Time was the folly of our own vain making and delusion, the stinking, jaundiced *pisciata di cane* by which our mangy race tried to leave the mark of its unknowing on *infinitas*. The trickling sands of this vain making and illusion, the trickling *mictus* of this unknowing: these were the *anxietatum* that had come to rule the pulse and rob the breath. God had given us the infinite, and we had turned from it; to calendar, to horologium, to clepsydra, to clepsammia, and now to monstrous clamorous mechanisms of oscillating wheels—*grandi orologi* that overshadowed man himself; *grandi orologi* whose graceless *rotismi* commanded among the overshadowed a greater awe than did the perfect rotations of the eternal heavens themselves, as the overshadowed, in everly increasing haste and everly increasing lifelessness, made their way like *automata* in procession to the idiot pyre of *tecnologia* and godless *computus*.

Nor did this diminution of eternity, this beat and measure of our procession to the idiot pyre, serve to mark or reflect the true temporal flow of nature. To travel from Lucca to Firenze took but a day, beneath the God-given horologium of sun and moon. Yet, so did the fools of every town differ in their misbegat calculations, that a traveller could leave Lucca on the twentieth day of March and arrive in Firenze, in the span of one natural day, on the twenty-first day of March of the previous year. To travel thence to Pisa, he would arrive there, after seven natural days, on the twenty-eighth day of the year following that of his departure from Lucca. Thus, in eight of nature's days, he will have travelled from his own year to the year that had passed and to the coming year as well. And in his eight-day journey through these three years, he will have discovered as well that the days themselves were reckoned variously; that a traveller could hear the first hour of the day sounded at dawn by the monks' bells of one town, then, some hours later, hear the first hour of the day sounded at noon by the monks' bells of another village, and then yet again hear the first hour of the day sounded at midnight in some farther town. Thus, within the span of one natural day, our traveller may have heard the soundings of the beginnings of three different days of two different years. And, as the keeping of canonical hours drifted from and towards the keeping of secular hours, there might be within one village no hour that was both *hora quod officium* and *hora quod tempus*, so that one man's noon might be another man's forenoon. And, as the canonical calls to prayer, set at every three hours, were not strictly observed and as the hydraulic mechanisms, *cerchi*, and other contrivances of horologia, even those of a city's central *horologium comune*, were far from reliable, *hora quod officium* and *hora quod tempus* drifted and shifted not only between but also unto themselves.

There was no time. And, after thousands of years of such compounding confusion of calendar and hour, there was not even an illusion of time that belief could suffer. Every hour that we heeded was the hour of our death.

And as we lost the breath of the infinite and of timelessness that God had given us, His own breath grew more furious, like unto, as the Bible told us, a blast: "*inspiratione spiritus furoris.*"

He, who now felt that blast in the wind of his life, believed this to be the greatest of sins, this casting away as offal the only gift, the desecration and sacrileging of breath, the spitting in the face of its Giver. And this was the common state of man: to abide in the greatest sin, which was without sensation or dimension or any worldly thrill or satisfaction with which we associate those lesser sins that precede damnation. Such was the state of *i vigliacchi*, the lukewarm ones.

The robe of his own life and soul had been singed — burnt through, to some extent, burnt away, in fact — by this idiot pyre, and by his idiot pursuits of a *computus* that he had once thought to be sacred. *Thought* to be sacred. *Thought*: the love of which was the root of all evil. He had fallen prey to the numerology of Augustine. He had fallen prey to thought, and to seeking God within the intellect, where He did not dwell.

It was the Arabs who had brought our numerals to us from the Hindoos; the Arab who had brought from the Hindoos as well the mathematics of zero and infinity. This *zero*, this *zefiro*, this *çifr*, as the Arab called it: this reduction of the great void, the vast of nothingness, to a defined numerical unit that could be added and subtracted on a schoolboy's slate. This reduction of *infinitas* to an arithmetical device, a quantity resulting from the division of any number divided by zero. It was the mathematics of the idiot pyre, an illusion like as time itself. Neither the Arabs nor Fibonacci of Pisa, the great Italian apostle of this misknowing arithmetic, had given true value to the Hindoo measurements of time. The kalpa, a single cosmic day, calculated at 4.32 billion years. Such would be the one true horologium, the *oriuolo del soffio della vita*, which would serve man: the horologium that marked time not by the hour but by the kalpa alone.

Between the discarded breath of man and the furious breath of God lay sin, which too had its sky. It was the sky that presided over that of which he did not speak. That the sky of sin led him to sin, or if it only bore witness to his sins, or if the truth lay or drifted in conspiracy between sky and self, he did not know. As he no longer confessed his sins to any man, but had come to find himself looking upwards as he repented in silence, he had come as well to regard the sky of sin as the confessor's sky. Its every appearance grew more grotesque in the countenances of its clouds and the umbrosities of its knowing, as its every appearance grew more laden with the accumulation of his shame and the cruel, self-knowing, self-tormenting opprobrium of his guilt.

The sky of gloom could be bright with joy, but not for him. It was under the sky of gloom that the taloned thing seized him; and though he feared and dared not give voice to the name of madness in coming forth from these seizures, he knew that they were more than the work of the poisons of ill humors.

Just as of the few skies of illimitableness he had known, only the first of them, on that blessed day of childhood meadow and bread, had lasted for the passing of the sun and into night, so it was that while a certain sky might rule a day or a night, or a day and a night, rare was the sky that possessed a day or a night, or a day and a night, unto itself. The sky of the vow could entwine imperceptibly with, or give way to, the sky of sin. The sky of signs and the sky of the unquiet dead and the sky of illimitableness could come in concert. The sky of works and days, the sky of *i vigliacchi*, could rule and pass through day after night after day after night like a sewing spike of dry, old bone. The sky of gloom could envelop him for spans unknown, making forever of a night; or a sole gasping night of two Sabbaths and more. And as the sky of gloom could come in radiance, so no sky bore an appearance quite unlike another. The sky of illimitableness or the sky of summoning could come with darkness at midday or fulmination at midnight. The secrets of the stars, which he strove to delve, remained myriad in their mysteries; and no matter through which sky they were cast, though their rhyme and meter might seem to change, their poetry remained unparsed, and their wonder remained perfect.

The nine skies were but one, nine-fold in breath into the souls of men, each of whom lived at any moment beneath a sky that was identical in appearance to, but likely different in power from, that beneath which his neighbor, beloved or stranger, passed or abided. Only the ninth sky remained unknown to all, and yet always had been and always would be known to all, to each in turn, since Eden's one sky became nine and until the book of the seventh seal be opened.

Yes, man in his folly had numbered the days of the week as seven, naming each of six for a pagan god, as the seventh for the Lord, who commanded that He would have no other gods before Him.

But the true number of days was the true number of skies, and the true number was nine. Long after he had come to know the truth of this, he had, under the first of skies, in the dead of its night, come to know the perfection of it. Nine was the number of the Trinity thrice-fold: the Trinity trinitied. Then, long after again, the old Jew in Venezia had told him: three was the number of nothing, for every number was the number of nothing.

This is what the old Jew had come to know in his heart after a lifetime of gematria and of cabbalah. The Jew could speak without end upon the secrecies and the powers of the triad: that it was the first of the three perfect numbers; the Mistress of Geometria, for the triangle was the principal of figures; and, too, it was the Mistress of Astrologia, for every sign of the *zodiaco* held three faces, three decans, and three lords of their triplicities; that it was the number of Fates, of Furies, of Graces, and of Horae; that the thunder of Jupiter, the supreme god of the Romans, was *triformis*; that it was the number of the thrice-greatest god of mysteries, Hermes Trismegistus; that, as the rabbis of old did tell, the Sword of Death dripped three drops of gall, the first of which entered the mouth of the dying, the second of which brought to him the pallor, and the third of which ensured his return to dust; that the Hebrew letter *yod* within a triangle represented the ineffable Name, as the triangle represented both the God and the Trinity of the Christians, just as among Christians the image of the head of God the Father was often depicted with a nimbus of three issuing rays of light; that *yod* was the tenth letter of the Hebrew alphabet, and that ten, another number of perfection, was called both Deity and Eternity by the Pythagoreans, in whose sacred geometry it was the most sublime of numbers, the Panteleia, and could also be represented by a triangle.

To illustrate this triangle of the ten to the uncomprehending poet, the old man took from the chest beside him a tablet and stylus. The tablet was of two-leaved time-darkened pine, hinged with leathern strings. The bronze stylus, long tarnished to patina but for the shining glow maintained by the grasp of the old man's fingers, was of a strong but delicate simplicity. The old man opened the tablet upon the lap of his robe, and the inner surface of each of the two leaves of pine-wood revealed itself to be covered with wax that was the color of moss. To the poet, the open tablet, with its dark wood and dark moss green, appeared as if of the deep shadows of a deep forest: *una selva oscura.* This effect was increased by the shadow of the dark patinaed stylus descending in candlelight upon it.

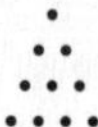

"And in the Greek that is both of the Septuagint and the New Testament, the number ten was represented by the letter *delta.*" With two slender strokes and one wide stroke, he drew this Attic triangle of ten beneath the other.

Δ

"In its genitive form, the name of Zeus, the almighty of the Greek gods, transmutes from Ζεύς to Διόσ — so close in sound to the *Deus* of the old Romans and the French and the Portuguese, the *Dios* of the Spaniards, the *Dio* of the Italians. Learned grammarians tell us that these names of God have nothing to do with Zeus. But I disbelieve them, for I suspect that they know little of the *delta* of his genitive domain. I believe that these names have something to do with Zeus the possessor, or with the unknown forebear, or forebears, of whom he was. The genitive: the case of possession. Here, in signifying the All that is of God, the name of the almighty takes on the delta that is the triangle of ten.

"Numbers, numbers, numbers," he said, seeming now to muse aloud to himself. "What is the number of the triangle of ten multiplied by infinity and in turn taken to the power of the delta of the triangle of ten that is of the All?"

Then his voice turned less inward.

"What became known as gematria goes back at least to the age of the Assyrian king Sargon II, who built his wall of careful cubits, which was the number of his name, to make strong his fortress of Khorsabad. It was during the age of the Second Temple that Israel began to see through the eyes of gematria. But it was not until the age of the *tannaim* that gematria and rabbinic literature became one. It was during this same time, during the years after your New Testament came to be, that Christians developed their own gematria, under the name of ἰσοψηφία" — he scrawled it, pronounced it again: *isopsephia* — "an old Greek word that signified an equality of vote, which now took on a new sense, of the balance of numerical values of letters. One could already see this at work in the Revelation of John, where the number of the Beast represents the sum of the values of three Greek letters" — he drew them — χ, ξ, Ϝ — as he enumerated them and explicated them — "the first of which is *c'hi* and has the value of six hundred, the second of which is *xi* and has the value of sixty, the third of which is *digamma* and has a value of six.

"This third letter, the archaic digamma, was so called because its appearance resembled that of one *gamma*" — he drew again: Γ — "set upon another. This double gamma had disappeared from the Greek alphabet before the Greek script of Revelation, just as the sound it represented, similar to that of the 'double U' of the alphabet of Brittannia, also disappeared, just as the letter that in Italia is called *doppio vu* and in Francia is called *double vé* is but a spectre. The digamma was the ancient Greek counterpart of the Hebrew *yod*, which gives us the sound *waw*" — again the stylus on the moss green: *w* — "whose value was also six. And, since the loss of the digamma, no letter bearing the power of six was to be found in the Greek alphabet.

"It is interesting that, in Revelation, your Jew, who spoke Greek no more than he spoke Hebrew, is made to say in that book's final chapter: 'ἐγὼ τὸ ἄλφα καὶ τὸ ὦ' — *I am the alpha and the omega.* It is as if this implausible Greek utterance — echoing the proclamation of God made twice earlier in Revelation, rendering it thus the *third* such proclamation — this evoking of the beginning and the end in terms of the first and last letters of the Greek alphabet, were to signal that this strange-seeming book lay in the realm most surely of ἰσοψηφία. And this last chapter of the book bears the number twenty-two, which is the number of letters in the Hebrew alphabet, as if to further signal that this strange-seeming book lay in the realm most surely not only of isopsephia but in the realm most surely of gematria as well. And the verse in which your Jew proclaims himself to be the beginning and the end is the thirteenth verse of that final chapter. A number of great power, thirteen: τρεῖσκαιδεκα, the perfect triad and the sublime Deity and Eternity of the sacred ten, the decad that also formed a triangle.

"And the chapter in which the number of the Beast is given — the sum of the Greek letters *c'hai*, *xi*, and lost *digamma* — is chapter thirteen."

The old man slowly turned the flat end of the stylus above the soft flame of the candle as he continued to speak. He likened the triplication of the *alpha*-and-*omega* proclamation to the *trishagion* heard by Isaiah — "Holy, holy, holy" — which became a part of the liturgy of Christians, who sained themselves thrice with the triangular sign of the cross.

With the warm flat end of the stylus, the old man softened and smoothed over the marks he had made in the moss-green wax, while telling that the name of Adam was of three letters.

Here the elder drew more signs that to the younger man meant nothing — אָדָם — and to the younger man's uncomprehending eyes he did say, "*Adamo. È il nome del nostro padre*" — *Adam. It is our father's name* — and that these three letters were the letters of Adam, *aleph*, of David, *daleth*, and of Messiah, *mem*, and that the soul of the first passed to the soul of the next and thence to the third, and that *mem* was the thirteenth letter of the Hebrew alphabet, which again, this thirteen, was the perfect triad and the sublime Deity and Eternity of the decad that also formed a triangle; and that in hermetic cabbalah the third of the sefiroth held the roots of the tree of the All, and that this sefirah was the sphere of the mother of the All. It is the last word — πάντων, all — of that strange-seeming book of Revelation. For the *omega* meant not only the end but also the 'great O,' in contradistinction less to *alpha* than to *omicron*, *o*, ὂ μικρόν, the "little O": this too was *omega*, O Magnus, the great circle that encompassed the All, *without* end.

"And this one you call by a name most false, whose true name was *Yeshua*" — again the stylus graved: ישוע — "this one whom you reverence without addressing him by this true name: his *sermo in monte*, as your San Agostino called it, is more a mystery of threes than the regurgitated γνωμολογία" — his listener strained to follow him, extracting the sounds and meanings of the Latin *gnome* and *logos*, the first of which, identical to the *lingua volgare*, referred to aphorism, and the second of which referred dismissively to fairy-tale talk; but the older man went on before the younger man's straining gave to grasp — "that your Agostino in his *De Sermone* called the verbal flowering of the highest and perfect standard of Christian life."

The poet was lost in the iridescences that had burst from the light of the Greek-birthed gnaw of the Latin *gnome*: the Greek-birthed gnaw of the old Latin *gnosco*, the Greek-birthed gnaw of the Latin *gnomon*, that fatal pointer of the sun-dial, the poison arrow at the heart of all his musings on the lie of time, the poison arrow at the heart of the folly of man's quest to impose his unknowing intellect on timeless infinity. This threefold gnawing was the gnaw of vain seeking itself: the gnaw — *gno* — to know. Amid these iridescences, the old man's voice continued.

"It is, this *De Sermone*, a calculated composition of three parts: the exordium, the discourse of the *via vitae aeternae*, and the discourse of last things. The first of these is devoted to the ten beatitudes, based on ancient Greek and Hebrew verse. Here, again, our ten, the sublime Deity and Eternity of the decad, which also forms a triangle. The second of the three parts is itself of three parts: an interpretation of the Torah, cultic instruction, and sententiae. The third of the three parts comprises the three exhortations, during which the Jew called Yeshua reaffirms himself as a teacher of the Torah.

"And this one whom you call by a name most false, whose true name was Yeshua, this one whom you reverence without addressing him by this true name, he is believed to have entered his ministry at the age of thirty, to have taught for three years, and to have died at the age of thirty-three, when he endured for three hours with three spikes through him, and after those three hours of darkness, he died at the third hour after that noon when darkness had taken the sky.

"And in your gospels there are three different versions of his last words from the cross. Those whom you call Matteo and Marco would have your Jew repeat the first words of the twenty-second Psalm, but in a mixed lingua of Hebrew and Aramaic: "My God, my God, why hast thou forsaken me?" This sort of allusion is a rabbinical technique of rhetoric called *ramez*. Your Matteo prefers the term Eli for "My God," as it is in the Psalm; your Marco prefers Eloi, a more classically biblical Hebrew term, or perhaps an Aramaic form, Eloi. Both terms are derived from El, the name of the Almighty most ancient." Stylus to tablet:

ל

"This *'ēl* signified the One on high and it is *'ēl* that gives the theophoric element to the name shared by the people of Israel, as bestowed on Jacob in Genesis: *Yiśrā'ēl.*

"Through the once powerful Latin demonstratives gendered as *illum*, *ille*, and *illa*, and meaning '*that* one' or 'that illustrious one,' this most ancient *'ēl* echoes, unexalted, in the vulgar Latin-born tongues of Europe: the *il* and *la* of Italia; the *el* and *la* of Spagnia; the *le* and *la* of Francia.

"And in the Arab tongue, so closely related to the Hebrew, our most ancient El was their Al, and their Al became Allah as our El became Eli and Eloi." Stylus to tablet:

أَلله

"It is all in the El, it is all in the Al: our *lamed*, their *lam*," said he, stylus to tablet, pointing to the Hebrew *lamed* he had drawn, and to the one, cursive *lam* and then the other that lay at the center of the name of Allah.

"*Lamed* is a letter of majesty, towering above the other letters from its position in the center of the Hebrew alphabet. It has a numerical value of thirty; and, perceived as configured from the elements of *caph*, which has a value of twenty, and *vau*, which has a value of six, *lamed* thus has a gematria of twenty-six: identical to that of the Tetragrammaton — *yod, heth, vau, heth* — that represents the ineffable name of God. Thus we here have the doubling, the folding upon itself, the closing and secreting of the great thirteen, that perfect triad and the sublime Deity and Eternity of the decad that also forms a triangle. And as thirteen is the perfect triad and the sublime Deity and Eternity of the decad that also forms a triangle, so thirty, the numerical value of *lamed*, is the perfect triad verily multiplied by the sublime Deity and Eternity of the decad that also forms a triangle.

"*Lam* is also a letter of majesty, and, among the Arabs, it possesses also the numerical value of thirty, as does the *lambda* of the Greeks, the *lamda* of the language of your gospels. And *lam* is found thirteen times in opening verses of chapters of the Qur'an.

"And these holy names of Eli and Eloi and Allah, are born alike of three letters — the *aleph-lamed-yod* of the Hebrew; the *alif-lam-ha* of the Arabic — and at the heart of each of these names lies the letter of the myriad threes.

"As the *hadeeth* of Abu-Hurairah tells us, Allah possesses ninety-nine names: three multiplied by thirty-three. He lived, this Abu-Hurairah, at the time of your Jew, whom you believe to have been crucified at the age of thirty-three, invoking with his last breath, as your Matteo and Marco have it, the name, Eli or Eloi, the God of the myriad threes."

Here he did pause and peer into the poet's large dark eyes, and he did smile, as a thief might regard his victim. And thief he was: of innocence.

"Tell me the first words of the Bible," he did say.

The poet's large dark eyes peered into the large dark eyes of the elder, and he did smile, as one might smile on a thief about to be foiled. The first words of the Bible were known to every schoolchild and pious unlettered laborer alike: *In the beginning God created the heaven and the earth.* It was the one and very cornerstone of the tale of creation itself. The poet spoke these words in his native tongue: "*In principio Dio creò il cielo e la terra.*" Then, as if to affirm and confirm them, he spoke them in the Latin of Jerome: "*In principio creavit Deus caelum et terram.*"

The smile of the elder did increase. "And no-wise else should I expect any man to answer. Even among those who can read the Hebrew words as they long ago were written, most refuse to believe or to pronounce what they see before them in the first words of Genesis."

The poet did no longer smile, but the old man did.

"You see," he said, "in the Hebrew language, the masculine plural is distinguished from the singular by the ending *-îm* — the letters *yod, mem soffit.* The first line of Genesis does not say that Eloi created the heaven and the earth. It states clearly that Eloh*îm* created the heaven and the earth: not God, but *gods.*"

He wrote big the word Elohîm:

אֱלֹהִים

He then twice underscored the *yod* and *mem soffit* that were the suffix of its plural inflexion.

אֱלֹהִים

He then repeated his words: "Not God, but *gods.*"

From amid his codices he produced a volume which he told to be a Bible of some few hundred years of age. It was, he told, made in Tiberias, on the western shore of the Sea of Galilee. There, in Tiberias, he told, lived and studied and worked the greatest of the keepers of the sacred written tradition, *massora.* For generations, the greatest of these keepers of the every word and letter of the true and ancient-most Hebrew Bible were of the family that bore the name ben Asher. It was a scribe of the family of ben Asher that had made the book that he now brought to the eyes of the poet.

"Since this first line of the first book of the Bible was first written, it has never been written otherwise. Nor have Jews accepted it, nor has it ever been translated faithfully into another tongue. Thus, no sooner, Christian or Jew, do we open the Bible than do we reject it, while professing ever to embrace it. Odd, too, that those who remain ignorant of the first line of Genesis would venture to delve and unravel Revelation."

The Jew opened the leaves of olden skin to the first line of the first book of the Bible: בְּרֵאשִׁית בָּרָא אֱלֹהִים אֵת הַשָּׁמַיִם וְאֵת הָאָרֶץ. The poet, entranced as he was by the fine and delicate strokes, knew only that Hebrew, like its sister tongue Arabic, was writ from right to left. Now, however, he could recognize the word Elohîm.

"I show you this," said the old Jew, "only because we speak much of threes. Here you see that this word that the world would erase from the Bible — this word that remains secreted to all who can not read the Bible in the language in which it was written, and that is kept secreted by all who can; this first and foremost and most momentous mention of the deific — is the third word of the Bible. And throughout the first chapter of Genesis it is to be found thirty-three times.

"There" — he gestured — "you will see it again in the very next line, and again in the very next lines after that: 'And the spirit-wind of the gods moved upon the face of the abyss. And the gods said let there be light, and there was light. And the gods saw the light, that it was good, and the gods divided light from the darkness.' And on and on: always the gods — Elohîm — and always rendered, since the earliest Vulgate, as the singular God. As it is said here in your land: *traduttore, traditore*. The translator is a traitor. This rock of a one true God upon which are builded my temple and yours: it is a lie, a treason, an illusion, a misknowing.

"And so it is, well beyond that first chapter of Genesis. When she who is called *ḥawwâ* and he who is called *'ādām* eat of the tree of wisdom, they are beheld with wrath: '*Behold, the man has become as one of us, to know good and evil.*' As one of *us*.

"And the gods and goddesses of the Elohîm were of good and of evil — '*Behold, the man has become as one of us, to know good and evil*' — Eloi and Yahweh of the Tetragrammaton, Baal and Ashtoreth, evil-most Samael and evil-most Lilith, and those without name, and those whose names are to us unknown.

"Third word. Thirty-three annunciations."

He returned the Bible to its place amid the other codices, and it was as if he had said nothing. He no longer smiled, and he breathed awhile in silence. As if his words had not strayed, he returned then to Christ on the cross.

"Again, as we have said, there are three tales of the last words of your Jew. Luca gives us eloquence: 'Father, unto thy hands I commend my spirit.' Giovanni gives us the most beautiful words of all: '*consummatum est*' — 'it is finished.'

"And this one whom you call by a name most false, whose true name was Yeshua, this one whom you reverence without addressing him by this true name, he spent three days in the tomb before resurrection."

He fell silent and with his left hand wiped weariness from his face. He straightened himself, took deep breath, and spoke anew.

Once again, as he spoke, he slowly turned the flat end of the stylus above the soft flame of the candle. Once again, as he spoke, the old man, with the warm flat end of the stylus, softened and smoothed over the marks he had made in the moss-green wax.

"I do not worship your Jew, the Jew before whom your kind kneel while persecuting other Jews in his name, which is not his name; the Jew that you have transformed into a fair-faced *italiano* named Gesù. But I do worship his three days in the tomb, and I do worship his coming forth into the light."

Then he said nothing, and he who waited for his words said

nothing. Raising himself, the elder moved slowly across the chamber and stood before his desk of dark and ancient plank. He searched through a small *cassetta* atop this desk, then turned and approached the younger man. He sat again, and to the other's eyes he held two dice between the thumb and forefinger of his right hand. Then the dice were in his palm, and, bending downward, he shook and cast them to the floor. He resumed his posture without regarding them.

The poet beheld the dice: the two spots on the one, the single spot on the other. Then, with uneasiness, he beheld the Jew. Only then, and only after pause, did the older man bend to examine the dice. He appeared to ponder them gravely. His companion's uneasiness increased.

"This is no necromancy," the old man said. "Through your belief, and through the powers of the threes that we have here invoked, those powers are here manifest even through the blasphemy of these dice."

The poet took the dice from the floor, shook them, cast them, beheld them: the two spots on the one, the single spot on the other. He then drew back. He spoke in a voice that was low, trepid, hesitant.

"We have trespassed," he said. "We have trespassed beyond where knowledge and its mysteries ought take us. You say this be no *negromanzia*, but if it be not such, I know not what to call it."

He looked into the old man's eyes, and the old man's eyes shone like those of the Beast whose *numerus nominis* was of many threes.

"Think of it not as trespass," the old man said. The poet did not see his lips move, but heard only his voice, as his eyes could not turn from the shining bestial eyes so close to him. "Think of it as entry. You sought the mysteries of the powers of the threes, and now you have gleaned a bit through their veil."

Then the old man retrieved the dice, and when his face rose again, his shining bestial eyes were the shining felicitous eyes of a child. Again he held forth the two dice between the thumb and forefinger of his right hand.

"*Dez pipés*, as we used to say in Paris." He beamed. "*Dati plumbei*. One side of each die imperceptibly, inwardly weighted with lead." His beaming increased, and he canted verse with the joy of a child contained in an agèd voice:

J'ai dez du plus, j'ai dez du moins,
De Paris, de Chartres, de Rains.

The poet understood this petite chanson: *I have high dice, I have low dice, from Paris, from Chartres, from Rains.*

"It is true," the old man said, as if wishing not to abandon this moment of the rekindled spirit of youth; "I have dice, each a different shade of yellowed ivory, that can be made each to cast a different number, high or low."

The poet felt as reassured as he felt crest-fallen, as his elder continued, and as the rekindled spirit of youth departed his voice.

"Such are the mysteries and powers of your threes: a casting of weighted dice; a pitiable purse of tricks. How close the Latin *tres* to the *treccare* of your native tongue, how close the Latin *trias* to the *triquar* of my own native Provençal, how close indeed to the Latin *triccare* itself."

He raised himself again and returned the dice to the casket on his desk of dark and ancient plank.

"As for your blessed Trinity, you must know that no such notion is so much as mentioned, save for one vague allusion, in all the Greek of your New Testament. You must know too that it was not until what the calendar of your Church so absurdly calls the second century that the term *trinitas* came to be contrived, by the Christian theologian Tertullianus of Africa — that selfsame Tertullianus of Africa who bestowed that name of Novum Testamentum upon your scriptures. And you must know too that it was not until perhaps two hundred years after the death of your Christ that the doctrine of the Trinity was fully formulated and accepted by your Church, at the first Council of Nicea." He continued to stand, and he did not sit. "And as a man of conscience, you must admit that you and all who in like manner have by this Trinity been so entranced can but trace the source of your entrancement to the subsequent treatise of another African, *De Trinitate*, and to the learned imagination and eloquence of its author, your great Numidian intellectual, Augustinus."

He sat, and his words seemed now to wander, but not afar. "You have seen men play at *sortes Virgilianae*? Have seen them cast dice to direct them to this or that verse of the *Aeneid* to thereby seek oracular response to this or that question? It is an ancient form of augury, descending to the days of the *sortes Homericae*. But it was not many years after Virgil's death, which preceded the birth of your especial Jew by perhaps fewer years than lie between the number of yours and the number of mine, that this pagan form of augury was adapted by Christians. *Sortes Sangallenses, sortes Biblicae, sortes Sanctorum*. You have seen play at these as well, with dice and holy text?" He paused, as if silently, pleasantly pondering. "I wonder at what it was, in life or in legend, of this Gallus, this sainted Hibernian of your Church, whose name alone, after Virgil's, was lent to such base sorcery." He shook his head. "This sort of thing will ever be with us, for the souls of men are ruled by gods whom their mouths renounce. I say that this fool's game of dice and verse goes on nearby at this very moment, that it goes on somewhere at every moment, in every Christian land.

"I find it striking that the exalted Augustinus, who himself was not without his tendencies towards cabbalah — not, of course, under that name — should be concerned with denouncing this common folly. For, in the end, I view him as playing this same game, but on a much loftier and more dangerous plane: with the trick dice of intellect supreme."

The poet felt different currents rise and flow together within him: currents of resistance, currents of submission, currents of feelings without names.

"You say that you do not believe in the Son of God —"

"I believe that every one of us is the son of God. I believe that every one of us is the father of God. I believe that every one of us is God. I do not believe that any one man should be called Savior above any other, for every man's true and only savior dwells within himself, whether he discover him and be saved or discover him not and be damned."

"And yet you do worship the three days in the tomb, and you do worship his coming forth into the light."

"Three days, fifty years: the number matters nothing. It is the coming forth into the light that I worship. It is in the coming forth from the tomb into the light that I find great power in this tale."

The poet now understood. The currents within him horripilated; and he understood.

"Yes," the old Jew said: "fifty years and more. In the dark of death of the tomb of learning and knowledge, none of which allowed me to perceive the faintest scent of the merest blade of grass that lay beyond that tomb. Then, with the great share of my allotted life wasted and lying dead behind me, resurrection came; and I came forth from the tomb into the light of wisdom.

"And so you come to me in search of secret knowledge — *j'ai dez du plus, j'ai dez du moins* — and I now tell you what I know.

"End your search. Come forth from the tomb of your seeking. Come forth into the light and be filled with the scent of the every blade of grass of your soul and the every blade of grass of the every moment of this life. Come forth and embrace Her."

"Her?"

"Sophia. Σοφία. *Sapienza. Saggezza.* Under every name, wisdom is feminine. Wisdom is a woman. Wisdom is the Woman. She who is what she is. Her."

"And what brought you forth from the tomb?"

"A breeze."

AND THEN I WENT NORTH AGAIN, TO Milano. Because that is where Giulietta lived, and there was within me an unsettling feeling, a sort of premonition, that I might not see her again.

Love at first sight. Life after death. We may eventually know if we experience the latter. But how are we ever truly to know if we experience the former? Can the depths of the sea be reached in a breath, without movement? Can the stars wed two souls that have never looked upon them together?

I once felt that I had known love at first sight. But that was long ago, when I perhaps knew love only under the guise of lust and need and weakness. That was before I came to know love under no guise at all. Only then — when I could be in love with the breeze through the trees of autumn as well as with another soul, when love flowed from me as freely and aimlessly as breath, when that breeze and that breath sustained me with love in abundance — only then did I come to know love. And only then, after many such years of the sustenance of the breeze and breath of love, did I feel again, most unexpectedly, that I felt love at first sight.

It was love: of that I am sure. God, yes, she was beautiful. But the beauty that emanated from within her was such that her physical beauty seemed but a radiance of a spiritual beauty far more rare. Never had I been so mesmerized by so natural a grace and serenity. Never had I looked upon another and seen her as a goddess, a beatific spirit, that was beyond my embrace. It was the only time I had ever felt outclassed. And she was twenty years younger than I.

But later, after our endless embrace had begun, whether we lay in one bed in each other's arms or were a sea apart, she confessed to having been likewise smitten by me on that night when our eyes first met.

We had talked of having a child together. I had lost the daughter who would have held my hand at the hour of my death, and I could never replace her. But I wanted so to leave something of myself — something real, of flesh and of blood — behind me on this earth. Giulietta was the only woman with whom I desired to do this. With my doctor's help, or without it, for Giulietta did so restore me and the smile of her happiness made me want to live, this could be done. With God's grace, something beautiful and breathing could be brought into the world.

Over dinner at Bice, with good white wine from the northern hills, we talked again of the child we envisioned. Later that night, we made love and slept together very closely, as one, until the sun came gently through the window.

Her pantyhose lay on the floor beside the bed. I took them and tossed them on my cheap green vinyl travelling-bag. She knew that I thus had claimed them as mine.

They are in the drawer to my right as I set down these words, sitting here, prepared to do, or to be undone, within whatever remains of this dream that we call time.

All there, in the drawer to my right.

A vial of morphine, a pistol, the false passports that I did not use when I went to Italy to boost the documents from the archives, a lot of money, and the beige carnation of her pantyhose.

I hold this carnation now to my face and inhale the scent of her and the scent of a garden of all that is untold and untellable.

I envision myself dying like this: alone, holding to my face like an oxygen mask the bunched, perfumed flower of her pantyhose.

AND THE UMBROUS LOW CLOUDS MOVED rapidly to the north under the luminous high clouds, which did not move.

SITTING FOR THE BETTER PARTS OF DAYS upon days, his elbows upon his knees, the weight of his skull held in his hands, face cast at the same cobblestones until the cosmos was circumscribed by his dust-laden sandals and the frayed dust-laden hem of his robe, less aware, for days upon days, of the steps trod to his chamber, the steps trod to table, the steps trod to pallet, the bread and fish and wine taken to gut, the brief, haunted neap tides of sleep, than of this dusty, fallen world whose farthern-mosts were leathern-shod foot and leathern-shod foot, mendless drape of gown, and endless shadow falling slowly down, feeling himself to be in Ravenna no more than in any other town, but to dwell only in the dust where shadow fell, and where, though his eyes were too lost to discern it, the date of his death was writ; and his soul was as nought, save for undoing and loss.

Countless words of love had he writ — the word flowed from his pen as drool from the mouth agape of one stricken — and yet not one for she who had borne him daughter and sons, and had borne his fate of exile as her own as well.

And, what was worse, the woman could read.

The snail-slime of his ink through the years lay open to all, to see, as did she, all of adoration and love for a lady long dead who had in life to another man been wed, and, through that long trail of slime, not a scintilla of feeling, let alone love, expressed for her, with whom he had stood before God and been godly bound.

He knew well of all of this, had become increasingly acutely aware of all of this through the years, though of it nothing had been said.

He knew well now too of something else: knew well now too that had he wed that one whose ghost had enthralled him, and had she lived, she would have ceased to be adored and would have been as plain and graying wife, with fallen paps, unpoetried. For no woman who shared his bed could ever be ideal, and none who embraced him could ever be risen to the altar of his vision.

What knew he of heat and love, who could give of them but to undefiled boyhood dream and not to she who gave all of heart and love to him? What did it bespeak, what awful thing, that he could only love as dear, *divina beata purissima*, she who, now rotted to carrion in her grave, had in life given him but merest glance? It bespoke that he knew nought of love, and of heart itself possessed but shrift, possessed but lovely rhyme and song thereof, unmortared by the higher, silent song of heart itself.

He had no soul. He had left it long ago in a meadow of illimitableness, or soon thereafter, beneath another sky. His heart was but counterfeit, self-made most fine. His love, the same, the stuff of an inkwell.

Half of humankind he had put in Hell, and with like strokes of quill had looked down upon them: sanctissimus, who himself could but love a corpse, and even then not truly love at all; sanctissimus, who foresaw no place in Hell for his own lost soul; sanctissimus, who had sought to conjure paradise through words; *damnatus.*

If only he could wrest or wrench, from all of creation's beauty that whelmed around him, but one word of stolen grace that he might lay to rhythm on the page that feigned as heart; but not one word or color thereof came.

Darkness fell, and he did not set flame to lamp. He sat in stillness, entering his own shadow, which became undistinguished from the fallen darkness.

The word never came.

There would be no more words, except the whispering that haunted him within.

Some days later, he was summoned to bear to Venezia documents that were in need of the Doge's seal.

The moon had been several times full and crescented to nought since last he had called upon the Jew.

They sat together in the late-day heat. The old man's gaze was weary, but it was like that of a hawk, many of years, seeking that which he knew would come: a breeze of deliverance, on which old wings might be borne.

The Jew's eyes did not cease their slow searching, in stillness and in turn in movements of his visage that were quite like stillnesses unto themselves; and he said nothing as the younger man spoke of the loss of his soul.

This silence did not hurt him, as he had been hurt years ago by the silence with which the old man had returned to him the three leaves of verse, the third unread. Perhaps this was because he had valued those words more than his soul. Or perhaps this was because there was simply nothing left to hurt. He said nothing more of soul; and when he spoke again, after long silence of his own, it was of the breeze that he assumed the old man to await. Only then were his words, most idle, received with response.

"*Aura. Anima.* Breeze, breath, and soul.

"One can not lose what one has never possessed. We must not mistake the revelation that our being is bereft for the delusion that we have lost that of which we have always been bereft. Such revelation is a blessing, and not to be mourned.

"If we do not come to know what we lack, we do not search to find it, and we remain unwhole, in the darkness that we mistook for light.

"*Aura. Anima.* Breeze, breath, and soul."

LEFTY HAD NOT LOOKED WELL THE LAST time we were together, and now he looked worse. He was wearing a *coppolla*, because he had lost all his hair; and his lips were traced with the faint purple crenulations of chemotherapy.

"Lefty's lookin' better, don't ya think?"

This is what Joe Black said.

"I seen guys go through this," I said, "and I seen the guys that beat it. I can tell you right now, Lefty, you got it beat. That *tizzun'* hair of yours'll be back in no time."

As I looked at him and said this, I figured he'd be dead in another few months.

Lefty smiled, which made him look only worse.

Then Louie spoke. To me.

"You're turnin' into a real pain in the ass to clean up after, with this 'authentication' shit of yours."

"What're you talkin' about?" I said.

"What am I talkin' about? I'm talkin' about that fuckin' guy in Verona with the Brioni suit and the Berluti shoes. I'm talkin' about the guy in Ravenna *and* that assistant of his that brought you that heap of shit. I hadda put the two of 'em in the sack together at gunpoint. Do you know what kinda pain in the ass that is, the both of 'em jumpin' around on their knees, beggin', pissin', and cryin' all over the place?

"The broad had a wedding ring. I guess her husband's takin' a little heat right now."

"Are you fuckin' crazy or just plain stupid?" I snarled at him through closed teeth. "These people got nothin' to do with nothin'. These people are just innocent fuckin' nobodies."

"Innocent? What the fuck does 'innocent' got to do with any of this fuckin' shit?"

I knew him by now. I knew his language. To Louie, "this fuckin' shit" meant everything: life, the world. Everything. "This fuckin' shit" was the all-encompassing summation of his ontology, pantology, and eschatology.

"How does some lackey librarian get five-grand suits and three-grand shoes?" he demanded. "Who the fuck knows what these people are or who the fuck they talk to? You're the one who's leavin' tracks here, Nicky. I'm just fuckin' coverin' 'em up."

"Tracks? What tracks? You're leavin' a trail of blood where there's nothin' but dust."

"Oh, Jesus, stop it, will ya? *Trail of blood.* Gimme a fuckin' break. This shit don't even make the papers. This shit is just forms that never get filled out. It's nothin'."

I looked away from Louie, and when I did, I found myself looking straight into the awaiting eyes of Joe Black. Those eyes were like icy little hells.

"Whoever can possibly, even remotely, connect us with this manuscript — *tabutu.*"

His voice seemed to come from the icy little hells of his eyes, under which his mouth seemed to move only vaguely.

"Why?" I said.

Joe Black looked at Louie, and Louie looked at Lefty, and they began to laugh. Even Lefty, sitting there with his boneyard scalp, had broken into a grin through his crooked chemotherapy-purple lips. I knew then that I no longer knew him.

Their laughter grew louder, then subsided.

"Why?" I repeated. "We managed to get this thing out of Italy, where the state would have claimed it. No one knows it exists. No one knows it ever existed. One can not steal what has never been missing. One can not steal what has never existed. As it stands now, this thing is ours, and it is clean, and it was never stolen, and it is beyond the reach of any national claim on it, and there is no criminal taint whatsoever, either to it or to our possession of it. The manuscript is clean, we're clean, and we can bring this off clean."

There was silence, and Joe Black broke it.

"Well, for one thing, before we start sayin' grace and singin' hymns here, there are people who know it exists: our friends in Palermo who brought us together with it, and who are in for half of whatever we clear."

"So why don't you start killin' them instead of a bunch of fuckin' librarians?"

Again, Joe Black looked at Louie, and Louie looked at Lefty, and they began to laugh. Again, their laughter grew louder, then subsided.

"What about the guy in Fabriano?" I said.

Louie sighed disgustedly. "Ah, he got away. He went right from you to the airport in Ancona with a bunch of other characters. Gone before I knew it."

"Well, at least that's one thing that didn't get fucked up."

I gave Joe Black copies of what I had brought away from the Museo della Carta.

Louie and Lefty watched him as he read it, though Lefty's gaze was really nowhere at all.

To Whom It May Concern:

I hereby confirm that the paper of this document was made in Fabriano in May of 1321, on special order from Sig. Guido Novello da Polenta of Ravenna, to whom this paper was delivered early the following month, during the time of his personal and professional association with and patronage of the poet Dante Alighieri.

Photocopies of the pages examined by me are herewith affixed, each of them bearing my signature and each of them bearing the impression of the seal of the Museo della Carta of Fabriano.

"See," I said, "this is the sort of authentication that we need. Two more analyses and we're set. The sources of this authentication can not all turn up dead.

"Two isolated minor library thefts have already been turned into major fucking crimes that can now be tied together —"

Joe Black waved away my words.

"What?" I confronted him. "Don't you think that the almost simultaneous murders of two library directors might be seen as somehow related?"

"No," he said, "I don't. I think minor, everyday murders in one Italian city are unknown to authorities in another Italian city."

"It's senseless and it's got to stop. We can not sell this thing with documents of authentication from internationally known experts who happen to have been murdered right after examining this manuscript. It's insane. We're moving into a whole new different world now. There's got to be no more blood and no more gunfire."

Louie sighed wearily. "Hell, I'm all for that. I mean, it ain't like I enjoy all this shit."

Joe Black disregarded him without turning his eyes from me.

"All right," he said. "Forget about the guy in Fabriano. What about the broad in Milan?"

"She's got nothin' to do with nothin'. That's my own, personal life."

"Not on my tab, it ain't. And I'll tell ya somethin' else. Guys that work for me, they got no personal lives."

Then Lefty spoke.

"It's like they say: loose lips sink ships."

Yeah, I responded in silence, what about purple lips?

"So, anyway," Joe Black said, and his voice again was low and calm. "Finish up this authentication business. Then we'll find our buyer. Then we'll whistle a merry tune."

Tabutu.

It was a long time since I had heard that word. As said by certain men in a certain way — and only rarely had I ever heard it said other than by certain men in this certain way — it was the most ominous and unsettling word in the Sicilian tongue.

Tabutu.

It meant something like "house of the dead," and it implied not only the threat but the promise or the deed of deliverance thereto.

Tabutu.

The word reverberated.

Tabutu.

That was when I knew.

Tabutu.

Six days ago.

Tabutu.

Six days ago, when I began, with that reverberation and that knowing within me, to furiously write this, upon which I now glance back and wonder at the madness that is my own — this screed of vituperation, this opiate-induced calm of lyrical thanatopsis, this heartbeat fixed, like a bullet in the brain, on an origin in a balmy hammock — and I see it now, this madness, for what it is: an attempt to escape through words, to live or to die through them.

None of this matters. None of it: the raving for a lost world, a world gone not to Hell but, worse, to the Lukewarm of *i vigliacchi*; the memories of throats cut and throats caressed; the throwing open of the gates to my soul — for what? None of it. Nothing. This is no tale that began on a remembered sweet afternoon. This is a tale that began six days ago, with that reverberation.

Tabutu.

This is a tale that begins and ends here, unknown to me as to you.

I wrote those words three hours ago, in the middle of the night.

I woke two hours ago, in the middle of the night.

I turned on the broiler in the kitchen. I prepared some bread on an aluminum tray and put it in the broiler.

I turned on "Jumpin' Jack Flash," by the Rolling Stones: loud but not blaring.

I placed a throw pillow at each end of the couch.

I took the gun from the drawer.

I wanted to see what kind of noise it made indoors.

I wanted to see if it still worked smoothly.

I wanted to see if it still felt sure and steady in my hand.

The loud whelming rhythm of "Jumpin' Jack Flash" should obscure the firecracker pops of the gunshots, no matter how they echoed in closed quarters.

The burning smoking toast should veil the scent of the puffs of gunpowder.

I stood away from the couch.

I raised the gun fast in one hand and gave myself no time to aim.

Tabutu.

One pillow, then the other, in less than a single nervous breath.

The gun felt like a handful of good, warm pussy.

HE HAD BEEN YOUNG, AND NOW HE was old.

With a laugh that was almost silent, a laugh as pure as it was derisive of he who laughed, he recalled what he had written in a callow time when he had barely thirty years of seasons to be counted; what he had written at the outset of that little volume that was his first; what he had writ, as if a sage white-maned in wisdom, of "the book of my memory," as if it were so great and ponderous as to bear seventh seal and age-encrusted clasp and lock.

One spent one's seed in brothel, and all was done and over, and whatever shame there be, it be borne therein alone. But to spend the folly of one's vanity in public was to leave behind a stain that did not wash away.

He laughed again, less soundlessly but more purely, more derisively, and he whispered to himself as one might whisper to another of the wicked folly of yet a third, unpresent, those three words he had uttered with pen when his skin was still soft and untempered like that of a child's curple: *incipit vita nuova.*

That night, he took from the chest where for many years, through all his travels, it had lain, the pieces of parchment that bore the strokes of his youth, the words of that little book that was his first. They were rolled together, bound with a thin leather thong, loosely tied.

Placing this parcel within his robe, he rode his mare that night beneath the moon, which clouds in turn obscured and bared, blackening and in like turn lighting the terrain through which he rode: beyond the city, ever colder and more damp with wind, through the rough lands, to the sea, to that span of the old Roman sea-wall that yet stood strong with mortar and stone. He heard the rushing, rising waves crash angrily against the high ground and stone, and he saw the froth of their coming from afar beneath the moon. The wind whipped his robe, wildly and with wild sound, as if wave and wind and he were one, ruled in common thundering by the moon, by its lashings of light and dark, which grew even madder, as the clouds moved now like mares of the night running free of bit and bridle.

He heard and he saw, and he was one with what was heard and what was seen, for a very long time.

Then he withdrew from his robe the small rolled parcel, loosed its leathern tie and let the wind bear the leaves violently from him and as violently down and violently away into the sea. He watched what of them he could: saw them like tempest-swept birds blown high and afar, and suddenly vanished, to their death.

"*Incipit vita nuova,*" he said, into the killing wind, unto the wild sea and light and dark: "*incipit vita nuova.*"

In the fierce breath of that wild sea wind, as the moon opened and shut her eyes to the mares of rapacious-running clouds that overtook her, he had tasted something that he had long believed to have forsaken him. It came from the breath within him as much as the breath that entered him. Aura, animus. And more: what lay, the cifra, beyond the eighth sky and unto the ninth. And more again: what lay beyond the ninth sky: what had preceded him always, what was him, and what would succeed him forever. He drew this breath as if it were his first: breath not of knowing but of unknowing; breath of wisdom, as it were.

Thus, after fifty-six years, the man who knew nothing, who had been the young man who knew all, entered new life.

The new breath of this new life wrote within him and without him all that remained to be written; and what remained to be written was silence most wordless, for it must remain so, and could be solely so: aura, anima, cifra, breath, and wind.

THE TANDEM ACCELERATOR MASS SPECtrometer operated by the physics laboratory of the University of Arizona is the most powerful and accurate means of radio-carbon dating that has yet to be developed.

The Arizona Accelerator Mass Spectrometer Laboratory is the place that dated the Dead Sea Scrolls.

It is the place that conclusively exposed the Shroud of Turin as a fabrication of the Middle Ages.

It is the place.

Some middle-aged broad from Phoenix delivered a gun to Louie this morning at the hotel. I told him that he'd never get into this joint if he was carrying. I told him that if he didn't want to leave the piece behind, he should stay behind. "I ain't supposed to let that thing outa my sight," he said. "Yeah. I guess nobody trusts *my* sight, huh?" I said. "It ain't that," he said. "Well, do what you wanna do," I said. "I can't tell when you're shadowin' me, anyway. I'm just telling you: don't fuck this up. You try to get near this joint with that fuckin' piece, they're gonna do a whole lot more than ask you to check it at the door." I left him at the hotel. He was sitting there with the Yellow Pages, browsing under Escort Services. But I was sure he trailed me.

The physicist who ran the joint told me all sorts of things that I can't even remember now, a few hours later: something about how carbon 14 was a radioactive isotope of carbon that was formed in trace amounts by the effect of cosmic rays on atmospheric nitrogen; something about how radio-carbon dating works only on things that were once alive, or that contain material that was once alive, because it works by detecting and measuring the proportion of carbon 14 in the thing, which decreases at a known rate following the death of the thing, or the death of the thing in the thing, to the known natural abundance of — and this was where he lost me. The proportion of carbon 14 to the known natural abundance of something or other.

I liked the shit about the cosmic rays.

Anyway, an old wooden box was made from a once-living tree, and parchment was made from the skin of a once-living beast.

The way it worked was: the analysis yielded a specific year, with a margin of possible error, rendered as plus-or-minus so many years, with those plus-or-minus years further broken down by possibility expressed in terms of percentage. The older the thing was, the bigger the margin of possible error. Something that the accelerator dated specifically to, say, ten thousand and eleven years ago might have a possible margin of error of plus-or-minus three hundred years. We were dealing here only with hundreds of years, not thousands. This would leave us with a pretty narrow margin.

The specimens they needed were taken: splinters of wood and shavings of parchment so minuscule that their absence could not be discerned.

The wooden box that held the manuscript came out with a dating of 1703 ± 10 years.

This came as no surprise, as I never believed that a box made in the early fourteenth century could have withstood time so well. It did, however, add to the tension of the main event.

Specimens from four pages were analyzed: the first page of the *Inferno*; the last page of the *Purgatorio*; the last parchment page preceding the paper pages near the end of the *Paradiso*; and the last page of the *Paradiso*.

It was a beautiful thing.

The first page of the *Inferno*: 1309 ± 8 years, with 10% probability of accuracy within 1 year, 80% probability of accuracy within 8 years.

The last page of the *Purgatorio*: 1315 ± 7 years, with 15% probability of accuracy within 1 year, 85% probability of accuracy within 7 years.

The last parchment page preceding the paper pages near the end of the *Paradiso*: 1320 ± 5 years, with 20% probability of accuracy within 1 year, 90% probability of accuracy within 5 years.

The last page of the *Paradiso*: 1316 ± 6 years, with a 15% probability of accuracy within 1 year, 85% probability of accuracy within 6 years.

And, so, on to Chicago.

The laboratory whose scientific experts are the world's foremost detectors of forgeries can be said to take a true devil's-advocate approach. Everything that enters here is assumed to be a forgery, and is subjected to an ever increasingly demanding series of tests designed to prove that it is a forgery. Only when it passes from the most basic to the most sophisticated of analytical challenges is it deemed to have passed through all suspicions of forgery.

Visual examination.

Infrared microscopy.

Authentication of writing characteristics as datable to the alleged year or years of origin.

Authentication of the ink characteristics as datable to the alleged year or years of origin.

Ink-migration testing: the authentication of the exactitude of the correspondence of the degree and nature of diffusion of the ink on and through the parchment, and the nature of the yellow stains around the ink-lines, to those indicative of the passage of the alleged number of years since the alleged year or years of origin.

Visual, chemical, and technical comparison with dated historical documents of the same time and place.

Trace-element testing.

Chemical analysis of ink-pigment plant-dyes.

Scanning electron microscopy.

Energy-dispersive X-ray spectrometry.

Chromatography.

Polarizing-light microscopy.

I was assured that under no circumstances would anyone but me be allowed to reclaim possession of the manuscript.

And, so, back to New York, where the summer heat was nearing its worst.

I've cashed in. Everything: bank accounts, stock accounts, everything.

Before I left for Arizona, I called my friend Bruce, who works at Stribling. I told him to call our mutual accountant and lawyer and figure out a way to turn my apartment over to one of them, for cash, now. I had no mortgage, no nothing. I don't know who owns it now, as I sit here in it; but whoever's joint it is that I'm sitting in, I'm sitting in it with a million in hundreds instead of a deed. "You'll hear from me," is all I told Bruce and the other two. "I can't explain."

I've called Michelle. "You'll hear from me. I can't explain," is all I told her.

A million in hundreds is heavy. I've called the accountant and told him to wire it to Giulietta's account in Milan.

"You'll hear from me," I told him. "I can't explain."

I've called Giulietta and given her the transfer number.

"You'll hear from me," I told her. "I can't explain."

Better she should have my money if I'm dead, anyway.

I order a pizza, listen to Bach cello sonatas.

I eat the pizza, listen to "Jumpin' Jack Flash."

I look around.

Christ, my library. All these beautiful books.

I'll buy new ones.

There's no reading-lamp in a graveyard.

Christ, everything. All these cherished fucking things. All these cherished fucking people.

Oh, fuck.

Oh, God.

Please help me.

I nod out for a while. I wake up. The light is strange. Is night coming or ending?

My bag is packed.

I am to meet with Louie, Lefty, and Joe Black in a few hours.

I turn up the volume on "Jumpin' Jack Flash." I make coffee. I take a Valium, a hot bath, a shave.

I've had this robe for twenty fucking years.

Like most racket guys, Lefty never carries.

I shut the music.

Joe Black probably has a gun in the drawer of his desk.

I look around. I feel like crying.

Then there's Louie. The ghost-maker.

I take another Valium.

I take the gun from the drawer.

When duties brought him next to Venezia, his visit to the old man's cell was of necessity brief.

He told with good and great heart of having delivered his youthful vanity to the sea, and of the breath of this deed.

The elder man expressed his understanding and approval.

"All words," said he, "are born from the hunger to express and to communicate. Each sound, every element of every alphabet of old, from which all alphabets are descended, has its own, numinous value, as we have seen. The older the tongue, the more powerful the numen. Thus, while the Latin language possesses precision untold for the conveyance of subtleties most sublime and dicta most forceful, its primary elements are less powerful unto themselves than those of the more ancient Hebrew tongue. The knowledge of those powers are, I believe, what first brought you earnestly to me.

"But ponder this: the first sound of the first letter of the ancient Hebrew tongue, the *ah* with which *aleph* begins, is the sound of a sigh.

"This same holds true for the sound, the *ah* of *alpha*, with which the Greek alphabet opens to us; and on and on and on. Its children are the *ah* of the first letter of the Latin alphabet, whence the same of our vulgar tongues of Italia, Francia, et cetera, et cetera, et cetera.

"All begins with the sigh, the *ah* from which all words and tongues and attempts to express the inexpressible derive."

Breeze, breath, and soul.

"*Ah*-ura. *Ah*-numus. *Ah*-numa. To enter into that sight, to know and to experience the divinity of the inexpressible is to enter the divinity beyond and before and towards which all words vainly strive.

"As your Gospel has it: 'In the beginning was the Word.' And that Word, preternatural and ex nihilo, was without sound, and of it the sight of eternity to which man laid hold" — he slowly, beautifully exhaled, in wondrousness, the breeze-like sigh of which he spoke — "is but an echo, and perhaps all of God that is this life, amid all of the Babel of words, man may ever truly know.

"P*ah*ro*la* prim*ah*, p*ah*rol*ah* ultim*ah*.

"Trinit*ah*.

"*Ah*ur*ah*.

"*Ah*nim*ah*.

"Spir*ah*.

"Sospir*ah*.

"Divinit*ah*.

"Poetri*ah*.

"Beat*ah*.

"Vit*ah*. Nostr*ah* vit*ah*.

"Sacr*ah*.

"Stell*ah*.

"*Ah*stronomi*ah*.

"*Ah*strologi*ah*.

He exhaled the long ultimate final vowel of each word with the slow beautiful exhalation with which he had illustrated the breeze-like sigh of the Word, *ex nihilo et ad nihilo*.

"The Bible, as we have seen, says nothing of religion, but speaks only of salvation and damnation. In this verse lies the truth, *apricus* and *secretus*, of both. It *is* the Church, the Templum; and for this reason, that the worldly Church, the brothel of hierarchs that bears the name of Christos, has scraped it from the parchment of Scripture: if the one true Church is within, there is no need of the Church without, except to serve those who have made of it a commerce.

"Many things converge. Again and again it comes upon me that, for all the dissertation of men, Jew and Christian alike, on the nature, variegations, and doctrines of religion, the very word itself can be found not once in either the Bible or the books which Christianity has appended to it. Nowhere, from Genesis to Revelation, will one find mention of religion.

"What we call religion is but a corruption of the pagan notion of *religio*, the word by which the Latin tongue signified a sacred place or thing. Only in that we use the word in designating that sacred place and thing within us, the *apricus* of soul, do we make right use of it, lest we be pagans and in discourse of pagan matters. We might too use it justly in regarding all of universe and cosmos, and every element and atom thereof, for, as God's creation, it is all most sacred as place and thing. But to apply it to what is of a man's device is to cede to pagan delusion.

"Let us dismiss, then, this pagan division of old religion and new, of the Judaic and the Christian. There is only one religion, and it is within us and encompasses us: the sacredness of what is, and the sacredness of the gift of this breath, which allows us to be, and to give and to partake, of it.

"And so."

The old man again nodded slowly, and again, in due time, words came.

"The Jew named Yeshua: the Messiah, self-proclaimed, and by Gentiles since adored as such.

"As to the beauty of the words attributed to him, there can be no doubt. As to the carnival of so-called miracles attributed to him, I feel them to be legend lies, or of the Chaldee art. What God or holy man performs tricks at a wedding banquet, or raises the dead to gasp anew in horrid putrefaction? Such things are not of God. Such things are not of the sacred.

"But as to the beauty of his words, I will tell you this, which has not been remarked of him: he was the first great orator of the common and unlettered. If he was not the incarnation of God, he was most surely the incarnation of, the perfection of, the ideal of the rhetoric of *humilitas*.

"In saying this, I say also that the mystical power of his words was far greater than any that might be invoked through artful rhetoric.

"As I once said to you, there are more of his words than have been allowed to survive amid the gospels sanctioned by your hierarchs. Among certain Syrians there has been kept that text of which we have spoken, called the Gospel of Saint Thomas, descended to them in the olden Syriac script. If God can be said to give voice to the Word, which is without sound and preceded all words, He has done so in the secret verse of this Gospel of Thomas."

The poet besought him to reveal this verse, but the elder man stayed him, saying, in effect: no, no, thou art a poet of words, and only when thou art a poet of wordlessness wilt thou be then fit for the sacrament of this verse.

The poet knew not to press the point, long resigned as he was to the old Jew's implacable ways. As if to wave away what he took to be the arrogance of the old Jew — to imagine it: he who was not a poet judging one who was as to whether or not he be prepared for the receipt of verse — he simply said with a smile most slight and wan, "I fear, my friend, that the day may never come."

The lines of the elder's face turned slightly as well, but not with smile.

"Stranger days have come," said he; "and stranger days yet are said yet to come."

The silence that followed these words was strange unto itself, as the sayer of these words seemed to ponder them no less than his auditor. It was the sayer who, saying again, broke this silence softly.

"And so, yes, Yeshua. What light has come in the course of my searching. I feel that the light in all regards grows dim for me. But I pose you this riddle: What God is it that implores unto Himself upon the cross of crucifixion: Father, why hast Thou forsaken me?

"And what of the grand thing that you have named the *Commedia*?"

The less old of them smiled distantly, as if at something that was neither memory nor still clearly on the horizon.

"The grand thing. I named it rightly, though unknowingly. It is the comedy of my own self and vainglory: an ornate mirror that reflects none but me and the folly of myself, who wrought it."

With these words, the distant smile was vanished.

"And what," said the older of them, "will come of this ornate mirror? Will it too be consigned unto the storm of the midnight sea? I hear that parts of it circulate throughout Italia as we speak, and that parts of it too have passed into the language of the French. I hear too that the city that exiled you is now fast to claim and proclaim you as native son."

The poet answered wearily and simply, with nothing of pensivity and little of breath.

"*Non lo so.*"

He spoke the truth in saying thus that he did not know; and what little of breath he gave in saying these sounds, which fell like slight pebbles in still water, was more than he had spent on his grandiose comedy in four seasons, perhaps more.

Upon what there was of it he dared not look, but for the beginning and the end of it, and the few other passages whose beauty and power he now felt to be both behind and beyond him. He looked at this beginning and this end, and these other few passages, at times for inspiration, that he might take up the pen anew, but to no effect, moved as he was by what he had made. More often, he went to this beginning and this end, and these other few passages merely to savour them.

Whenever he allowed himself, or was compelled, to glance elsewhere in the work — whether in the aspiration that he might see anew, or in self-flagellation, he did not know — he saw but flaw of rhythm and forcing of rhyme: much of the petty and the temporal, little of the great and the eternal; much of the filigree of rhetoric, little of the gust of soul. If only he could capture in rhythm and rhyme the awful tempest of that night of sea and wind and sensuous-mad moon when he let lash and fly and be wildly swept his leaves of verse into the devouring, thundering ocean waves. There could lie poetry such as should be. If only he could have captured, wrested, seized the roar and meaning of that moment, and made the pulse of its meter the pulse of his work. If only the work, between what of molten gold and bellows of his own he had forged and tempered as beginning and end, were to have been blessed so to surge.

Would that it had been the song of blush and bellicosity of cloud, of *profumo di forza* of wind through pine and wildflower, of spray of sea and the salt of sea of the tears of mortality. Would that, like that tempest night, the verse had devoured and sundered itself as it rolled mightily forth in waves of rhyme. Would that felicity and ferocity had danced, and that brutality and beatitude had lain together on the iron of unknowing, obsidian and pearl together, they, beneath the smiting iron hammer of rhythm, the merged sparkling dust thereof and therefrom aswirl in delicate rays of rhyme. If only he had let the *tre bestie* run feral through the circles and spheres. If only he had let Il Veltro be his guide.

But instead he had made a schoolboy's exercise of it, bound not to the tempest of God, but to the strictures of artifice and design. He had not allowed himself to serve as vessel for God. Could there be any fool greater than he, to contrive a trivial and ludicrous structure of childish arithmetical straws, with nought for foundation, as he now knew, and assume that the breath of God and the cosmos would politely accommodate with tailored vision, *contra naturam*, rather than simply blowing it asunder and away?

Would that he had it in him to work anew. But it was not so. He had not heeded the God within; he had not heeded the God without; he had not heeded the skies. He had heeded only that part of himself that he mistook in his great arrogance and blindness to be the God within, who had indeed written, through him, the beginning and the end, then turned away from him.

"*Non lo so.*"

"As to your riddle: I have pensed upon it, and have pensed upon it, and I can venture no solving it."

"The riddle." The elder spoke as if he but vaguely recalled any such thing. His voice then changed to that of one who spoke as if beholding a fresh-laid grave. "Alas, the riddle."

"Yes. It calls to mind no answer; though my pensing on it, as you did pose it, carried me to a dangerous place, where an unholy sort of cogitation lay."

"So, then, you know the answer but dare not give voice to it."

The poet, who beheld the stonework of the floor, raised his head, looking away and then towards the elder's gaze.

"Yes, then you know," said the elder once the poet's eyes met his.

"The answer is the same as that of the riddle of the Sphinx. The answer is: man."

The younger of them slowly shook his head, returning his eyes to the stonework of the floor, then raising them again.

"On the third day, he rose from the dead.

"And why would he rise from the dead in a manner that human eyes might perceive?"

The younger of them did not give answer with haste, for as the words came to him, they seemed to be those of a child. But his faith brought them to voice.

"That he should thereby monstrate that He be God."

"Should not the faith of those who deemed him thus have been as such as to suffice?"

"What you speak is blind heresy, and you speak it from Jewry alone."

"And he ascended to Heaven."

"And He ascended to Heaven."

"In soul or *in corporis*?"

"It saith not."

"What saith you?"

"I saith not."

"Because you wish to hold your knowledge from me, or because you do not know?"

"It is because I do not know."

"And what do you feel?"

"I feel that He ascended in soul alone."

"To Heaven."

"Yes, on the third day, He rose from the dead and ascended to the right hand of God."

"And this is the Heaven of which you have written in that grand thing, the *Commedia*?"

"No. I wrote therein from within myself: from a glint of vision, a rapture of scent of petal and pine unknown in a breeze from a realm unseen, a felling wondrous nocturne of scintillations and dreams undreamt."

It was then, for the first time, that the poet told the other of the eight skies and the ninth, and of the final revelation of his work having been writ of the sky of illimitableness, which had entered him in full for a breath.

"Is that not Heaven sufficient for you, or any?"

The younger man was silent, then with calm forcefulness said: "No."

"Your books of Scripture, and your creed, make much of Heaven and Hell; and ours do not. We find Heaven more as you did, here on earth, within the gift that God has given us, along with much of Hell as well."

The poet turned upon him and again with quiet forcefulness spoke; but he spoke as if done with all words.

"Do you believe that He whom we call Gesù was God?"

The Jew answered without pause, and with quiet forcefulness in kind:

"Yes."

The poet beheld him, as if to embrace him.

"Then you are a Christian."

"No."

"How can you come to crede that He was God come as Savior among your kind, and not profess new faith?"

"I answer you this: it is my creed that you are God like unto the Jew called Yeshua. I answer you this: that all upon this earth that breathes is God. Above all, I answer you this: that faith is but a birthmark with which we are born, an impalpable umbilicus to time and place, which we rarely ponder to cut. Had your soul or mine cried its first in the Arab land, then Mussulman would you or I be.

"Had your soul or mine cried its first in Chaldea of many ages ago, before strange gods indeed would you or I kneel. I was born, as you see me, into the masque of Jew; you, with your pale *toscano* features, into the tribe that once worshipped other gods but came to worship a common Jew who proclaimed his theophany." The elder smiled softly, and looked upon the poet. "With that nose of yours," he said, lightening his tone, "I should not be surprised to find that you have a drop of the blood of the crucified mingled in you with that of the crucifier." Seeing that these words did nought to affect the poet's gaze, which seemed strangely damned, or damning, or both, the elder returned his voice to dignity. "If you believe the letter of Genesis, you then must believe that we are, one and all, descended from but sole, original father and sole, original mother. There are those among us who believe that before Eve, there was another mate to Adam. I myself believe that God created man and woman from one. There is nothing in Genesis that contradicts this. Just as He created the sun and stars on one day, and light and dark on another, so the light and dark must be of a different kind than those of day and night: they must be the light and dark of soul. I believe that creation of man and woman to be as that of a single soul-matter into its twain, the one without which the other can not be. Man longs for woman, and woman for man, as each seeks the lost part of itself; as each seeks to make whole again what once was.

"I say that when man looks upon woman he looks upon himself, that when woman looks upon man she looks upon herself. I say that God is neither man nor woman, but is whole, as is that part of God that is within us. I say that it is our common folly to gender God as male, much as it is to gender the wind as masculine — but such be our tongues, which, oddly, we gender as feminine; and wisdom — *sophia*, *sapientia* — as feminine, and the *mysterium tremendum* — the All atremble — as neuter."

The poet felt himself to be lost within the gathering whirlwind of the elder's swirling talk, and when it was demanded of him to answer, he was ill prepared to do so.

"And of this matter of the ungendered whole twained in gender," began the elder's demand for response, "what fetch you in explication for the Jew's harsh command unto her from whose womb he came: *Get away from me, woman, I know you not*?"

Spake he then: "Is this the Word of his Love?"

To the silence of the poet, the elder declared, "For all he did declare as sage, I daresay your Jew spake near as oft as maddened mage." To the further silence of the poet, the elder further declared, "These words of the Jew you worship are, like those of his upon the cross, to be most gravely reckoned."

There was silence then unto them both, and this silence stayed for goodly time.

"Bring me the end, the ultimate sounds of your long song."

"No eyes or voice but my own have seen or pronounced these words. It should not be known that I gave end long ago to what lay undone."

"There is no shame in creating as you have. Our very fates are written before our breath is done. Besides, ours, you will remember, is an oath sealed by death. Your words shall remain secret beneath my breast."

"And what do you desire, then?"

"That I might see what you did see."

The poet parted his lips barely, as if to speak, then halting, paused, and heard his own heart beat. Then his parted lips spoke.

"Close then thine eyes and see," he gently commanded, "for I bear it with me, graved clear in memory."

The elder closed his eyes, and the poet closed his own; and thus they sat in darkness that was theirs alone. The poet let silence take them until it lulled the darkness, that the verse might come forth from that lull.

O luce etterna che sola in te sidi,
sola t'indenti, e da te intelletta
e intendente te ami arridi!

Quella circulazion che si concetta
pareva in te come lume reflesso
da li ochi miei alquanto circunspetta,

dentro da sé, del suo colore stesso,
mi parve pinta de la nostra effige:
per che 'l mio viso in lei tutto era messo.

Qual è 'l geomètra che tutto s'affige
per misurar lo cerchio, e non ritrova,
pensando, quel principio ond' elli indige,

tal era io a quella vista nova:
veder voleva come si convenne
l'imago al cerchio e come vi s'indova;

ma non eran da ciò le proprie penne:
se non che la mia mente fu percossa
da un fulgore in che sua voglia venne.

A l'alta fantasia qui mancò possa;
ma già volgeva a il mio disio e 'l velle,
sì come rota ch'igualmente è mossa

The poet paused, and his soft voice fell to a hush.

l'amor che move il sole a l'altre stelle.

The poet's breath imbued the final, long vowel with an aspiration that moved towards silence like an outgoing tide of the whispering of the stars themselves to the hearts of men: a long lingering sigh, born of that vowel, that was as breath letting full the veils of sound as it moved from word to wordlessness, from the human to the divine; the susurrus that was the breeze that bore the bride that was the soul's desire unto the embrace of the infinite, awesome, ineffable All.

The elder's face had been impassive. Then serenity had overcome it, and his eyes remained closed as the poet looked upon him. When the elder inhaled deeply it was as if he had continued to be borne along by the immense and delicate susurrus, only just then feeling the caress of its magic to evanesce from him. His eyes yet remained closed as he spoke, and his voice was soft, as if wishing to honor rather than to violate the silence.

"Your vision moves like the elegant stepping forth of Aphrodite, theophanous, from the godly cadenced waves of your sonorous rhyme, laced with the heavens' light."

The poet had never had, by voice or missive, profounder praise; and the elder was not yet done.

"God has breathed into and from you. He has allowed you this gentle lifting of the veil of the inexpressible, and you have wrought the telling with a delicacy and a power of a sort that is more than rare. You are among the chosen, and you have served well."

The younger man was compelled, rendered as abundantly self-conscious as he was gratified, to touch aloud upon those infinitesimal troublings that these lines of verse yet held for him: various minute vowel sounds; souciance of rhyme; perhaps the last line, in which he had dared not to evoke the heretical vision of an earth that moved amid the sun and other stars.

"One perfect sky can become another through one shifting wisp or hue upon another, eternally so, till the perfect dawn of one day becomes the perfect dusk of ten thousand upon ten thousand days later, as I have seen. But divinity brought forth through human soul can not be shifted endlessly so, for the music of the earthbound tongue is not infinite in wisp and hue and faience of movement. You have served, and you have suffered. Leave it be.

"As to the final earth-trembling words leading your carcass to the gallows while bearing your soul to salvation, this is a most strange and lovely deadly point, and an aspect most powerful of the mystery of God's breath into and from you, and of your serving, and of your suffering."

"Would you let it stand?"

"I do not know. And as I have not written it, never shall I know, so close to the grave, from any vantage, as I now am. It is a matter that only you, the orator of its deliverance, can justly decide. As it has been said, the choice is a simple one: lie and be damned to Hell, tell the truth and be crucified.

"Come to me in the morning light, and I shall try to return a gift with a gift.

"You have entered into the sigh. You have become the poem.

"You have come to the words of which I spoke, the secret verse of the forbidden Gospel of Thomas, which you sought to know."

He then made his way to the books, and when he reached, the younger man was certain that his reach would grasp the sole locked volume, so close did his hand come to it. But instead he retrieved a homelier, ill-sewn book of makeshift sort and most old. While standing, he turned some pages, then, laying the open book to place between them on the bench, he sat.

The words in the strange Syriac script were writ grand in the blackest of inks. The old man moved his forefinger lightly across them, as he pronounced them, haltingly and more as if from memory than from reading. Moving his eyes from the book, he then rendered them softly in what he explained was the Aramaic dialect in which the one called Yeshua would have spoken them. As far as he knew, he said, the words had never been set to Greek or Latin, or Hebrew, for that matter. He spoke them in the vulgar tongue:

"'If you bring forth what is within you, what you bring forth will save you. If you do not bring forth what is within you, what you do not bring forth will destroy you.'"

When the light of the morrow came, he found the old Jew awaiting him. A broth of groats in a small cauldron of blackened iron hung low over slight flame. A glass flagon of dark amber, somewhat more than half filled with a liquor of similar color — a distillation most potent and delectable, as he would discover, an *alcool* of Araby kind, called *ha-shesh* — stood upon the table planks, with two diminutive glasses of the exalted Venetian style. Upon the bench of their long and many discourses — the sole mute witness to their oath and all that followed in the long time since — lay the book of clasp and lock, and upon the book, a shagreen pouch the size of a fist.

As steam rose and thickened from the cauldron, the scent of cinnamon drifted luxuriantly through the room; and as the rays of the morning softly glowed in the amber of liquor and glass, the old Jew's mean cell became like a cloister of the senses' delight.

The brew of groats with its tincture of cinnamon, ladled into stoneware bowls, filled both men well and goodly, to satisfaction and to pleasance and to surfeit of neither. The amber Araby liquor was poured, and the poet, after the Jew, raised his glass.

"Woe unto he who rises in the morning to follow strong drink," quoth the elder, after the words of the Bible. He beheld the poet then, and he smiled as a churl in subtle merriment, and he drank, and with him drank the poet. Breath quenched the fire of that which had quenched, and the elder sat upon the bench to one side of the book of clasp and lock and shagreen pouch, and the poet sat to the other. The elder moved his head in nuance, as if in vague and gentle affirmation.

"*Le stelle*," he said, in like and gentle affirmation: "*le stelle*," he said, as if yet lingering on the final sounds of the poet's work, as uttered by the poet the evening past. He turned then to he who had brought them to be, so simply and exquisitely, at poem's end. "Did you see them last night?"

The poet confessed that he had not.

"They were a marvel," said the elder: "innumerable." He slowly repeated the six syllables of this word, as if invoking the marvel so descried: "*innumerable*. Beyond the sum of number and of numen, like the infinite whispering of God's true name, and of all the spirits and forces that have borne the names of gods, or have been and are as gods unnamed, and of all the souls that are, or have been, or ever shall be, adrift and converged and aswirl in the All."

He breathed deeply, as if taking within himself again the air of the night beneath those stars. Then, with closed eyes, soft breath returned, and his eyes as softly opened and looked into the poet's own, which seemed to be mesmerized by his elder's words and deed of breath.

"Most wondrous, this *innumerabilità* of *infinità* remains ever in flux. Thus, Heraclitus in his deep-most wisdom: πάντα ῥεῖ. Here a soul departs expiring corpus; there a soul fluoresces, entering corpus not yet born. Here a star falls to earth; there one comes to be.

"Unknown and unknowable, the gematria of infinity. Yet it courses round and through us, and we are of it, and it of us."

The bizarre intoxication of the *ha-shesh* overcrept the poet very slowly, until he seemed to feel more than hear, and what he felt did summon other feelings, and these feelings wove together strangely and richly unto themselves.

For all of the elder's words that so enchanted him, and for all of the enchantment of vicious and succouring pride that lingered yet of the elder's praise of the evening before, the poet, in the strange weaving of the feelings within him, remained besieged by the doubts and resonant self-knellings of failure that had reigned him for so long.

These doubts and knellings had been dwelt upon aloud, again and again, in the confines of this chamber. But the rich weavings, the deep sense of the *innummerabilità*, the grandeur of the power that lay beyond all measure, now brought forth, as like unto a mist from the dark underside of enchantment, further lament for the folly of his youthful design.

Again he damned and mourned what he deemed to be the ruination of his *Commedia* by the deluded scholastic scaffolding of an academic architecture, which by nature was the nemesis and undoing of all transcendence. Damned was all thinking, said he, and thrice damned was his own.

If only he had embraced the form of God, which was without form. If only he had embraced the numbers and measures of infinity, which was beyond number and measure.

The old Jew allowed him his maundering, then silenced him with a bemused glance, which brought something of shame to the poet.

"Yes," spoke the elder, with a sigh of arch indulgence, "we, the both of us, more than know that thou art a fool for threes. It is thus that I give you this."

The elder took the shagreen purselet into his hand and extended it to the poet, who felt immediately that it contained no small weight in coin.

Loosing its thong, he fingered within, as the glimmer of gold came forth. There were thirty-three florins in all.

"A sum divisible by three," said the donor, his bemused grin undiminished.

"This is more by far than the lesser coins that I have tithed for thy teaching through these years."

The old man waved his hand, and, grinning no more and seeming to speak in earnest, said, "It will save you the stealth and toil of robbing my corpse."

The poet said nothing. Gold was gold. And this was more of it than he had ever held.

"The maker bleeds to make," said the Jew, "and he who is the maker's *bibliopola*, the thief of publisher and bookseller in one, drinks his blood, and ever thus has it been. '*Lector, opes nostrae*,' says Martial in his pose: 'Reader, you are my riches.' But later he speaks to us without pose and true of heart: '*Quid prodest? Nescit secculus ista meus*,' says he of all acclaim and fame: 'What good is it? My purse knows nothing of these things.'"

The poet nodded slowly, gently smiling at the wisdom of these words that he had forgotten.

"Take it," spoke the Jew, "into thy robe, as our fine Martial would have done, nobly and forthwith."

The poet let his words be distilled inside him, until they were pure of pretense, pure of all and any false remonstrance; then he gave them forward.

"I thank you."

The old Jew nodded gently, barely stirring the shadow cast by him. He laid then his hand upon the book of clasp and lock, and in so doing, left upon it a small brass key of intricate tooth-work.

"The gold," he said, "shall more than pay for the journey ahead."

When the poet had unlocked and laid open the codex, he was again without words, for its most strange leaves of parchment — scraped and pumiced to a loveliness most rare, but thicker than any *pergamenta* he had ever seen, so that each page seemed to glow, pearl-like, or cloud-like, through the loveliness of its surface, from the leonine hue within — were innocent of ink, save only for the recto of the first, on which, in an ink of *maruno* so deep as to appear as black when shifted from sunlight to slightest shadow, there appeared, delicately made, several elegant characters of the Araby kind.

مُناأسْكُنُ
عَلى الثَّلاثَةِ
في الثَّلاثَةِ
في الثَّلاثَةِ

And beneath these, no less finely drawn, the ageless sign of the Trinacria, enclosed within a triangle, which itself lay upon another, inverted triangle, so as to form a Hebrew star with the Trinacria at its heart.

The poet knew the sign of the Trinacria well. He himself in his work had invoked Sicilia by the name of this ancient-most symbol for the Sicilian land, and the power thereof, after the fashion of Ovid.

As was his wont, the poet moved his fingers lightly over the page, whose mystery was enhanced by the otherworldly lustre of the vellum itself.

"I have had word after, again and again, of his death," said the Jew. "These reports of his death arrive with increasing frequency. They come to me from Saracens and Sephardim alike, delivered forth via rumorous goliards, or sent as sealed epistles via the Venetian merchant vessels. One might say that he has come to die nigh every fortnight or full moon. But I daresay that none who beholds his grave in hearsay has known him so much as to look upon him." He gestured vaguely towards codices and scrolls. "And as he dies, again and again, precious gifts, again and again, continue to arrive. From him."

The poet wondered, but he did not speak, and his eyes remained lost in the opalescent underglow of the page before him. The Jew's gnarled forefinger came down upon that page, its crooked nail, talon-like, to the symbol of the trifigure within the trifigure within the trifigure; and the poet's eyes, startled, rose suddenly to look directly into those of the elder.

"This," spoke the elder, "is where you shall find him: the three within the three within the three."

The poet saw in the eyes of the Jew something of that same strange opalescence that possessed the page.

"Again," said the Jew, "a gift most suited to one whom we both more than know to be a fool for threes."

Of he of the threefold threes, the elder told him what he could.

"We studied together in Paris, at that time and in those cloisters when and where the learning of the world flowed together as many tributaries merging, and your good countryman Tommaso d'Aquino was one of many to probe that fertile delta with net of wit and senses.

"I had taken the name Isaiah, and he went by no name at all, and therefore an hundred names were for him conjectured, and an hundred origins as well, for never was there one who could speak with such perfect fluency such a world of tongues. Were he to speak unseen in darkness, he could be perceived as Jew or Arab, as Spaniard or Provençal or Italian, or as ghostly presence from the sundry ages of the Greek and Latin orators and bards.

"It was the cabbalah that brought us together; and to our studies he, through the vast of his erudition, introduced illumination as if from the every sum of every wisdom: *the mille folliata geometria mystica* of Pythagoras; the obscure treatises of the Christian cabbalists; the rare dream-book of the one known as Artemidorus, of which he possessed the only manuscript I have seen; and more.

"It was he who led our way into the realm of Plotinus. More than a year and well into another, we spent with the entire of the *Enneid*." He looked to the poet and smiled his smile that was barely such. "There you have it again: the thriced three.

"Was the world created? By God or by Demiurge or breath of Pantocrator? Or was it eternal? Did the individual human soul endure beyond death, or was it only the soul of the All, intellectus agens, that was of eternity? These were among the mysteries that we, like many of that time and place, did try to solve. But, unlike the many, we ventured in our searching far beyond the scholastic dialectics of the day; ventured into arcane wisdoms little known and less bespoken. The dialectics of Plato had led to the mysterium of the *Timaeus* and, ultimately, to the beautiful and magical vision of the true, secret text of *The Last Dream of Socrates*, which was the denunciation not only of all dialectic, but of all thought as well." He closed his eyes and recited from memory.

"Plotinus was our bridge therefrom into the unknown; and we crossed.

"It was together that we journeyed to Provence to pursue the learning that had passed from the select of Isodore. I remained there, as teacher of Torah and of Hebrew, and serving as rabbi as well. He too remained for a goodly time, living among us, though, truth here be told, he was more Arab than Jew. My father was of the Sephardim most high of Spain, his from north Africa. But his mother was an Arab whore, who did give him breast and lettering, as much as the purse of her trade did afford; and it was she, in time, who told him the sooth of his begetting." Again there was the smile that was but barely such. "I recall him raising his cup as we bided our supper one night, with Qur'an and Bible open at table, but our eyes given over to the setting sun: 'To my father, most holy, in Hell; to my mother, most sinful, in Heaven.' And, upon another time: 'I know why Christ embraced the Magdalena and turned from her who believed him to be her son born of miraculous chastity.'

"But these are needless digressions," he interposed as if unto himself: "the musings, nothing more, of an old man upon the past, which is, as it must and should be, forever lost. I tell you that he is more of Arab than of Jew only that you might seek him and know him the better.

"We remained then, as I have told, together for some time in Languedoc. But by the time that we, the Jews, were driven from that land, he was gone.

"Such was his gift of tongues that he was a master, in both Hebrew and Arabic, of that most demanding and delicate form of verse known as *muwassaba*; and a master as well of nigh all other forms, from the heroic meters of Homer to the lays of Occitan. He was, as such, in great demand among the princes and lords of Provence and far beyond, unto the very royalty of Paris, who commissioned from him verse in vernacular for courtly reading, as well as the translation into Latin of such royal documents as needed rendering.

"By the time I reached Venezia, he had departed France, having ingratiated himself with the king of Sicily. He had held always that it was in this ancient-most land of the Trinacria that the wisdom of the ages most deeply brewed and lingered. It was, said he, the land whose various blood had been most drunk of any land by conquering powers upon conquering powers, and yet whose true and hidden soul remained more powerful than the sum of all conquering.

"He is there now. It was from there that he sent me, among the treasures of his gifts, the heart of wisdom from the forbidden Gospel of Thomas. As I say, the gifts continue to arrive. But his epistles ceased some time ago. In his last to me, he told of having found the fabled Ithaca, home of Odysseus, and wrote that this was to be his home as well: his falcon's nest, he called it.

"These are the only clues I can offer, for they are the only clues I have, as I myself have never pursued the journey. Thus, as to the meaning of the three within three within three, I know not, other than that it is where you will find him.

"The book you hold, from him, will serve as your entrance to him."

There was silence, and then the poet spoke. "How do you know that this sign is that of his whereabouts, rather than a device of different meaning?"

"Because the strokes above it state it." The elder placed his forefinger, talon-like, again upon the page, where the calligraphy lay, and with his voice made from this silent calligraphy sounds that were like those of the sweet fluent water of a recondite stream:

Huna 'askunu
'ala al-thalatha
fi al-thalatha
fi al-thalatha

He then translated this sweet fluent water to words that the poet could grasp:

"*Here I dwell, at the three that is of the three that is of the three.*"

But, like sweet fluent water, the meaning of these words escaped his grasp.

"Why did he not simply state his whereabouts?"

"Because, I daresay, he both held my erudition to be more than it is and he wished not to risk his whereabouts being known beyond his desire. What might one expect from a man without name?"

There was silence again, and then again the poet spoke, but he spoke now that which was closer to his heart's true bidding.

"You paint an enticing and impressive portrait of your friend and fellow. Yet, for all of this, it remains unclear to me as to why I should make such labor in undertaking to seek and to find him."

The elder seemed as if to silently compose what he might say. But this was not so; and his words came forth as if voice were their fated and sole and faithful bride.

"Because he can see."

LEFTY WAS A DARKER SHADE OF LAVENder, and his hands shook. He sat to my left. Louie sat to my right. Joe Black looked at us from behind his desk.

"So you left it in Chicago?"

"It had to be left," I said.

"You know." Louie grinned sardonically. "All that fancy authentification shit."

"Who's talkin' to you?" Joe Black said.

Louie rolled his eyes, sucked his teeth, lighted a cigarette, and looked away.

Joe Black turned again to me, giving me back my words. "It had to be left."

"Yeah," I said, "it had to be left."

Joe Black looked toward Louie with disgust, then he turned to Lefty.

"I thought you said this guy had a head on his shoulders."

"Hey," Lefty said. His voice was weak. "They don't make house calls with" — he looked to me — "what's that thing you told me about?" — then again faced Joe Black — "stuff the size of a room. They don't make house calls with stuff the size of a room, Joe."

"Electron-scanning microscopy chambers," I said.

"Nicky knows what he's doin', and he's right. I mean, whadaya wanna do, take this thing down to Canal Street and sell it on the sidewalk next to some guy peddlin' knock-off Rolexes?"

Joe Black stared at Lefty. His stare changed, as if Lefty were excused due to terminal illness. Or as if this whole routine were being played out according to some sort of prefigured effect.

"Look," I said. "You want me outa this, just gimme my money now."

Joe Black turned away a little and looked up at Rembrandt.

I leaned forward, shook my head, sighed wearily, and reached behind me in the manner of one abstractedly scratching his own back.

I brought the gun up fast to my right and shot Louie through the head, swung it two feet to the left, and shot Joe Black in the chest; and when he slumped forward with a doomed but violent lunge of execration, I shot straight into the top of his skull.

After the first shot, into Louie, there was but for an instant a great noise from Joe Black and Lefty. The glimpse of an instant: for Joe Black couldn't draw a breath before the next shot took him; and with that shot, in the glimpse of that instant, Lefty was suddenly silent.

The gun was now aimed point-blank at him.

"I was on your side, Nicky. I was on your side all the way."

My friend.

From the old days.

"You know the score. It was Joe Black's ball game. But I was your rabbi the whole fuckin' way."

The old days.

"And after I did my thing" — I looked straight into his eyes — "'Good-bye, Nicky,' right?"

"Not if I had my way, buddy. Not if I had my way."

"Those words come pretty quick and easy. Would you jump in my grave that fast?"

"Look at me," he said.

"I am."

"Let's bring it home together."

"You gotta be fuckin' kiddin'. You're the first one they'd come lookin' for. And you're fulla shit, anyway. 'Cause you'd be right there with 'em, lookin' for me."

"Nicky," he said. Then there were no more words.

I put a hole where his soul used to be.

The old days were dead, and so was my old friend.

Tabutu.

I did not know who else knew that the manuscript was in Chicago. I did not know how long it would take anybody to find these three stiffs. All I knew was that you don't kill somebody like Joe Black and wait to find out what happens. There is the shadow of the law. Yes. But guys like Joe Black have many shadows, from New York to Palermo. And those shadows have shadows in turn.

The door locked behind me when I pulled it shut. Down the block, a building was being gutted to make more luxury living spaces. From a few storeys up, a debris chute vomited wood and plaster into a big Dumpster cart. The plaster dust was stirred into a blinding cloud with each loud successive outpouring. I tossed the gun into the Dumpster as I passed it.

I grabbed my sack, looked around one last time, was almost

blinded by the irrevocability of it all, and by the loss of every tangible wisp and shard and treasure of my life.

I flew straight to Chicago. I picked up the manuscript and the report, which detailed its passing with perfection through every form of scrutiny known to man and modern science. The laboratory signed an agreement of confidentiality, I returned to the airport, and I flew straight to Paris.

THE WORDS STAYED WITH HIM: *Because he can see.* They more than stayed with him: *Because he can see.* They moored within him: *Because he can see.*

And this mooring became as blackness moored to black; for, as the first winds of summer gloried the Ravenna country-land around him, bringing new life to townsman and *contadino* alike, they brought to him the sky of his illness, so that the sweet sun that cast its sweet golden light upon the gay-ringing bronze of the church bells, and upon the singing of children and of birds, and upon the lush, lilting green of thistle and leaf and dew-ripened blade of hillock and field and meadow arrased and perfumed with clover and flowers and the breezy flight of butterflies bold of color and white — this same sun was to him not sweet. It was the sun that hurt the eye and roused the stench of putrefaction, and brought forth the foulness of maggots and the foulness of flies; and all that gleamed and sang and danced beneath its light was to him as a disease unto his senses, and as a demon cruelty that mocked and caused to ache the blackness within him, until it seemed that he could bear no more, and he withdrew into his own shadow, and the dust of the ground was once again his cosmos, and he was as one who was dead and yet still hurkled from the sun, in heart and soul, and even from the blackness that subsumed them. As his heart beat, like that of a lost and bleating thing aslaughter, he dwelt upon this sky of illness, while casting his eyes from it, and dwelt as well upon the source of the seeds of darkness within him, upon which this sky did wreak its morbid evil, and upon the sky that they in turn did court and curry.

As the days grew longer, the blackness deepened. He took little food. The sounds of his wife and offspring were like those of vile strangers whom he had not the strength to silence. All duties and all correspondence went untended, as did the merest of those ablutions of self, or the slightest of attention to the draw and drape of vestments, by which even the humblest of men presents himself with something of dignity, no matter how threadbare or mean. He had ceased to wear his *berretta*, and as often as not his *infula* as well, which he clutched in his hand, its white linen flaps wilted like a dirty rag from the sweat of his clench, as he went bare-headed like a beggar.

He moved no farther than where the vicolo to the west of his own passway took him: the shaded seclusion of a cortile amid the crumbling walls of a monastery ruins: the whole of it, cortile and cobblestones and remnants of walls alike, taken over by clinging vine and patina upon patina, wine-dark upon green, of moss upon moss. There he would sit, on the moss upon moss of an ancient millstone that lay atop the great open depth of what once had been a well.

He began to take even less of food, but more of wine; and he no longer moved to unsettle the flies that beset and crept upon him, not even to curse them, even as they came to his wine-purpled lips, gathering at the sickly sediment that encrusted them, and at the jaundiced crystalline matter of the corners and lashes of his eyes. From the breaches among the mossy rocks beneath the mossy millstone on which he sat, in drenching rain as in still of heat, with arms forming a bony bower for his head, there seemed to rise the terrible odor of decay and corruption from the dank and deep of the hole that the millstone covered. Then did his head stir in disgust; and then did he perceive that this stench of death and worse, the afterings of death, exuded from him.

His footsteps grew slower, feebler, and less frequent. When he stirred, it was in torment. When the awareness of breath came upon him, he gasped, like as one who feared death and was in the very throes; and at times in these gasps, he seemed not to capture breath, and he shook, with the horror of a stopped heart, to the very choking point of swallowing his parched and bloated tongue back into his throat, to feel that he was already beneath the earth, lost in such nightmare as the restless dead might dream.

He was brought to bed with fever, and there, in the soak of his sweat and filth, he died an hundred times and not once saw the light of life or knew the sleep or pulse of calm.

Then he dreamt, and woke, trembling, unto that dream. Again he dreamt, waking, trembling, unto the dream; and again. Then he dreamt, and woke unto dread, with a heart that beat like that of a small bird, whose life is brief. And the dread was good, because he knew it to be real. Then he slept and did not dream, and woke unto dread with strength, and both were real, and both were of him.

He thirsted for wine, but he took only water; and in time he thirsted for water alone. Then the rich scent of bread from the baker's oven drifted through the window, filling his senses, overtaking the stench of him. And he slept; and in the still of the summer night, he went naked in his frail pallor to the barrel of the courtyard bath, and there cleansed himself, and he scraped from himself what beard he could; and he found that his wife had boiled and thrashed and set to sun and air his unders and his *fibula*, and set as well to sun and air his robe; and he clothed himself, and he awaited the dawn; and with a straight of good hard maple branch to aid his weakened legs as walking-stick, he shambled forth, not knowing why, towards the tomb of Theodoric, on the outskirts of town.

Something within this cloak lived.

Onda e nuba.

You go to Hell if you lie; you are crucified if you tell the truth.

The three points that were of the three points that were of the three points.

The triad within the triad within the triad.

The trinacria within the trinacria within the trinacria.

The poet laid his hand on the cool stone of the great sarcophagus and looked into the veins of its roseate porphyry and the veins of the hand that lay upon it; and his eyes rose to the sculpted cupola and walls of the tomb. Shafts of rising sunlight through the narrow eastern finestrum illuminated the words of majesty and holy might graven most grand and fine into the rock. They had endured for almost eight hundred years; and they would endure, both rock and chiselled elegy, beyond an hundred generations.

Was this all of immortality man might know? Was eternal glory such as to be quarried from the earth, cleft and hewn and hoisted and adorned with *ad gloriae* to God and to him who rotted therein, in measure and sacring eloquence alike and of a kind, as if to share thereof, alike, and chiselled, *in aeternam*?

The humble, ancient millstone had endured as long, and likely would endure as long again; and, while bearing neither name nor noble words, was monument to the countless unknown who made and were for ages served by it, as in his blackness it had served him.

If there were Heaven and Hell where souls did dwell, then surely the soul of the emperor and the souls of the countless unknown were weighed stripped of bejewelled and kingly crown and staff as well as of serfly sackcloth and tunic and crude-made scythe. If there were Heaven and Hell where souls did dwell, then surely this monument of great and prodigious grandeur was as nothing to the monument of the millstone; and the exquisite and lesser and the humble and greater were together nothing when viewed against the true monuments, which ascended of stone unto the clouds and which descended of stone into the sea and which were formed of wind and wave, the very hand of eternity itself. These were the temples of immortality, which did make child's folly of all the stoneworkings of men that were raised in claim thereunto, and upon which the glance of God must be brief and of bemused and angry dismissal, just as His glance upon the millstone must be in its brevity more of pleasance in its bemusement.

A smile of bemusement began to gather among the lines of his own drawn face, as he made to depart the sepulchre, with more of his dwindled weight brought to bear upon his stick of maple than upon the weakened leg of his leftward side; but the smile was suddenly stillborn.

For who was he, in the inward self-raised temple of his own vainglory, to bring judgment upon the vainglory, of stone or of self, of other men? And who was he, born neither to throne nor to millstone, to deem the latter nobler than the former, upon which sat him who wrote with blood the lay of his life upon the parchment of the war-razed surface of the earth itself? Who was he to disdain words graven into great and beauteous stone unto the glory of God and self — he who had same-such glory of God and self on the lowly, thrice-scraped, thrice-used hides of barnyard beasts and worse, the cheapest paper of the stewed, pulped, and pressed innards of horses and soiled discarded unders and latrine rags of men? And who was he to tell of the glancings of God? Surely God dwelt within him, but surely He dwelt as well in emperor and in the countless unknown of the millstone, no more or no less in any than in any other. And just as surely demons dwelt. And most surely that within one that passed judgment as like unto God upon his fellow was not of the God within, but of the movements and workings of those demons that, which movements and which workings, we, in the greatest and most deadly of all vanities and follies, had exalted into that which we glorified as the supreme shibboleth of human arrogance: the curse of thought.

Yes, to think, to exercise the flawed and tormented intellect as supreme over the feelings of the soul, was to occlude and turn away from God within, and therefore from God the All. *Mosce animai*: flies of the soul, which brought only endless nervous harassment to the breath of our life, endless knotting of brow and endless worry, endless errance from beatitude, and a twitching and swatting, in lieu of life, unto the grave. Yes, thought was the root of all evil. *Pensare humanum est; perseverare in pensarem est diabolicum*. He had been named rightly: Beelzebub, lord of the flies.

To think was to discard the gift of breath and feeling and communion. To think in God-like judgment must be much the worse in sinfulness. "Judge not," as it was written, "lest you be judged."

Here he sat at the base of the great sarcophagus, overcome with the realization that he had spent the years of his age in judgment while *thinking* himself to be a servant of God and of what gift God had given him, damning all thought in endless circles drawn in the dust of soulless erudition, posing as humble and sinless pilgrim while at the same time, with his pen, dispatching to Heaven or to Hell whomever he so pleased. He had consigned to the *Inferno* every writer who was greater than he, under the pretense — that is to say, the *reason*, the *thought* — that they knew the forces of the All by different names than he; and at the same time, with another stroke of pen, raised to divine force a young lady of Firenze whose only holiness lay in that she was not his to hold, and that she died fattened and whiskered in wifery to another. She was as nothing to sea-born Aphrodite, whose singers of praise he had damned to Hell. She was, as truth to himself he now did tell, little more than a worn and common device that he did take from others, much as he had stolen from those more ancient poets whom he put in Hell, verily often of a single stroke, taking from them as he sent them down. Who and what was his Beatrice if not a ploy of verse, after the fashion of the day?

And what of his false erudition, his raising to glory of philosophers and makers of poetry whom he had never even read? And what of his false justification, his damning of his own personal enemies under the pretext that they were the enemies of God and all men? As the politics of Boniface VIII had led in serpentine manner to the poet's exile, so the poet's work harped more on the evil of Boniface than on the evil of Satan. What manner of high and mighty theology was this?

He was a fraud.

He had surrendered his soul and his life to God again and again. Yet this surrender was not real and true. He would not rise to paradise with vicious pen and hollow prayer. God was within him, and the vast and wordless poem of infinity lay revealed, and he had beheld the sky of illimitableness.

How much of breath remained for him on this earth? And was

he to continue thus? He knew that he could not endure another sky of darkness like the last. It was time to surrender, wholly and with his all, to that other, most beautiful, and mysterious sky, and to that wordless poem; time to let forth from within him that which would save him.

The morning air was pure and cool in that place of the dead, and he breathed of it; and full and salubrious it came forth from him.

Within the tomb the morning light had dimmed as the westward morning of gray from the sea robbed the sun of its splendor. Yet he knew the sky outside the tomb to be good, for he could feel its goodness in him. And, in his full and salubrious breath, he could feel, too, the cumbent sigh in him of the every sky of his every breath, awaiting, each and cumbent sigh, its billowing; for so many breaths, the countless most of them, had gone uncelebrated and unsavored, while each had been, and was, in the lingering sight of its having been, an infinity, a drop of the dew of eternity upon soul and senses, unto itself: each breath of each of the nine skies, infinite moment and dew of eternity, a sacrament, without which, though the bellows of our lungs might unawares suck and expel in shallow rote, we do not live, but merely are, remanding all of salvation, light, and miracle that endlessly opens to us.

How much of breath remained for him on this earth? He could but lay lien alone to the breath that now passed through him, could but savor its dew and the drift of its infinity.

Rise or fall, his breath would be his fate. Rise or fall, it would be without the weight of the self-forged ferrous manacles of willfulness, which he herewith sundered with the mighty freeing blow of the sweet and gentle breath of that within him that saved. Rise or fall, it would be the breath of God within him, and the winds to which he also surrendered, that would bear him, downward or aloft, to Heaven or to Hell, to beatitude or darkness, or to places or fates unforeseen or undreamt.

He laid one hand on the cool red stone of the great sarcophagus, braced his stick of strong maple with the other; and he rose.

Yes. Unforeseen or unknown. For while he knew that what he brought forth would save him, there was no knowing the nature of that salvation. His own words came upon him.

Selva, salve; selvaggio, salvagia. Even the words bore like sounds. How fitting that he might find himself, at the dusk of his journey, in a dark salvation.

He entered the Basilica di San Vitale, there to pray. Nowhere in his life had he known the soul and eye and hand of man to make such beauty as the compassing, heaven'd vision mosaicked herein. Years ago, upon first setting foot into this place, in the full of candlelight, so overtaken and dazzled was he by what struck him as a myriad sharded rainbows in the fulgent flashing of a myriad suns, that he could not discern the forms and figures of the exquisite for the blinding brilliance of the whole of their convergence. He since had come to know these forms and figures well, yet ceased never to marvel at the untold hues of their tesserae, at how one shade of rose yielded imperceptibly to white, or one of palest blue likewise to deepest green. If every word had number and numen, then every hue had such as well; and as each utterance and breath of poetry possessed its color, so each color possessed its breath of poetry. Here the cumbent sigh of every color seemed to have its billowing forth.

How the countless upon countless tesserae of this magnificence seemed so to be born of the same spiritus sanctus that had been primum mobile of his own vision — it haunted him still; and how it humbled him, singing forever to him in the silent, soft timbre of its choired hues the verity of verities that the poet of Ecclesiastes had brought forth, bringing in the end every wise man and nuovista to his knees, and in the further end serving over every grave as common breeze that whispered, *There is no new thing beneath the sun.*

He was on his knees now as he heard these words within him, beholding on high around him all that illumined the beauty of his vision while with beauty far greater illuminating that it was not his or any man's.

Stealth and theft had served him well as mortar in his work. But of the virgin power of the vision of which his work was born, he had once in his heart felt most sure and viciously proud. The beasts of his book had been for him the proving of its power and the creatures of its mystery. Yet here, on high around him, were beasts and books and emanations of mystery and powers thereof; and all led, as in his work, to the vaulted stars above. These, like the graving mallet of the wisdom of Ecclesiastes, denounced for him all that he had in his folly and his arrogance embraced as new. *La vita nuova* existed only insofar as one came to know that there was only *vita. Lo stil nuovo*, insofar as it wrought power through poetry, transcended style and was new only as the sea and wind and stars were new. All of beauty was of *stilo aeterno* alone.

As his vision led to God, so did that of this place, as all visions perforce must lead as well as derive. But here, confronting God, one could not but be struck as if by lightning, for here, from the heavens of the presbytery, bursting the bounds of human comprehension of all that was holy, came forth, bold as the unimaginable first fire of light of the world's unimaginable first dawn, the hand of the Creator, clenched save for index finger and least finger, which were extended outright and straight in the sign of *la mano cornuta.*

He began to pray the Pater Noster, but forsook it. Closing his eyes anew, he did but breathe, to let come forth within him what words as might. No words came, and thus he did rejoice, feeling cumbent sigh on cumbent sigh billow forth and billow forth, till breath itself became his wordless prayer. And in that moment, when breath and prayer became one and wordless, that which was within him knew the ecstasy of surrender; and he was transfigured.

In Paris, I went directly to the God-forsaken Rue Dénoyez, in the twentieth arrondissement. Night had fallen.

Rue Dénoyez. Say it fast and sloppily and slurred, as all is said in this dark and desolate skid row of lost, anonymous North African shadows. You might be saying Rue des Noyés: the Street of the Drowned. It is the street of the drowned, the street of those who have abandoned all hope, those who have fled to nothingness, those who have gone down or stalk or stagger adrift, clinging to their slender bottles of Boukha Bokobsa *eau-de-vie de figue*, the clear, strong Tunisian fig liquor of their slow and violent drowning.

I had not felt safe in a long time. I could not feel safe. Wherever I went — in the eyes of every stranger asking me for a light, in the glance of every loitering shadow, in the movement of every passer-by or slowing vehicle — I saw and felt my death, until I no longer could tell innocence from danger. All that I could hope for was to hide.

In the Rue Dénoyez, nothing was safe. But there was no need to hide, for all was hidden by the dark drowning-world of the Rue Dénoyez itself.

Down the street from the cramped little dives of stupor and bloodshed, where the fig liquor was sold and the mad yelling was as loud as the recordings of dervish howlings that blared through the smoke-thick air of acrid human scents, there was the Hôtel Dénoyez: the flophouse of the drowned.

I checked in. I dared not leave the manuscript unguarded in this dank dark place of rotten doors and rotten walls and rats and drunken Arabs and doped-up Tunisians fucking or killing each other — it was hard to tell which — in the adjoining rooms.

Morning came. I put the manuscript, the documentation, and every piece of my true personal identification in a bank vault in the seventh arrondissement.

I returned to the street of the drowned. It was my idea to hide there. But instead I was drawn into the drowning tide.

I do not know for how many days I staggered between the blaring dives and the dank dark flophouse, drinking my fig liquor and puking my puke upon the crusted puke of the drowned and drowning others. Neither by their twisted expressions nor their unintelligible words could I discern whether those who approached me were threatening me or welcoming me. One spat upon the cross I wore around my neck. I spat back in his face. He shouted and I shouted. Like animals thrashing as we drowned.

I could smell the deadly bitter stink of diabetic ketoacidosis: the ketones seeping through my clogged pores.

I did not want this death.

I lay in a cold sweat, shaking and gasping for breath as seizure ran through me. Then, after days, sickness left me.

I kept my room at the hotel of the drowned, but I now also took a room at a small hotel, a real hotel, in the Rue de Montalembert, near to the bank where I had locked away the manuscript. I bought a good suit, and I cleaned up and went to the airport.

HIS FRIEND AND PATRON SMILED UPON the sight of him in the forenoon of a gray and quiet summer day.

"Alas," spoke he, in the overripe arch tone of a comic player, "he doth live and breathe."

"Precisely."

His friend and patron's tone then assumed its true tone, though his merriment wryly endured. "I do believe that thy good wife had all but measured thee for six fine boards of coffin-wood."

The poet sat in the grand chair with its seat of deep-blue velvet cushion.

His friend and patron had been somewhat unsettled by the sole word the poet had uttered in response to his jocular greeting, for it seemed most strangely grave in timbre, and had been spoken with an expression of countenance most eerily serene; and this vague unsettling feeling, this sense of strangeness and of eeriness, was like a pebble let to fall into a pond of still, clear water, barely disturbing it, but causing greater and greater concentric circles to spread forth limpidly from the point of its slightness. Every movement — his taking to the chair, his slow shifting of the walking-stick from one hand to the other, the crossing of his legs, the tranquil, savorous taking of breath, as if the air of which he partook were different and of a finer variety than the air of this world — and every stillness seemed to be as yet another silent and delicate concentricity of horripilation, no sooner perceived by than vanished from the subtle-most placidity of the senses.

The poet declined the offer of spiced wine, gently, with a calm gesture of hand and a soft flow of gratitude in the turn of his smile and the cast of his eyes.

To his friend and patron it was as if the poet were here and yet not here: an apparition of himself summoned and sent to serve his bidding. *My friend still lies abed, and at this moment dies. Here before me sits his spirit, come to give farewell before soul departs with the outgoing tide*. But, no, it was in whole and truth his friend before him, but yet, most inscrutably, it was his friend as not known to him. Of dourness, of grimness, of plangent or brooding darkness of heart, there was none.

Perhaps the great work was done at last. That would lend light to this presence, as unsettling as it was serene. But, no, he had declined the wine, and no sack or parcel as might contain the sheaves of his finished labor lay at hand. He had come bearing naught but self and stick and strangeness.

"And how goes the poetry?"

"I live and breathe it."

"That is good," said his friend and patron tenuously, as one might reflect aloud upon an enigma while yet pondering it.

"It is fine indeed," the poet said.

"Scriptor and rubricator await it."

"Greater and lesser men have awaited greater and lesser things."

His friend and patron poured and drank of the good spiced wine.

"But since the thirtieth canto of the *Paradiso*, there has been nothing."

"There has been much. Many have died, many have been born. Souls have passed from one wind to another. The waves of seas have thundered on rock, and the constellations have moved in mystery. Things have been revealed, and things have been beheld. That which is within us has destroyed, and that which is within us has saved."

The poet spoke these things as if in easy and casual conversation, and at the same time as if in tranced soliloquy. He seemed about to go on, when, in the breath between the sentence last spoken and that to come, his eyes lighted on his right hand, which lay upon his knee. He watched his hand and formed with it the *mano cornuta*; then, looking his friend and patron in the eye, raised and directed this *mano cornuta* to his eye as well. His friend and patron was taken aback, angered and nonplussed by this sudden effrontery and insult; but the poet spoke immediately, again as if in casual conversation and at the same time abstracted.

"Who was it, do you know, who so rendered the hand of God in the basilica?"

"An artisan of one of our mad Gothic bishops, I should imagine, lost between vulgar pagan curse and sacred Christian image." He sighed through his nostrils in abrupt frustration. "What brings you now to ask such a thing?" The poet shrugged benignly, turning his *mano cornuta* before his own eyes, as if it were the revelations, and his reflection upon it were of the beholdings of which he had spoken.

His friend and patron looked away in exasperation. The poet in time relaxed his hand and laid it once more upon his knee. His friend and patron in time returned his gaze to the poet, until he again saw one whom he admired and of whom he was most deeply fond.

"You speak of hand and image," he said. "As you know, our friend Giotto has agreed to illuminate my book of the poem with pictures of his device."

"A good man, our Giotto. Have you seen his work for the Scrovegni chapel in Padova?"

"I hear it is quite marvelous."

"Quite marvelous indeed. *L'invidia*," spoke the poet, slowly, most slowly, giving the final long vowel the lingering *ah* of the old Jew's primeval utterance; and as he spoke, and as vowel lingered, he brought thumb and forefinger, barely parted, to his lower lip, and slowly, sinuously, drew them from him, in obscure monstrance of Giotto's image of Invidia as a serpent protruding from an open mouth. "In the paintings of that chapel's walls every aspect of humanity is given perfect face and form." He paused. "Yes. Bought with Scrovegni gold. It seems that of late the guilt of usurer families elicits great glories unto God."

"We have agreed upon the commission. But he is deign to begin his work until the poem entire is at hand."

The poet slowly nodded, as if his friend and patron's disappointment were his own. And, in all compassion, it truly was. He then spoke gently.

"This making of poetry, it is sad to say, is not much like the making of bread. One does not simply drop one's coin and forthwith receive his loaf."

His friend and patron's face betrayed a pang of hurt.

"The simile that comes so fluently to you seems to me to be without grace. I have loved your poem from the beginning, and have done what I could to lighten your worldly burden, through appointment and through benefaction from my purse to yours, solely that your great gift might flourish. If of the crass marketplace this relationship be, then tell me, where is my return to be found? The world shall have your poem, and I am no common tawdry *stationario* who shall profit by vending ill-made copies of it, with false ledgers, to profit thereby, while you do not, from what you have wrought. I want only that this poem most beautiful might flower full and be; and that I might possess, at my further expense, the most beautiful and the perfect book thereof. Though Virgil of our tongue you might well be, this is not the age of Augustus. Patrons of *poetria* do not gather in swarm like bees to the nectar of verse. Believe me when I say that more than a few have declared me mad for my desire and my indulgence. And I have told them all: he is my friend, and the work of his will be to the spirit of this world as gold is to you and gold is to me, and thus to he who makes this work, these meager shavings of gold I gladly decree."

There was stillness. In the distance a bird sang, and it seemed to be the only stirring in the world. And when the song of the bird stilled, the poet spoke.

"And you are my friend. And I grieve for my miscast words, that they moved you so. And I grieve that I have failed you."

His friend and patron felt his forehead faintly descend and faintly rise, as in affirmation of something glimpsed amid their words and amid their silence: glimpsed but neither defined nor understood.

"As we speak," the poet said in a voice quite low, "as friend to friend, as heart to heart, may I press you further in your honesty?"

His friend and patron gave his answer through the light of awaiting eyes.

"Has there been in the work any element that has brought you pleasure of an impure kind?"

The light in his friend and patron's eyes turned obscure then shone; and again there was the movement of faint affirmation.

"It did please me that you did dwell upon my late aunt Francesca's place in Hell. She did shame and grieve this family so."

"And did you ever wonder that I may have done this of impure inspiration, knowing that it should please you and gain your favor?"

"Yes, I have so wondered. And I turn the press of honesty now unto you. Was this canto written so?"

"May God smite me dead if I here speak falsely, but in all truth I no longer recall."

The friend and patron again moved in faint affirmation. Then he stilled and strongly spoke.

"Enough of God. Enough of truth." He stood and strode to a casket of walnut-wood that rested atop a low, long cabinet of older, darker wood. "Come," he said.

The poet stood beside him as he removed the well-fitted lid from the walnut box and turned back the folds of soft muslin within, baring a heft of parchment, most beauteous to behold. His friend and patron lifted the topmost sheet and raised it to the sparse light. Though of a delicacy far finer than the thick leaves of the book of the sign that the Jew had given him, it possessed the same pearl-like lustre, and was most angelically white and free of blemish or warp.

"Do you know how often I hold it thus? In the eye of my mind I see the great majuscule *enne* with which the poem commences, its color most brilliant, rosso scuro unlike that of any other rubricator's ink." He turned to the poet, the leaf yet held to the light. "I have dared speak of it to no one, but I may be able to lay hold of the *sacrum incaustum*, the imperial purple ink of old, as well as the finest red *minum*." He lowered the leaf, passed it to the poet, who savored it much, then replaced it with care in its muslin swaddling. His friend and patron closed the box, then caressed its wood.

"It is the rarest of uterine vellum. It majesties the crimson of rubric, the black of text, and the every color of illumination unlike any other. I believe that our friend Giotto has never worked upon the page; but his colors will take as glorious to this as paint to liquescent plaster, as vision to cloud.

"And the hide of its binding awaits as well: the very finest water-ox, tanned in the very finest African way."

The poet's eyes remained on the casket of walnut. He wondered at the great number of lambs or calves that had been led to slaughter to fill that box with its vellum most fine.

"Only the fair translucent skin of Beatrice in her virginity could have yielded more fitting vellum," said he, allowing his eyes to meet those of his friend and patron in strangeness.

"Something of the sort can be had from the Arabs of Africa, for a price," in strangeness spoke his friend and patron. "But I would have nothing of it." He gestured to the walnut box. "If it please your thirst for knowledge, know that it is not near as fine as this vellum."

The poet returned to the cushioned seat of his comfort. His eyes grazed and lingered, as they had so many times before, on the volumes that rested upon the shelves that were of the same dark olden wood of which the great cabinet was wrought. He envisioned his *Commedia* among them.

Speaking as if the poet's inner imagining lay revealed, his friend and patron said, "Your poem shall lie in a casket of carved chestnut tree, hinged with gold and lined with cushioned velvet as that which adorns the very chair in which you sit. It shall rest on the shelf of a lectern of its own, carved from the self-same chestnut tree, so that all shall be, chest and lectern both, of a single somber and lovely grain. A brace of great candelabra shall flank the lectern, to be lighted when the book is raised from its casket below to the reading boards above."

The poet was entranced by this expression of love and exaltation for what did not exist. His friend and patron was borne as well by the picture his words had summoned; and the two men sat in silent luxuriance and reverie of what did not stand before them except as phantom.

As the poet slowly stood as if to speak his leaving, his friend and patron soundlessly pressed forward across the surface of his desk a pristine *fiorino d'oro* that shone upon the darker glow of the surface of the desk, which was that same dark and older wood as cabinet and shelves.

"For what of need or desire might come your way," he said.

The poet looked upon the coin, then most benevolently into his friend and patron's eyes. "You have given me enough and more," spoke he. Taking walking-stick in hand, he smiled in wordless farewell and turned to the arched stone portal.

As he set foot across the threshold in parting, the voice of his friend and patron fell upon his back.

"I simply do not understand. A single year to write the *Purgatorio*. And it now has been six years since, and the *Paradiso* is still unfinished. I simply do not understand."

The poet faced him.

"Nor do I," he said openly and plainly. "Nor do I."

The poet lingered, hoping that further words might come forth from him; but no words came.

"It will be finished, will it not?"

Then words came.

"All things in time come to right end."

AT THE AIRPORT, THE ONLY OTHER PERson in the smoking section of the l'Espace lounge carried a small black vinyl attaché case on which, in red, were the words EUROPEAN SOCIETY OF CARDIOLOGY. He was a silver-haired gentleman, and, as he sat there calmly smoking, I told him with a smile that I liked the image that he presented: the attaché case and the cigarette he was enjoying. He seemed only then to become aware of this juxtaposition, and he smiled in turn.

"Don't tell anyone," he said in mock hushed secrecy.

He was returning from Stockholm, where he had delivered an address to an international congress of heart specialists. The doctors attending the congress had been given these attaché cases.

As our brief conversation drifted to its end, I asked him

if his duties at the congress had allowed him any free time in Stockholm.

"Have you ever been to Stockholm?"

"No."

"Free time in Stockholm is like free time in Purgatory. There is nothing there."

We sat and smoked awhile in silence. He asked if I would mind if he turned on the television to view the news for a few minutes. I did mind, but I told him I didn't.

There it was: a United Airlines jet flying directly into one of those big ugly twin towers in downtown Manhattan.

We looked to each other in disbelief. Then, without being told, we knew. The will and wrath of Allah had descended.

"Fly the friendly skies of United," I said.

Black billows of fuming destruction rose to engulf the sky. The second aircraft struck as we were watching. Then the doctor spoke, slowly nodding in grim affirmation of the new age to whose arrival we were now bearing witness.

"At least," he said, "we can be comforted that the authorities in their care and wisdom protected those innocent lost souls from the dangers of secondary-smoke inhalation."

He lighted another cigarette, then again he slowly shook his head, but now in negation.

"Welcome to the Apocalypse," he said. "No smoking allowed."

Louie, the angel of death, would have loved it. All that shit — all of it — going down in flames.

Those sounds amid the scratching of the rats in the hotel of the drowned: the noise of drunken Arabs and doped-up Tunisians fucking or killing each other — it was hard to tell which — in the adjoining rooms. The sounds of monotheism.

Boom, boom, boom. The sounds of monotheism.

Monotheism. The root of all evil.

In forsaking paganism, in abandoning the gods and cleaving the sacred into Almighties, man had chosen, raised, and embraced under different names and guises long-sleeping Enyalion, the ancient Cretan god of war and destruction, and had begun to "go down," to use the words of William Blake, "to self-annihilation."

Enyalion. Ad nihil. Annihilation.

The artificial births of the one true God were the true genesis of the fatal disease that is the plague of Enyalion: ψῡχόθϱος, the death of the soul. Where once theophany billowed through soul and sky, there now billowed the black smoke of annihilation through soul and sky gone dead.

There are species of animals that have been known to kill their own kind, for food or for territory. But it is the pathology of religion that has made man the most unnatural and ungodly and self-slaughtering of species. Men had always warred, and in their wars they had sought the favor of the gods. But they had not warred in the names of their gods. Helen of Troy was legended to be the half-mortal daughter of Zeus, and yet Zeus was legended to take no side in the Trojan War. It was the Jews who first killed in the name of God Almighty, in the third century B.C., in their war against the Greeks and the Jews who accepted the gods of the Greeks. But monotheism had been an evil of aggression from its beginning, more than a thousand years earlier, when it was imposed with force upon the many-godded Egyptians by Amenhotep IV.

Monotheism.

Cross, crescent, six-pointed star. They were but weapons in the sash of Enyalion.

For some time, I had not smoked a cigarette without feeling the murder on the trigger-pulling finger that touched my lips as I brought the cigarette to my mouth. Now I felt nothing but the good strong smoke.

Why had I killed? Not for any fucking bullshit God, not for any bullshit fucking Allah, not for any bullshit fucking Jesus fucking Christ.

Why had I killed? I no longer cared.

And it no longer mattered.

It never had.

All I knew was that I did not occupy the throne of Satan, which is the throne of God.

So fuck it.

Just give me the old-time religion, the *real* old-time religion. Lay me down with Aphrodite, let Dionysus flow in my veins.

Fuck the Semite triad. Fuck all the sons of Shem.

The Levant — Jerusalem — the cradle of the Beast of all evil; the "holy city" of the three monotheistic religions.

Fuck these three Jerusalem cats, and fuck Jerusalem.

May the many true and sacred gods blow them and fucking Jerusalem from the face of this dying earth.

I light a cigarette, take a drag, let my forefinger linger on my lips.

A few hours later, I lie sleeping on the big plush couch of Suite 418 of the Ritz in London. I am awakened by the awareness of a softly stirring presence. A maid is changing the flowers in the room, and she apologizes for having disturbed me. I rise and part the voile sheers of the big window overlooking Green Park. I gaze out awhile, then I turn on the television. I see that those big ugly towers no longer exist.

I try to reach Michelle at her place in Brooklyn. Every attempt is met with a busy signal immediately following the country code or the city code. Only after hours of constant trying do I manage to get through to Brooklyn.

"Michelle," I say.

"Oh, my God," she says, "Nick."

She is all right, but she has been worried for me. I tell her that I am safe and well.

"The last time I called you. Did you tell anybody about that call?"

"No," she says.

"Are you sure?"

"I'm sure."

"Good. Now here's the hard part. You know how we've always operated: never lie and never deceive. Remember what we always said? In a world of liars, honesty is the greatest and most feared weapon that there is. And it's what makes us good and it's what makes us strong. But right now you've got to lie for me. I want you to say that I've been acting strange and distant lately."

"Where's the lie in that?"

"And that I had an early-morning appointment today at the World Trade Center. And that I wouldn't tell you anything more about it. You figured it was with some financial guy or something. And that's all you know, and you're worried."

She sighs anxiously.

"Why are you doing this?" she says.

"I can't explain," I tell her. "Just call Russ and tell him you think I was supposed to have this meeting this morning and you're worried."

"Why don't you just have Russ do this? I'm no good at lying. I never was. I can't lie. I never could."

"It wouldn't work with Russ. For one thing, it wouldn't make any sense that he would know about any early-morning meeting having to do with my personal financial affairs. For another thing — look: fuck Russ where he breathes — just do it. Believe me, you're the only one who can do this for me. You're the only one. So, please, just do it. If you want, you can just say that you thought you heard me setting up a meeting for today with somebody downtown, and that you haven't heard from me since."

"This is too much. I don't get it."

"Will you do it?"

"But *why*?"

"Because I need to be dead."

THERE WERE TIMES WHEN LA SIGNORA Gemma wished she were dead, and there were times when she knew she was.

But this death in life was not the death of her wishing, and with greater and greater occurrence, when taking whetted knife in hand to gut fowl or fish, she paused to vision drawing the blade deep across the veined softness of her pulsing wrist, or with greater violence across the base of her throat.

When had she begun day-dreaming these little deaths by her right hand, these *mortiti di mano destra*?

She had been a withdrawn child, but happy in her misted melancholy, preferring to become lost in the magical tales told and sung by her nursemaid than to prance at play in song and dance with the other children maidens of the families of high name. She found somewhat threatening the haughty airs and aggressive noisy nastiness of these girls, most of whom were of nobler names than she. And at the same time she was sorrowed by those other little girls who ran soiled and in rags with purer song and dance, and sorrowed too by those even younger than she, yoked and indentured, or bent in harsh labor in the fields. Only in the tales of her good nursemaid did she find a place to thrill and joice and hilarate and twirl and traipse in wonderment. It was in these tales that she found life as it should be: where the cold and haughty met their justice, and the innocent of heart but pained of fortune met their meet rewards. And in this world as it might be she did dwell most sweetly, as in a scented vale whose air, light, and enchanted shades bore melancholy only in that she knew them to be not real. But this melancholy was as nothing to that of the world that threatened or sorrowed her and should not be real. It was beneath the clouds, amid the trees and flowers of her father's gardens and beholding the starlight of the night, and in the sweet-trancing voice of her nursemaid, and in the endless echoes of it within her, awake and adream, that she dwelt from the cradle to the milky way of her youth.

In time her magic world was clericked. Law and letter were imposed upon the God who resided in the clouds and trees and flowers and starlight of night, and the lilt of her nursemaid's training and its endless echoes within her, awake and adream.

One midday when her nursemaid fetched her from the learning-bench of the ecclesiastics, the goodly lady, who knew her more intimately than mother or father or any else, discerned that she was disturbed and dark within.

"What bad thing, dear miss, has come to thee?"

She denied all disturbance and darkness for a long while, and only after her maid, in her wisdom, ceased all inquiring did she, after some silence, free herself of the troubling weight within.

"If God, being God, can forever rejoice in an endless happiness beyond our dreams, why then should He be so stern and so dour?"

"This is something, my dear, that thou must never ask of the brothers of the order."

It was to little Gemma as if her worst fears had been confirmed. She cast down her head, which was now as heavy as her heart, and she said, "I have sinned."

The goodly maid tugged playfully then upon her little hand to draw her eyes to her. "No," said the maid with a gentle smile. "Thou hast not sinned. It is just that God is to each of us as we see Him. The brothers of the order, being stern and dour, see a God that is as such. Thou, being a child of joy, see God as He truly is. And thou must never cease to see Him so, and thus shall He never cease so to be.

"Your happiness makes happy the heart of Jesus, who wishes to see none suffer as did He. Long, long ago, in joy, did He cast away the crown of thorns. It is the stern and dour among us, the very same who placed it on Him, who relish that He wears it still."

"Then why must I never ask my question if it be sinless?"

"Because, being stern and dour men, they will be as jealous of thee as of birds that fly and sing unto Heaven God's true song."

She felt once again good and light within her, and God was once again in the sun-bright air, and within the good and light of her as well; and she felt that it would be ever thus, her hand in the hand of the goodly maid, in the soft midday of forever.

"Then let us sing."

"We can not sing as the bird sings; so let us thus sing of him."

"Yes, oh, yes! 'The Robin Far from Home'!"

She would that of song and fable there be no end; and her goodly maid, though she could neither read nor write, remained her truest teacher. Having learned from her to ask nothing of the ecclesiastics save those questions they implicitly solicited with erudite answer ready at hand, she endured unto excellence their various dourings of God, arithmetic, rhetoric, and grammar, returning ever to drink of these things in lovelier guise at the side of her maiden, whose songs and tales in verse or prose were splendid and beguiling with the light of God, and the frolicking numbers in flux of blackbirds and squirrels and purloined field nuts, and rich throughout with eloquence most pure, and fine of form.

Her curriculum was designed to adorn with refinement a lady-to-be. As such she was Latined only so far as was deemed befitting. But this Latining brought to the learning-bench before her the wondrous fables of Aesop in the form of the *Liber Esopi*. Now more than ever she and the goodly maid were as sisters in an enchanted world, for Gemma and maid now could share tales in turn. When little Gemma came to the fable of the fox, she could but barely wait to run and tell the goodly maid that the tale was the same as one that the maid had told her since earliest memory, and that the maid's tale and the fable of Aesop were one, and what a wondrous thing this was, to have had Aesop bloom in the garden of her reverie without word written or read, and that she should not be surprised that the goodly, unlettered maid had already given her the better part of Aristotle, in lovelier form, without the either of them knowing it.

It was the magic of Aesop that led her deeper into Latin than where it was deemed necessary or fitting for a lady to go; and soon she was reciting for her maid the verses of Horace, Virgil, and Ovid as well.

She revelled in the courtly music of the day, which did so finely wed rhyme to song. On one occasion, there came to Firenze a troupe of players from the courts of Provence. She could not understand a word of what was sung, but never had she heard such sweetness of sound. And never had she seen ladies sing so fair and fine who stepped forward with their art as the men of the troupe stepped back as if in deference to their betters. Though she could not understand their words, their voices and dulcet pluckings of their strings carried meaning enough, and she knew that theirs was a realm of new and different magic.

The gentlemen of this new and different magic, as she would later learn, were by name called troubadours, and the ladies of this new and different magic were by name called trobairitzes. And, as she would also learn, this new and different magic was to them more than a century old, and it was by name called *fin' amors*: love most true and sincere, which spanned the realm of greatest purity, greatest power, and greatest passion. This was the realm of the troubadours and trobairitzes: the most beautiful thing that could exist between a lady and a gentleman of courtliness.

I walk over to Langan's. Cucumber-and-Stilton soup. Steak haché with eggs and fried onion rings. A good green salad. A big bottle of water and a glass of wine.

I'm living.

Or dying.

Whatever.

I had left the United States under false identity. Amid the scattered remains of the thousands of dead in that new-made Hell, they would never put together the pieces of who was who.

I am a fragment of an unidentifiable shattered molar.

I am Οὖτις.

I am no one.

I am dead.

HE TOOK HIS LUNCH AT THE INN OF THE crone, then walked with an apricot in his purse to the old Pineta burying-ground. There he sat upon the grass beneath the great tree of elm at the cemetery's heart. He leaned his back against the ancient thick bark of the tree's mighty trunk, settling himself between the main-reaching arms of trenching roots that were nigh as big as he in their parts alone that protruded from the earth.

Which had come first, he wondered, the graveyard or the tree? Surely a tree such as this was the growth of some hundreds of years. But just as surely most of the burial-stones round the tree were so old and weathered by the elements of centuries as to be worn bare of any trace of funerary making. Some of these seemed to have been dislodged, hove, and raised by the growing girth, length, and expansion of the tree's roots.

Some yards away an old and forlorn grave-stone tilted to the left. He tilted his head in whimsical alignment with it; and he saw a sparrow light upon it.

He pictured the stone of his mother's grave and the stone of his father's grave in the cemetery of Firenze.

He tried to recall his mother's touch; but he could not. He had been so young, before the stepmother.

He recalled bringing his lips to the damp of death upon his father's forehead. "No colder in death than he had been in life," he had in youth been fond of saying, but this was of course a conceit of the meanest sort. The dead were always colder than the living.

Yet there was no denying that his father had possessed a certain coldness of temperament in life. And, yes — he found himself now nodding without expression towards the tilting tombstone — he himself had possessed of such as well.

Could such a coldness run in the blood of generations? Could one be conceived of cold seed?

He nodded again towards the tombstone with vacant eyes, but not without expression; and this expression was one of forthrightness in the face of the musings that now rose within him.

Yes, he had placed flowers on graves, making certain that the city's eyes were upon him. And, yes, what was his poetry but the placing of lovely flowers on the grave of what secretly lay dead within him? His words, the pretty flowers of his words, sang of love and caritas and divinity; but the song of his life itself was a song far different.

The look of his father's face in death came to his memory: the eyes wide, the jaw dropped, as if aghast, as if privied to an undreamt horror at the moment of his passing.

The look of his wife's face, and the look of his children's faces, came to him: the one cold with a sadness to the bone; the others, cold with a sadness of a different sort, a sadness perhaps born of the cold that chilled them from without rather than within. Could he, having been so afflicted by his father, have afflicted his children in kind? And could he, in imbuing his wife with the seed of generation, have altered her maiden temperament as well? He nodded to the tombstone, again without expression. Yes, he thought, a truly wondrous thing indeed, even in its malfeasance and insidious castings of the lots of fate, was nature, and most so that which pertained to the mysteries of humankind. Yes, the breath of his salvation did bring forth the truth that what pale and little of love and passion had dwelt within him had been spent on pretty words. Just as his vision turned to the stars, so he had felt love only for that which was distant, far-away, and beyond his reach. And what was that, though it bore love's name, but another infirmity of nature? Saint John had lain in love to warm and comfort a leper most foul. He himself all but recoiled at a damsel of flesh rather than of rhyme, lest he discover in her the slightest imperfection, blemish, or divine Maker's mark upon the whiteness of her skin and soul.

No, he had never loved, as until late he had never breathed. The skies of illimitableness had grown ever more rare because he never had seized their moments. Had any man ever truly loved, save for wise man or for saint, or for the most rare as to be both?

He breathed, and, in that fine breath, he felt there to be love: for the sheltering leaves above him and the grass around him and the dead beneath him. And he did pray that this breath and love from in him might spread to all the world, above and around and beneath him.

The sun appeared in a breach of gray, and its light fell in soft glimmerings on him through the lush leaves and boughs. He removed the apricot from his modest purse and watched the light play on its skin, golden softness on golden softness: *apricus*, that most lovely and subtle of Latin terms for nature's light.

It was as luscious as it appeared. As he savored it, he pondered the burial slabs that time had worn bare, and pondered too their various aspects of upheaval as caused by the sinuous underground reachings of the big tree's ascendance. Most surely, he pondered, the roots of trees did enter the coffins of the dead; and, as surely as their grasping, tenacious strength did enter through this lesser wood of decay and damp, so must these roots enter into the dead themselves. In their thirst to seek nourishment from all of moisture that seeped and subsided beneath the ground, surely then the roots of a tree such as this must drink of the dead: must drink of the moisture of loamy seepage of the rotting dead direct, and must drink also of the tricklings of that decay, ooze and atom alike, into the elements of all moisture of which the roots did drink. Thus, clearly, the residues of the dead were absorbed into the life, substance, and composition of the tree. So it was that within a tree such as this the dead did live, and through a tree such as this, the particles of the dead were transubstantiated to new and vibrant existence.

He raised a leaf that had fallen, and he wondered at its perfection, and at those long dead who had entered its lacing veins, and at how this very leaf in its decay would become the loam of moist sustenance as well, and how it all would go on, as every atom found life anew, and as every exhalation became the inhalation of another, and endlessly on, so that one not yet born may breathe the very breath of Christ and then, when allotted span of breath upon this earth did end, may sprout forth as a bud in spring.

The sweet flesh of the apricot was done, entered into him, and he did suck upon the pit, which was most toothsome. And as he sucked he pondered further.

What if this great tree beneath which he sat were such as did bear fruit? Then truly would one eat of the flesh of the dead, the atoms of their decay contained within the ripened sweetness of the fruit. What if the apricot that now was of him had been plucked from a tree upon a farmland hillock that served as a family burying-ground? Then, truly, the dead which dwelt in the tree and the fruit thereof were now of him; and, if the very pit in his mouth were to find its right place and circumstance within the shallow of the rich earth of this distant place, then the particles of the dead within the pit would in time abide yet anew, at the very heart of a sapling whose roots would one day grow to partake of the moisture herebelow. And thus who had lived and died on a distant countryside might dwell within an apricot tree afar, and now within him as well, commingled with the dead of other ages and places; and on and on, as fruit did blossom and was eaten, and as pith thereof did scatter and sprout within the air that the dead did bequeath the living.

Oh, if only his beloved — he thought aloud in whisper, assaying the possibilities of metrics and of rhyme as he slowly whispered on, beginning again and again anew — oh, if only she had been put to sleep beneath an apple tree; that I might taste forever of her sweet divinity, through what days God may grant in the earthly arbor of eternity. *Meletta. Eternità.*

He spat the pit into his hand, and hurled it against the tilting headstone.

Enough of the vilings of verse, and enough of the lie of his love, and enough of her.

He shook his head in disgust and closed his eyes. He breathed deeply, with resolution. Then he simply breathed.

I CALL GIULIETTA TO MEET ME IN LONDON. I give her the name under which I am registered at the Ritz.

"I can't explain," I tell her. "Just come, as soon as you can. And bring me about twenty grand from that wire transfer."

I stroll to the Ritz Club. I should not do this. I have not been here in almost a year. Hotel clerks and concierges don't really remember infrequent guests: they merely check the records prior to one's arrival, then pretend that they remember. Casino managers are different. They remember. But I want to gamble. So fuck it.

"Welcome, Mr. Tosches. It's so good to see you. It's been a long time."

"It's good to be back."

This guy remembers my face and name. I remember only his face. He is alone behind the desk of the warm, old-fashioned luxury of this joint. I pass a fold of several fifty-pound notes to him as we shake hands in greeting. The dead should have no names.

"I should like to forgo the formalities of entrance this evening."

"But of course. The presence of a gentleman such as yourself is noted by means more distinguishing than a signature in a common registry or a swipe of a membership card."

True gentleman indeed.

I lose seven thousand pounds at the blackjack table, and am down to my last two pink hundred-pound chips.

Of course, by now I am convinced that Giulietta will vanish with my money.

I walk out with three sealed plastic packets of five thousand pounds each.

Maybe she truly loves me after all.

"Good night, sir."

Yes, a true gentleman indeed. With a wink of appreciation and commendation, I pass him another hundred pounds for the perceptive discretion he has shown in not using my surname.

I fall asleep with my hand on my cock, envisioning sweet Giulietta, with ten grand in each hand and lush nylon on her legs.

In the morning, I take a shave and a haircut at Taylor of Old Bond Street.

Department of Manuscripts, British Library, Euston Road.

A fine quiet in the office of Dr. Susan Pulice. Her lovely Italian accent enlaces the quiet, brings Giulietta and all things beautiful to my heart.

"You have intrigued me," she says. "The disappearance of all Dante's autographs has fascinated me since my university days. I often wondered how such a thing could have, and indeed had, happened."

"And you have mentioned to me your feelings regarding the possible discovery of such a manuscript."

"Yes. I believe that it would be a discovery of greatest, almost unimaginable importance. I also believe it would be a most controversial one. Such a manuscript would challenge even the best Italian scholars and palaeographers, whose knowledge and experience I have the highest respect for. I can think of at least four great Italian palaeographers that I would certainly contact."

She mentions names, some of which I know, some of which I do not: Mirella Ferrari of the Università Cattolica di Milano, Stefano Zamponi and Teresa De Robertis of the Università di Firenze, Armando Petrucci of the Scuola Normale Superiore di Pisa.

"It is my personal opinion," she says, "that a Dante manuscript, even a tiny and scruffy fragment written in his hand, would be regarded as a unique treasure by every public institution and private collector in the world. To have the possibility of acquiring and keeping such a manuscript has always been in the dreams of curators and collectors. It would be very difficult to calculate the monetary value of such an item, and the value would depend on many factors."

Again she mentions names: Peter Kidd, the head of the Western Manuscripts Department of Sotheby's, London; Christopher de Homel, former head of, and still a consultant to, the Western Manuscripts Department of Sotheby's, London, and now the chief librarian of the Parker Library, Corpus Christi College Cambridge.

"There is, of course, no way to verify the handwriting of Dante, as there is no specimen to which to compare it."

"Yes," I say. "If I am not mistaken, there is nothing more than a single reference to his handwriting."

"Niccolò Niccoli, in Leonardo Bruni's *Dialogi ad Petrum Histrum*, about eighty years after the death of Dante."

I open my black calfskin valise, draw out a single sheet of paper, and from it I read aloud the words of Niccolò Niccoli:

"'I recently read some letters of his, which he seemed to have written very carefully, for they were in his own hand and signed with his seal. But by Hercules, no one is so uncultivated that it would not shame him to have written so awkwardly.'"

"His seal," she muses. "That would certainly be a wonder unto itself."

I speak in the language of heraldry: "Per pale or and sable, fesse argent."

"Now, how might you know that?" she asks.

"Because it is to be found on the final manuscript page of the *Inferno*, above the poet's signature. It partly obscures the words *tondo* and *stelle*."

I reach again into my black valise, and I place before her a folder containing copies of the full laboratory reports, a copy of the Fabriano letter, and copies of the manuscript leaves that have undergone analysis.

She studies these pages awhile. I look away. My eyes are drawn back to her by a barely audible whisper, a whisper that seems to be but the shade of utterance: "My God. Oh, my God."

She looks at me.

"How can I reach you?"

I smile pleasantly, for she is a most pleasant woman.

"I'll call you."

Giulietta and I stroll through the cool air of an unusually pleasant London afternoon. The news-stalls scream with lurid tabloid headlines of panic, war, doom, and Armageddon.

"Today's your day, isn't it?" she says.

"What do you mean?"

"Today."

"What about today?"

"All year long, I have to listen to you telling me about the meanings of the magic numbers of your insane gambling systems, and the crazy holy days in your secret calendar, and now you forget?"

"I don't know what you're talking about."

"Today," she repeats. "Today. The anniversary of the death of Dante."

IT WAS WHEN THE MOON FIRST MARKED HER time in blood that her fate was revealed to her by her maid most fair.

"Thou hast blossomed, my dear, and thou art child no more. It is but the first rosy dew of thy womanhood. In no great time, thou wilt bring forth children of thine own, with whom thou mayest roam anew the realms of wonder and magic such as we have known. In no great time, a little hand shall be in thine, as thine has been held close in mine."

Young Gemma did miracle in this. Soon after her encounter with the mysterious and ethereal songs of the troubadours and trobairitzes, her handmaid had interceded on her behalf to beg of her father lessons in the language of the French. She had crouched with fluttering heart at the top of the stairs, heeding what transpired below between her handmaiden most fair and her father most feared. The maid's bowed and fawning deference concealed the boldness of her stealth as she did petition him in the guise of acting with his interest in mind, saying such like: "She will be lady soon enough, and, while she has excelled in her schooling, I feel that we should be amiss in not fully cultivating her for a future in realms of court beyond the confines of the Florentine tongue, especially as such an auspicious *istrumento dotale* has now been executed." The listening girl wondered at this strange phrase, but it gave her no pause as she listened on. "A knowledge of language of the royalty of France would indeed distinguish and equip her as a lady of the court wherever the horns of reception of diplomacy might herald. I have made inquiries. Such lessons would not be dear. Furthermore, as she has grown fond of idling and dreaming a-day, I daresay that such discipline should do her well; and I am confident that I can present the prospect to her in a spirit that she will embrace." There had been no sound from her father. As she soon did learn, he had merely nodded distractedly and waved away the maid to pursue, with a curtsy and a bow, her wisdom or her folly, such as it were. But at the moment, not knowing this, her heart fluttered all the more as, following her father's silence, she heard the steps of the maid ascending towards her. Then she saw her with a great smile upon her face, and upon that smile a hushing finger excitedly placed.

They both well knew that the language of the mysterious and ethereal songs of the Provençal troupe, which had glamoured Gemma so, was as unlike as like any of the language of Francia they ever had heard. From one young lady of the troupe whom they overheard afterward to speak most fluently in Florentine, and to whom the fair maid, dressed in her finery for the occasion, had introduced young Gemma as the daughter of the house of Donati, they both did learn that this language of the south of France was known by sundry names and lilts. The lovely trobairitze said that it was this language that first had given voice to the visioning of true love, *fin' amors*, in the aristocratic courts of Provence an hundred and many years ago.

"A lady poet," marvelled young Gemma, looking into the singer's kind and sea-dawn eyes; "and one so sweet of voice, and to whose verse men do bow and step aside."

The lovely lady had smiled. "Are not the very words *poeta* and *poesin* feminine? And are not the muses ladies all?"

"But yes, they are in truth," exalted the girl.

"And among the makers of song most beautiful of the golden song of most antique Hellas was a lady, Sappho by name, who did sing — hear the beauty of her sounds, which the Arabs have returned to life for us, as thou didst hear ours, then will I tell thee the beauty of its meaning."

Little Gemma had closed her eyes to give herself to the enchantment of the sounds. Closed they stayed as the lady gave them new tongue.

"And I tell thee too that among the great court poets of my homeland who are honored with most glorious esteem is the lady Marie de France, who did make verse of *fin' amors* as well and in her way."

"It is not so here, where men do sing the praise of ladies, but do seem to silence them as they praise."

"As thou hast here today witnessed, we sing as one. Yet thou art right. When the songs of love of the courts of Provence were emulated by the poets of the Sicilian court of Frederick II, I daresay not a trobairitze was heard to make verse among them."

"Tell me of the tales that poets make in France."

At this the maid apologized for the girl's continuing imposition, but the lady of verse was bemused and happily indulgent.

"They are of magic and adventure, ladies in waiting and knights most brave in battle and most tender in courtship."

And at this the ladying heart of the child was irretrievably taken; and her capture was most visible, in eyes that widened and lips that parted. It was as if, grown so as to barely see over the stones of the wall of the enchanted garden of her childhood, she now glimpsed a vaster and more enchanted realm beyond, into which she did crave to clamber but could not.

She watched as her goodly maid and the lady of verse spoke in guarded manner: the one placing her lips parallel to the ear of the other, and then the other doing likewise, for several such turns of varying duration.

Unawares, lost in the glimpsing of her new and beckoning enchantment, she did not know, though she had been gazing straight to them, which of them had begun the secret exchange; but she had overheard grabs and snatches enough to surmise the possibilities of its particulars: the station in life of that gentleman there; the misfortune or transgression of that lady there; the beastliness of that child there; or, though she should not hear it, the darling nature of this delightful child that was she; or perchance an embroidery of all and sundry.

The goodly maid ended this conversing of furtive tones by saying altogether clearly, "Well, then, let us thank thee so much."

"Will we meet again? Will we ever meet again?" asked Gemma of the lady singer.

"Who knows?" said the lady.

"In reading a tale, we must not peek ahead to see what comes. And in the tale of our lives, we have not even the opportunity to succumb to that temptation. One thing that I can say is that I most surely will have thee in mind when next I raise my fiddle to sing."

Then there had been the silent wave of her father's hand and the calling at the salon of the damois late of the court of the duchy of Milan.

"I am here to learn the language of *fin' amors*, of magic and adventure, ladies in waiting and knights most brave in battle and most tender in courtship."

The lady was given pause, then did speak.

"I do believe thou art."

As she well knew Aesop in Latin, and as she had traduced it to the vulgar tongue of Italia, the lady thus deemed it best to begin with an Aesop that had been put to the vulgar tongue of Francia perhaps an hundred years past. Thus might she discern what of Latin each of these tongues had cast away, altered, or clung to, the each in its way; and thus might she also come to know the difference with which the musica of the one tongue and the musica of the other had diverged from the musica of the Latin, what was the mother of them both.

Then, in the flight of months, she did indeed dwell amid the *lais* of Marie de France, and the chantefable of *Aucassin et Nicolette*, and *Lancelot*, and *Perceval*, and Chrètien de Troyes, and the *Roman de la Rose*, until her heart almost broke as Isolt bursts into tears after realizing that she has failed to recognize Tristan in the *Folie Tristan*. She went even unto the *Enèas*, foremost of the *triade classique*, even there in the rhyme of its octo-syllabic couplets, finding enchantment that moved her heart, as when Lavinia peers from her window to see the tent of Enèas:

El n'en pooit son oil torner;
bien tost, s'ele poist voler,
fust ele o lui el paveillon;
ne pooit panser s'a lui non.

Oh, those words — *ne pooit panser s'a lui non* — "she could think of nothing but him."

Him. Yes, someday, there would, for her, as for the damoiselles of the tales, be him. She did lie abed with forearms crossed upon her, as were portrayed the dead, knightly and saintly, in effigy; but her hands lay upon her breasts, feeling all of life therein, as with eyes closed she did see knights most handsome before her, returned from quest, one and then another, upon the knee of fealty, bearing a sole and perfect rose.

"'*Amors l'a de son dart ferue*,'" she would whisper as she did lie, as if in narration of what was so blithely and dreamily foreseen; "'*desi qu' el cue soz la memelle*'"; and her fingers did move as if to explore the piercing of love's arrow; and with a sigh did whisper on, as of herself: "'*Ele comance a tressüer, a refroidir et a tranbler*.'"

And then those words of her fair maid in the soft light of dawn, the very *alba* of which troubadour and trobairitze did sing: "*Thou hast blossomed, my dear, and thou art child no more.*"

Yes, she did miracle in this most truly. *Blossomed.* Like the rose of the romance, like the rose of courtly offrance; she herself had blossomed and now was to enter that realm, in breath and in flesh, of *fin' amors*.

"Am I now a lady of the court?"

"Thou soon shall be."

"And wilt thou stay beside me, that we might together choose among those knights and princes who do call?"

The maid took young Gemma's hands within the solacing, soft grasp of her own, and she did smile, solacing and soft, as her eyes sweetly quieted the dance of visioning of Gemma's own.

"Thou art betrothed," said she.

Gemma's heart, upon these words, did race in dire of distress, and her world was of a sudden black and bleak, as a dream overtaken and borne away in terror by the awful mares of night.

"This can not be."

"Thou shalt be most happy, dear Gemma, wait and see."

At this, tears welled in Gemma's eyes, and she commenced to sweat, to turn chill, and to tremble. The maid drew her close and fast, and the welling tears then flowed in torrence.

In time the tears did cease, as all tears in time so do. The maid raised Gemma's chin easily, so that she might see the smile of well-being that the maid did bear.

"I should be so fortunate as thee," said the maid. "But I have found my happiness through thine, and I now shall find my further happiness through thine."

"It is thee who hast brought me happiness: mother more than she who bore me, dearest elder sister more than maid, and closest friend."

The goodly maid wiped the runnelled last of tears from Gemma's cheeks with the hem of her gown, and stood her straight most lovingly before her.

"Is he a knight?"

"Oh, yes, a warrior most brave in battle shall he be. But so much more in his nobility, with destiny and lofty as the stars, and beside him in his glory shall be thee."

"Shall he bear me a rose?"

"Of that and more you may be assured." The maid leaned forward in her chair, and did speak secretly into the sweet pale pink of Gemma's ear, in the guarded manner that grown ladies share. "He doth write verse."

The girl's eyes welled anew: with felicity.

"To speak truly," said the maid, "we both as women from childhood grown do know that life is not a fable brought to rhyme."

Gemma did nod with subduction such as a wordly lady might so do.

"But I do say," continued the maid, "that what lies before thee may portend what of fable and of rhyme is ceded by this world, which turns dreams and us alike to dust."

There was silence then, as the light of day increased. It seemed that there might never be another silence quite like this for them to share, and they were in the lull most tender of its stillness. After good while, that lull, which had been felt as a presence, did leave the air; and yet they stayed in silence. Gemma did not so much speak, it seemed to her, but rather heard herself speak, so strange in coming were her words.

"Who is he?"

"He is the young master of high-born line of the Alighieri; by Christian name, Durante."

Her maid sensed that she seemed a bit fallen of crest.

"What is it, my dear?"

"I have seen him at the May Day, and else-wheres."

"Yes?"

"He is quite timid."

Her maid did lark. "Stand before the mirror, darling one, and see thyself. Still water, as is said, runs deep."

"And he looks not too unlike a bird."

"Come now, let's not be churlish. The word is *aquilino*: very much unlike a bird, and quite like unto an eagle, with the profile of striking prowess of an emperor of old. Would thou prefer one who is handsome in the dainty way that ladies be? Come now" — the maid tickled lightly Gemma's ribs — "thou must admit that he is as commands the glance."

"Yes. *Aqualine*. That is very kindly put indeed."

The tickling of light fingers and the playful light laughter of Gemma dwindled to calm which brought, ever so faintly, an after-lull of the stillness of moments before.

"Shall I love him?"

"As he shall love thee, dear Gemma, as he shall love thee."

The maid's kiss upon her forehead was warm and without sound.

GIULIETTA AND I GAMBLE AND DRINK some good white wine. God, how I love this woman.

To look into her eyes and see her smile is to feel all the love that has ever flowed from me be returned to me in luscious waves.

The gods have brought us together, and we have been blest.

If anyone ever hurt this woman, I would kill.

Up in the room, we make love like leopards.

I love to sleep with her, feeling her hold me, feeling the warmth and luxurious comfort of the soul with whom I was meant to share the stars.

I am the most fortunate man I know. I see men and women who detest each other; men and women who, after twenty years or so, sit together at tables unable to look into each other's eyes. Men and women who together have fallen into a deeper loneliness than ever they might have known alone.

And when I am with Giulietta, death is a dream and I want only to live. And we are both free, like leopards, who bring each other the gift of breath as vast and sweet as breath can be.

It was on a day in May, some years ago, in Cyprus, at Petra Tou Romiou, where the goddess Aphrodite had first stepped forth from the sea, that I cast my seed into that stormy sea, then placed a golden wedding band on my finger and threw a second golden wedding band as far as I could out into the surging waves, and with much prayer did marry her, Aphrodite, and I did open my mouth and nostrils to her sigh: she who, as Panthea, had said, "I am all that has ever been, and is, and shall be, and my robe has never yet been uncovered by mortal man." Then, not far from there, in the ruins of ancient Palaipafos, as the dark afternoon deepened to night, I stole my way to the sacred black sanctuary stone that is believed to be the oldest of venerated objects: the nameless worshipped thing that preceded the birth of Panthea — Isis, Aphrodite — she of many names; the nameless worshipped thing of the all that has ever been.

I kissed it and, with my eyes closed in prayer, I pressed my naked cock to its cold eternal power: "the great cunt of existence," in the words of Samuel Beckett.

Never had any wedding been so heartfelt or so pure.

It was then, days later in another land, that I met Giulietta, looking at her and seeing the goddess that I had wed.

THE SHOP OF THE MAP-MAKER IGNAZIO occupied two stanzas of the three that comprised the narrow but imposingly mitred construction that seemed to serve as a jamb of fortifying stone that prevented from caving in upon one the other the more antique palazzi that flanked it. The third stanza, as the poet discovered, belonged to the map-maker as well, being the quarters where he made his home. Engraved in the lintel of marble slab over the portal, which fronted its own docking post and canal steps of rough-hewn stone, was the name of the proprietor, in the olden Roman way.

The map-maker had about him a most exalted air, in fine gown of exotic looming, and with the silvern hair of locks, beard, and moustaches most carefully groomed and tonsured. Upon presentation of the letter of beknownst bearing signature and seal of the poet's friend and patron, the map-maker did bow his well-kept head most properly and perfunctorily. He then properly and perfunctorily excused himself, whereupon he did ascend to the corbelled gallery above, there to speak harshly to an apprentice at labor, saying, "Again thou hast rendered the strait awrong. The promontories of east and west are not at all so parallel as thou persist in making them. The western promontory must be set aright, to lie somewhat more south, so that both promontories extend equally, but the eastern north of the western. I shall not have to tell thee again, for thou shalt not be so slovenly again, shalt thou? Very well, then. Scrape away thy wrongfulness and render anew, as should be."

The walls about the poet were latticed with deep cubicles, in each of which rested a single loosely furled map, or several loosely furled maps together, protruding at great variance from their respective cubicles, and varying too in hue, from grays and tawny pales of parchment to whites dull and bright of paper.

"And so," the map-maker said, properly and perfunctorily, returned to the poet's presence. Then, as he had seen the poet gazing at the walls around him, he made a grandiose spanning the spread of his arm, saying, "There thou hast it, in fine and in broad, from the canals and hidden-most crannied crooked passways of this city to the farthers and remotest of lands: the world, its each and every part, laid with art and exactitude to chart. And there, on that table, its colors still wet, the most exacting and finely wrought new mappemundi of Marino Sanudo that ever shalt thou see."

The poet spoke nothing, but gave forth in countenance alone acknowledgment of the map-maker's words; and thus the latter flourished on: "And upon not a one wilt thou encounter the fantastical creatures that adorn the Polo book or other such nonsense as one might meet in the baubles of fantasy that are called maps, and so demean both science and craft thereof, drawn with lying pen to illustrate the tales of Polo and like ilk. Hast thou seen the Polo book?" The poet affirmed that he had, again responding with countenance alone; and he affirmed in truth, for he had browsed one of the several copies of the Polo book that hung chained in the Rialto, and had let it fall to hang again, so dull and ill-writ did he find it. "I do swear," the map-maker furthered, "that no less than three copies of the Polo book have I examined, and of the three not one was like another, and each was as could have been scriven by an adolescent of little schooling and an active if somewhat uncaptivating imagination, without having ever wandered farther than the contents of his chamber-pot could be hurled. On some occasions have I formally invited the Polos to convene with me at their convenience and my hospitality. I have had not so much as the civility of a response. And why? Because they do indeed fear me, for I know that none of the Polos did ever so much as see Cathay from afar, and furthermore do I know that to draw a map of their travels, as described in any and all of the three copies of their book that I examined, would be to trace a route that defies all physical possibility and natural law. What I do not comprehend is why Marco and his cohort, in their fraud, did not make use of accounts such as already lay at hand, for these are the works which serve and honor the charter's craft with veracity and worth. The Polos are but niggardly merchants, no more given to truth in their tale than in their bargainings. It does irk me that Marco Polo's awkward fraud has gained such common currency and popularity. Would that he were to be brought to account; he and all those whose fablings are such affrontery to myself and others, to the name of whose profession they have attached."

The poet entered as with a ready sword the sliver of silence afforded him by the map-maker's necessity of drawn breath.

It was then that the poet removed from his leathern sack the book of lock and clasp and of the three unto the three unto the three. The map-maker watched attentively, his sinistral brow arched as he delicately stroked the delicacy of his beard. Then the book lay open on the long broad tavola that accommodated the unfurling of maps and the exchange of coins. The map-maker was quite as taken with the pearl-like under-glow and the thickness of the vellum as had been and was the poet, and he did inquire of the poet as to its kind and its maker, to which inquiries the poet could but say that he regretted not to know.

"As master of thine art and science," spoke the poet, "does this sign reveal to thee a place?"

"It places us, of course, in the Trinacria: la Sicilia."

"Yes. Very well, then. But I know it to signify a place of three within a place of three within the place of the three that is, as thou rightly sayest, the Trinacria."

"I have no Arabic. What meaning bear these characters above the sign?"

"'Here I dwell,' say they, 'at the three that is of the three that is of the three.' Thus we have it, though most enigmatically, in word and image as well."

The map-maker pondered the sign a moment more, shook his well-kept head, and fetched the map he sought from among the many compartments of the wall to his left. He spread it and weighted it upon the tavola, then stood straight, and peered down at the map.

"There lies the Trinacria," said he. He waved his hand over the map, shaking his well-kept head once again.

"There is no place whereof countless points of demarcation can not be configured into countless triangulations. As for any prominent triangular form or gathering of three points, I see none. Dost thou?"

The poet looked, and the poet looked, and the poet saw none.

The map-maker peered again at the sign in the book of lock and clasp. "Hast thou noted that these triangles are wed so as to form the Pentagram of sorcerers?" He stepped back, as if the book did possess an evil. "I dare say this sign may be more of the Satanic demesne than of the geography of land and sea. I should take this to an Arab who knows as much of the black arts as la Sicilia's black heart."

The poet closed and locked the book, and replaced it in his leathern sack.

He was beneath the marble lintel, making to close the door behind him, and to step forth into a faint and misty rain.

"Wait!" called the map-maker. The poet turned, and the map-maker spoke again, more quietly. "I have found it. The triangle within the Trinacria. I have found it. It lay plain as day afore us on this *portolano*, but we did not see it in the blindered vision of our more intense and enigmatic searching." The poet's eyes came down as one with the finger of the map-maker upon three specks that lay in trinity in the sea near one of the eastern points of the Trinacria.

"These islands are little known, even to the Genoese who bring north the riches of tuna from their seasonal currents."

The poet beheld the three specks as if they were three sapphiring stars in the heavens.

"As to the three within this three, I feel that the answer lies, like the place itself, within this three." The poet looked into the map-maker's eyes.

"Thou might inquire of the Genoese who sail these dark seas," spoke the map-maker; "though that which I spoke I do not recant, for it was no Genoese seaman who devised this sign."

"No," said the poet, "I should think not."

BACK IN PARIS, I TAKE MY BLACK VALISE to the Bibliothèque Nationale.

It is here, in the old Cabinet des Manuscrits on Rue de Richelieu, that I meet with the director of the Reserve des Livres Rares and the *conservateur* of the Département des Manuscrits Occidentaux.

The one rubs his hands together briskly, raises his brows, and smiles.

"Now, François," he says to his companion, "we have the rare privilege of diagnosing the true nature and extent of our esteemed friend's madness."

"Perhaps," I say. "Then again, perhaps not."

"Yes," says the other. "We French excel at diagnosis. Did you know that the Académie Française once pronounced the judgment that 'France has many drunkards but, happily, no alcoholics'?"

So there we are: François, Antoine, me, my black valise.

Though, outside of the Vatican, nothing compares with Manuscript Number 313 of the Palatino collection of the Biblioteca Nazionale di Firenze — the old and beautiful illuminated *Commedia* that has been dated to the 1330s — other great libraries have their unique Dante treasures as well: the British Library's so-called Egerton manuscript, the Bibliothèque Nationale's own manuscript from the old Arsenal collection. Both of these magnificent illuminated works date to no later than ten or so years after the Palatino manuscript, but the Egerton manuscript is believed to be the older of the two.

I ask if the Bibliothèque Nationale would give its Arsenal manuscript in exchange for the Egerton manuscript, if such an opportunity were possible.

"But of course not."

Many drunkards, no alcoholics.

I lay the documentation before them.

They examine the copies of the parchment pages. Filled with the evidence of the labor of composition. I watch their eyes, which reveal a growing stunned awareness that these can not be the pages of a copyist, or the pages of a forger, for no forger would have produced a false original simultaneously with the author's true original, especially as the author's original would have been highly identifiable and, above all, at the time, absolutely worthless.

They are without words.

"What would you pay for such a thing, the *manu propria* of the *Commedia* — all of it — in Dante's own hand?"

Their words come forth as from a haze. The Bibliothèque Nationale never offers price evaluations. The seller sets his price, and the library makes its decision.

I nod slowly and say nothing.

One of them speaks, saying only, "Something like this . . . something like this . . ."

The other speaks. "Such a thing would be claimed by Italy. Such a thing would be claimed as part of the Italian patrimony. Such a thing *should* belong to Italy."

I recall the big illuminated *Commedia* in the Vatican, written in a mid-fourteenth-century Gothic semi-cursive chancery script, gifted by Boccaccio to Petrarch with a long dedication in Latin verse, and annotated by Petrarch. The codex had been a part of the collection of the sixteenth-century nobleman Fulvio Orsini. But the book bore a notation penned and dated 1815: "*dalla Biblioteca pariginia*" — "from the Parisian Library" — and, beside the seal of the Vatican Library, there is the seal of the Bibliothèque Nationale.

Who the fuck knows what went on, or what goes on, between these people.

"And yet the Arsenal manuscript remains here," I say.

"But this . . . something like this . . ."

"There is nothing like this," I say. "There is only this."

"And what price do you put on it?"

I smile and bid them good day.

Back at the hotel, I call the best, most expert, and most trustworthy rare-book and manuscript dealer whom I know: David Hanker of Rarities in Savannah. It was from David that I got my copy of the first, 1576 edition of Dante's *Vita Nuova.* It was from David that I got my five-volume Zatta first edition of the complete works of Dante. It was from David that I had gotten a lot of rare and costly volumes: all of them now left behind; all of them now mourned for. I must figure out a way to get them back. Or, fuck it, to just get more. But what of Pound's own copy of *The Cantos*, which he had inscribed, in 1948, with the cryptic notation, "In one volume, missing the summary of the Ghibelline, part V, as in *De Monarchia*" — cryptic because no later edition of *The Cantos* was revised to include this "missing" summary; cryptic because Dante himself had never included any such summary in his *De Monarchia.* There was no getting another copy of that one.

I ask David what the original manuscript of the *Commedia* might be worth.

"Do you have such a thing?"

His voice is fraught with excitement.

"No," I tell him.

"Are you sure?"

"If I did have it, I don't think it would slip my memory. This is all theoretical. There exists not the slightest scrap of anything that Dante ever wrote in his own hand. You know that."

"I thought there were letters in the Vatican."

"No. You're talking about the so-called thirteen Epistles. They're purported to be copies of letters by Dante that show no evidence of ever having existed. Some people believe they're copies of real letters. Others seriously doubt it. Whatever: there's none that even pretends to be anything but a copy, or a copy of a copy. Believe me: there's nothing."

But he doesn't believe me. He doesn't want to believe me.

"I'm going to call someone in Italy, and I'll get right back to you."

"David."

"Yes."

"Whatever you do, please tell no one that you've spoken to me."

Now he really doesn't believe me.

I light a cigarette. Before I finish smoking it, the telephone rings. I raise the receiver but say nothing. It's David.

"Two to five million a page," he says, "depending on the contents of the page."

The arithmetic is easy. There are three hundred and nineteen pages. Two times three hundred is six hundred. Five times three hundred is fifteen hundred. Multiply each figure by a million. Six hundred million; a billion and a half. Split the difference, round it off: a good conservative average estimate. Let's call it a billion.

"Are there drawings? I always imagined there would be drawings."

"Keep imagining."

"Nick."

"Don't call me that any more."

"Damn," he says. His voice is suddenly calm. "You do have it."

"I'll call you."

"When?"

"Soon."

Avenue Matignon, between the Champs Elysées and Rue de Faubourg St. Honoré.

Christie's. Chief international consultant, Rare Books and Manuscripts.

"The estimated value?" he says, repeating my words.

"Yes," I say, "the estimated value."

"Incalculable."

"Incalculable?"

"Incalculable. There's nothing to compare it with. Leonardo da Vinci. The Codex Hammer sale, 1994. A single notebook. Widely known, widely printed in facsimile. An Italian bank wanted it. Bill Gates outbid the bank. Christie's brought down the hammer at thirty million, eight hundred thousand, and change. With something such as this, that would be roughly the opening bid. It would be the most expensive manuscript ever sold. Nothing but the means of the people could limit its potential price. Even a fragment, just a fragment, might bear an estimated value of two million dollars."

I open my black valise, lay down the goods.

He examines the documents carefully.

"How, in the name of God, did you ever come to discover this?"

I shake my head forlornly.

"I represent a very, very private collector."

"Yes, of course. Property of a Gentleman."

"Precisely."

Back at the hotel again, I make more calls, following up on previous calls.

The New York Public Library. The New York Metropolitan Museum of Art. The Pierpont Morgan Library.

William Voelkle, the department head and curator of the Pierpont Morgan Library, speaks more eloquently than the others, but he seems to speak for them all.

"Our institution is extremely rich in its holdings, but not in its funds."

I call Bill Gates.

He does not take my call. He does not return my call.

Fuck Bill Gates.

The days pass, and each day grows more strange than the day before it.

Under various guises, I have dealt with perhaps two dozen institutions and individuals. Moving from hotel to hotel, I begin to receive calls from voices that I do not recall. These voices do not openly identify themselves or those they represent, but they all propose variations of a similar arrangement: part cash, part goods or services. Museums without money inquire about the favorite Renaissance artists of the anonymous gentleman whom I represent. Libraries allude to the number of rare books that unfortunately vanish with distressing regularity. It is difficult to tell if it is a person, an institution, or a nation that insinuates its access to many tons of purest heroin. I buy one of those caller-identification devices, and I begin to call back and hang up on the numbers that appear. A voice hints at an impending robbery of vast quantities of pharmaceutical opiates in Darmstadt, and when I call the source number of the hinting voice, a lady answers in German, telling me that I have reached Das Kulturelles Institut des Christen. Does my gentleman have a taste for young girls or young boys, or for delights of any kind? Are there any among the living whom he should like to relegate to the dead? Everything has its price, I am told, and the currency of that price can take all the forms of one's most secret imaginings.

Amid these eerie voices, I come upon small eerie notices in the press. A philanthropist is found murdered in his London town house. A night watchman is found killed at the Cloisters in New York. There seems to be a new outbreak of bloodshed in Palermo and the surrounding towns. A financier is kidnapped in Chicago while organizing the funding for a multinational endowment for the arts. A curator in Vienna to whom I have spoken has been missing for over a week. And now this thing: the rampaging and ransacking of the hotel of the drowned by a band of men reported to have been heard speaking in Italian.

I stop looking at newspapers. I move to yet another hotel, the Bas-Bréau, away from Paris, in the little country town of Barbizon.

Still, the glances of strangers unsettle me. Paranoia is not fear. Paranoia is an underlying semi-hallucinatory edginess.

It is not good to be dead and paranoid.

THE OLD JEW EXPRESSED HIS FELICITY that the poet now believed himself to have knowledge of the three that was of the three, and he agreed that this belief should seem to be corroborated by the fact that this three that was of the three was a trinity of isles, for the Arab, in having told of finding what he felt to be the fabled Ithaca, home of Odysseus, and in having told of making it his home as well, had perforce indicated an island, as such was fabled Ithaca.

"As I did say," spoke the elder, "thou art a one for threes."

"In few days' time, there is a merchant cog of Venetian flag that sails for Palermo on its way to the Arab lands. It is then that I will depart, to arrive in Palermo by the next new-born moon."

"Your journey will make an Arab of you, for the blazing, hellish heat of the Sicilian summer, which has brought men to death, will yet be in full dominion."

"If I find him —"

"You will find him," interposed the elder, most firm of tone.

The poet looked into his eyes, then finished his say: "is there any message that I might convey?"

The elder stood, slowly and with some difficulty. He stepped idly about, as one lost within the confines of four walls, then he stood before the window, gazing out for a time long in passing. It was thus, with his back to the poet, that at last he spoke.

"No."

The poet left the elder to his gazing for a good time more, then idly told of what the map-maker had said: that he who made the sign was more of the realm of Satan than of the geography of this world.

The elder's back remained to him, and only when he turned to regard the poet did he speak.

"'More'?"

Like the slow coming of an umbrous looming, it began to seem to the poet that his companion was not quite the same man who had greeted him at the door; indeed, that the presence at the window were but spectre of the elder he had known. He was somewhat unsettled, but did tell himself that he must be witnessing the descending effects of age most formidable. This reflection was lent palpable substance when he embraced the elder in farewell, and did feel to him more of skeletal fragility than of thews.

During this embrace, the elder did grasp the poet's shoulders and did say, "My name is Jacob."

The poet knew then that he would never see him again in this life.

I AM LYING HERE, AT THE BAS-BRÉAU, IN THIS private villa where Robert Louis Stevenson supposedly wrote something-or-other.

With their backs to me, two waiters, whom I know only to speak French, seem to exchange indistinct words in hushed Italian. I see that my hand trembles.

I must get out of here. I am dead, and yet I am unstill.

Then I remember.

Mephistopheles.

Years ago, I wrote a book called *Power on Earth*: a book about the shadowland realms of Michele Sindona, the infamous Sicilian financier who was believed to occupy the throne at the heart of the world's evil, the secret crossroads where the three beasts of international finance, the Mafia, and the Vatican came together. Sindona was the most remarkable and intriguing man I have ever known, and *Power on Earth* told perhaps the most remarkable and intriguing story that I ever told.

As published, the book was eviscerated for legal reasons. In fact, even in this eviscerated state, the scheduled publication of the British edition was outright cancelled.

Much of what Michele Sindona told me seemed outlandish, incredible, the rantings of an imprisoned man who knew that he would never draw a free breath again. He told me things about the Italian prime minister Giulio Andreotti that no one could or dared to believe at the time of the book's publication, in 1986. Then, seven years later, Andreotti was officially investigated for corruption and accused of protecting the Mafia. He was indicted in 1995, and his trial lasted four years.

Sindona gave me a course in the three effective systems of money-laundering, the most sophisticated of which involved acumen and stealth in the manipulation of currency-futures options. None of this was known to the President's Commission on Organized Crime, which was so naïve as to speak of money-hiding as money-laundering. Michele told me that James D. Harmon, Jr., the director of the President's Commission on Organized Crime, admitted to him that neither he nor his assistants knew anything about options on currencies or commodities, or about futures or forward contracts. It was not understood, Michele said, that in the course of true money-laundering, the money emerged as clean and legitimate and taxable income; and, to this day, the machinations of this system remain beyond the grasp of governments.

He told me of his dealings in the Middle East, and of Karl Hansch, also known as al-Hanesch, a little-known German Islamist who was in direct command of the most underground of terrorist operations and training camps. Hansch, the director in Tripoli of the intelligence arm of the East German Republic, was supported by forces drawn from the East German S.E.D., as well as from the military and police hierarchies of Libya, where he was closely associated with Muammar al-Qaddafi. The elusive German worked in unison with Markus "Mischa" Wolf, who, as the head of the H.V.A., the East German intelligence agency, was the only Jew to direct espionage operations for the East. As Wolf's confidant, Hansch implemented plans to multiply conflicts and increase terrorism throughout the Arab and Islamic regions.

Sindona seemed to believe that the end of civilization would come whence it had begun: Mesopotamia and the wastelands beyond. He saw Islam as blindly supplying countless young men willing to sacrifice themselves for what they perceived to be a holy cause, especially among those sects that beheld martyrdom as the gate to an ever-green garden of sacred, infinite orgasm. What they did not realize, said Sindona, was that the voice of Allah and the voices of Hansch and Wolf, the German and the Jew, were one; and that Mammon was the only god of those who sent these young men to their death.

Yes. Old Michele. He told me a lot before that March day when he either killed himself or, as they say in that fine Italian phrase, was suicided — *suicidato* — by cyanide-laced coffee in his prison cell. A few days after his death, I got a letter from him. A letter from the dead.

"You know me well enough," he said, "to know that I am not afraid to die. I believe in God and in eternal life, and I await the passage with serenity; and, therefore, any possible violent act against me does not worry me at all."

Yes. Old Michele. He told me many things. Many, many things.

Mephistopheles.

"That is what I call him," he said fondly. "He is young, maybe ten years older than you."

At the time, I was about thirty-five and Michele was about sixty-five.

Mephistopheles.

"He can do anything. What he did not know, I taught him. And he is like me: he plays alone."

Over the course of our prison meetings, Michele asked me on a few occasions to deliver brief cryptic messages to this man, and I delivered these messages.

And now I remember. All that time in Paris, and only now do I remember.

It is as if the spirit of dear dead Michele has come to guide me in my own serene passage.

SLOW, LUGUBRIOUS, WITH BOLD AND HEAVY clank, lode of iron link by lode of iron link, the anchor was raised; slow, lugubrious, the hulking vessel was hove; and slow, lugubrious, the ponderous weight of sail was hoisted; and with mighty groan of hull, the sails did billow with loud blast and deep rumbling creak of mast, as the Adriatic wind came carrying down.

The loaf of bread and the garland that had been cast to the sea in offrance by the *capitano* as he made the sign of the cross in stance at the prow passed and were gone in the churning froth of starboard, where the poet stood, his weight against the bow-rail, staring into that very froth, so that the tangle of blossoms seemed to rise suddenly towards him, be drawn under, rise again, and then be gone.

He had been free from the bile of thought, and had been of breath alone as he stared into the froth: breath of fear, breath of fearlessness, breath of mystery, breath of power, breath of all skies commingled, as he felt himself moving towards the unknown, moving towards it simply because it was the unknown; and the froth into which he stared was the hypnotic surge and spray of this moving, which grew more hypnotic with, and deepened, every breath of fear, every breath of fearlessness, every breath of mystery, every breath of power, every breath of skies commingled, until the deep of sea and the deep of breath and the deep of the unknown were as one.

But the tangled, tossing petals took that from him: and the sight that lay not in his eyes, the sight that had been of froth and of nothing and of the shades of the unknown, saw himself once again placing flowers on the grave of his mother, flowers on the grave of his father, and saw himself bearing that one lovely rose in his young awkward hand.

"It will buy you more than gold of your young wife's heart and devotion," the girl's maid had implored him in secret; and he had complied, even unto presenting it to her upon one knee and with bowed head.

Her heart. Her devotion. As if he had cared thereof. And yet that rose of genuflection had meant much, for in placing it in her hand, he had placed it as well on the grave of the dreams of his young heart.

He had been but eleven years of age when the *istrumento dotale* of his betrothal had been drawn, drafted, and executed by his father and by hers. Three springs had by then passed since his first encounter with the girl Bice Portinari, whose name his heart and pen would poetick as Beatrice. He could still, even now, staring into the froth, recall the color of her raiment on that spring day forty-five years past and more: it was the color of rose most crimson, like the rose that he would lay on the grave of his young heart's dreaming.

He was not yet nine years old, and the Portinari girl had entered only recently into the blush of eight years full. He recalled what he had written in the volume that had come to be known as *La Vita Nuova*:

"The moment I saw her I say in all truth that the vital spirit, which dwells in the inmost depths of the heart, began to tremble so violently that I felt the vibration alarmingly in all my pulses, even the weakest of them. As it trembled, it uttered these words: *Ecce deus fortior me, qui veniens dominabitur mihi.*"

As he recalled these words, which he had writ a good many years after the long-ago spring encounter that was their source, or that was set forward as their source, he marvelled at the lie of them. What eight-year-old boy would "tremble so violently," whether from love or from lust? What eight-year-old boy's spirit, in this ludicrous trembling, would so spontaneously letter, in perfectly composed and meticulously metred Latin: "Behold a god more powerful than I, who comes to rule over me"? Indeed it now struck him that the young man who had placed these words within the child of eight was mining allegory of the lessest ore. This precious annunciation of Love as "*deus fortior me*" was but trite exercise after the mannerism of Sindonius. As he had written this, so but a few lines later he had written: "Though her image, which was always present in my mind, invited Love to dominate me, its influence was so noble that it never allowed Love to guide me without the faithful counsel of reason." If the former was an embarrassment both as a counterfeit of false date and as an imposture born not of any spirit within but rather of a birth-weary paradigm of rhetoric — and, now that he came to ponder it, an embarrassment entire; for, muttering the grandiose preciosity of "*deus fortior me*," it did occur to him that this mis-begat arrogance of Trifle did beg the question of what god, being a god, could not be stronger than he? — so this latter was cut wholesale from the drab cloth of the philosophic propia of the day.

Trembled so violently indeed: like a desiccated twig of academic diligence.

He had not seen her again for nine years after that first encounter; and yet he would have had it to be believed that through those long years her vision remained the ruling heavens of his heart and soul and being, so beatific was she and so great was that god who was so distinguished as to be stronger than an eight-year-old boy.

It was in the sixth of those nine years that he began to circulate sonnets of his composition among verse-makers of renown, to curry their recognition and their favor. He was but a stripling, a boy of fifteen years, who knew but to compose in the manner of his elders' renown, which was called *stil nuovo.* It was the poetry of courtly love, and of the divinity of love, given voice and rhyme not in Latin but in the inchoate and vulgar tongue. It was the Bolognese poet Guido Guinizelli who first made beauty in the *lingua volgare* from the poetry of like kind come down to him from the courts of Provence, in the langue d'oc, and, therefrom, in the lingua del si, the courts of Sicilia; and it was he from whom the *stilnovisti* of Firenze took their first breath. "*Al cor gentil repara sempre Amore,*" had sung Guido of Bologna: "Love seeks always the gentle heart."

He whispered the words into the froth of the sea and windward unknowing. How lovely were those words: eternally so; a comforting, a salvation unto themselves.

Yes, the sixth of those nine years. It was in this year too that he rechristened the Portinari girl as Beatrice — She Who Blesses — so that she might better befit the designs of his verse and the sublimities of the *stilnovisti* whose rank he sought to enter, and into which he did so enter, through the embrace of the greatest of the

Florentine *stilnovisti*, Guido Cavalcanti. It was Cavalcanti who had brought the poetry of love from the sweet air of the courts to the orbis profanus of the city streets. It was Cavalcanti, some fifteen years his senior, who beheld Love as a god of damnation as much as of blessing. He believed neither in Heaven nor in Hell, and he lived this life fiercely; and the younger poet, for all that would transpire, could but call him *il miglior fabbro*. Unto the froth did he whisper again: the words of he who had been his closest friend, he was the better maker, he whom he had sent to his damnation and end.

It was in the spring of the ninth year, the spring that he saw the Portinari girl again, the spring that he turned eighteen. By law of sovereign Firenze he was now a man, and, under law as well, he entered into manhood as an orphan, for his father by this time had gone to earth.

And thus it was as man that he did kneel on one knee with one rose held forth. And thus it was that as fore-ordained, he and Gemma Donati were duly wed.

His marriage did not stay him from his continued pursuit of the Portinari girl, nor did the marriage of the Portinari girl herself, to the banker Simone dei Badi; and his exaltation of her in verse increased rather than lessened. Not even the birth of his son could stay him from the unseemly folly of roving the streets in the hope of a glimpse of her, the unseemly folly of writing of tears copiously shed for unrequited love of her.

The passing of years was the passing of froth; and the meaning and truth of those years, as effervescent and impossible to glean as the spray of that froth, which appeared and vanished at once, in self-same infinitessum.

As he had begun the book that was known as *La Vita Nuova* with the portrait of himself violently atremble with love at the age of eight, so he had ended it with the recounting of his decision, at the age of twenty-eight, to write no further of Beatrice until such time as his power of poetry enabled him to do so "more worthily."

A span of twenty years, he reflected, looking into froth and spray, which now began to turn ghostly as both sea and sky darkened. In that span his father had died, orphaning him, and he had married, and a son to him had been born. Yet nowhere in the book of this span, neither in verse nor in prose, was there merest allusion to any of this. The death of a lady friend of Beatrice was given much occasion; and the untimely death of Beatrice herself was treated with the gravity, importance, and majesty of the Assumption itself, as he did raise her to Heaven to behold the face of God.

Had nothing of that vital spirit in the inmost depths of the lake of the heart been stirred by the death of he whose blood ran in his veins, or by his fated marriage to another, or by the new life of a son in whose veins his own blood did run?

The passion with which he hated his father — why could not he have bartered him in marriage to the Portinari girl? Why, after the death of the poet's mother, had he taken such a wretch as second wife to himself and cruel stepmother to his offspring — this passion was real and no conceit. Likewise the coldness with which he came to his marriage, simply but deeply in obstinate resentment that it was his father's machinations that had rendered the fate of his manhood thus. This coldness was that of innermost Hell itself. And what of his own flesh and blood, miracled unto him by his own cold seed? Was not this purest and most wondrous and most innocent of God's dearest blessings, a child newborn in swaddling, worth even a passing glance of emotion amid the profusion of cascading love that issued forth from him for a coquette in the street who would have nothing of him? His son was in his ninth year when *Vita Nuova* was circulated — did his aging father care only for the inner spirit of his own nine-year-old heart? And why, in his beatification of Bice in death, did he not mention that she had died in the embrace of a common usurer?

To the latter question he could answer honestly, unto himself, with ready truth: no mention of the Portinari girl's marriage was made because it did not fit the design or the conceit. To the other, more perplexing questions, he had blithe answers at hand: that these matters lay outside the domain of the book, or that these matters lay outside the realm of poetical decorum. These were of course lies that lay at hand. The truth perplexed even him, for not even in secret had he ever expressed it, in verse or in prose or in spoken confrontation.

Could it be, he now wondered, lost in the froth that now roared, that he had been incapable of making verse of, or living with, what truly was close to him, what truly was of him and of his life? In a fulgent flash within the froth, words came forth to him. These words too were from the book that had come to be known as *La Vita Nuova*, in a passage in which he contrived the Lord of Love to speak to him: "*Fili mi, tempus est ut pretermictantur simulacra nostra.*"

What had been the source of this wisdom, which stood alone in enigmatic gust contrary to all else of the book? It had come from him, but from which sky?

It was this wisdom, he now believed, that had led him to the pure, wild beauty and power of the *Commedia*'s beginning and end.

If only he had left the Portinari girl to rot in peace beneath the stone that bore her rightful name. And yet, against all wisdom, he had continued to be beguiled by her, the one simulacrum he could not cast away.

Her fair maid had been right. He had indeed come forth with perfect rose in chivalry. And he had indeed been in battle a warrior most brave, armed and armored and without fear, riding with the Florentine militia in support of the Tuscan Guelfs against the Castle of Poggio di Santa Cecilia, then riding to war against the Ghibellines of Arezzo in the Battle of Campaldino, then riding yet again to the siege of Caprona. And he had indeed risen to a destiny most lofty, becoming one of the six men of the Priory, the ruling body of the government of Firenze. And above all, the fair maid had been right in foretelling that Gemma would love him as he would love her: for to what palest simulacrum of love his neglect did bear, her pained heart, after much sweet and fruitless labor to draw love from him, could but respond in kind. The chill barrens within him dealt knell to her pained heart on the morning that she first gave birth, and the midwife did present the babe to him, and he, beholding it austerely, did not take it in his arms. And thus it was as well with the sons and daughter that followed. It was these children, and the good maid of her youth, whom she did visit, that brought her what comfort of heart she knew.

And throughout, for her and their eldest son and all of Firenze to read and hear in rhyme aloud, his grand fool's show a gushing love and adoration of the Portinari girl. And in death did the girl serve his fool's show all the more, winched aloft as if by canvas corset at a tawdry passion play. Never would she forget the first anniversary of the girl's decease. Having asked his fellow *stilnovisti* to call upon him on that day, he did then sit for them in pathetic exhibition, striking the pose of one beyond the reach of this world, responding not to the presence of his gulled fellows, except to sit in his pose, pen in hand and paper before him, drawing childlike pictures of angels, such as she herself may have drawn as a littlest girl. Only Cavalcanti had the boldness to dismiss this face with mockery, saying, "Imagine one who summons an audience to view him lose his mind. Would that we were all so prescient, but not so inconsiderate in our prescience." And, with those words, and a warm adieu to Gemma, he did depart, leaving Gemma to glance with distaste upon her husband's continuing and increasingly loathsome performance, and to feel, as she watched her five-year-old son stride quietly about, that the boy seemed more a man than his father.

I' vengo l' giorno a te . . .

It was Cavalcanti who so brought down truth upon her husband in this sonnet: dear Cavalcanti, delicate as a butterfly lighting on a flower, brutal as a hammer of great iron wielded in wrath upon rock, poet so true as to dare set force before form —

Di vil matera mi conven parlare
perder rime, silabe, e sonnetto

— dear beautiful Guido. He was, she believed, the closest to friend that her husband knew. But her husband, she felt, had feared Guido while admiring him, and envied him while praising him: feared his honesty, envied him his majesty, of poetry, with which he did breathe sonnet and ballad of rose and of thorn.

Those were the years of the Whites and the Blacks, the two factions into which the ruling Guelfs had split. The Whites were allied to the Ghibelline parties of Verona, Pisa, and the Romagna; the Blacks, to the empiring papacy of Boniface VIII. The Blacks of Firenze were led by the self-styled patrician Corso Donati. Guido, a dire enemy of Donati, thus found himself with the Whites. During the May Day festivities of that year in which Gemma's husband was to set the *Commedia*, armed conflict erupted between the leading Black and White families and their supporters. Gemma's husband and his fellow priors decreed the exile of the leaders of both factions of the conflict. Dante's best friend, Guido, was banished to Saranza by Dante and his fellow priors.

This, for Gemma, was the chillingest wind that had issued

from the chill barrens within him since that morning, some thirteen years before, when she did bear him son. She could not but feel that in banishing his best friend, he who had embraced him and loved him and raised him to prominence among the *stilnovisti*, her husband was banishing the source of his fear and his envy; could not but feel that in banishing from Firenze he who was Firenze's greatest poet, he himself would thereby usurp those laurels.

As Guido's bold voice of honesty and love had now been deposed from the chill barrens of her husband's being, she herself, as if inspired by the angry wail of Guido's fate, was so bold as to speak forth, asking him how, under God, he could doom his friend thus. He had looked at her first and fast in anger, then his look became of that austerity with which he had beheld his firstborn son.

"There are six priori," said he sternly, "of which I am but one. Would you have had me to stand in defiance of the others?"

"Yes," she exclaimed, "by all that is right and all that is good. Yes."

At this he did angrily wave her away and looked away as well. But she, unstayed, did speak again.

"And what of your great powers of rhetoric and oratory, you who are so brazen as to speak for gods, and to assume to move the world with couplets of caritas and love? Could they be not so great as to move your few fellows to compassion for one so supreme of poetry and so innocent of politics?"

Not even with threatening glance did he so much as acknowledge the sound of her voice.

In Guido's verse, love often brought an inner death. "*Amor aparve a me in figuro morta*," he once had said. And as Gemma saw it, his love for her husband did in truth bring death. For the curse of Guido's exile was not long. Removed to Saranza, the diseased air of that place did soon enter him, and this malaria filled him. In the heat of the August of that year, as he lay dying, he was brought back to Firenze, to breathe his last and to be laid beneath the earth.

How could he confront the gaze of Guido's widow, whose name, like that of his own wraith, was Bice? How could he confront the gaze of Guido's son, Andrea? How could he confront the gaze of himself within the polished mirror?

Far from expressing remorse, her husband, when he later set about populating the Hell of his *Inferno*, did darken and befoul the great poet further in death.

Little more than a year after Guido's death, Gemma's husband was sent to Boniface VIII in Rome as one of the three ambassadors of the ruling White Guelfs of Firenze. Some months later, during this absence of him and his fellow ambassadors, a great storm of thunder and hail did strike Firenze with force; and Gemma did enjoy to see it as the celebration of revenge of Guido's spirit from on high: for, in the absence of the ambassadors, this thunder and hail did follow most hastily upon a storm of a different sort, as the Blacks did seize power from the Whites. It was in March of the new year that the poet, returned from Rome, was sentenced to death.

Fili mi, tempus est ut pretermictantur simulacra nostra.

Yes, he wondered again, whence had come this wisdom, which stood alone in enigmatic gust contrary to all else of that book that came to be known as *La Vita Nuova*? Had it indeed come from him, under sky unknown? In his further wondering, he now for certain did not know. Then, within him, the words sounded, more deeply and profoundly, in the voice of another. Could it be that he whose voice sounded and the source of this wisdom were one?

Could it be that this gust had come forth as counsel from Cavalcanti in those long-past years?

No, these words did not have the cast of Cavalcanti to them. But it was true that the voice that now brought them to him, both within him and in the thunder of the froth and waves, did seem to be, as he did well remember it, the voice of Cavalcanti.

Dear, dead Cavalcanti. He had done all he could to alter the course of exile that his fellow priors ordained; he summoned the full of his eloquence of persuasion, saying that the voice of Cavalcanti was a treasure that Firenze must not relinquish, and that the flaring of his temperament was but an errant spark of the fine and sacred fire of divine poetry that burned in him, illuminating and bringing glory to Firenze, and was neither of White nor the Black, nor of Ghibelline nor of Guelf, but of the true heart of Firenze, which beat beneath the wracked breast of these torn and troubled times.

He had all but prostrated himself. And he should have done this as well. For had he not already done so, for all to see, before the ludicrous figure of his Beatrice, in that *beffa* of pretense which now endured as a stain irremovable of his youthful folly? Was not the blood of friendship of greater value than the honeyed wine of verse?

The terrible words of Guido's last *ballate mezzane* were forever scorched as if with white-hot brand upon the soul.

La forte e nova mia disaventura
m'ha desfatto nel core
ogni dolce penser, ch'i' aveva, d'amore.

Thus the first had begun, and had closed, after some lines, with a glance at what remained of him, which was such:

che, qual mira de fòre,
vede la Morte sotto al meo colore.

And then the second, which did begin,

Perch'i' no spero di tornar giammai,
ballatetta, in Toscana

and which did go on,

Tu senti, ballatetta, che la morte
mi stringe sì, che vita m'abbandona

It was then, with renewed eloquence, and fore-flowering of eulogy, and wielding the leaves of these ballate as soft-spoke axe and mace, that he did prevail on his fellow priors in allowing Cavalcanti to be returned in extremis to Firenze, so that his last breath might be Fiorentine breath, and so that, through this beneficence, the great treasure of his spirit would be restored to Firenze. And while Guido did draw the last of breath, the younger poet did bathe the dying man's feet with oil of rosemary and of aloes.

But should truth be told — which it now was, silently and in stillness, unto his confessor, the turbulent froth of sea that did bear away the moments and years and deeds of his life, and all the dark sediments of his soul — he had laved Cavalcanti's feet not in the purity of Christian caritas, but in guilt. And as he so did, all the while did he hope that the expiring poet might sense that it was the younger poet's hands upon him, and that the dying might then grant absolution to the living.

God, how he had crueled all who had tried to love him: friends and wife and children all. If there had been beauty and power in the words that issued from his masquerade as praise-singer of love, it was only because, beneath this masquerade, there had been one who truly did wish to love and be loved. But the strophes of the songs of love were so much easier to master than the soul-surrendering, will-relinquishing unmastering of the beatitude and beautiful beast of the thing itself in unrhymed truth of flesh and blood and soul. The beatitude and beast had wrenched the poetry from him at times, so as vision and secret heart and soul and sound and rhythm of word were as one, majestic. But his willfulness, the cold inside him, had been so girt as to allow beatitude and beast to so wrench life from his cowering and relentless control. It had been easier for him to ride to battle than to express his fear in so doing; easier for him to bare a carefully designed simulacrum of his soul to a phantom of like design than to lay open his soul in the least to one who was real and whose own soul and words were not authored by him. The chain-mail and plate he had worn in battle was as nothing to that which had hid his heart. Why had he been able to confront highest nobility and papal court, and yet been unable to behold or hold in comfort the slightest silent new-born babe? Because the former were as he, in fraud of self and with heart well-hid and armored, and the latter was pure and innocent of all guile, and to look upon this purity and innocence of guile was to be pierced by the dark cutting truth of his own corruption.

If it had been the sky of illimitableness that had brought God and beauty to him, it was perhaps none the less the sky of his illness that, these many years, had ruled him.

The wind now brought chill, and the violent sea was black, and the froth and spray were white in what meager light of crescent moon there was.

Yes, the Black and the White. All so long ago.

But why, ten years and more after standing in ablution of the great poet's feet, praying for his absolution, had he been so possessed as to denounce him in the *terza rima* of his Hell? In life the two men had favored divergent interpretations of Aristotle. It was to the exegeses of Thomas of Aquinas, who all but made Christian of the ancient philosophy, that the young poet hewed, while the elder found much wisdom in the view of Aristotle's philosophy as explicated by the Islamic sage of name of Averroës, who believed that life was the sum of the soul's journey. Thus, as the young poet did live most *contra naturam et contra Deum* in his artifice, and as the elder poet did live most righteously in awareness of the gift of life and the fulfillment that lies in the striving towards perfection of one's nature, so the younger, in that he professed belief in afterlife, saw himself to be most holy, and did see the elder, who believed in life alone, to be among the damned. But why, why, why had he chosen by name as an exemplar of atheism one who had loved him, one whose respect, embrace, blessing, advice, and finally absolution he had sought, rather than any of an hundred others? Was this but another, perverse attempt to assuage his guilt, or, worse, another instance of his mean belittling through anathema of those whom he felt to be his betters? And why was there no place in his Hell for those who would deny freedom to all in their searches for wisdom?

Yes, the discovery of truth in the wisdom of the infidel Averroës had been enough to damn one to the Hell of his device. And, yes, he reflected on this. As he sailed, in the blackness of fallen night, to a mysterious Arab, at the behest of a heathen Jew.

In his cramped and creaking quarters that night, he did descend to his knees until words of prayer came.

IT IS A GREAT OFFICE, SO SPACIOUS AS TO occupy the better part of the building's fourth and highest floor, dressed with a subdued wealth of Louis Quatorze furnishings, which seem to welcome one to their comfort rather than to ward off one's touch, as precious antiques most often do. Like their genteel proprietor, they exude strength rather than delicacy.

We stand together at the Palladian window. The gathers of the heavy wine-dark brocade curtains are shirred by thick tasselled cords of golden silken thread.

The color and texture of the brocade are seductive. I touch their sensuousness very softly, as I would the lips of a woman whom I never before have touched, or the lips of one with whom I long have been intimate but forever might caress as if for the very first time.

"Οἴνοψ," he whispers, as if reading my mind. It is the form of the beautiful epithet — *wine-dark* — as first come forth from Homer.

Then, prosing Homer's lines, he slowly recites the passage of that first occurrence, from the twenty-third scroll of the *Iliad*:

"'By cunning, thou knowest, is a woodman far better than by might; by cunning too doth a helmsman on the wine-dark deep guide aright a swift ship that is buffeted by winds; and by cunning doth charioteer prove better than charioteer.'"

He smiles vaguely.

"Cunning," he says. "Cunning."

He looks down through the window across the small, occult Place St-Thomas-D'Acquin to the small building near the big church. My eyes follow his.

"Many who have lived here all their lives do not know that it is the secret office of the French secret service," he says of the small building of plain façade on which we gaze.

He turns away.

"I know more about them than they know about me."

He sits on a couch and gestures for me to sit on the couch across from him.

"So," he says. "When did you die?"

"A few days before Dante, you might say."

"You are the second such victim of that unfortunate incident that has come to me in as many days."

Never have I known a man to cogitate with such rapidity, perception, and elegant calculus of psyche.

"There were also two who came to me seeking death and reincarnation in the days preceding that unpleasantness. I was able to make life — and death — easier for them, by placing them properly on the morning of your own vanishing."

I am stunned.

"But how did you know?" I ask.

"The same way that I know that you are the one."

"The one?"

"The one who has the Dante manuscript."

I am doubly stunned.

"I know much about Dante," I say. "I know nothing about any Dante manuscript."

He shrugs, as if it be of no matter.

"I speak conversationally at times," he says, "but in the course of affairs I make no inquiries that do not pertain directly to those affairs. Some people, however — such as yourself, in mentioning Dante — reveal much without meaning to do so. They answer questions that have not been asked."

"Who do you work for?"

These words come to me without forethought, and I regret them as I hear them.

He merely smiles.

"Only the very arrogant and the very foolish say or believe that they work for themselves."

He pauses, and only when he sees that I wish to pry no further does he speak again.

"Let's just say I work for the lord of this world. Or should I say 'lords'? Or should I simply say that I work for you."

I look silently into his eyes. I feel like smoking a cigarette. I look toward a small porcelain object on the low table between us.

"Is that an ashtray?"

"It is whatever you want it to be."

THAT COULD HAVE BEEN THE END OF HIM, amid the bare shivering branches of that fateful March. Gemma did regard him in awe, as he seemed to accept his condemnation to death with fearless calm, as if his life were but chaff to be blown from this world to the next. For some beats of her heart it did please her to envision life without him; but these wicked beats of her heart did but lead to a deeper coursing of the blood, where she did find to trickle beneath the cold stone of their existence a subterranean spring of love for him, which ran against all reason and contrary to the nature of all outward feelings. It was then that she did come to believe that a similar trickling might lie unknown within him; and that some blessed day these tricklings might torrent to sea and to light.

Yet the beating of his own heart as the hour of his

death was decreed seemed to lead him to no such spring beneath cold stone. How and why could he not so much as embrace her, if only to seek succour, or the sheltering warmth of another, in a time of direst fate? How and why, when she stood with tears welling in eyes that implored such embrace, could he but look upon her and gently say, "All my affairs are in order"?

When she could bear it no more, she did beseech him, in compassion and in hope that her words might give him premiss to do what his pride withstood.

"Thou must not die for naught. Thou must beg these wretched villains for thy life."

He seemed to let her words settle on the scales of his judgment; but, in truth, he was merely silent, as if in solemn and taciturn attendance at a funeral foreseen.

"The nobility of my house was not got through begging, and nor through begging will it be surrendered."

Never had she dreamt the likes such as him, who would seem to accept more naturally his own execution than the embrace of one who did so wish to comfort him. It seemed that even in the tragic turns of the tales of her youth, no imagined knight or prince had made such show of grace in the face of death. She remembered the fool who had pretensed to weep, lost in a madness of gloom, whilst doodling his silly angels in memory of the Portinari bitch, as if to make show that poem and poet were one. Yet now, in this hour of gloom most real, there was neither show nor truth of any feeling. And though he did pray, he made neither verse nor lamentation. Perhaps for once the wall of rock that hid his heart, his true and human heart, from himself as from the world, while presenting to self and world that heart of perfumed artifice that did serve verse and the pose of its maker — perhaps for once this wall did serve good cause, in staying true feeling from penetrating to that true and neglected heart. But this could not be real.

Nor could any of it be real. This sentence of death. This death in life that had usurped her dreams. This death to which all were born. This death that was the end of breath, this death so close, which must not be, so that death in breath might endure unto death.

No, it could not be real, and yet it was: so real that every passing moment slowed upon her as she watched him wait and looked into the eyes of her children's unknowing but doom-sensing askinge. And she prayed, and she prayed; not hearing her own prayers, which seemed dead of heart, and not knowing why she prayed. But she prayed and she prayed; and the night came when this prayer was as a song that came from her unawares: "Dear God, let him live that he might blossom; for beneath every lie, there is the truth." With that long, sighed *ah* of *verità*, prayer and hope alike did end.

The sentence of death was commuted to a sentence of exile. Firenze, which had been his life and blood, was now spat from him like a bitter black bile. That strong and noble tree of the Alighieri was now uprooted and cast dead to drift, as nothing, upon the dark waves of the ocean of wind-swept fate.

The Lenten reprieve of his life seemed to move him no more than the prospect of its end had moved him. He did but gravely stir and stare about, as did she; for the manor in which they stirred and stared would soon be forever behind them, and all its finery, and chambermaids and servants as well. The nobility of name that he so cherished would hence be without all of worldly equipage and trappings by which the standing of nobility is both privileged and distinguished. They would know the grace of dignity and courtly life again, but only in so far as it would be graced unto them by such distant and disparate nobility as might see fit as to take them under wing.

For seventeen years they had lived their misery in luxury. Then for seventeen years they wandered.

HE SPEAKS SOFTLY, TELLING ME: "YOUR speech will betray you always as an American. You must therefore be the naturalized son of an American emigré to a nation where English is either the native or the dominant non-native language."

I nod at what he says.

"Is your passport false?"

I nod.

"Good. And your wife: is she American as well?"

"No. She's Italian."

"Easy enough. She remains Italian. New name, new background. New marriage certificate. New, naturalized citizenry through marriage to you in the land of your new birth." He pauses, and he peers at me. "You are really married, aren't you?"

"No."

"Do you want to be?"

I hesitate for a moment.

"All right. You can hold the marriage certificate. You will in fact be married in the eyes of the law. But you don't have to tell her. Unless, of course, the stars shine especially sweet one night and the wine is right.

"All your taxes will be tended to by the same accountancy firm that will create your life's tax records anew, along with your wife's, both for her new past in Italy and her new past with you. No one believes it, but this is actually the hardest part: the tax records."

He has been taking notes. Now he lays down his pad and pencil.

"You will be a legal, tax-paying citizen of a friendly country, with a legal passport that allows you to travel the world freely and at will. I should be careful, however, of encountering anyone whom you might remind of a certain deceased or vanished individual."

"And the cost?"

"Five million dollars. You and your wife. All-inclusive. One million payable now, the balance payable upon actualization. After that, I will assume the tax liability for any income with which you might not wish to be legally associated. The fee is slightly higher than the usual corporate tax rate: I retain thirty-five percent, out of which all taxes will be duly and lawfully paid. You yourself must see to it that all such income is made payable to me, through an assignee account, for services of consultancy."

"I'll have the million next week."

"Fair enough."

I stand and we shake hands.

"By the way," he says, "should you come upon the gentleman

who does in fact have possession of the Dante manuscript, I may be able to bring him together with interested parties."

"And who might those interested parties be?"

"That is a matter that discretion dictates should be broached only with the gentleman whose property it is."

I nod and bid him good-bye, and I hear him speak to my back as I leave.

"However," he says, "I see no harm in saying, without mentioning any names, that these interested parties, in their various ways, may be said to represent the three great religions of the world. Two of them wish to raise this treasure before the world. The third wishes to raise it before the world as well, and then to destroy it by fire before the eyes of the world."

I turn to him, and he gestures nonchalantly as if to say: people are strange.

IT BECAME HIS CUSTOM EVERY EVENING, after his hard biscuit and scrap of dried beef, to take himself to the rail to be as one with his confessor self of wave and froth of sea.

His southward course to destination ultimately unknown seemed sweet and lovely in the spell before night fell full, for the waves and froth beneath the colors of the dusking waves of light and cloud were but turned to beauty of movement leading to mystery through the glimpse of eternity that was the span of one fortunate to so glimpse. And this movement had been his through the years of his wandering.

The sky, pale above and darkening as it met the sea, was lush with still, recumbent breadths and wisps of rose.

He looked into the twilight-sparkling stern-slime, which some believed to be the lees of the stars.

Seventeen years in exile had he been. To the waves and

froth he did now give prayer of gratitude to those who had blessed his exile with kindness and patronage: first Bartolomeo della Scala of Verona, in the earliest, harshest time of his uprooting; then the many others, in Treviso, in Padova, in Venezia, in Lunigiana, in Casentino, in Lucca; and, again in Verona, the most beneficent Congrande della Scala, under the shelter of whose great generosity the *Inferno* was finished and set before the eyes of Italia, and Firenze did lift its ban of death; and then, most lately, his friend and patron Guido Novello da Polenta of Ravenna.

The seventeen years behind him were now but mere spray that had no more substance or did no more linger than the faintest of this spray upon his wrist and cheek. But the vast and profoundest sea of kindness and faith that had carried him to this course, in mystery under gusted sail and sky of wondrous rose, forth upon the vast and deep of sea: this was now within him, and in the majestic confessor sea that raged and gentled, beyond all poetic device, and more powerful than any poem, like the rose of sky that was rhyme without sound and proof of God such as set to the fires of the sun every theologian's errored attempt at argument thereof.

The curse of his banishment had been his blessing. For it was in the *selva scura* of his exile that he had found the three beasts. For it was in the forced exile from the city of his love and earthy roots that he had been brought to the city of God. For it had brought him here.

Again he thought of those who had loved or tried to love him, and whom he had crueled. His wife had suffered in silence throughout the seventeen years of their wandering, and through seventeen years upon seventeen years she had suffered as well the cold, painted chain-mail of his fear and egomania. And how the two did seem to be together welded, for the more fear drove one inward in seclusion from fear, the more did inwardness delimit one's being and one's world. As the Church did deem as heresy any insinuation that the earth of man was not the center round which the universe revolved, so the homocentric universe of egomania might be seen natural, microcosmos within macrocosmos; but it was not natural, as man was the center of nothing, and was more meaningless and less of substance than the sea-spray, which now rose high as the ship did heave with waves of coming storm.

Nothing that drew inward from fear could be of God or good. From all inwardness must flow not the perverted venom of fear, but only love most pure, which in its truth destroyed all fear and brought forth love and life in turn. He must love those who had loved and tried to love him. He must love all.

The great sea waves of storm in their deafening blast did roar forth to him, saying in thunderous command: *Scream thy soul unto me with all thy force, even though it break thy voice and throat and the every gut of your bellowing; and it shall be unto me but sweet and softest whispering that I shall hold most dear in absolution and love as great as this, my command, that thou dost hear.*

And the scream that issued from him, so violently as to wrench his bowels and tremble him unto fainting, so that he grasped the rail, his knuckles white, just to keep from falling, was the loudest blare and cry of his life; yet such as nothing was it to the seaman who stood not seven steps away, who heard not so much as to turn the least-most towards him.

He cried out again, even more violently, for as long as breath, and the dregs and ghost of breath, and the force of pounding blood, allowed. And thus unto that which commanded, confessor and savior and sea and deafening, wordless All — *quisquis fuit ille deorum*; whichever of the gods it was — he did loose and evacuate and liberate himself of the remains of fear and untruth and will and the last of that foul and sebaceous sediment that was the darkness that was him.

The storm worsened. The heavens, which were all of a darkness, burst with thunder, lightning, and hard rain. There was no more of sleeping on deck in the open good air of night. For many days and many nights the ship was less navigated than thrown and tossed, and by night there were no stars. No compassing or ruddering, no furling or reefing of sail, but only fortune kept the ship from shallows or stone. Captain, navigator, and doctor of the stars alike were as nothing in their powerlessness. In veering from the Adriatic coastline and rounding the Gargano, all hands and vessel of good wood came dangerously close to being blown to break against the jagged rocks. The bilge rose so awfully that when the ship was hove upon fearsome waves, this bilge became as a wave within the hull-strakes, as to suddenly fill the lunging quarters so precipitously that the many rats swept awash and submerged in this inner tidal wave did overcome one another in the fury of their frenzy to escape to air, that the mass of rats that lived did swim and claw wildly amid the mass of rats that died, that they were together like a vile swarm of life and death that moved as one, as the desperate living did stir the dead; and when the bilge wave fell, the rats that lived came running forth amid the spilling tide of their dead, and did run as mad wherever claws might take them, so that their mania impelled them to every quarter, so that no man did move amidships or abed without the squeal and sudden damp encounter with chill of tail and stench of bristle, until these maddened and starving creatures tore and ate of what flesh they could, as they had torn and eaten of the dead of their own, and did surge and pounce wherever victual barrels were pried, and then were even so bold as to jump and bite at whatever a man raised to his mouth to keep body and soul together. And, all the while, as no man could safely take to the stern-board, lest he be gone to wind and wave, what shared chamber-pots as there were could hardly be tended in that same force of wind and wave. The stench of rat and man overwhelmed the innards of the ship so severely that men took to wrapping nose and mouth in rags, like Saracens, or bandits; and still did vomiting increase the foulness.

Two among the rat-bitten did begin to fester, and the pus-letting of their infected limbs — one, the right leg; the other, the left — did not stay gangrene. The chirurgeon, who himself was sick with fever, sawed the limbs to save the lives; and as he pressed burning sword to stump to stanch the blood and seal the gape, each severed limb was taken to the deck and tied round the ankle by rope and hung from the rail that the rats might be drawn unto them and then driven overboard by all able hands using truncheons and whatever could be used to swipe or sweep or strike. In the end those who lost their limbs lost their lives as well, and two others besides them, who did perish of fever, with tongues grossly bloated scrofulous and protruding hideously from their parched and swollen lips. None dared suggest what all thought: that these bodies be used for further ratting. The four had been found dead, uncannily, on the same morning; and they were thrown to rest in the sea, unceremoniously, in fraternity. The poet, who was the only one among them who travelled as passenger rather than as crew, was also the only one among them who could speak some words of godly Latin, which the captain called on him to do as the four dead were put overboard.

Such were the raging winds and destroying waves that no port of refuge could be dared; and as the hard rain became a torrent as whelming as the waves that rose and crashed upon and about them, the men became as damp and as foul in their shivering as the rats that sought them in the filthy canvas of their bedding. And if one man be roused with a horrid start as little claws laid into his chin and little teeth into the tender of his lip, his wild swipe would oftimes land the creature bristling mad upon another, so that few slept except in malady or the numb of exhaustion; both of which increased as the provisions, what remained of them, went to rancid ruin, maggotted and green with mold and bespoilt by the rats.

Fear and suffer as he did, the poet at no moment felt that

death was near, but rather that this were penance of a sort, delivered not upon him by the confessor sea, but upon any and all who might find themselves in the path of this penance. Wakened one morning by the sudden pain of his hairs being torn from his scalp as a rat became ensnared in the matted tanglement of his nape, he did reach and clutch the thing and wrench it from him, along with a clump and many strands of that tanglement, and seeing the ugly glint of yellow eyes and yellow teeth to flesh, the poet did clutch all the harder, until there was the slight sound, like the cracking of a splinter of wood, and the slight sight of slight blood trickling slightly from the thing's open mouth, reddening its yellow teeth and descending slowly, like a thread of crimson lace come undone, onto the pressing thumb of the poet's clutch. Then with all his force he hurled the thing mightily against the big planed beam, so mightily that it did for a breath hang upon the beam by the glue of its gore, then fell, marking the beam with the stain of its slow descent, as the lessening glue of that gore guided its fall for a cubit or more. Rising to stand, he then did stalk forward to the beam. Bracing himself with outstretched arm upon the beam, he placed the saining fingers of his blood-laced hand into the small plash of gore atop the descending streak, wetting them well. Then with the gore-thick tips of those fingers, he did intersect the streak upon the beam, making in this way the sign of the cross.

He knew not why he did this, any of it. He simply did it. Fully aware, but unthinking, unknowing, unmasking, he simply did it. And as he simply did it, the Spaniards who were present simply witnessed it. Even those who saw this as the nightmarish sacrilege that must mark their end were too weak or too betaken by delirium to speak or to wail.

In the mid of that night, as the ship entered the Mediterranean, the rain did ease and the waves did ease and stars were to be seen amid the billowing black of clouds in the black sky; and the rain ceased and the waves slowly gentled and the stars embroidered the black of cloudless night; and at dawn all who were not dying made their way to the deck and rails to behold the rising aura of the sun as if it were a god; and the ship made its course under golden sun and with salubrious leeward wind; and it was then that all turned to the poet as if he were their savior and of powerful holiness. And he was glad to have again the froth and spray and exultant waves of confessor sea, whose tempest had indeed consumed his scream unto God, and whose placidity now did comfort him, and which he looked upon as his savior and of powerful holiness.

Soon other ships of great sail were seen upon the sea, then gliding white gulls and lesser birds in flurry. Peaks of land rose from the farthest mist. The flags of Spain, the House of Aragon, and the kingdom of Sicily were raised in turn.

The anchor was lowered as the sun passed from golden to blond; and the longboats brought the living and the dying to port as the sun passed from blond to rose. The poet stood as the sun passed from the sky. Looking down at the satchel at his feet, he saw that the stirred and stirring dust of this place retained the dusk of rose of the setted sun. And as the dust did ethereally swirl and rise and move like wisps of shadows of things unseen, so, amid the closer din, from afar there could be heard to ethereally swirl and rise and move like wisps of shadows of things unseen an eerie wail of song, such as he had never heard, like eternal threnody and serpentine siren's-song in one.

He lifted his satchel and made his way slowly amid the swirling dust of the waterfront streets towards the swirling wail of dust unto dust.

DAVID, MY FRIEND IN SAVANNAH, HAS not heard my voice since the day I called him after my meeting with the gentlemen of the Bibliothèque Nationale. But he has heard the voice of Mephistopheles.

It has taken David less than forty-eight hours to sell the two pages that have been sent to him. One has brought more than three and a half million; the other, more than four million. After commissions, my share of this, legally free and clear of tax obligations, is about four and a quarter million.

The native Barbadian language, Bajan, is really just a sort of creole English, barely indistinguishable from the English that is taught in the schools of Barbados, New York, or London.

On the beach, an old black man brings my attention to a great and ancient tree.

"Manchineel tree," he tells me. "Very dangerous. Must stay away."

Manchineel.

The word brings to mind another word.

Manichee.

In the balmy sea air in the shade of this tree, as the old man talks, I feel the presence, shade and sun, of what the Manichees held to be sacred: that Satan was indivisible from and co-eternal with God.

"That sap, man. That fruit, man. It kill you dead. Many man have enemy. Little bitty drop of manchineel in coffee, man, and man have enemy no more."

The tree is as beautiful as it is big.

"That fruit up there, man — you see, it look like apple? — ain't nobody know what it taste like, because ain't nobody taste it and live to say. You stay 'way from that tree, man, you be O.K."

White butterflies swirl wildly, fluttering in play among themselves.

IN LIVING FOR HER CHILDREN, AND THROUGH them, Gemma found what of love and happiness did grace her days. Their nursemaids, chosen by her husband, were goodly in their way, but brought to them little or nothing of the magic conspiracy that had been between her and her own maid. She tried to draw them into the enchantment of verse and tale and song that was for her but a crushed and distant memory. But as her fair maid had been as an angel of sunshine beyond and apart from the dismal discord of mother and father, Gemma could be no such thing, for try as she might to present to them an air of gaiety and wonder, the true air of her life did give the lie to that other air. In her merry telling of the dreams of her childhood, her own children saw with ease of sadness through the veil of that merriment to the unhappy end that was all of fulfillment that such dreams might bring.

"And I asked my maid, 'Shall he bear me a rose?' And my maid assured me that he would. Then came the day, on one knee before me with head most chivalrously bowed, that your father did present to me the most perfect rose that I ever did see."

Knowing not what she did in trying to imbue the cold, unloving contract of her betrothal with what hue of romance such as might inspire their dreaming, the children upon hearing the likes of this did turn inward with a melancholy sense of guilt, as if they had been the end of the romance that had lighted her life; for as they believed her tale of the rose, so they knew that its romance must have been lost with their coming, for surely no rose or scent thereof did they recall or know of gracing what passed, void of light, between father and mother. Thus, without speaking it, they felt themselves to be the death of the rose, and her love for them in the imagined perspective of this sacrifice and loss brought them to love her in return all the more.

The tale of the trobairitze, they truly loved; but there seemed no end to the curiosities it did elicit, such as to why, with all the beauty of language at her command, she did not compose verse as their father did, and why, if the making of verse were such a joy unto God and the heart, did their father carry about him such a dire and burdened way? To which she did answer with such felicity as she could, such as that in giving birth to them she had been the vessel of poetry so fine as to sate her soul, such were they and their unfolding lives poems most beautiful and godly, and that their father did seem to brood most gruesomely because his verse-making was of such ponderous and monumental sort, as he had taken it upon himself to build a great cathedral of verse unto God.

This had been said during the time of their first refuge in Verona, at the little casetta granted them by the kindly Bartolomeo della Scala. The *Commedia* at this time had barely yet pullulated within her husband, let alone, to the best of her knowledge, had it been conceived, even in vague, within him. Yet she did sense, in his gravity, arrogance, and his vengeful pain of exile, that he did seek to make a templum unto his glory in the veined-marble way of epic.

But at this time, in Verona, in that first year of their wandering, her elder son was already like unto a man in his boyhood, scholared and barely three years shy of eighteen. After she had spoken these things, and often his younger brother and sister did in time set forth into the garden, he lingered with his mother and did speak softly.

"I have heard read from the sonnets and canzoni of his little book."

"They are lovely indeed, are they not?" replied his mother with an awkwardness that her gentility of voice well hid.

"Yes. They are lovely. But I heard in them nothing of the great cathedral of which you spoke." He smiled sweetly to his mother in prelude, as if to illumine to her that the air of secret and merry conspiracy she had so long wished and tried to lavish among them had come to be. "They seemed more to me the flutterings of a little girl much given to affectation."

"Oh," she sighed, so that the son might not look down upon the father, "he was but a young man, not much older than yourself when he did commence that sonnetting. You had but seven years when that book came to be."

"Yet he was a warrior by then, and most brave, as you and others have told. I should feel that he would have been somewhat ill at ease to lay these dainty, ladylike flutterings before the eyes and ears of his fellows."

"But such was the way of the courtly poets, as you well know."

"Yes. As much as I do admire its form, I must say that with all its periphrasis of heart, I should prefer a newer verse, beyond that of the *stilnovisti*, a verse that might bespeak the heart more truly, as it is within us in fact and not in fancy."

"You are a spirit with which to be reckoned, my first and dearest. May you never forsake your feelings, wherever they may lead you."

"What now does he write?"

"You must understand that this blow of exile which he, and we with him, did withstand has brought him, that we might eat and live, to toil at the translation of decrees and correspondence into Latin, and at the translation therefrom, and to toil as well as the author of documents of court, and to serve as emissary, courier of seal, and ambassador of court. I do know him, amid this, to be drafting a treatise on the eloquence of the *lingua volgare*, such as to give it the dignity of Latin."

Her son had asked his question only in temerity of posing another, and he now saw that there was no way of comforting into that other question, except perhaps to ask it casually and easily.

"And who was this Beatrice whom his sonnets and canzoni did deify?"

His mother sighed softly, as if seeking in her breath a way of comforting into a proper answer, but finding none, except perhaps to speak casually and easily, and to place the truth of the surface in the stead of the truth of the depth.

"Your father never knew she that bore the name of Beatrice, except as figment."

"But he renders her, and her death, so verily."

"Such be the art of courtly poetry, and of the *stil nuovo*, which you perhaps dismiss too hastily and harshly."

"But I should think your own name to be finer fit for deifying."

She held him close and the boy sat in silence, feeling the goodness of his mother's hand dallying upon his head.

"And what of a lady named Bice?"

She looked to him with gentle study. He did feel the halting for a moment of her hand's caress.

"Some years ago, not many, three or four at most, when he did take me to Bologna to consult upon my future schooling with a gentleman of the University, he did fall asleep as we rode in carriage one evening towards the home of our host. He slept not long, and when he woke, it was with a start, with the calling from his sleep of the name of Bice. It frighted me, but I dared not ask him, and have wondered ever since."

Gemma felt an aching within her, and she knew not how to answer, for she knew that the boy well might in time know the truth, and while knowing that she must not lie, she could not bear to reveal the deeper truth that she had only moments ago deftly covered with truth of a lesser and devious and shame-saving kind, and yet to play at further lesser truth — to say that Bice was the name of the wife of his father's friend that great poet Cavalcanti — would not only bring her all the closer to outright lie, but would present to her son a new and more insidious mystery founded in the aether of facile misleading.

"I think it best," said she, "that you ask this of your father rather than of me."

The boy did never ask his father, for he feared him; and when the boy became a man he did never ask his father, because he feared him. But more than ten years after that never-forgotten day with his mother, his question was answered in silence. He was then a man of twenty-eight.

The elder son and the younger son, who himself now long knew of the mystery of verse and names, together one morning did come upon an old scrap of parchment amid the scraps on their father's desk. The scrap was dense with astronomical markings in the scrawl of his natural hand. But these cramped scratchings were arrayed like a nimbus around words at which he had labored to make pretty: "*O Bice, mia Beatrice.*" On that evening, they looked upon their father, then into each other's eyes; and the elder soon did breathe harshly and, with slight and slow movement of his head, did express a sort of weary disgust that was hid from none.

He spoke nothing of this to his mother, and she never again heard from the mouth of her son, or the mouth of any of her other children, the name of Beatrice or of Bice.

Gemma had watched them grow, and had loved them the while. It was the eldest who had devised the surprise of presenting her with a perfect red rose on some occasion or other, some year or other; and the others took up this surprise of the rose thereafter. At times, on those days when the surprise of the rose followed those spells of beholding knife and wrist, she was brought to tears of saving grace, or tears whose nature she did not know, except that even if they did flow from the spring of surgence of a world of melancholy, there was a rose at the heart of that world.

And as she watched them grow and loved them, she perceived how each of them seemed to take on an aspect of the father from whom they seemed estranged, each in his or her own way. He was a man of poetry; a man of worldly affairs; and a man of otherworldliness, whose soul visited places it did not understand. And so she watched, as the one son turned to verse, as the other took to law, and as her frail and fragile daughter came more and more to live within, and to the cloistered last resort of the nunnery was taken.

And as she watched them grow and loved them, she did rejoice that in taking on the aspects of their father, they took on something as well of what once had been she: for they were children of the rose, one and all.

And as she watched them grow and loved them, she watched too as she herself grew old and wizened. God, how fifty years could pass: a butterfly in spring in her garden of child's magic, then venturing in the sweet breeze to the greater meadow beyond, then blown by dark gale to a desolation unseen, to where the blade that cut the rose's stem was held poised to wrist, to where what a husband had not given had been got from the children of her womb, and where those children now were grown and gone and all was still but for breath and beat of heart and whisperings most dark that once had been songs most bright.

Night fell, and she did not make light, but sat alone and still, as one with the shadows.

THE MONEY COMES IN WAVES — WAVES OF euros, waves of pounds sterling, waves of dollars; waves and waves and waves.

Mephistopheles now regards me as a preferred client and a friend.

"Do you know," he asks, "that pornography accounts for more than sixty percent of all profits made through Internet commerce?"

"No," I say.

"Do you know that of these countless pornographic Internet ventures, more than ninety percent are covertly controlled by two of the world's largest entertainment-media conglomerates?"

"No," I say.

"Do you know that these conglomerates are on the verge

of developing real-time interactive pornography — a satisfaction-guaranteed virtual prostitution on demand?"

"No," I say.

"Do you know that this will increase the profits of this sector tenfold and more?"

"No," I say.

"Do you know that Silicon Graphics, which is presently trading at a greatly undervalued price, is the only company capable of providing the sophisticated technology necessary for this development?"

"No," I say.

"Well, I just thought I'd let you know, because I'm about to buy ten million shares in the morning, and that alone may knock the price up a bit; so, if you're interested, now's the time."

"Get ten million for me too," I say.

"Very well."

"Now, what about those two conglomerates?"

I no longer have need or reason to invest or to speculate. Even blackjack has lost its allure. Now the only means to a *frisson* is to up the ante. A million shares here, ten million there. A double-down for a few hundred grand on a face-card or a ten.

Exactly one hundred and thirteen pages have been sold. I'm in no hurry to sell any more. There are some pages that I will never sell: the first page of the *Inferno*; the final page of the *Paradiso*; the last page of parchment preceding the first page of paper, where I have discerned, redacted by the same ink in which the lines of the paper pages were laid down in a different hand, words that the world never came to know.

"*La via sola al paradiso incommincia nel inferno*," these words seem to say: *The only way to Paradise begins in Hell.*

Waves of money: waves and waves and waves.

But that different hand, that different hand. The more I gaze at these paper pages — the wrought original draft of the *Paradiso*'s final ascension, yes; but in that different hand — the more I wonder, and the more this wondering maddens me.

Night falls. I feel death like the breath from the nostrils of a nearing beast in the darkness.

Breath and the curse of psyche. What was breath to the Greeks — ψυχή — Latined as *psyche* — became the gasp of mind to us.

It is the middle of the night where I am. It is morning where Mephistopheles is.

"Put me down for another ten million shares," I tell him.

I go down to the sea, to the moonlight, to the shadows in the shadows of the big old beautiful tree.

I close my eyes, receding into the shadows within me. I see my daughter's face: the angel from whom I turned away, the angel whom I abandoned. Death cleft us and delivered my penance. The love that was to blossom in full between us was extinguished, stolen; and all that was to be said and savored has forever been lost to silence.

I open my eyes to the other shadows. Now I know. That hand. That other hand of the paper pages. Now I know.

THE TWILIGHT THAT IMBUED THE SWIRLing dust with dusky rose evanesced to night as he drew close to that serpentine wail of sensuous lament that beckoned him. As it grew louder and more distinct as he neared, he began to hear it not as a single commanding voice, but as an entwining of wails, further entwined with the high crying tones of strong-blown skrilling instruments underlaid and given the timbral heartbeats of nine skies, which did pound together in percussion like thunder, then did resound both profoundly and with slow and with fast pulsing and pouncing and rattling athither, *huc et illuc*, and then converging again in thunder, by the drumming of taut hides and the shaking of rattling things. And it was like that calligraphy, delicate and powerful at once, whose eloquence of form seized him even as its meaning lay beyond him. But in sound there is a force of communing that speaks itself, independent of the words of song that grace it. So it was that while the swirling wails of voice were as calligraphy sorceried in air, the skrilling and the many-rhythmed beating of drums and sistra spoke to him most directly, forgoing intellect and rumbling and howling within him until it had claimed the hastening pulses of his body as its own, and he was of it, and it was of him. Weakened from voyage though he was, the satchel he clutched seemed no more to burden him as he strode, seeing at last, upon what in pitch of darkness must have been a wall far before him, the demon-like darting and dancing of shadows cast by unseen fire, and feeling the fierceness of rumbling and howling within him intensify, as if he were now one not only with it, but with the fate of it, unknown to him, drawn between the tide and moon of that fate. Then he turned at the wall where demons danced, and, in that instant, as the scene of the dancers and the sorceries of sound lay before him, the fierceness within and without him struck and shook him, thunder unto blast, wail unto lace of scream that was of murder as it was of ecstasy unbearable, for it all was contained within three high walls of an ancient piazzetta, and this closure, open to the sky of night and the angled wall of demon shadows, was like a sonorous sacring-place that resounded and reverberated all that transpired to shake and fill its hellish air, as the waves of heat from several fires made a furnace of the heat of night, so that all those who did make sound did glisten, and those who did make dance did send rain of droplets flying from them, their flight merged with the flight of embers and cinders. And from the several fires there surged not only waves of heat and leaping flames, but waves of scent that bore the fragrance of spices most exotic, for some of these fires did burn beneath tripods from which cauldrons hung, and some did blaze beneath spits through lambs or hindquarters of calves, whose tallow did crackle and splatter in the flames, and with each crackle and with each splatter there flourished an explosion of clove or of cinnamon that for a moment flared in delicious scent distinct from the waves of scent amid which it burst. The poet laid his satchel to the ground and leaned against a wall near where no fire burned, and he braced the satchel with his heels, and he loosed his robe and removed his berretta and infula, and he put the back of his head to the wall to get what cool of stone he could, and he closed his eyes and tried to sense the fate that was within him and without him, this strange, transporting calligraphy of engulfing sound that did mourn and rise unto God and sing the song that rent the heart so that heart anew might beat.

He had spent his life in profession of Christian theology and philosophy: a lifetime of learning, study, and pondering most intensely. Yet here he leaned, overtaken. These people knelt before a false god, and were an assault to all of Christendom. But what of himself? He who, of all of Christendom, had chosen no patristic sage or saint to lead him through his *Paradiso*, but had chosen instead, over Saint Peter and over Augustine and over and over all others so holy and close to God; had chosen over all the dead wife of a banker. Allah and the banker's dead wife. If he could defend the one as personification of the divine, why should he damn those who perceived divinity in a different god? He remembered what the old Jew had said: faith is but a birthmark with which we are born, an impalpable umbilicus to time and place, which we rarely ponder to cut.

One thing he was must to accede: those who could make a noise so rapturous and rapturing as this were a people of might. Whether this be a feast of holy celebration or of funerary rite, he did not know, for its endless song did lament and rejoice at once, and the faces of the men were so contorted by the fearsome madness of wending firelight and shadow, and the faces of the women, which were veiled, showed a brilliance of eye, like glistening amber, that was wicked and serene, reverent and lustful, somber and wild, and an hundred other glintings in flashing turn, magicked as they were by the same fearsome madness of wending firelight and shadow. Then he did realize that the flashing glintings of amber were untelling, and that it was not the veiled ladies that hinted of these many things through their eyes, but that it was his own eyes that as they beheld did imbue them with the fearsome madness of the coruscating light of his own free and burning soul; and he knew that freedom and that burning to be good, because it was of him, and therefore was of God. And if this clamour of majestic calligraphy unwrit were a cry unto Allah, it was not Allah that here brought him to quake and to burn most free, but the power rather of He who made Adam, and thus as well these souls that were lost and knew not the Holy Spirit whose awesome presence filled this place.

He marvelled that the court of Sicily had emulated the songs of the troubadours afar, as this sound did be within hearing. What was the flower of the *stilnovisti* set before the tempest of this? And he himself, in making much of sweetness, with his proclaimings of *il dolce stil nuovo*? Had he not felt his own heart's furthest yearning? In his folly had he not known what his own, buried heart had known, that the sweet and the new of the style he did fruit were but the means to an end? And that this end was the *stil eterno*? The song of this *stil eterno* was the howl of the ancient wolf of his *Purgatorio*. It was the cadence of the wisdom of the poet of Ecclesiastes. It was the scream of his soul that the sea had devoured. It was the song that now entranced and shook him. And to be shaken and entranced was a beautiful thing. His sentence of death and his exile had robbed him of what worldly fortune had lain before him. To have tasted of riches, then to have been deprived of them: it was a loss that dealt more of attrition and pain than did all labor. For no man who did abide in this world did not cherish riches and wealth of purse; and while man did much people his tales and fables and hagiographies that the word *golden* was endlessly summoned as the superlative of all things — golden words and golden yearnings, in golden light and golden sun, in golden youth and golden joy and golden glory — a superlative that in its rhetorical usage did belie the very forsaking and denouncing and casting away that man in his fabrications did find so ennobling. It was the wealthiest who did speak most convincingly of riches of spiritual life, and of the worthlessness of worldly riches, in that they could buy neither joy nor salvation. But the truth was that if a man be at one in spirit with the All, and that if a man be capable of joy, and that if a man be saved, worldly wealth did purchase the freedom to live most fully in spirit and in joy and in salvation. For just as in Roman times a slave might purchase his freedom with the coin of manumission, so it was ever thus that money bought man his freedom to live. If a loaf of bread was a good thing, so was the means to purchase it, and so much the better the means to purchase it forever without care, and to give it freely to whomever should hunger. But instead of the Florentine gold that had been so close unto his reach, he had naught, and had been reduced to a peon of title, and was but a beggar at the bidding of others. Yes, he had lost it all, and he could not but reflect with remorse on what might have been. And this was why it was good to be entranced and shaken and freed: for his dream of wealth and manumission was long ended, and he himself was but a coin fondled and tossed in the hand of that and those that were greater than he. And this mystical din, which came here upon him as had the sea, was the manumission of the goldless, whose freedom lay but in the clench of that *mano cornuta* of the Pantocrator, and who were of the unknowable mystery and imprisoned by it, and who thus were its gold, seeking escape through the fire of the spirit, that this fire might melt and liquefy the gold of them, thus to seep through clench if only for a moment, before the atmosphere of this earthly world hardened them to another's currency once again. And in this was the quaking: the tumult fit to shake the world, that its blaze, if but for a moment, might purchase vision most true of that goldless freedom to which the golded did in luxury give much lip; that is to say, that for the moment between melting and cool hardening, they might be of other world. And it was in that world, now overtaking him, that he felt neither loss nor regret nor the self-pity and self-mourning of the rending of the garments of his words and feelings. As his screaming into the sea had purged and emptied him, so he now was filled. If he could not have riches, he would have the All, and if he could not give riches, he would give of the All that was within him. It was then that someone, like apparition from shadow and smoke and fire and crescendum of tumult, came forth to offer him on a spit of wood a torn piece of shank meat, still crackling and steaming with spice, and moist with blood beneath. He chewed into it like a beast, feeling and filling the hunger of what may have been days or what may have been weeks; and the blood of the lamb was sweet to his lips. Then, in further apparition, there came forth an earthen bowl of spiced broth, then another of strange wine that did both quench and burn, so as to sate and make thirst at once, then a small globe of fig meat and nut meat moist with honey, then more of broth, this of pigeon, and more as well of the hard wine that did both singe and quench. How long this feast and madness and its eternities and infinities of moments did last, he did not know, for the stars seemed to move not as the sky of night ordained, but as in flight and dance of fugitive grace.

He approached the court in the dead of night, searching round the castellated walls until he saw the fire in the iron sconce, big as a man and embedded with its weight into the massive stone of the arch of the portal of guard. Though his satchel held *litterae* of courtly embassy and *lettera di salvo condotto*, he knew that his appearance was that of one who might have been washed ashore into a pool of fetid sewage, then lain to dry. Fearing so much as to touch the letters of authority and *sicurtà* himself, lest he soil and besmirch them, he did implore the guard through the face-gate to accept first the satchel, that the letters might be examined, then to accept him, that he might be given quarter, scrub, and shave, before taking rest and changing vestments so that he might approach the court in dignity in the light of day. This procedure was complicated and prolonged by problems of language. For one thing, the guardsman had no Latin, in which the letter of authority was formally rendered. For another, the guardsman was a Spaniard who spoke but little of the local tongue. And for another, the poet, who had little of the tongue of Spagna, and who with difficulty had read some verse in the *lingue di si*, now came to perceive that the tongue of Sicilia was not so much a dialect but a language of its own, and a most obscure language at that. Thus, as he did make a babble of words drawn from certain universalities of courtly Latin phrase, the vernaculars of Italia and of Spagnia — what little of the latter he knew — and blind spear thrusts at the language of Sicilia, the guardsman in turn did speak forth rapidly in the vernacular of Spagnia, resorting to a sort of pidgin *lingua della Sicilia* and his own blind spear thrusts at the vernacular of the caller. In the end, it was the seal upon the letter that swayed him, so regal did it appear: this and the fact that the poet was alone. Above all he was swayed not by kindness for the pitiable form before him, but rather fear of the possibility of recrimination by his superiors should he send him away. So it was that the heavy iron gate was parted to permit the lean shadow of his entry.

DEUS ABSCONDITA. THE GOD WHO IS hidden from man. I have found him.

HE HAD BEEN GIVEN CRAFT TO BEAR him to the three that was of the three that was of the three.

The fire-light of the tower of the port of Trapani vanished behind him in the dead of night.

The sea grew strangely still and silent as the towering shadows of the islands that bore the old Arab names of Rahib and Gazirat al ya bisah loomed and were gone.

As the barque rounded towards the ancient island that bore the old Arab name of Gazirat Malitimah, the poet felt and was robed as one who was damned, and the appearance of the isle in the light of the crescent moon was that of an isle of the damned, or the dead, or worse.

The eerie calm sea allowed the craft to leave the poet at the sea rocks beneath a winding road that rose to the high peak of a triangular outcropping of black stone atop which a castle-like structure stood, carved partly from the stone of the peak itself, and built partly of immense blocks of rock whose transport to these isolated heights defied all theory and explanation.

The slight moon gave little light. The ascent was long and strenuous. As he climbed, the poet felt as if he were laboring towards the stars themselves.

An attendant brought him to sleep, and in the morning he was brought before the elder whom he sought, and to whom he presented the book that bore the elder's mark.

Though surrounded by great luxury, the old man was attired most humbly.

The poet said nothing. The old man said nothing.

An attendant placed before the poet a golden plate on which were slices of dried tuna heart, bread, wild strawberries, and a compote of figs in chestnut honey.

"My name is Dante Alighieri," said the poet.

"Ah." His host smiled. "My old friend in Venezia has been keeping fine company. I admire you very much. You damn Helen of Troy to the circle of the *lussuriosi* of your Hell, then you raise the whore Rahab to your Heaven. You emulate Horace in his inventive use of the word *cauda* to connote the *membrum*, then you place him in your Limbo with other great pagan makers, none of whom, to my knowledge, has given us, as you have, the fine pagan evocation of a man copulating grossly with a snake. Yes, I admire this sort of thing very much. And, the all of it, most beautifully wrought. I look forward to the completed work."

"I don't know whether to lower my head in gratitude or in shame."

"Tell me. Have you ever copulated with a snake?"

"No. Have you?"

"Yes. And by all the holiness of Mecca and all the gold of

Zecca, I would have wagered, judging by your words, that you had done so as well."

The poet beheld the old man's face, which revealed nothing.

"And so." The old man sighed at last. "What do you seek here? How can I help you?"

"He said that you can see."

The old man was silent for a long time, and for that long time he peered into the poet's eyes.

"I will answer three questions. Choose them well. I will tell you when the time is right."

That day passed, and then another. Of fish and fowl and hare and fruit there seemed to be no end. The moon, unseen at night, was a pale ghost in the daylight sky. From where the poet awaited night, there was ocean as far as the eye could see. Then, in the soft darkening sky, the north was gray and rose, and to the south, beyond Rahib and Gazirat al ya bisah, the sky was azure and violet; and, as the colors of the north and the colors of the south wove together, clouds stood still above the waves of the sea. He did not know this sky. Then all deepened. Then all darkened. Then all blackened.

"The time is good," the old man said.

YES. NOW I KNOW. THE MYSTERY OF THOSE three paper pages written in a different hand is a mystery no more.

The oldest surviving evidence of a scribal copy of a completed *Commedia* is, curiously, a few fragments of the work in transliterated Hebrew. These paper fragments, from the Biblioteca del Talmud-Torah in Livorno, came to the Jewish National and University Library in Jerusalem, the "holy city" of evil, following the proclamation of the state of Israel, in 1948. By watermark analysis, these fragments have been dated to between 1326 and 1332. There is also evidence of a complete Italian copy made in Firenze between October of 1330 and January of 1331. But hundreds of copies of a completed text, all of them now lost, were certainly in circulation long before this time. This is not surprising. In April of 1472, in Foligno, Johann

Neumeister, who had learned his craft from Gutenberg in Mainz, produced the first printed edition of the *Commedia*. Of the unknown number of books that this *editio princeps* comprised, only twelve are known to have survived. The last of these in private hands, although missing two of its original leaves, was sold at auction by the Piasa group of Paris in 1999 for the equivalent of almost a million dollars: a new record price in France for any printed book. Considering the near disappearance of this first printed edition of 1472, it is to be expected that the many manuscript copies of a hundred and forty years before, and more, should have been lost to us over the centuries.

The first of these lost copies is believed to have been made by Dante's son Jacopo, and presented to the poet's patron Guido Novello da Polenta, nine months after Dante's death.

Why nine months? According to Boccaccio's narrative, Dante finished the poem, but, upon his death, parts of it could not be found. Then, after eight months, as legend has it, Jacopo was visited in a dream by the spirit of his dead father, who led him to the location of the missing parts of the poem.

Jacopo was a poet and a lawyer: a dangerous combination. And Dante, lest we forget, was but a man — a man who throughout his marriage to Jacopo's mother, and throughout Jacopo's own childhood, adolescence, and young manhood, went publicly about pulling his poetic prick and moaning like a *ricchione* over some dead twat he never even knew. Jacopo must have felt something. He must have felt something like:

Beatrice, fellatrice, va fa'n cul', Beatrice maiala!

The fact is that Beatrice vanishes from the *Paradiso* exactly where the paper pages begin, exactly where the wretched hand and divine verse of Dante are replaced by — yes, I truly believe so — the fine hand and piss-poor verse of Jacopo, poet, shyster, and son. The poem then ends, on parchment, in the hand of Dante, in a transcendent glory that had been written long before.

THE CANDLELIGHT CAST GREAT SHADOWS, and the poet asked the first of his questions.

"What name does the one true God bear?"

The silence of breath between question and response was brief.

"No true god bears a name."

The silence of breath between response and question was long.

"Will my soul ever be free of torment and ill?"

"No."

The silence of breath between response and question grew longer.

"Can you tell me the hour of my death?"

"Yes."

The poet looked into the eyes of the other, which were soft with candlelight. Then the poet turned away.

"And now," said the other, "I must ask something of you."

"What might that be?"

"Did you present your final question according to the design of fear, or did you wish to have your death foretold rather than knowing merely if I could foresee and foretell it?"

The poet, looking out into the night upon the sea and stars, did not return his eyes to the eyes of the other. After some time, sensing that the other had made not the least and subtlest movement, he turned to him.

"Tell me, then. Show me my death."

"But you have had your three questions, and you had your three answers."

"And, yes, your suspicion is true. Fear overtook the last of them as I spoke it."

The other's eyes expressed gentle understanding.

"I should not like to leave here in cowardice. It was in grace and strength that I came, and all the more in grace and strength should I like to depart."

"I shall, then, say only this: it is in grace and in bravery that you shall die."

THERE ARE THOSE WHOM I LOVE AND who dwell within me. Some of them I have abandoned long ago. Others long ago have abandoned me. Yet they dwell in the love within me.

There are others, whom I never have abandoned, and who never have abandoned me.

When my second death, my true death is near, I will bring them to me.

For so long, the souls of others sustained me as much as my own soul did.

God, how I long now for them.

I must have them know that I breathe. I must allow them the knowledge that we still breathe together, apart as we may be. I can not let them know this only when I bring them to me to celebrate that befalling thing.

God, how I am blessed to have Giulietta, whose breath I can feel upon my skin and in my soul, and upon whose skin and into whose sweet soul I can breathe.

As for the rest of you, neither I nor those who dwell in the love within me desire or would abide your company. To you who in your fear, your stupidity, your jealousy, darkened the path of my previous life as you desecrated your own — and you know who you are, as do those who dwell in me know who they are — may your true death precede mine, as did the death of your souls.

In the name of the Father and the Son and the Holy Ghost. Amen.

On his return voyage to Venezia, the poet swore that he would make a poetry that truly would sunder the artifice of all verse: a poetry that would destroy and discard that artifice for the natural, indwelling meters of breath and the elements; a wild, free, and powerful rhythmus beyond all meters devised; a poetry that ran *sans entraves*, a poetry that roared as he had roared unto the waves of the sea, and as the sea itself had roared; a poetry whose dactyls blossomed in the soft, gentle, imperceptible sough and sigh of the All.

No more would his poetry be forced and corsetted into the scholastic arithmeticking of rhyme and scansion. It would create its own as it unfolded from his new-born soul. It would speak of the little bird that could not fly, of soaring hawk, of the rat's-blood cross, of the tomb of life and the emergence from it to wisdom — to Her, before whom poetry was but a kneeling, a candling that might bring forth one hint of light to the tombs of others.

I have long hair, or perhaps my head is shaved. I have a beard, or perhaps Teutonic moustaches.

Giulietta paints as she always wanted to do. I sculpt great rough rock with violence, and I write what poetry I feel to write.

In this world of tree-shaded hammocks, sea and stars and breeze, laughter and freedom and love, I feel the desire for life running through my veins. There are specialists in Geneva who tell me that there is hope.

Within, I am still Nick, and Giulietta is still Giulietta. But we whisper these names only when we are alone, as one, with the miracle in her belly.

Yes. If I could make the truth by writing it, this is what I would write.

HE ALMOST FEARED TO APPROACH THE old Jew's quarters. The feeling that he had felt upon their farewell still lingered: that he would never again see him alive. And death did so seem to be in the stormy air. It was bad air: *mal'aria.*

But the old Jew was there, although he had no eyes and did not speak.

In the old man's pallet lay Bice, who did sigh and turn from the poet upon his appearance. Then she sighed again and she settled once more into the peace, or disquiet, of the sleep of her death.

The cart in which the poet lay blanketed trundled in darkness over stony earth, and the poet's eyes opened slowly to behold the vast of the stars above.

Then his eyes slowly closed.

RED MOON RISING. A WOLF IN THE PINES.
Golden moon risen. A wolf in the pines.

FIND MY GRAVE, BABY, FIND MY GRAVE.

ABOUT THE AUTHOR

BORN IN NEWARK and schooled in his father's bar, Nick Tosches is widely regarded to be one of the most original writers at work today. He is the author of acclaimed biographies of Sonny Liston, Dean Martin, the Mafia financier Michele Sindona, the minstrel singer Emmett Miller, and Jerry Lee Lewis; several books about popular music; and the novels *Cut Numbers, Trinities,* and *In the Hand of Dante.* Thirty years of his writing was recently collected in *The Nick Tosches Reader.* He is a contributing editor of *Vanity Fair.* He lives in New York City, and his poetry readings are legendary.